My Holy Satan is an ex
ing story of one of the gr
aspects of the human spiri
the search for truth against
odds, even torture and death.

Richard, a young serf of the
Middle Ages, has this great
urge. Fortunately, he is be-
friended by Hillel, a Jew, a
scientist, a man who pledges
an awful oath of brotherhood
with Richard.

Richard and Hillel are not
able to pursue their search for
truth. About them lie the
threatening forces of human
defeat: the feudal system, em-
bodied in Baron Guillem and
the baronness, who becomes
Richard's lover; the total dark
power of the Church, em-
bodied so strongly in Father
Luce, member of the Inquisition.

Richard faces the Inquisition and its terrible torture
and imprisonment in one of
the most vivid accounts of human degradation ever written.
How human hope and the
human spirit still manage to
triumph is a part of this magnificent story.

Recently I v
near Hagerma
had picked to
who had, with
houses.
Beyond evei
the Testament
himself, Vardi
he not only di
a master biblic
and journals s
single library 1
it told Fisher
three times; a
in the rare boo
Fisher is a gr
bodied in the n
that one did so
The Testamei
mately, a vast a
publishing the S
mankind." It is
conduct. Going

nd Springs valley,
ty of the spot he
ergy of the man
ter and built two

ich has gone into
iis home he built
lking-writing that
ey. After making
ier had the books
ie nation. Not a
the item wanted,
s he read two or
purchased, often

his labor is em-
scholarship, and

or, but it is, ulti-
'hen I took over
: consciousness of
ources of human
iself into various

innocent
8. Jesus Came Again
9. A Goat for Azazel
10. Peace Like a River
11. My Holy Satan

levels of human existence and into meanings and situations, stark and plain
then, but long ago mossed-over with a huge accretion of concealment and disguise. His wife says that at times she feared for his sanity, and at no time
more than when he entered the dungeon in *My Holy Satan*.
The inception of the gigantic work was in a feeling that his important
Vridar Hunter tetralogy had not done the job. Interestingly enough, the re-
written tetralogy will form the twelfth volume in the Series, to be called
Orphans in Gethsemane.

Alan Swallow

MY HOLY SATAN

A Novel of Christian
Twilight

Books by Vardis Fisher

THE TESTAMENT OF MAN:

Darkness and the Deep
The Golden Rooms
Intimations of Eve
Adam and the Serpent
The Divine Passion
The Valley of Vision
The Island of the Innocent
Jesus Came Again
A Goat for Azazel
Peace Like a River
My Holy Satan

THE VRIDAR HUNTER TETRALOGY:

In Tragic Life
Passions Spin the Plot
We Are Betrayed
No Villain Need Be

OTHER NOVELS

Children of God
Dark Bridwell
April
Toilers of the Hills
Forgive Us Our Virtues
City of Illusion
The Mothers
Pemmican
Tale of Valor

NON-FICTION

God or Caesar?
Neurotic Nightingale

Vardis Fisher

MY
HOLY
SATAN

A Novel
of Christian Twilight

ALAN SWALLOW, *Denver*

Library of Congress Catalog Card Number 58-13022

FOR ISIDORE H. REITER

of those walking with Hillel

"The divine morning star, that has shed its sparkling beam on Socrates, Archimedes, Plato, and once and again inspired them to sublimer efforts, what is it now?—a devil, the great devil Lucifer. . . . If Satan does this, we are bound to pay him homage, to admit that he may well be after all one of the aspects of God"—Michelet

". . . but for Damian there is Hildebrand's lightning-flash of genius, 'My Holy Satan'."—Helen Waddell

I

His tread was stealthy, not because his feet were bare but because his senses were alert to the presence of danger. Richard was eighteen and his whole life as far back as he could recall it had been lived in fear—not only in fear of the terrible and powerful men on earth who did dreadful things to persons like him, impoverished and defenseless, but in fear of the sky above, where God and Satan and the host of demons manifested their anger or their diabolic treacheries. He had always walked like a terrified one, driven forth, unarmed, to meet a foe.

He was not sure that he had a right to do what he was now determined to do. What right had any serf, save to toil for his master, accept without murmur his brutal tyrannies, and fall at last upon his hard bed and die? But there was in Richard, as there had been and still was in his father, a deep and brooding sense of outrage, of rebellious hate, that drove him now and then beyond the boundaries of his small ugly and degraded life, to see, to inquire and to think. Not that his father Victoir was a bold man. He was on the contrary a timid, ineffectual, discreet and secretive man, who had never taken more than a minor risk, yet was a rebel at heart, in spite of the meek and humble countenance which he always turned on his superiors. Victoir was so discreet that he had got the habit of whispering, even when alone with his son, safely beyond the eyes and ears of the Church's spies, or the baron's.

It was posted on the church door, Victoir had said, and he imagined it was there for all people to read. For all people to read! Very few people could read in these times—not Victoir, who could not even write his name; not any of Victoir's serf

9

neighbors; not even the baron, it was said, or the baron's wife, nor most of the priests. But Richard could read; he had learned a little from his mother and a great deal more from Hillel, a friend, who could read in several languages. It was Richard's dream to be some day as learned as Hillel. . . .

On naked feet he went softly through the dust of the village, slowly, humbly, as a man will who wants it known that he intends no offense; furtively, for he did not want to meet one of the Baron's men. He saw Elie, the crippled beggar; and then Ambre, the witch, who had just slipped in from the hills; and Chretien, the father of Madelon, a terrifying man, hawknosed and with eyes out of hell. Richard came to the hill—all churches were set on a hill to overlook the village or the town—and walked more rapidly, since there seemed to be no one in sight.

This is what he read:

. . . . having heard the plea of the mighty Baron Guillem Maurel Philippe Délicieux; and whereas small moles and other beasts and certain insects do consume and destroy the branches and fruits and grains in the fields and vineyards of the said Baron Guillem; and whereas all powers come from God, whom all creatures must obey, even the unreasonable and disobedient ones; and whereas when temporal justice does not prevail we must invoke divine intercession; therefore having fortified ourselves with the Holy Cross, and having before our eyes the fear of God, from whom alone all just judgments proceed; and having been advised in this matter by a council of men learned in the law, we do acknowledge that the said Baron's appeal against these detestable vermin is valid and that they shall be exorcised; and in conformity herewith we charge and burden them with our curse, and command them to be obedient, and anathematize them in the name of the Father, the Son and the Holy Ghost, that they turn away from all fields, grounds, pastures, vineyards, seeds, fruits and produce, and depart. We declare them to be banned and exorcised through the power of Almighty God, to be accursed and daily to decrease, to the end that of them nothing shall remain save for the use and profit of man. If said offending vermin do not cease and desist they shall be summoned to appear before the court, to show cause why they should not desist, under penalty of banishment and confiscation.

Some of the words were unfamiliar to Richard but he understood the proclamation. His father, with what had seemed to be a twinkle in his eye, had whispered, "So it is, my son. The Church is going to banish the moles." Richard looked away across the lands which the baron owned. It was true that small beasts and hordes of insects were destroying a part of the produce. So it had been many times. But was it true that the Church had power to exorcise and intimidate and banish these things?

If intimidation failed, did it have power to curse and anathematize them, so that their will would fail and their fertility perish? Richard did not know. It was said by Church leaders that even inanimate objects had in ancient Greece been prosecuted for homicide, as when a stone fell and killed a man and was then taken to court and found guilty and cast into the sea; as when, after a drunken rowdy was killed in a fight with a bronze statue, relatives hailed the statue into court and had it condemned for murder. Church leaders appealed to these ancient analogies when prosecuting beasts or insects, thunder and lightning, or any other creature or power that appeared to be an enemy of God's chosen people.

Now and then Victoir voiced gentle skepticism, but only to his son of all people, for the skeptic's life was not worth a fig, once his heresy became known. In the awful slaughter at Beziers, when of ten thousand people not a man, woman or child had been spared, Victoir had heard the judgment: We the said Bishops and Judges, sitting in tribunal as Judges judging, having before us the Holy Gospel that our judgment may proceed as from the countenance of God and our eyes see with equity, and having before our eyes only God and the truth of the Holy Faith and the extirpation of the plague of heresy, against you, Giraut of Beziers, in this place on the day and at the hour before assigned to you for the hearing of your definite sentence, we pronounce that you have truly fallen into the sin of heresy; and as one so truly fallen you are cast forth from this our ecclesiastical court, and delivered to the secular arm. But we earnestly pray that the said secular court temper its justice with mercy, that there be no bloodshed or danger of death.

The concluding words made Richard shudder whenever he thought of them. For where had justice been tempered with mercy? In all the raping and torturing and butchering that had been the nightmare of his childhood, and in the wild screams

11

still wrung from the nightmares of his mother, where was the mercy? The prayer that there would be no bloodshed meant only, his father had said, that the luckless one was not to be beheaded but burned alive. And this was so because in the Old Testament there was an injunction against the shedding of blood.

Shuddering—for what child anywhere had seen more horrors than this youth had seen?—Richard returned to the village street and slipped into the gloomy stinking hovel that was his home. His parents were outside at the moment but his tall frail skinny brother was there, pale and sad and silent. The whole family lived in this one small hut, with its floor of earth and its ceiling of dead branches through which the rains came. They slept on the earth floor on old foul vermin-ridden mats; and when Richard sat on his mat he began to scratch himself and feel for vermin, because it was too dark to look for them. There was no window in this hovel, no opening but the low doorway. He scratched and felt hunger-pains and thought of the strange world in which he lived.

Was his father a heretic? Richard did not know and would never have dared to ask. He did not know how much his father believed of the holy faith. It was not what his father had said but the way he had sometimes looked at his younger son: as when, for instance, Richard had said that the crusaders brought back from the holy land milk from the breasts of the Virgin, and portraits of her, and two fingers from the Holy Ghost. Victoir had then looked deep into his son's eyes, and in the father's eyes Richard had seen something that had startled him. Had his father doubted these things?

Richard had heard that in one place or another, where treasures were reverently preserved, were the diapers and swaddling clothes of the holy babe; portraits of Mary painted by St. Luke; the seamless robe of Jesus; the cloth on which had lain the head of John the Baptist; many pieces of the cross; an arm of the apostle James; the wings and tail feathers of the Holy Ghost; a phial of the sweat of St. Michael, shed when he struggled with Satan; and even the umbilical cord and the prepuce of the holy infant. Were these stories true? Was it true, as Hugues de St. Victor said in his treatise on beasts and other things, that the dove with her right eye contemplated herself, and with her left eye, God? Was it true that the holy cross now and then appeared on the altar-cloth;

12

that blood had been seen to move and flow in statues of the Virgin; or that when a man accidentally broke an arm off a statue of the Virgin and Child, blood flowed from the stone?

There were so many stories, known to the people far and wide. There was the tale of a varlet who on his way to a contest found an image of the Virgin. He had a ring given to him by his lady-love, and now, to protect it from loss while fighting, he put it on a finger of the statue, and at once the marble finger bent firmly around it. On this man's nuptial night, it was said, the Virgin suddenly appeared and bitterly reproached him for his faithlessness. Shamed and confused, but with ardor beating strong within him, the man turned again to his bride; whereupon the Virgin manifested such rage and jealousy that he abandoned his wife and became a hermit. Was it true? What man on earth could tell him?

There was the story, known to everyone in the village, of the young abbess who fell into sin and became pregnant. The nuns wrote their bishop about the horrible scandal and at once he set forth to see the abbess himself; but before he arrived the abbess slept and the child was born and the Virgin came softly and took the child away. Was it true? Were *all* the tales of the virgin-birth true?—that Mary, as Augustine related it, was impregnated by God through her ear?—or as some of the painters had represented it, that the Holy Ghost had in the form of a dove entered her ear?—or, as still another painting was said to reveal it, that a fully formed babe descended in rays of light from the outstretched finger of God?—or, in the manner of still another, that the dove descended in blinding glory and entered Mary's navel? The followers of Mahomet, Richard had heard, believed still another version, that the angel Gabriel opened Mary's garment and breathed upon her womb.

Was it true, as so many people seemed to believe, that women could conceive by wind, lightning or water? His own mother had failed in all these and many more. She had eaten the bark of cypress and mulberry, she had drunk mare's milk, she had choked down a goat's testicles and a hare's uterus. She had chewed the roots of valerian until for days she had seemed to be out of her mind. And one time—but Richard shuddered, for he dared not think of that.

13

He raised his eyes to look over at his brother Pascal and after a moment he became aware that Pascal, still bowed as though in grief, was fondling a small scrawny kitten which he hugged to his chest. For Pascal cats had a strange and for Richard a horrible fascination. So for that matter had many beasts. Pascal had gathered stories about them and all the stories he believed: that the lion, for instance, had three astonishing habits: it slept with its eyes open; when pursued it obliterated its tracks with its tail; and the cubs on being born remained three days without life, until the father breathed upon them. Pascal believed the tale of one Gerald de Berri, that a sow suckled a hunting dog, which, on being grown, had strength that exceeded that of the lion. Pascal believed that if a pup was fed on cat's milk it would develop a passion for catching mice. . . .

Well, even in the pulpit tales were told of marvelous things. There was the sciapod which, though having but one leg, was able to run at incredible speed, and which when in repose used its one foot as a parasol to protect its head from the sun. There was the hippopod, with the torso of a man and the feet of a horse; and the Ethiopian with four eyes; and the dwarfed man in some far-away land who was only two inches tall; and the griffin, which was half-eagle and half-lion. There was the whale which, covering its back with sand and resting exposed at the surface, became a floating island, because birds dropped the seeds of grass, tree and shrub upon the sand and these grew into the most verdant plant-life. Told in the pulpits, the wineshops, and written down, Richard had heard, in books, was the tale of a novice who stole into the graveyard of a certain priory and saw by the dim light of lanterns of the dead a group of exhumed and desiccated monks sitting in solemn assembly, discussing what should have been heard in neither earth nor heaven.

Richard's eager and inquiring mind wondered about so many things. There was the way the Church leaders related the marvels of bestial history to the miracles of the Lord: the lion slept with his eyes open because so slept the body of Jesus on the cross; the lioness brought her cub forth dead and for three days it was dead because Jesus died for three days and was then awakened by his father; and when young pelicans struck at their parents' faces and by their angered parents were slain, and the mother then opened her side and let blood flow on them to make them alive again, it

14

was only because God after the Fall cast mankind down and then in pity awoke his children with his own blood. If the unicorn could be captured only by a pure virgin, this was so because Jesus took on humanity in a virgin's womb. There was no end of these wonders; they were proclaimed year after year from every pulpit in the Christian world. But were they true?

Richard drew a sigh from the dark chamber of his doubts and glanced again at his brother. He then turned to look at his sister. He then sighed again. He needed someone with whom he could talk about all these things; but if he approached his father there came into the man's eyes that strange searching look which seemed to say, My son, don't ask me questions, for would you have me delivered to the torch and faggots? His father might have been less prudent many years ago, before the Pope in Rome resolved on the extermination of the tens of thousands of people called the Albigenses. These were heretics, it was said, though what part of the true faith they had rejected Richard had never learned. Did they doubt the story of the unicorn, the lion, the griffin? There was something they questioned, and for this they had been massacred by the thousands and the massacre continued unabated. The horrors of those early years, when Richard's family had fled in hiding from place to place, had so deeply seared his soul and mind and had made him so abnormally sensitive that he would sometimes tremble for hours as if chilled. He could never forget how terror of the inquisitors had driven a whole people to such madness that they flung themselves prostrate before the accusers and slavered like beasts. There hadn't been enough prisons to hold them nor enough executioners to destroy them. Little wonder that Victoir's eyes beseeched his son not to ask questions. Little wonder it was that his brother had taken to fondling cats, his sister to a deep quiet sadness out of which she rarely spoke.

Nor would Hillel, his Jew friend, discuss any of these things. In 1204, when Richard was two years old, Nicholas, the most renowned painter in France, had been burned alive at the stake. Richard mentioned this one day to Hillel and in his dry cryptic way Hillel said, "Have you heard of Vilgardus of Ravenna? He brought to light again the great dreams of Virgil, Horace and Juvenal. It is said that he was burned alive but I do not say it." Regarding Richard in his faintly whimsical way but with his eyes

15

veiled and subtle and with the record of some bitter unhappiness everywhere in his face Hillel said, "O nightingale, give over for an hour till the heart sings!"

Quickly Richard asked, "Did you write that?"

"No. How to be a beggar and a fool? Would you know it? Then go read books and learn to be a poet."

After reflecting a few moments on the words Richard said, "But isn't it good to read books and know things?"

"Cato said to know anything is praiseworthy. Abelard said the beginning of wisdom is found in doubting. By doubting, he said, we come to examine; by examining we reach the truth."

"Ah, but you've told me what happened to Abelard!"

"I've told you what others have said."

That was the way with Hillel. Never once had he told Richard what *he* believed; in his subtle way he seemed to reveal it by quoting the words of others. Richard well knew that Jews, hated and degraded by the Church and forced to wear the badge of what Christians called their shame, did not dare to utter words that might be used against them. Yet Richard trusted Hillel and wished that Hillel might trust him. He needed someone to love, to trust, and even more than these, someone to instruct him and lead him to the light. He had no doubt that there was light somewhere. Hillel had once said to him, "One of your Christians spoke a tremendous line—lux immense Deus." The immense light of God! But where was it? Hillel had told him of the great line from Boethius, who saw infinite darkness as a multitude of stars and exclaimed, "If light can thus conceal, wherefore not life?" Yes, yes, Richard had thought many times, the words singing in him, but how was he to find the light which life concealed, if he was to have no teacher, no books?

That was when he was sixteen. A year later Hillel seemed to trust him a little more; he told him of his great admiration for Averroes, the Arabian philosopher, recently dead, who had translated Aristotle and made him popular with certain schoolmen. Averroes, Hillel told Richard, had said, "Among dangerous fictions we must call those which tend to make us look upon virtue as only a means to happiness. If that be so, virtue has no meaning, since we abstain from self-gratification only in the hope of being repaid with interest." Richard had got the words by heart and had then asked himself, Don't Christians abstain because they hope

16

to be repaid with interest? It was also Averroes who had said that of all tyrannies the very worst in the world was that of the priest.

"Please tell me more!" Richard had begged Hillel. "I'll never betray you!"

"If they put you to torture?"

"They can kill me but I won't."

"Richard, you know very well that no tie of kinship, no love of friends is allowed to conceal heresy. Your Church demands that the son must denounce his father, the husband deliver up his wife. You know that children are called on to desert their parents if they suspect them."

"I know, I know! That's why my father won't talk to me!" He moved closer to look deep into Hillel's eyes. "I swear—"

"No, don't swear."

"But I must know, I tell you! I must know what Abelard knew and Averroes and what you know!"

"You'll risk your life if you try to know so much."

"Then I'll risk it. I'll join the poor students in Paris you told me about. You say they sleep on straw they buy in Straw Street. I don't have straw. You say they're so poor they share a single gown which in turn they wear to their classes. I have only these rags."

"They're burning the works of Aristotle at the university in Paris."

"All right, then I'll go to the school of Geneviève, where Abelard taught. Or I'll go to Toulouse or Bologna."

"But how?"

"Yes by the mercy of God, how? How can I, a slave—"

"Please don't say it."

A little later Richard said to Hillel one night, "Maybe I've found a way. If I could be some lord's jus primae noctis child—" He faltered on the Latin; it was a phrase he had heard Hillel use. Richard meant that if he were a bastard, if he were the fruit of some lord's right to the peasant girl before she lay with her husband, he might establish a claim to freedom. As for bastardy, he had no shame in that, nor had the Christian world, for bastard was a common surname.

After he had blurted out his hope he thought that Hillel was looking at him with pity. Was is because physical love for Jews

17

was a holy thing, but for Christians only a necessary evil? "I was only wondering about it!" he cried, confused and abashed. "I—O God am I to be a slave all my life, beating the moat to silence the frogs so that the baron and his knights can sleep? The son of a bitch! If I ever have children are they not to be my own, but divided up among monks and lords to be their slaves? If my lord's beast dies must I forever go on soaking it in salt water and trying to sell it to some fool? That or be flogged? Am I to live in rags and filth and eat bread made of twigs and soup made of barley husks, while the lord who owns me copulates first with the girl I marry, sells me with his land, beats me and starves me and at last casts me out to die?"

He was speaking with hysterical anger. Hillel raised a hand to silence him. "You should never say such things, to me or to anyone. You well know—"

"Yes, I know, I know it all! I know that the baron owns me and the Church owns the baron, and God—"

"Richard!" Hillel said sharply. "May your memory be for a blessing, but don't say these things to me. You know that if your bishop were to hear them or Father Luce—"

"That boar!" said Richard and spat with disgust.

Father Luce! He, Richard, the slave, had hoped to marry Madelon, the strange ecstatic and dedicated daughter of Chretien and Noelle, but Father Luce was taking her into his gentle, pious and sinister custody. How he hated the man! He still hoped to wed Madelon, but more than that, deeper than that, was his wish to be a learned and enlightened man, like Abelard, like Nicholas, like Pierre de Bruys, who for expressing his contempt for the vices of the clergy had been burned alive. Richard hoped to be a free man, free not only of the baron but free of fear, free to express his thoughts, free to think...free, God willing, to write books. But how vain and foolish his hope was!

It had been Hillel more than all other people on earth who had fired him with the hope. He wanted to ask Hillel so much but he knew that the man had to be prudent. It was Pope Innocent the Third himself, now dead these four years, who had said that all Jews were outside the bounds of humanity, a subhuman people apart from all people. The Church and the aristocracy hated the Jews, and many of the common Christians hated them. The Church was determined to obliterate from Christian ritual and

18

practice all traces of Jewish influence; to stop Jews from prose-
lytizing; to prevent Christian Jews from reverting to Judaism;
and to stop Jews from associating with heretics. From his father
Richard had learned: Jews were not allowed to build their synagogue on higher ground than the Christian church; Christian
women were forbidden to enter any Jewish place without an es-
cort; Jews were believed by many Christians to use the blood of
Christians in their Passover bread; and Jews, when represented in
Christian dramas, were always odiously grotesque or malformed or
avaricious and stupid. Jews, like an accursed people set apart in
the contempt of all men, had to wear their shameful telltale badge,
as the leper had to wear his own. . . . Yes, Richard understood
why Hillel had to be prudent, why he did not wish to talk to a
Christian about many things; but Hillel was a doctor, and Jewish
doctors, let the Church say what it would, were popular with most
of the common people. Jewish men of learning were for Richard,
as the Arabs were, fascinating intimations of the lux immense
Deus. . . .

He would not be put off but became an almost insufferable
nuisance. Again and again he slipped over to the small house
where Hillel lived, and gently knocked, and when the door was
opened walked in, even though he knew that he was interrupting
a scholar's labors, even though he knew that Hillel was alarmed,
not alone for himself but for both of them. But Richard had nobody else to turn to, and he must learn, *he must learn,* even at the
risk of being accused, at the risk of being burned. He must know
what the wise men had said. Every scrap of learning which Hillel
dropped he seized and possessed, memorized and treasured, and
whispered over and over while lying on his mat and scratching at
vermin; while toiling bare-footed and half-naked and more than
half-starved in the baron's fields; or while beating the moat to
silence the frogs, so that the proud fat baron and his knights could
sleep. He remembered them all!

> O nightingale, give over for an hour
> till the heart sings!

And Boethius:

> Look to the highest of the heights of heaven,
> see where the stars still keep their ancient peace!

He remembered word for word what an Archbishop had dared to say: The wretched world lies now under the tyranny of foolishness: things are believed by Christians of such absurdity as no one ever could aforetime induce the heathen to believe. He had a priceless collection from Abelard. All error, Abelard had said, came from four major sources: authority, custom, opinions of the ignorant, and the concealment of ignorance with a pretense of knowledge. Abelard had said: All knowledge is good, even that which relates to evil, because a righteous man must have it. To be righteous? Richard wondered. Abelard had said that no act is sinful if the person is not conscious of it as a sin. He had said that it was impossible to believe what was not understood, and ridiculous for anyone to set forth to others what neither he nor they could rationally conceive. He had said that among Christians the blind were still leading the blind, and for that he was condemned at the Council of Soissons. He had pointed out the discrepancies in the holy texts and the absurd contradictions among the Fathers themselves; and for that he had been condemned. He had said that the first key to wisdom was questioning, diligent and unceasing; and for that he had been condemned. Yes, yes, but the Old Testament said that in much wisdom is much grief and he that increases knowledge increases sorrow! Yes, and St. Paul had said, If any man is ignorant let him be ignorant!

But Abelard, Richard had gathered from Hillel's words, had not been a great man in all ways, especially in his early years. When young he had been a vain inconsiderate rakehell, as Francis of Assisi had been; and solely to satisfy his lust he had seduced the innocent and unsuspecting Heloise. The outraged father had then had him castrated. Then there came to Abelard a great and tender love for a woman, so rare among Christians, so common among Jews. Richard had begged to know the whole story, and Hillel had told him that the story was to be found in the letters, written over many years, after Heloise was immured as a nun and Abelard became the most brilliant teacher of all the monks. Scandalous songs had been written and sung about them in the streets of Paris but their love had become like the stars which Boethius saw.

Hillel had read to Richard from one of Abelard's marvelous letters: "Dearest, you know—who knows not?—how much I lost in you, and that an infamous act of treachery robbed me of you and of myself at once. The greater my grief, the greater need of consolation, not from another but from you, that you who are alone my cause of grief may be alone my consolation. It is you alone who can sadden me or gladden me or comfort me. And you alone owe this to me, especially since I have done your will so utterly that, unable to offend you, I endured to wreck myself at your command. Nay, more than this, love turned to madness and cut itself off from hope of that which alone it sought, when I obediently changed my garb and my heart too in order that I might prove you sole owner of my body as well as of my spirit."

Richard wept to hear such words. In those two, Hillel said, it had been a bitter struggle, before in God and their own great compassion they found peace. Abelard had died first and was laid away in the monastery of Cluny; and a good and holy abbot, Peter the Venerable, wrote a letter to Heloise, telling of the end. Twenty-one years later she died and was laid at his side.

The sad and pathetic and tragic tale had moved Richard so deeply that he had wept for hours and his thoughts had turned with fierce protective tenderness to Madelon, who seemed to him in her spirit and holiness, her selflessness and trust, to be so much like Heloise; and to himself, in whom he wished to find, not the young Abelard of unbridled passions but the older Abelard who was a great scholar and a great saint. "Madelon and Richard!" he had murmured, for he was only seventeen. He had even felt an urge to unman himself, and then, liberated from passion, to give his whole mind and soul to the joy in books. He thought it might be well for Madelon to become a nun, if this were possible, for she was as poor as barley chaff and her family was of no social worth; and for him to become a monk, when they would then exchange their sweet and tender letters, while love ripened to its final consummation of a common tomb.

But his romantic dream was not to be. Even while he dwelt on its tender intimacies, Father Luce caressed Madelon's arms and with his ardent black eyes looked deep into the cloudy gray of her own.

II

Father Luce, friend of the baron, had a countenance that held a person's gaze and aroused his wonder. His eyes were close together; deepset, and so morbidly intent that they looked like two shining black discs when his upper lids were lowered, and like two glowing black stones when the lids were raised. His stare was hard, direct, hypnotic. Above the eyes were large brow ridges thatched with heavy black brows. His forehead was narrow, his temples sunken, and these and his sunken cheeks gave extraordinary prominence to his cheek bones and to the large ears standing behind them. His nose and his chin were large and strong; his upper lip was wide; and his mouth was wide, with lips that looked as firm as leather. The lips were always parted when his intent eyes studied a woman. Above his low and deeply wrinkled forehead his hair was receding on either side of a black bushy forelock.

Since it was his habit to spy out heretics, and since on their conviction he got a part of their confiscated property, he had amassed considerable wealth, including several houses. It was in one of these, a cottage with two rooms, that he had persuaded Madelon to spend a part of her time, so that in privacy she could commune with her Lord. Father Luce's passion was seduction but he would have been astonished and offended if anyone had called him a scoundrel. Sincerely, in the depths of his strange heart, he saw the matter this way: there was only one true faith in the world, that of his Church, and he was one of its holy men. A holy man could do nothing unholy; he sanctified those with whom he was intimate, he ennobled and strengthened them. He delighted in visiting the nunneries and debauching the virgins there and he believed as fully as he believed in the risen Lord that every virgin who accepted his embrace would inherit a higher glory. He might have accepted the doctrine of Illuminism, popular with some who wore the cloth: "The body cannot contaminate the soul; we must, by means of sin, which makes us humble and cures our pride, destroy sin." Still, he did not think of himself as a sinful man, nor an imprudent man either: before entering the house to visit Madelon he always asked her father to come with him to the door and to wait there.

Madelon in her own way was as remarkable as Father Luce. She was hardly more than a child—she was barely fourteen when one Sunday in the churchhouse Father Luce first saw her and fixed his enraptured gaze on the corpselike whiteness of her skin. Like all peasants and serfs she had been undernourished; unlike most of them she had never cared for food but from early childhood had dedicated herself to the sacred heart of Jesus and to her dreams and visions. She was a very frail and delicate girl, almost an invalid, with a thin white delicate unsmiling face. Her cloudy gray eyes were filled with otherworldliness; her lips were soft and tender but without color; her cheeks were and had always been as white as death. She felt deeply because she had suffered deeply and still suffered, though the cause of her sorrow had baffled her tired and prematurely aged mother, wearied her sardonic father, and amused her roguish younger sister. She had, even as a small child, devoted herself to the sick when she was allowed to; with little acts of charity she had tried to lighten the poverty of the poor. Charity was her passion and her heart was pure love.

Like most girls of Provence, with its hot burning sun and its periods of drouth, she had a nervous and excitable temperament, and had suffered, like so many women in this area, from what was known as vapors of the womb. Some women in this climate became wanton, carnal and self-indulgent. Some, like Madelon, turned with intense devotion to the spiritual life. At fourteen she was like a child of four, and it was her helplessness, her sad white face and her purity of soul that appealed so deeply to Richard.

From her earliest years she had seen visions. At Mass one day, when she was only a child, she became convinced that the holy wafer, drawn to her by the depths of her love and longing, had entered her mouth without assistance from her. Years later, when she went to Confession, though she had nothing to confess but her strange imaginings, the priest said to her, as she reported the matter to her parents, "I've been expecting you." She had rarely left the hovel of her home save to go to church but had sat hour after hour in her own quiet brooding, melting in the wonder of her marvelous visions.

When Father Luce with the most exquisite kindliness suggested to her that she ought to spend a part of her time in his little cottage, because it was a holy house and she could there commune with her Lord undistracted by evil forces, she did not protest at all. Like the child she was she went with him; and still with the utmost delicacy he showed her the two small clean rooms, the wash basin, the window which looked south to the baron's castle, and the bed. Madelon was hardly conscious of these things. She was so little conscious of him that she was unaware of his rapt gaze or of his lingering handclasp.

Madelon spent a part of her time there, and Father Luce came to visit her, after posting her father at the door so that the village louts would not gossip. His manner toward Chretien, the father, was casual and worldly; he remarked on the condition of the baron's fields, on the prowling of wolves at nighttime, on a new bell that had just been installed in the church, whose tones, he said, were far mellower than those of the old; but the moment he was inside and the door was closed behind him his manner changed. Then his black eyes darted round him, looking for Madelon, and if he did not see her at once his whole face took on an expression of crafty vengefulness. The moment he saw her his manner again changed. He would then rush over to her and clasp both of her hands in his, her small white hands which had no strength to resist him or withdraw; and he would lead her to the bed, explaining in his soft sibilant persuasive voice that she could commune more fully when lying prone.

After Madelon lay on the bed he would sit at her side. When not clasping her hands or trying to fondle her his own hands would finger the chain of his pectoral cross, while he supplicated her with a whispering voice. He told her that he loved her. But he never said, "I love you dearly" or, "I love you deeply" or, "I love you with passion"; these were profane expressions which his Church did not approve. He would say, "I desire your company in the name of Jesus." He would say, "I wish to embrace you in the Holy Virgin."

On the day when Richard sat in the hovel, looking now and

24

then at his brother or sister, thinking of Hillel, of Abelard and Heloise, Father Luce was sitting by Madelon.

"Did you know," he asked, bending low to fix her with his hypnotic stare, "that my name means light? It is the same as Lucas or Luke or Lux. . . ."

If Madelon had been alert she could have read the man's soul in the quality of his voice. But Madelon, though vaguely conscious of him, was filled with that ecstasy that never left her; she knew that the holy man was there, sitting at her side, whispering to her, but these were only a dimmer part of her cloudy consciousness, in which a feeling of intense sweetness was the core. She was vaguely aware of the way he fingered the cross, which hung down his bosom; and when he clasped her hands she was vaguely aware of that. She knew that he was a friend of the powerful baron. With happiness that was deep and hushed and still she knew that he was a holy man. But her passion was communion with Jesus, and even when he caressed her frail arms or touched her white cheeks she gave her soul to that.

"Madelon?" he said.

"Yes, Father."

"You must put yourself completely in my hands and give yourself up to me."

"Yes, Father," she said but she did not know what she was saying.

"I will embrace you in the Holy Virgin."

"Yes, Father," she whispered but she did not know what he meant.

"The deeds of holy men are holy."

"Yes."

"You must endure all things for me."

"Yes, Father."

No other woman had ever made such tumultuous appeal to his erotic passions. He trembled while clasping her hands and staring into her eyes or gazing at her soft childlike face. He did not know how much longer he could control the passion that assaulted him and flowed through him with the yearning of springtime; and while he was thinking of the matter she startled him with childlike words.

She said: "Last night I dreamed a dream. In this dream—" she was speaking like one who spoke not to him but to herself or her Lord "—I saw a soul tormented, oh, so awfully, by the lusts of flesh; and I thought if only one of our Lord's holy men—"

"What, what?" he said, interrupting her. "Madelon, do you know what you are saying? I am a holy man."

"Yes, Father." She was silent a moment; when, as though he had not interrupted her at all, she went on in her dreamy child-like voice: "This soul was in mortal sin and our Mother said to me, You must save this soul—"

"Madelon!" he cried and clasped both her arms.

On his next visit she startled him again. She said she had had another dream. In this dream she saw a wild and angry sea, filled with pirates, and on a tiny piece of wood she saw a priest, buffeted by the waves and the storms; for it was storming from a black sky and she cried out, "O Lord, O Lord, save him!"

Father Luce arose from the bed. "Madelon," he said gravely, "I think that sometimes Satan is in you. You have wicked notions. You must deliver yourself to me, completely, your whole soul. For I am a holy man. Do you understand me?"

Madelon began to weep. She wept, as she always did, in a soft gentle way, her whole being melting into sorrow. It was when he saw her weep that Father Luce's passion almost breached its walls. Hastily he sat by her and with one hand covered her eyes, so that she could not see. Then his hot gaze searched her frail body, only partly concealed by her garment. Her legs from the knees down were bare. She seemed to have no breasts; indeed, in no part of her did she have a womanly form. But the fact that she had no breasts and was so weak and defenseless and girllike only made his passion the more intense.

Of all the women this man had embraced that one had most completely enraptured him, had most completely torn him from his moorings and delivered him over to blind passion, who had been thin, even emaciated, who was little more than skin and bones. When he reached under her to press deeper his hands had found no buttocks or almost none but only the hip bones, the outline of which he had sharply felt; and in that moment a terrible groan had been torn from him, a deep anguished cry from his throat, and with all his strength he had crushed the frail thing to him. He thought later that for a few moments he had lost consciousness.

26

Now, with his gaze roving over Madelon's form, he felt a return of the same impulse to crush and rend; to sink deep and inside and out of memory; to absorb and leave nothing; to possess utterly, losing himself in the possession or to destroy the possessed. He was bending over her, his emotions so hot and naked that he was gasping; and he was reaching round her to draw her to him when with a low scream Madelon strove to throw him off and sit up.

The cry sobered him. He clapped a hand to her mouth and bending to her ear hissed, "You fool! It is I, Father Luce." Madelon was babbling under his palm and he crushed the palm down until her struggles ceased and she was still. After a little while he took his hand away and looked at her accusingly and said, "Madelon, Satan is in you. You are wrestling with the Devil. You must give yourself to me or the Devil will take you. Do you understand?"

Momentarily in possession of her faculties Madelon said quietly, "He has taken my father."

"Your father?" he said, his eyes looking into her eyes.

"My dear father," she said.

Still looking into her eyes Father Luce considered the matter. Then with the exquisite gentleness of which he was such a master he said, "I will save your father, Madelon, if I can. But first I must save you."

Madelon whispered, "Yes." She had no one to tell her of the dreadful power of the priest and confessor over women and especially over nuns, and in her whole heart and soul she was a nun. She had no mother to advise her, for her mother had been terrified into silence. She had no father, for her father was a crafty rascal intriguing with the Devil. There was Richard. . . .

Father Luce left her now, knowing from long experience when to proceed and when to desist. He chided her gently and told her to humble herself and she promised that she would seek a deep and abiding humility. He went to the door and the moment he opened it he looked at Chretien's eyes to read the man's thoughts there; but Chretien was unruffled and unalarmed. Many times he had heard his daughter scream in her sleep.

He said: "Has she been dreaming again?"

Father Luce seized his cue. "Yes," he said blandly. Looking at Chretien's huge curved nose and low recessed forehead he added:

27

"I think there is a devil in her but I will cast it out. It will take time."

"Yes," said Chretien tonelessly, "it will take time."

"She's all right now. I'll see her tomorrow."

"You'll see her tomorrow," Chretien said.

Father Luce walked away, erect and proud, as befitted a holy man, and Chretien stared after him, his eyes narrowed to sly lights. The two men looked much alike. Chretien looked like a Father Luce whose huge nose had been curved into a beak and a part of whose forehead had been lost in the sinking of his skull. They had much in common in their attitudes toward many things, though the one was a holy man of the cloth and the other was an impoverished vendor of old clothes whose secret deity was Satan.

"So the devil is in her?" Chretien thought, after Father Luce had disappeared. "Well, that much is good." In the darker recesses of his crafty mind a wicked design was taking form. He softly opened the door to look in and to listen but, catching no glimpse of his daughter and hearing no sound, he shut the door and turned away.

Chretien, whose name in the language of Provence was the word for Christian, believed that no person on earth knew as much about Satan as he knew. He was not for Chretien or for anyone else in this time a physical monster. For such as Father Luce he was a man degraded and corrupted by his own evil; for Chretien he was the Lord of the Lost and the Morning Star. It was possible, he admitted, that Satan had a huge chest and gaping mouth and fierce teeth, a low forehead and red flaming hair, and powerful jaws like those of a wild boar. But for Chretien he was not a monster, no, but a being with a devilish sense of humor, who delighted in practical jokes upon such self-righteous hypocrites as Father Luce. If the clapper of a church bell refused to ring was it because, as the faithful said, Satan was sitting on it? Perhaps. Chretien knew of a certain prior who was so afraid of being carried off by Satan that he had a guard day and night. Was Satan delighted by the man's foolishness? Knowing very well that he was, Chretien opened his mouth in a wide grin, revealing the stained snags of his teeth.

Glancing slyly round him, for he was on his way to the wine tavern, he saw Elie, the crippled beggar, and concealed a grin of delight. Elie was one of Satan's most enterprising imps: if relics were brought to the village Elie always dashed into hiding, lest he be cured of his infirmity and deprived of his way of making a living. But that, Chretien supposed, was only Elie's manner of showing his contempt. Elie's father had been a priest who, to get rid of a woman of whom he had been enamored, held the Holy Wafer in his mouth instead of swallowing it; whereupon he had swelled up until he could barely pass through the doorway. He had then told the story of a woman who had placed a wafer among her bees, which at once built around it a lovely little chapel, and inside it an altar, at which they worshiped the Virgin. Such tales, with which Chretien's world was filled, indicated to him the fertile resources of Satan's wit. Though Elie, the rascal, concealed himself when holy relics were brought to the village, sometimes, in imitation of wandering vagrants, he appeared bearded and tonsured and wearing a religious habit, and peddled false relics and summoned the people to witness his miracles.

But for all his resourcefulness Elie did not have Chretien's knowledge of Satan or close kinship with him. Christians said that Satan's sin was pride, and certainly he had a right to be proud, for had he not made fools of millions of Christians? Jews said his sin lay in envy of man; for when Adam was created, all the angels bowed to the new king of the earth, Satan alone refusing; and when God rebuked him Satan replied, "I will exalt my throne above his and establish my dominion over him." Possibly, then, the Jews were right. But Chretien preferred the explanation of a wandering impostor: Satan, this man said, committed the great sin when he dared to think for himself, and all his imps were sinful for the same reason. Satan was the great opponent, in Chretien's opinion, of ecclesiastical tyranny, and some day would return triumphant to heaven.

How many followers did God have? No man knew but a prominent churchman had computed the number of Satan's—7,405,926, divided into seventy-two companies, each under a captain. Chretien thought of himself, quite naturally and with glowing pride, as one of the captains; for he had made a pact, and though it had not been written with his own blood—Chretien could neither read nor write—it had been sanctified and sealed with his blood, while the words were spoken: I, Chretien, give myself to Satan, body and soul, now and forever, to use me as he will, to the end that I may assist him in restoring reason and joy to the earth.

How many titles did God have? He was called Father and Almighty and a few others but Satan's names and titles had the magic of a jongleur: he was prince and god of this world, prince of the powers of the air, prince of the devils and of hell and of darkness, the angel of the bottomless pit and the dark son of night, the black archangel in the midst of the infernal, the genius of evil and the piercing serpent, the great red dragon and the roaring lion, the adversary of the Almighty himself and the infernal and potent rival of God, the Good Man, the Good Fellow and Gentleman Jack. He was his Satanic Majesty and Infernal Highness, but more than all these, above all these, he was the Star of Morning. How large was God's kingdom? The Star of Morning ruled over the four dominions, the four limbos. Two were on the borders of hell, the Limbo of the Fathers, inhabited by pre-Christian men who, though holy and righteous, were not as accessible to God as Father Luce; and the Limbo of the Infants, in which wailed in torment the unbaptized children. The third was Purgatory, a kind of ablution chamber in which dead Christians washed themselves, in preparation for the intolerable monotony of the Christian heaven; and the fourth was Hell, the region of eternal flames, from which, the priests liked to intone, Nulla est redemptio!

The words of priests were like soft falling rain on the fertile areas of Chretien's wicked soul. How he loved the verses from the book called Revelation, "These both were cast alive into a lake of fire burning with brimstone"; and the one like unto it, "But the fearful and the unbelieving and the abominable and murderers and whoremongers and sorcerers and idolaters and all liars, shall have their part in the lake which burns with fire and brimstone, which is the second death." Setting his wine-cup down Chretien snorted with joy, for he knew that Satan had no fires save the fires in men like Father Luce. How the holy men had been deceived! Matthew had written, "But the children of the kingdom shall be cast out into outer darkness: there shall be weeping and gnashing of teeth." Mark had written of the burning in fires of hell that would never be quenched, burning and screaming in pain that would never be stilled. Reflecting on how completely Satan had duped the offspring of Adam, forcing them to live in dread of torments and terrors, driving them mad with fear, he chuckled deep inside him and looked with renewed relish at the world roundabout. His contempt for his fellowmen was utter. His admiration for Satan was boundless.

Though only an illiterate rag-vendor Chretien was no fool. He had his joys and nobody suspected him, not even that godbelly of righteousness who looked like his own brother. He also kept a sharp eye out for heretics, not to inform on them but to warn them; and now, sipping cheap wine, he wondered about Richard. He wondered about Madelon. He was not sure that she had not suspected him. The scheme evolving in his mind was to encourage Father Luce to find in Madelon a heretic, after he had exhausted his lust, and then to blackmail the priest. If Madelon knew about his pact with Satan she might some time in her hysterical babbling reveal it, and to Father Luce of all people. Well, he would destroy them both. He wished also to destroy his wife, Old Noelle, for he imagined that she had put on him the curse of sexual impotence.

She was called Old Noelle by her neighbors, though she was not yet thirty-five. She was a sad, quiet, wrinkled, graying, defeated and frightened woman. She had had nine children and all but two of them were born dead or had died at birth. Believing that God had cursed her with a dreadful curse she had found a frog and spat three times into its mouth. Because she suffered from sleeplessness she had taken a louse from her hair and put it in a small piece of hollow bone and sealed it in with wax from her ears; and this she wore around her neck. Because she had heard that witches could accomplish wondrous things with human blood, fat, guts, or with almost anything from the human body, she ate her fingernail parings and sometimes her hair. Chretien thought that Satan had made a more complete fool of only one person, a monk who had appeared one day to announce himself as the Angel of Philadelphia and the special envoy of God.

When, toward evening, Chretien entered their hovel, Old Noelle had just returned from the fields where, barefooted and in rags, like most people of her social level, she had been toiling for the baron. She was sitting, as was her habit when in the shack, on her mat in a corner, her hands piously folded, her bloodshot eyes fixed on nothing. Her younger daughter Simone had come in and was sitting on a segment of tree bole in another corner. When Chretien filled the doorway the hovel darkened, and when he stepped inside there was light again.

31

He looked first at his daughter and in the pert and impish way she had she looked at him, her brown eyes as round as her small round face. Simone was ten and unlike nearly all children of serfs and peasants looked well-nourished and healthy. This was because she was resourceful and daring. She foraged in the baron's woods and fields, though she had no right to, but she was wise for her years and she had seen him looking at her and she knew that if she ever married he would take her as his own for the bridal night. And, too, people liked her and sometimes gave her things to eat.

Chretien looked next at his wife and went over to the few broken pots which they owned, to see if there was anything for supper. There was nothing of course except some barley flour, a double handful of small withered beans and some acorns. There was no bread. The bread of the well-to-do was made of a good quality of wheat flour but that of the peasant was coarse, of gray or black color, baked of barley meal mixed with chestnuts or peas, or with powdered twigs.

Simone hopped off her stool and drew from a hiding-place a bone with some flesh on it. She showed it to him, hoping he would be pleased.

"Where did you get it?" he asked.

"A friend."

"Who?"

"A friend," she said, smiling up at him.

He took the bone and sniffed. It seemed to be fresh enough, though that hardly mattered, since the poor ate decayed and stinking meat when they could get it. The bone and its shreds of flesh would make a soup. He turned to a stone jug, used to bring water from the village well, and saw that it was empty. He took it up and left the hut but turned to look back and say, "Madelon has been screaming again." Then he chuckled in his deep and diabolic way and went off to replenish the jug.

To reach the well he had to pass the alley between the wineshop and the cobbler's hut. In this alley was a wooden plank, placed across from wall to wall, about two feet above the welter of human excrement below it. This was the village's public privy. Just before Chretien came on the scene a drunken lout had been sitting on the plank and had fallen off. He had toppled backward into the depth of filth and two drunken companions were dragging him out and hustling him off to the village well to cleanse him. With no sense of outrage at all Chretien followed them. The people had no knowledge of the relationship between polluted waters and disease; no suspicion that the filthy conditions in which they lived caused plagues, epidemics, diarrhea, vomiting and a host of other ailments; and no approval among church leaders of bathing and cleanliness. The Arabs, known as the cleanest people on earth, were despised by Christians for their cleanliness; and whenever possible Christians destroyed their public baths, calling them temples of the body, which they abhorred. Even the wealthy ones, like the baron and his wife, never bathed but drenched themselves with scents or carried bouquets of fragrant flowers and herbs. Though Pope Boniface had proscribed mixed bathing, lovers in the upper classes did sometimes begin their trysts by bathing together and searching one another for lice. Elienor, the baron's wife, and her lady friends had a Latin maxim over which they laughed with obscene relish: dum paro mempirium, sub grumpho murmurat anus. Mempiria was used as a toilet paper, or, more commonly, grass or hay. The monks, who called their privy a necessarium, arranged the seats so that they could see one another while squatting.

So it was with no sense of anything improper or dangerous to health that Chretien waited until the drunk had been lowered into the well. He was dragged out, gasping and drenched and half-drowned and dripping with his filth, and marched off by his hilarious companions; and Chretien pulled the bucket up to fill his jug. He bore the jug over to his hovel and looked round to see if there were sticks for a fire. His shack, like those of most of the poor, was made of tree branches and mud and leaves; it had no floor but the earth, a sagging roof, no chimney, no fireplace, no sewage. The fire was laid by a wall lined with stones and the smoke escaped through the doorway. Most of the poor people suffered with eye trouble, as Old Noelle did, because of the smoke. After Chretien had torn twigs from a wall and kindled a fire the smoke-filled hovel sent Simone coughing and choking outside. Old Noelle did not stir.

Because she did not stir Chretien was angered and he strode over and smote her. He knew his rights. The baron and his underlings had a legal right to beat his serfs, and often did for the most trivial offenses; and in turn a Christian husband had the right to beat his wife and children. Chretien was not a very brutal man—not so brutal as some men he knew, who had so brutally flogged their wives that they were maimed and stiffened. He struck her one sharp blow and said, "Get up."

The woman was almost too tired to rise. She struggled, turning first one way and then another, like a beast, and at last over to her hands and knees. She thrust her rump up and was wracked by a fit of coughing. Then, when it was stilled, she rose slowly and painfully; wiped at her running eyes with a forearm; and began the preparation of supper.

Chretien went outside and sat by a wall. He looked over to Father Luce's house where Madelon was and again his eyes became sly and crafty. He heard Old Noelle coughing and for a few moments thought about her, wondering if he ought to put her away. If a husband found that he was related to his wife he could kick her out, and some of them accomplished this by faking a relationship. But never mind about that now. He was more interested in knowing how long it would take Father Luce to debauch Madelon and what he intended to do with the girl after he had done it. Chretien intended to have something to say about that. He bent forward, his arms clasping his knees, his shrewd mind bright with cunning, and stared at the house and matured his plot

III

Just after daylight the next morning Richard and his father, both barefooted, both garbed in rags, were hoeing weeds in one of the baron's gardens. Back and forth, up and down the rows, they moved side by side and did not speak, the one beyond hope, the other determined with all his heart to have a better life than his father had had. But how was he to do it? Richard asked himself, feeling the sweat run down over his face, feeling the old despair within.

He knew well that the serfs were bound by law to the soil: the sequela, the law called them, as distinguished from the freeman's liberi; they could be bought and sold or given away or flogged or killed. If they dared to poach on the lord's domains, including his wooded areas, or to filch from his crops, the punishment was terrible. If they needed twigs for their fires and with a crooked stick pulled down a bough out of reach, they were known as those who by hook or crook poached against their betters. Their religion forbade their labor on holy days but if they did not labor on holy days they were fined for idleness. If too sick to toil they had to hire someone to take their place.

He knew it all, O Lord, he knew it all!

At Easter they must plow, sow, harrow; in June, cut and pile the hay and carry it to the manor house; in August, reap the grain. In October the wine was made; in November, the pigs taken to the acorn forests. Their house was commonly a hut in a field, fenced with a thorn hedge; it might have a tiny chamber for grain, one for fodder, and one in which the family lived. The serf might hope one day to own a pothook, a trivet, a kettle, a shovel, a sauce pan and a ladle, and one bed in which all his family slept. He might, if very lucky, own a cupboard, a cheesepress, a crock, some baskets, a ladder, a plow, a billhook, shears, harrow and a litle cart. He might own two or three scrawny beasts.

But from year's end to year's end he would know that taxes were determined as the lord willed. The lord could tax for his ransom, for the knighting of a son, the marriage of a daughter, or for a housewarming. The serf had to grind and bake at the lord's mill and oven and pay whatever percentage the lord decreed. If he owned anything and wanted to sell it he had to get his lord's permission and pay a percentage on that. If a serf died the lord claimed his best chattel, and the rector the second best. The serf sinned if he married a relative, yet was punished if he tried to marry into a clan not his own. The lord's favorites were men and women with strong backs and weak minds, who would have many children to labor for him; and if a man serf lost his wife and did not marry again within a year he was fined by the lord, for loss of offspring.

O God, he knew it all!

He knew that the manor was the center of life. Customs, arbitrarily determined by the lords or abbots, varied from manor to manor, and Richard admitted that Guillem was not so ruthless and exacting as some lords of whom tales were told, including those in the cloth. A serf on Guillem's domain could take as much grass as he could lift on the point of a scythe, as many oats as he could take thrice with one hand. Some lords complained of large hands but not Guillem. He could pile his stall full of hay as high as his loins—and some lords who abided by this custom hated tall men. A serf could have as many sheaves of straw as he could carry under one arm while holding the lap of his tunic in his hand. If a plowman broke the lord's plow he was fined a loaf of bread as tall as the plow wheel. If a serf wished to learn what his rights were under the law he had to pay a fee for the information.

But all these and many more things like them were not the worst. The lord, in his frequent hunting forays, had the right to dash across the serf's crops, if one were lucky enough to have a small plot of his own. If wolves and boars and other beasts from the woods came in and devastated the serf's grain or vegetables he risked the most dreadful punishment if in driving the beasts away he injured one. All wild things belonged to the lords. Nor were

36

these yet the worst of it. Some lords had informers who not only spied on the toilers but tempted them to break the rules, so that they could be fined for the lords' enrichment. Even extortion was sometimes employed. Richard had known an old crippled serf, bent, gray, gnarled at forty, whose limbs had been twisted and broken when the man was young, in an atempt to extort money from him.

He knew it all and he hated it.

And what were the hours of toil? From daylight until dark the year around—and sometimes after dark as when, exhausted from a hard day in the fields, Richard had to go over and beat the waters of the moat, so that the baron and his idlers could sleep. Was this to be his life all his years? He'd rather die, he'd rather be clubbed to death or delivered over as a heretic, than to live as his father had lived, or Old Noelle, or most of the helpless slaves who were his neighbors. If this was the Christian way, then by the living God he would not be a Christian! If this degradation of man to a level below beasts was what Jesus had taught, then he would no longer believe in Jesus. But where could he go, what could he do?

His father, in his tired hopeless way, would have him continue to pay crushing taxes to lord, Church and king; to toil most of his time in the lord's fields and pay most of what he received in taxes, dues, fees and fines; and when he was too weary to move, to labor for several weeks in every year on the public roads. His father would say, If you are lucky you will have enough for yourself and family to eat, of the coarsest fare; enough to clothe yourself in rags; and if you are unlucky you will be flogged to death for breaking some law you had never heard of. You will have a mud hut, his father would say; a hard bed crawling with lice; children who will die at birth or live through scrawny childhood; and a wife who will be bony and broken at thirty, and you with her. His father would say, If you are lucky you won't be burned alive.

Glancing around him for sign of a spy and then pausing to lean on his hoe, Richard dashed the sweat from his brow and said, "Blessed are ye that hunger for ye shall be filled! Blessed are ye that weep now for ye shall laugh!"

Startled, his father looked at him anxiously and again wondered if this rebellious son was his own. Quietly he said: "In another life."

"Says a dirty lying thieving priesthood!"

"Richard—"

"Blessed are the meek for they shall inherit the earth! What earth? The little piece they're buried in. Blessed are the pure in heart for they shall see God! What pure in heart? Church leaders in their jewels and velvets and silks? Father Luce? Do you know what he is doing now?"

"I don't want to know."

"Why not? Are you afraid of me, your son?"

"If they should torture—"

"I wouldn't talk!" Richard cried. "They could kill me but I wouldn't talk."

"You are young," his father said sadly. "But you are old enough to know that spies are everywhere. It's true we have nothing. If we were condemned they would get nothing. But if you anger Father Luce—"

"I know, I know what you'd say! You'd say I must keep my mouth shut, I must let him rape the girl I love, I must—"

"Richard, come, we must labor."

"All right, but I can talk while I labor. If my own father won't listen—"

"But no good can come of it."

"I must understand these things. Is this what Jesus meant, this wealthy Church, and us the slaves toiling to make it richer? Is this what our religion means? If it does, father, I'm not a Christian. I'd a thousand times rather be a Jew. I'd rather be the lowest heathen in the whole heathen world."

"Richard," said his father, "listen to me. Please listen to me. You can say such things to me, for I'll tell no one; but if you begin to say such things to others, even to Father Raoul—"

"Father Raoul is a good and holy man."

"Yes, so he is. But he's a churchman first, Richard, and a friend after that."

"Yes, maybe. But I'll never say them to Father Raoul."

"You might say them to—well, to Madelon."

"You think she would betray me?"

"Ah, Richard, see how young you are! Would you trust such things with a woman?" They were hoeing again. When Richard did not reply his father said: "You shouldn't say such things to anyone, not even to me. There's no person under heaven that they can't make talk with torture. Always remember that. Please for your own good remember that." Victoir paused to scratch himself and with a faint smile said: "If a man itch they say he should roll naked in a field of oats. But whose oats?"

Richard looked at his father with a bitter grin. "Those words could be used against you."

"Yes," Victoir said, "they could. The only safe way is to say nothing at all."

"But do you mind if I talk to you? I have to talk to someone."

"If you talk to anyone it's best if you talk to me."

"Then tell me what you think of the followers of Peter Waldo."

Victoir stiffened and shuddered. Not long before Victoir was born, Peter Waldo, a rich merchant of Lyons, had been deeply stirred by a wandering minstrel. At his own expense he had had the New Testament translated into French and had read it; and then, after dowering his wife and portioning his daughters as nuns, he had taken up a simple evangelical life and preached a return to the humble spirit of the early Church. The Archbishop of Lyons excommunicated him. Priests would not give him permission to teach. Since Pope Lucius the Third had banned him and his followers those who believed with him had greatly increased in numbers. Pope Innocent the Third had then imposed a more drastic ban at his Lateran Council in 1215, and now the Church was exterminating Waldo's followers as a specially odious kind of heretic. . . .

"He only taught what Jesus taught, didn't he?" Richard was saying. "He taught poverty and love and kindliness and all the things that used to be Christian virtues. Didn't he?"

"I don't know," said Victoir, busily hoeing.

"I'll tell you what Hillel told me."

"Don't tell anyone what he tells you."

Richard considered a few moments. "I've no right to, have I?"

"You have no right."

"Then I'll tell you what I heard another man say. The Archbishop of Besancon was denounced for incest. That wasn't long ago and you must remember it."

"I don't."

"I've heard that there have been popes guilty of incest or murder or both. There was Pope—"

"I don't want to hear about it." Wiping sweat from his face

39

and glancing anxiously round him Victoir said: "Won't you ever realize that if you keep saying such things there can be only one end for you?"

"But I'm talking to my father who will tell no one. Would you have me talk to someone else?"

"Never."

"Will there ever be a time in this world when men can say what they think and not be tortured and burned for it?"

"If God wills it."

"But why shouldn't he? Is he our loving Father?—or is he what the priests say, a being who calls into life millions of souls doomed from the start? They tell us that for these millions he prepared hell in the center of the earth, down there under our feet," said Richard. "Would such a God ever want men to speak thoughts that aren't the thoughts his priests have?"

Without pausing in his toil Victoir said, "I can't answer such questions. Our Church has the truth—"

"Oh yes, you say that but you don't believe it. When you were a young man you saw hundreds or thousands of people tortured and killed. My mother was raped how many times by men doing what the Church says God wanted them to do? She still screams in her sleep. Were these people wicked, these Albigenses? I've been told—oh, I won't say who told me—that they were the most civilized people in this part of the world. Doesn't God like civilized people?"

"Their doctrines were not those of the holy Church."

"Maybe not, some of them. But if they made them a good people—"

"They said the Church in Rome is the synagogue of Satan."

"You don't know that it isn't. When you think—"

"Hush," said his father. "Here comes Fleur."

To eat the noon meal which Fleur brought to them they sat in the shade of a tree. For each there was a piece of dark gray barley bread and a handful of peas. Richard crushed the peas in one palm and made a paste to spread on his bread. Fleur, wearing only one patched ragged garment that fell to her knees, sat before the two men and watched them while they ate, her eyes grave and her small sensitive mouth set tight.

Richard looked at her and smiled and said, "Would you like to be a nun?"

40

Fleur glanced at her father before she spoke. "I don't know."

"Children of slaves," said Victoir, "don't become nuns."

"But if she could somehow would you let her?"

"What would I do?" asked Fleur.

"Well," said Richard, "as Father Raoul tells it you'd have seven offices to say daily. At two in the morning there would be the night office; you would all get out of bed when a bell rings and go in darkness to the church choir and say your Matins, and then your Lauds. You'd return to bed but at six you'd get up to say Prime. After that, during the day, you'd say Tierce, Sext, None, Vespers and Compline. You'd have a little food after Prime, food at noon, and again after Vespers."

"All I could eat?" she asked, studying her brother's eyes.

"Father, would she?"

"I don't know about such things."

"I've heard that the nuns talk in signs as much as possible. If Fleur wanted fish she would wag her fingers in the way of a fish-tail. If milk, she would draw on her left little finger. If mustard, she would hold her nose in the upper part of her right hand and rub it. If wine—"

"Wine?" said Fleur.

"I've heard that the nuns get wine. To ask for wine you'd move a forefinger up and down at the end of a thumb before your eye. Like this," he said, showing her.

"Watch what you're saying to your sister," Victoir said.

Fleur looked back and forth from father to brother. "Father, is he lying to me?"

"He talks too much," Victoir said.

That was so, Richard admitted to himself. He wanted to tell his sister, with a touch of malice, that she would neglect her offices and get so that she mumbled her words, the more quickly to be done with them. She would become so lonely that she would sneak animals in. She would die of absolute boredom in ten years but before she died she would be debauched by some priest like Father Luce.

In her soft small voice Fleur said, "Pascal has found another cat."

"Another cat!" said Richard. "We have so much food to eat that he can bring in all the stray cats!"

"It's very scrawny," said Fleur, "and it's blind in one eye."

41

"Blind and scrawny. That's Pascal."

"And it's covered all over with lice."

"So is everything in our house."

"It's an awfully poor little thing," said Fleur.

Feeling anger against his brother Richard got to his feet. Pascal! Pascal had been born on Easter Sunday and his mother had named him Pascal, meaning Paschal, her Easter egg. Pascal, who worshiped two things, cats and the Virgin, and who would if he had his way bring in all the stray cats in Christendom and fondle them and weep over them!

"Another thing," said Richard, when he and his father were again hoeing, "I'm tired of being a slave to feed my brother."

"He's sick," Victoir said.

"He's no sicker than I am. He's a loafer and a no-good. Why should I slave to help feed him and the cats, when all he does all day long is sit and pick lice off them?" He drew a sharp breath. "I tell you, father, I won't do it."

Victoir paused in his labor and turned, and saw that his son was violently trembling. He felt deep pity for him but he felt pity for Pascal too. From early childhood Pascal had been a strange child and had grown stranger with the years; but he was older than Richard and had seen more of the terrors. He had seen his mother stripped naked and raped by a mob destroying the heretics. Richard did not know that and Victoir would never tell him. Victoir would never tell him that his mother went mad with the shame of it and lost the child she was carrying, or that Pascal ran away screaming and was not found for days. He would not tell him that when Elise was shrieking with birth-pains a man thrust into her some kind of instrument to baptize a child that was already dead.

"We must work," said Victoir. "If they see us idle we'll be fined."

"Yes, father, we must work." Richard was weeping. "I—I'm going to see Francis."

"Francis?" said his father gently.

"He's an old and holy man. He'll tell me what to do." Tears mixed with sweat were blinding him. He mistook a bean plant for a weed and struck it, cutting it off; and then, perceiving his error, he knelt quickly and dug a hole and buried the plant. Then he looked round him but he could see no spy in sight. "Or should I see Dominic?"

42

"Francis, if anyone."

"But how can I get away?"

Victoir considered a moment. "Well, you might confess to some sin and ask for a pilgrimage to Francis. Father Raoul might ask the baron to let you go."

"But when I came back what would the baron do to me?"

"Nothing, if Father Raoul sends you."

"Do you think I can trust Father Raoul?"

"I've told you that you can trust no man."

"Not even Francis?"

"No man."

"Do you know of any country in the world where I could go to school and read books?"

He asked the same question of Hillel when, one night after dark, he slipped into the Jew's house.

"Jews have no country," Hillel said.

Richard did not at first grasp the implication in the simple reply. When at last the meaning opened like a light in his mind he said, "You mean if your people had a country I could go there and think and believe as I pleased?"

"If you were a good citizen and did not blaspheme the Holy One or profane the sacred places."

"Has it always been that way with your people?"

Hillel said he did not know. He thought it would be that way now.

"Then," said Richard earnestly, "your people are greater than Christians."

Hillel's face was touched with a faint subtle smile of amusement. "We'll not discuss that."

"My kind of life has been this way as far back as I know anything about it. We've always been owned by someone. Will we always be?"

Christians, Hillel said, had approved slavery for a long time. His people once had. His people did not any more, or at least those did not whom he knew.

"My father tells me I can trust no man. Is it true? If it is true then what are men?"

Hillel's brown eyes were small, and when quizzical, as they often were, they were only points of light. The points of light

43

were now fixed on Richard. "What are men? That, Richard, is probably the most terrible question you could ask."

"You don't mean it."

"Look round at the world. What do you see but arrogance, pomp, slavery, greed, torture, war? All these are men."

"But if there's no man another man can trust, Satan has won, hasn't he?"

For a little while Hillel was thoughtful. "Well, yes, in a way he has, at least for a time. Do you have such deep need to trust someone?"

"Yes."

"A woman?"

"No, a man."

"I suppose you wish to trust me. Is that why you come?"

"Yes!"

"But I'm a Jew."

"Men were men, weren't they, before they were Jew or Christian."

"Your Church says Christians have always been. Didn't Augustine say it? My people say the first man was a Jew." Hillel smiled at Richard's open earnest eyes and added drily: "Possibly they are both wrong."

Richard's face broke into a smile. "Possibly," he said.

"Now suppose," said Hillel, his manner again grave, "some person were to repose trust in you, some person who doesn't happen to believe all the dogmas of your Church. Suppose—God forbid it—you were some day accused of heresy. Suppose that to drag confessions out of you they put you in the torture chamber. Do you know what that would be like?"

"I can imagine it."

"Perhaps a doctor can best imagine it. Before torture they might keep you in a dungeon for months. Do you know what those places are like?"

"Terrible."

"Cold, wet, filthy, full of vermin and rats. Day after day in that utter darkness you sit or lie on a cold floor, with nothing to eat but a little bread and water, with no light, nobody to see, no sound of human voice, until you are weak and sick and dying and almost out of your mind. Then they take you to the torture chamber, a big sinister room shrouded with black and with men in black

44

robes; and they show you the instruments, the pulley, the rack, the boot, fire, all of it, and they explain how horribly they can make you suffer. Probably no man in the world can endure the agonies."

Richard sucked in a deep breath. "A few have," he said.

"You have heard that a few have but I don't think any man could endure all of it. A stupid man more of it, but a sensitive man who loves truth—"

"Truth?"

"Truth or his friends."

"I could," Richard said.

Hillel responded with a gentle shrug. "You're sensitive and highstrung; and physically Richard you're not very strong."

"You mean I couldn't endure it?"

"Nor I. The occasional fanatic can, the person utterly convinced that he is right and that for all his hideous suffering God will give him great glory. But you're a kind of skeptic, aren't you? I don't think any skeptic in the world can endure the pulley or the rack or the boot."

For a few moments they were silent. Richard was wondering about his strength when Hillel said: "I suppose you would like to have your freedom."

"Freedom!" Richard cried. "My God, can you ask me that?"

"But again, do you understand? Your Church doesn't bother the serfs very much. It looks for heretics—"

"Oh, I know! I will say it. No, it doesn't bother the serfs because they have no property to confiscate. It looks for heretics among those with wealth. But if I were free it would not mean that I would be rich."

"No, it wouldn't but you would more likely be a marked man than in your present condition. Serfdom is a terrible thing but it does offer protection against persecution."

Staring at Hillel, wondering what he had in mind, Richard blurted: "I would take my chance."

"Well, I have money—the baron is very generous with me. If you really want your freedom—"

With a strangled cry Richard flung himself to his knees before Hillel. He was weeping again, and with the sobs shaking him he looked up at Hillel, and Hillel looked down at him, his face luminous with compassion.

45

"I wonder how much Guillem would want for you."

"I—O God, I don't know!"

"You understand, of course—Richard, are you listening?"

"Yes!"

"You understand that it must never be known that the money came from me. A Jew's life is hard enough as it is."

"I'd never tell!"

"I wonder who could arrange it. Father Raoul?"

"I could ask him."

"But he must not—"

"I wouldn't tell him, so help me, God!"

"Well, you might speak to him, you might have him ask the baron how much he wants for you. Father Raoul could impress on him that you're not very strong."

"Yes, yes, I know what you mean. He would make the best bargain he could."

"I suppose," said Hillel, with a grimace for his want of prudence, "that it would become known where the money—"

"I'd never tell."

"You're so young. You have so much to learn." Richard got to his feet and was turning away when Hillel said, "No, don't go yet. There's one thing I must tell you. You are young and impulsive, idealistic, trusting. Those are virtues if managed but if not managed they can be the death of you. The thing I would tell you is this, never trust a woman, and above all a woman you love. For the time might come when you would not love her and a woman who turns on a man can be worse than hell itself."

Richard turned his tear-stained face and looked at Hillel. "You mean Madelon?"

"Oh, why do you limit it? I mean any woman. You think you love Madelon?"

"I do love her."

"I think you're too young to know what love is. In any case, Madelon or another, you are so impulsive and idealistic that you'll wish to tell your woman, possibly to tell her everything and certainly too much."

"I'll tell her nothing."

Hillel's smile was weary. "You'll tell her too much, I'm afraid. But try to be prudent. Understand that Father Luce can destroy you."

46

"I think he wants to destroy Madelon."

"I know nothing about that. I'm thinking that the time could come when he would want to destroy you."

"You think I should give her up and let him have her?"

"I'll not advise you in that. I doubt that you have any choice. Well, I must now return to my work—" He went to the door with Richard and touched him lightly and said: "Be prudent. May your light shine on and may your memory be for a blessing. Goodnight."

"Goodnight," Richard said, and slipped away into the dark.

IV

Hillel did not return to his work at once. He watched Richard
disappear in the direction of his home and then closed the door,
thinking, What a dreadful fool I am! For why should he, a Jew,
risk his profession and possibly his life to help a young man who
seemed headed for trouble, in one way or another? Why, but for
the reason that persecution had taught the Jews greater compassion.

He lay on his bed and closed his eyes in thought. He was alone
in the world, for his parents were dead, and his brothers and sisters if not dead were in parts unknown to him; and though twice
Richard's age he was still unmarried. Provence had a number of
Jewish poets and philosophers who were protected by the wealthy
seigneurs, and a few doctors who were also protected, though any
doctor if he followed the best mind he had lived in constant danger
of his life. Hillel scorned the commonly accepted medicines, such
as the blood of bat or badger, the dung and urine of beasts, the
skulls of criminals hanged by moonlight; bee glue, eel grease,
viper flesh, woodlice, wolf-guts, the omentum of the ram and the
secudines of the woman, the saliva of the fasting person, wax
from ears, nail parings, burnt hair—for him what a mess of superstition it was! Actually there were Christians who drank two or
three cups of human urine during their morning fast to cure gout
or what they called the hysterical vapors; and those who balked at
urine went out in the dark of night to consult the witch Ambre.
He was not at all sure that a part of his materia medica was not
superstitious nonsense, or that Herophilus and other doctors of
ancient times had not erred in accepting the humoral pathology of
Hippocrates, who had thought all disease a result of abnormal con-

ditions in the body's blood, phlegm, black bile and yellow bile. He thought that Vesalius had been wrong in believing that nasal mucus was a secretion from the brain and that the brain could be purged with drugs to increase the flow of mucus. He knew that a red-hot iron sometimes helped to stop bleeding but he doubted that fires burned before a house purified the air. He had long ago rejected the widespread belief that all disease was a punishment from God.

Because his approach was scientific he was not popular, and because he sometimes employed surgery he lived in peril of his life. A doctor, when summoned to prescribe for the ills of the princes of earth, was usually told that if successful he would be handsomely rewarded but that if he failed he would be hanged or skinned alive. Under the Church the practice of surgery was largely confined to barbers, hog-gelders, or to any wandering impostor who fancied his skill with a saw or a knife. An honorable surgeon was looked upon as a menial if not an actual criminal. . . .

So why, he asked himself again, should he whose life was in constant peril run the risk of being found abetting a heretic? That Richard was a heretic or would be with a little more thinking he had no doubt. The Council of Avignon eleven years earlier and that of the Lateran six years later had proscribed against the Jews, and Hillel felt in his bones that as the mighty movement against heretics gathered momentum and violence the Jews would be flung down to deeper degradation, even though non-Christian Jews were thought to have souls not worth having, or possibly not to have souls at all. In the professional calm of his life Hillel for more than fifteen years had noted the prodigious slaughter of people in the area all around him. He had thought of going to some other land—but where? Jews had no land, no home; they were as likely to be persecuted in one place as another. If they traveled it was safest to disguise themselves as Christian priests or itinerant beggars. To escape notice, some cut the hair of their boys to leave a curl on top, in the fashion of Christians; but how could a Jew escape notice, since he was cursed with his yellow badge! If he went away from home he had to wear it, for if he did not wear it he was discovered and flogged.

It was folly for one whose lot was so heavy to take on greater burdens. Why had he made this promise to Richard? Was it because he was so lonely and unloved and so in need of love? Was it

49

because of his yearning for a friend to talk to? Or was it because—

Agitated he arose from the bed and paced the small room. After a few moments he paused and snuffed the candle and then paced in darkness, thinking of himself and his life and his problems. To him, who had read many of the great writings left by the Greeks and the Romans, it seemed that the world had sunk into a worse barbarism than any it had ever known. Would the light ever come again?—or would new and ever more resolute Augustines pile banal analogies upon banal analogies until human reason was snuffed like the candle a moment ago? Would intelligence some day win? Would the Fredericks prevail, or the Father Luces?

Thought of Frederick forced a wry smile. That ruthless and butchering but in his strange way enlightened despot had ordered certain mothers not to talk to their babes at all, to see if at last when the children spoke they would speak in the language of Jews, Greeks, Romans, Arabs or in the speech of their parents; for the reason that different peoples argued that it was in their language that God spoke to Adam and that all other languages were bastards. He wondered if Frederick's experiment was successful. Thinking next of Frederick's atrocities his mind turned to that of a wild longhaired Christian who decided to crucify himself and who was able to drive nails through both feet and one hand but could not then manage to spike the other hand, and was taken down and rushed to a hospital. It was true, as Richard said, that some men could endure a lot of pain; but not men like Richard. Poor Richard! Even if he were ever to marry this girl Madelon he would have to go with her humbly to the baron's castle, his soul debased and outraged and sick, to offer her up as Guillem's bride for the night. Hillel had known a peasant who had married an attractive girl and who had taken his wife to Guillem to be deflowered; and he had seen the husband and wife the next day, their shame and despair. . . .

Richard meanwhile had slipped quietly into the hovel and lain down on the hard mat of his bed, his heart racing and his mind singing. Hours later, after he had fallen asleep, he was aroused by a dreadful scream. He sat up, rubbing at his eyes in the gloom and peering round him; and saw after a moment the scared white face of his sister, and then his father sitting astride his mother. Horrified, Richard moved over and perceived that his father was thrusting fingers into his mother's ears, while at the same time with a knee he was trying to gag her mouth. Elise was struggling like a beast thrown down for slaughter, and Victoir with all his strength seemed to be trying to kill her.

"Father!" Richard shouted. "What are you doing?"

At once Victoir removed his fingers and his knee and slipping off the writhing body turned to face his son. Appalled by the passion in the face Richard backed away on hands and knees, going to the doorway; and Victoir on hands and knees came after him. When he was outside Richard leapt to his feet and stood ready to flee, yet waiting for his father to come out. Victoir came out, still on hands and knees, and like a beast looked up at his son; and Richard said:

"What is the trouble?"

"There is no trouble," said Victoir, his voice quiet.

"Then why were you killing mother?"

"I wasn't killing her," Victoir said.

At this moment Elise, recovered from her terror or her strangulation, rushed up and seizing her husband's feet ended him up and over, and there Victoir sprawled on his back, his eyes looking up. White and wild and terrible Elise looked at her son.

"Mother!"

"Take him away!" she shrieked. "I hate him! O God how I hate him!"

Looking at her Richard backed away. Then he turned and fled, going he knew not where and not caring; hating even with more furious passion than his mother hated; hating his parents and his brother and himself, his stink and his lice and his rags, hating almost everything that he could remember in eighteen years of living; going blindly, sick and blind, filled with nausea, and wishing with every ounce of his strength that he could fall dead. For there was nothing to live for and there would never be anything to live for.

He went away to the shadows of an old wall and sat on his heels, trembling, trying not to vomit, looking back at the hovel he had left, thinking of it and its mice and lice and rats and filthy belongings, of his parents who hated one another for reasons dark to him, of his brother with two scrawny cats cradled in his arms, of his frail white little sister whose eyes had shone like lights of terror.

"My God!" he whispered, choking. "O my God!"

51

He bowed to his arms, trying to keep down the sickness, feeling himself lost in an engulfing darkness; feeling the wet and salt as he opened and shut his eyes; feeling the tremors running through his body; feeling the vomit that strove to come up. He murmured a prayer against the vast and encompassing tyranny around him which he could neither live with nor breach. After a little while he tried to think and as he struggled to clear his senses there came to him like weird mockery out of the night a story he had once heard, the story of a peasant who in some city was leading a donkey and by mistake entered the lane of the perfumers' shops and instantly fainted dead away, being brought to only when a shovelful of manure was held under his nose. That was it! he thought, turning a sickly grin on the night: scents from far lands for the rich, a spadeful of dung for the poor.

He was relishing the bitter jest when he saw his mother leave the shack and go away. She went away into the night toward the hills. He thought he should follow her and then he thought he should go over to see if she had killed his father. His mother was a very strange woman; that is all that Richard knew about her. She thought the stars were the glorified souls of saints; that the ringing of a church bell was the clear musical voice of Jesus. Because the cock, for having crowed at Peter's denial, was regarded by the Church as one of the Devil's voices, Elise was afraid of it and visibly shuddered at daylight when the roosters began to call. She sometimes collected dew in a cupped leaf to wash the faces of children and make them as beautiful as angels. Had she gone out to gather dew?

Or had she gone to see Ambre, the fat witch with the evil face? The people roundabout thought Ambre was a witch but Richard saw in her only a filthy harlot who lay with any drunkard who could afford a coin. Witches, he had heard, were old, lame, bleary-eyed, foul and full of wrinkles and sullenness and silence. Ambre was not like that. Witches were thought to copulate with Satan. Possibly Ambre did, for she seemed wicked enough to copulate with anything, imp or beast.

His mother, Richard was now thinking, while hugging his knees and waiting for daybreak, suffered from what was called vapors of the womb. Maybe she had gone to Ambre to get some magic for it. Women did not dare to consult a male physician, of whom there were none but Jews and Arabs. Or maybe she was muttering her penitentials for some sin old or new. Of how many sins was she guilty? Those who befoul their lips shall do penance for four years; if they are accustomed to the habit they shall do penance for seven years. God knew she had befouled her lips, for she could curse like a pirate. If polluted by a violent assault of the imagination you shall do penance for seven days. Maybe she had had an evil dream. That many of the serfs were incestuous was a fact known to Richard and to everyone; but in his home, so far as he knew, there had been none, though he sometimes wondered about Elise and Pascal. There was a queer relationship between them. Was that her sin? He who defiles his mother shall do penance for three years, with perpetual pilgrimage: perhaps Pascal should be driven out to a pilgrimage to the Holy Land. . . .

Whatever it was Elise spent a part of her time trying to cleanse her soul. Her lips were often moving, over the Beati maybe, a favorite; how many times he had heard her muttering, Let them now that fear the Lord say, that his mercy endureth forever. I called upon the Lord in distress: the Lord answered me and set me in a large place. The Lord is on my side; I will not fear: what can man do unto me? . . . Elise also punished herself, in the manner of some penitents, with long vigils, fatiguing postures, or by allowing without protest the lice to feed on her flesh. She would stand for an hour with her arms extended in the form of the Cross; or when in a violent mood she would flog herself with nettles and thorns. Daily she said the Pater Noster a dozen or a hundred times in honor of the wounds of Christ, the Ave Maria in honor of the seven joys of the Virgin. She strove to protect herself with every sign and substance she had heard of, with the Cross, holy water, blessed oil, candles, wax, salt. . . .

Richard had supposed that her wild grief and penitence were because of one of her babies that had died unbaptized. The horrors which awaited the doomed infant were enough to drive any mother to despair. Terror-stricken women fought with every possible means to save their stillborn children from eternal damnation: if holy waters were sprinkled on the womb too late the mother might then supplicate the Holy Spirit to purify it or herself seek absolution and try to apply it to her dead child.

Or possibly she had gone to see Old Jeanne. This was the story: when a young woman Jeanne had committed a dreadful sin and had been immured in a small dark cell at the edge of the forest.

53

Nearly all people had forgotten her sin and now, thirty years later, when Jeanne was an unsightly halfblind old hag, she had the stature of a saint and was venerated. Many persons went to consult her. Elise had gone a number of times, and Richard had wished to go, to peer into the hole and catch a glimpse of the ghastly face. It was said that Old Jeanne had lost her powers of speech and now addressed her visitors in an unintelligible babble, which some took to be revelation in the gift of tongues.

Anyway, she had gone, though only God knew where: to gather the herbs of consolation or to beg Ambre for magic; or to commune with old Jeanne; or to thrust her hands into an anthill. He did not greatly care. He had no affection for his mother, only incredulity and pity. He wanted to get her out of his sight forever. Thinking of her had filled him with weariness and he thrust his legs out and let his head sink to a shoulder. When he awoke the stars were still bright and no bells were ringing. He thought he saw a wolf in the village street, for these beasts came into the villages; but he decided that it was a pig, a privileged scavenger protected by the baron's men. He slept again. When he awoke daylight had come and the church bell was ringing. He listened to the bell and loved it. All over the broad land bells were ringing and their music, like the stars, like hawthorn in bloom, like the sweetbriar and the wild thyme and olive trees and fields of jasmin, and hillsides of mimosa like draperies against the sky, was pure and good. The music went into you sweet and mellow and sang in your bones and your soul. It was nice to think that this was the voice of Jesus calling. . . .

He went to the shack and looked in; his mother had not returned, his father, brother and sister seemed to be sleeping. He could make out the form of Fleur lying on her back, her thin little arms folded on her breast and her small face looking like a white flower. Pascal still hugged his cats. Victoir was snoring. There they were, his family, and there it was, his home. Out in the woods somewhere Elise was plucking bitter herbs and chewing them; Hillel might be bent over his studies; Father Luce was yawning and looking forward to another day of lechery; Madelon was arousing herself from an ecstatic vision; the baron. . . .

The baron and his knights were preparing for a day of hunting, and a little later they came rushing across the landscape with the baron in the lead. For the poor there were few greater terrors than that of a lord of great estates riding to the hunt: he and his men went where they pleased, trampling crops, running over stray cats and dogs and children and scattering everything before them. Richard moved to higher ground for a better view.

Baron Guillem had a deep voice and he loved to sing when he rode to the hunt. Walking his beast as he approached the village he was singing now.

> Though lords and kings contrive
> to get their little share
> of earth, why should I care
> how kingdoms rise or tumble,
> since my delights are humble,
> to love and to be alive! . . .

A moment later he had changed:

> Western wind, when wilt thou blow,
> the small rain down can rain?
> Christ, if my love were in my arms
> and I in my bed again! . . .

Staring at the fat pompous brigand Richard reflected that hunting was the exclusive privilege of nobles, including the lords of the Church: the peasant or serf dared not catch even a rabbit, or to protest if his crops were beaten into the earth by the hooves of horses or his children run down and killed; for the baron, God bless him, sat as judge over his people and if he needed to enrich himself he could have his henchmen incite the poor to riots or misdemeanors so that he could levy fines. There he sat in his rich garments on a clean white horse and Richard hated him.

Those behind him now came up and the baron galloped into the village, singing:

> Lady Venus, what's to do
> if the loved loves not again?
> Beauty passes, youth's undone,
> violets wither, spite of dew,
> roses shrivel in the sun,
> lilies all their whiteness stain:
> Lady, take these home to you
> and who loves you, love again!

Richard hated him but he was fascinated by the man's splendor and arrogance. Guillem and his entourage came galloping through the village, every one of them splendidly mounted and caparisoned. Red, the color of infidelity, was Guillem's color and he loved it and made the most of it: his horse was white and he was red and they made an extraordinary picture, though the baron was not a handsome man. He was fat and thick with a round fat face and a high forehead that was bald halfway to his crown. The ideal of lordly beauty was golden curly locks, frizzed and plaited but what hair Guillem had was neither golden nor curly. He should have had eyes like the falcon's, large and luminous and glowing with pride and spirit but his eyes were green and small. He should have had a nose straight and slender but his nose was fat and short. His ideal body would have been tall and strong and hard with muscle and sinew, and long legs well-shaped for the saddle; but he looked only like a fat man on a big horse. He did have of lordly beauty a white complexion with rosy cheeks and a smiling mouth that revealed perfect teeth.

Off he went, and what he lacked in beauty he made up with verve and dash and a tremendous love of food and wines and beautiful women and killing. Many stories were told about him; the common people gossiped about him endlessly. It was said that when young and a knight a beautiful lady sent him her chemise and a command to fight with no armor but his helmet, his chausses-de-fer, shield and sword. Badly wounded and knocked off his horse, Guillem had writhed on the ground and rapturously kissed the blood-stained chemise so many hundreds of times that it saved his life. He then returned it to the lady, who made for him a silken banner to carry in the tournaments, into which she had woven some of her pubic hair.

Another story related to his present wife, the Baroness Elienor. Guillen fell madly in love with her but she loved another knight; she promised to surrender to the baron if she lost her true-love. She married the other knight, whereupon Guillem took his case to a Court of Love; and solemnly deliberating women decided that she had lost her true-love when she married him, since among the highborn it was believed that marriage and love could not exist together. She was commanded to take Guillem but whether she was now married to him none of the common people knew. Richard had heard that she detested him and that while he devoted his ardent nature to any attractive woman he could find, including daughters of the peasants and serfs, Elienor found lovers where she could. Many times Richard had seen her riding her palfrey, with an ivory saddle and stirrups of gold and a housing of scarlet. She usually wore a great surcoat of white satin, a wimple of linen and silk and a kind of silken hood to protect her from the sun. Attached to the housing were many small bells that made music when her palfrey trotted.

Baron Guillem was off to the hunt, for stag or boar, his wolfhounds trailing and baying, ferocious creatures that had to be muzzled when not at work. Or perhaps he was off to war. When hunting he and his men usually played music on the long and elaborately carved horns of slain beasts and kept up a ringing cry of Soho! When off to battle his horse over its coat of iron had a caparison of cloth emblazoned with the armorial bearings of its master and the whole beast was garnished with little bells of two shapes intermingled. Richard did not remember having heard bells.

But what difference does it make to me? he thought bitterly. The son of a bitch with his horde of parasitic knights lived in a castle and had heaven knew how much rich cloth embroidered with gold and ate the finest food in the world—black puddings and sausages, venison, beef, eels, herring, fresh water fish, spiced pottages, roasts, pastries, entremets, pungent sauces and wines and spices from all the lands of the earth. Richard stood in a ragged garment of sackcloth and ate barley gruel. Guillem took lovely women as he found them; Richard knew that he would do well if he ever had a wife at all. Guillem had many servants to dress or undress him, massage his aching muscles, bathe his feet, shave him, drench him with costly scents, prepare his great feasts, care for his horses, dogs and hawks, collect his taxes and rents, hunt with him and go to war to fight for him. Richard had a stinking bedmat and not even that was his own. The squires and knights spent all their time polishing their weapons, currying their steeds, training their hawks, crossing blunted lances, preparing for jousts and tournaments, feasting and fornicating—and Richard toiled from daylight to dark in the baron's fields. So it had been as far back as mind could run; so it would be, so far as he could tell, to the end of time.

Choking with hate and bitterness he watched the last horseman vanish into the woods and thought of their gay pennons flying and their voices ringing after bear or boar; and then recalled a curious thing that Hillel had said to him. Fixing him with his quizzical stare Hillel had said, "Don't you ever bathe? God, you have an awful stink about you." Richard had been astonished. He had said that the Church did not approve much bathing and Hillel had said, "Have you never washed yourself in all the years of your life?" Richard admitted that he had not, nor had he since the rebuke; but now, itching from both filth and fury, he felt that a bath was what he needed, possibly more than freedom or learning. There was a small river not far from the village and he hastened to it.

Sitting on the bank and concealed by a thicket he took off his ragged one-piece garment and laid it across his lap and looked at it. He could see no lice crawling but he could see them when he examined the seams. The rents were patched by drawing the torn edges together and making them fast with thorns; he pulled a thorn out and on turning back the edges saw a pocket of lice. He next looked curiously down over his thin body, at his knees almost black with soil, at his calloused scarred feet, at the broken toenails, and then scratched in his pubic hair and between his thighs. Sliding down into water until immersed to his waist he washed his garment by forcing it roughly through the water, back and forth, up and down. After he had laid it aside he wondered about his hair. He then knelt and doused his head under and roughly massaged and scrubbed it, digging in with his nails, delighted by the itching and tingling and the water's coolness. Have you ever bathed! he thought and snorted with fury. Who among the serfs ever bathed! Good Lord! Too weary from labor to move, too tired to sleep, too full of hate to care they did not have time to cleanse themselves. Still, he realized, that was not all of it. Bathing was not a habit with Christians and he doubted that Guillem had ever bathed or even Elienor, or Father Luce. Cleanliness was all right for Arabs and for Jews like Hillel; but for Christians it was a form of self-indulgence, a pampering of the flesh.

Having scrubbed his head so violently that he had dislodged a part of his hair he sat on the bank, breathing hard, and thinking with bitter mirth about himself. Examining his pubic hair he found in it tiny sores and scabs and knew that these were from scratching himself during his sleep. He was torn and raw in his armpits. He was raw at the nape of his neck and around his anus. He slipped into the water again and using wet earth as soap and his fingernails as probes he scoured himself from head to heels and was astonished to learn that the true color of his flesh was not what he thought it was. His skin was quite fair when the dirt was off. He drew one foot up and the other and abraded the calloused soles and the thick hide over his toes and heels. With handfuls of mud he scoured in his crotch. With mud he washed over his face and into his ears and around his neck. Feeling half-skinned he lay on his back and rubbed his back over the earth, turning in the water to wash off the mud, falling back to rub again. When it seemed to him that he must be clean all over he entered a thicket and found shrubs in bloom and stood among them naked breathing of one blossom and another to find the sweetest. He gathered armfuls of bloom and crushed and macerated it in his palms and rubbed his palms over him, over his face and throat, his chest, his belly, and, looking round guiltily, over his private parts. He was not accustomed to such sweet clean odors and he felt a little giddy and horribly naked. He washed his garment with mud and rinsed and washed and rinsed and squeezed out of it all the water he could and put it on. It felt cool and nice against his flesh. It seemed to him that his hearing had improved and his sense of smell; he listened, he sniffed, it was a different world, a cleaner and more pleasant world.

But where in the world would he sleep after this? Not on his old mat, not in the hovel: never again would he sleep in such filth. He was not aware that this act of cleansing himself was symbolic; it was a gesture toward freedom and clean air and an unclouded soul and a way of life that would be good as orchards were good. He would never go back. Like an Arab or an enlightened Jew he would now bathe regularly and get a new garment somehow and keep it free of lice and keep himself free. Had Abelard kept himself clean? Had Heloise? How often did the Holy Father in Rome bathe, and his cardinals and archbishops and bishops and abbots? Had Madelon ever bathed? He knew that she had not, any more than Old Noelle and Chretien had bathed, or Elise and Victoir and Pascal and Fleur, or any other serf in this whole part of the damned world. Very well, after this he would be different, he would not be like his people but like the Arab philosophers and poets and Hillel.

Thought of Hillel filled him with eagerness. He gathered more bloom and rubbed it into his ears and stuffed petals up his nostrils and rubbed the essence between his thighs and over his hair and his naked arms, over his lips and eyelids and in his armpits and set off at a fast walk to Hillel's house. It was still early morning and he was sure that no spies would be abroad.

V

The day before Richard took his bath Father Luce came to Chretien's hovel. For a few days he had been busy with his priestly
duties and had told Madelon to go to her father's home and remain there until, again free of responsibilities, he could care for
her. That had been only a pretext on the Father's part, to give
himself time to reflect on the matter and decide what to do. For
the truth was that Madelon's behavior baffled him; he did not
know if this pallid and scrawny girl was in the possession of Satan
or if she had established a deeper communion with God than any
he had known as confessor and priest.

The thing that baffled him most was the suddenness and ease
with which she became unconscious when his gentle caresses became too intimate. If he fondled her hands or arms she remained
conscious but when he touched the area of her breasts or softly
stroked her loins or belly her eyes closed at once like a drowsy
child's and she sank into a strange state that was deeper than
slumber. This frightened him a little. Though priests had great
power over women and especially over nuns and though the common people did not dare to question their practices or their holiness, still there was, as Father Luce well knew, a limit to what he
could do without arousing scandalous outcry. He was determined
to possess the girl body and soul but he was very sly and crafty
and he was resolved to proceed with infinite prudence. Besides,
he was afraid of Chretien. He had looked into that man's eyes one
day and had known that his motives were suspected.

Father Luce was resolved to be prudent but passion in him was
stronger than prudence. When away from Madelon he was able
to cast off the spell which her helplessness and white skin and frail

body and childlike eyes put on him. He could then consider the dangers in the course he was pursuing. But when with her his passions overpowered him like intense August heat and he could not keep his trembling hands off her. He did not understand why she affected him so deeply. He had known other women, he had known more than he could recall the names of and they had been all kinds of women, but he had known none who had brought the full measure of his lust boiling to the surface until his mental faculties darkened and seemed to fade out and all his senses burned upon her like the Provence sun upon a delicate flowering plant, until he could not only see and feel and hear her but could smell and taste her. . . .

Chretien was not at home. It was Simone who came to the doorway.

"Good afternoon, my child," Father Luce said, smiling upon her, his hypnotic eyes looking into the soft brown depths of her eyes and beyond the depths into her soul and then down to see if her breasts were yet budding. "Is Madelon here?"

"Yes, Father."

"Tell her to come."

Madelon came eagerly and this startled him; he had not suspected that she would be fretful and unhappy during his absence. She came like the frail child she was, breathless, her lips parted, her eyes wide and expectant and holy, her pale hands clasped at her breast.

"Madelon, have you been to confession?" He knew she had not, for he had commanded her to confess only to him. The question was for Simone.

"No, Father," she whispered.

"Then come with me."

He was leading her away when it occurred to him that he must be prudent. He turned to Simone. "Child, you come with us."

With the two girls he went to the house and then touched Simone gently on her dark brown hair and told her to wait at the door, while he heard Madelon's confession; and he took Madelon inside, leaving the door behind him slightly ajar, and went with her to the bed-chamber. As in former times he told her to lie on the bed and he sat at her side, looking with that dreadful intentness into her eyes.

62

He took her two hands in his own and said, "My child, have you been virtuous?"

"Yes, Father," she said, with a pale joyful smile. She struggled a moment to get her breath and added, hardly above a whisper: "Under your holy guidance I will become more virtuous, and more and more."

"Have you anything to confess?"

Madelon was staring at the ceiling. In her weak tremulous childlike voice she said, "Father, I had another vision."

"Tell me about it," he said, his gaze on her lips.

"In my visions I travel everywhere," she said, forcing the words out in whispers. "I go all over the world. Wherever I go I write letters like the blessed Saint Paul and I tell people to repent and to come to the sacred heart of Jesus and to his blessed Mother. I—"

"Yes?" he said, gently urging her.

"The sinful people come to me and together we go into the Sacred Heart!"

There was silence while Father Luce considered her words. Then he said: "Is that all you have to tell me?"

"No, Father. I feel that I will die soon."

"My child, you'll not die until our Lord calls you."

"Yes, Father."

"Have you been to Mass?"

"Yes, Father."

From under his robe Father Luce drew forth a small phial of wine. "I have something here for you to drink," he said, bending forward, looking into her eyes and breathing into her face. Madelon closed her eyes. Father Luce slipped an arm under her neck and gently lifted her. "I've blessed it," he said. "It's the blood of our Lord and I want you to drink it."

"Yes, Father," she whispered, her eyes still closed.

He put the glass to her lips and obediently she drank but the wine strangled her and she broke away from him to cough. When she was done with coughing he held her again and proffered the wine and again she drank. "You must drink all of it," he said.

"Holy Father, I'll do what you tell me but first I must cough."

"Madelon, I'm your master, I'm your God, do you know that?"

"Yes, Father."

"You must endure all things in the name of obedience to me. When I command, you must obey."

"Father, I will."

"Then drink this."

Eager to please the holy man, who was one of God's saints, she gulped the wine down, spilling a little of its grape red over her bosom. Father Luce then eased her down to the pillow and she lay there, her breathing slow and deep, her eyes hidden behind pale eyelids. He again clasped her hands and let his gaze search out her emaciated body, the lust in him rising and the point of his tongue moving slowly back and forth across his upper lip. Now and then he glanced at her eyes to see if they were closed, or peeping, and explored again, his own eyes burning with ardor. Madelon was breathing like one asleep.

"Madelon?" he whispered.

"Yes," she said faintly.

"My dear child, do you feel better?"

"I feel funny," she said.

"Do you feel warm and happy?"

"Yes."

Releasing her hands he gently clasped her frail naked arms and felt her shiver. He felt her tremble as he softly caressed down her arms and down again, from her shoulders to her wrists, barely breathing himself but listening to her own deep breathing. Feeling that he should take his time with this, yet unable to subdue the hot impulses that were flushing him like fire, he released her arms and moved a hand gently over her tiny breasts. At once she came up like a wild terrified thing, writhing and choking back a cry, her feeble hands trying to push him away and her clouded gaze sweeping his face. She would have struggled up and fled if he had not firmly clasped her and forced her back down. Then she lay still but for the tremors in her body and the spasms in her face.

"Madelon, my dear child," he said but she did not reply. She was trembling as if chilled. Her eyes were closed fast. Tears had filled her eyes and had been forced out between the lashes and now fell down to her white cheeks. He patted her hands gently and waited. Little by little the tremors subsided: she would be still a moment and then shudder, and again be still, as still as death. It was her frailty and her helplessness that overpowered

64

his will, these and her wasted form and her delicate pale angelic face.

He patted her hands, his eyes all the while closely watching her face. He saw tiny spasms in her eyelids. Once she drew a sharp gasping breath and then seemed to relax and sink, as if despairing. When again he touched her breasts she shuddered and seemed for a moment about to rise; but the shudder passed and she was quieter than before. It had happened again, though he did not understand this at once: Madelon had sunk into that deep comatose state which was her only defense when she could endure no more. Her pure soul was unable to see or at least unwilling to see in Father Luce what a shrewd woman would have seen so quickly: there was no escape but utter unconsciousness and she sank into it as into blissful oblivion, knowing no more. . . .

When convinced that she was unaware of him he gently maneuvered her and slipped her garment up until it was above her waist. Then with morbid curiousness he looked at her flesh, at the strange deathly pallor of it, at her small hips and half-fleshed thighs, his gaze roving over her, until with a start he saw what looked like a wound in one of her feet. As a child she had suffered from sores and the skin had never entirely healed but had remained reddened. Lord, did she have stigmata? Only the most blessed of the saints had the stigmata of Jesus' wounds. He bent low to examine the foot, when, with the flood in him breaching its levies, he arose in haste and looked out into the other room and listened. The door was slightly ajar, as he had left it. He could hear no sound. Turning back, he covered her, drawing her to him in fierce embrace, his hot lips kissing deep into her white unresponsive mouth. . . .

Chretien meanwhile had come to the door, having seen his daughter there. With mischievous eyes Simone looked up at her father, her round roguish face giving him an impudent grin.

"Is Madelon in there?" he asked, whispering like a conspirator.

"Yes," said Simone, whispering.

"And Father Luce?"

"Yes. He's confessing her."

"I can't hear voices," said Chretien, putting an ear to the door.

"They're praying," Simone said, with whom it was a habit to say the first thing that came to her mind.

Chretien turned and looked all around him like one plotting a move. "How long have they been in there?"

"Quite a while."

"You go now," her father said.

"Must I?" she asked, pouting. "I want to stay."

"You go now," her father said.

Simone went away, looking back, her bare toes kicking angrily at the dust; for she was a bright child and she knew that her father suspected something. She knew a great deal about men. She knew about her own father, more, God help her, than she would have dared to tell. After she had gone a hundred feet she stood and looked back at him.

She was still standing there kicking her toes into the dust when Father Luce came out. He came out with ecclesiastical dignity like one who had done his duty and must now hasten away to other priestly chores; but a part of his poise left him when he saw Chretien, and, looking away, saw Simone.

"How is she?" asked Chretien blandly, his small black eyes searching the Father's face.

"All right," said Father Luce, his voice controlled and dignified. "She has confessed and now she sleeps. Your daughter is a strange girl."

"That's true," said Chretien.

"I wouldn't bother her," said Father Luce. "She's tired. She has had many visions and they exhaust her."

"You think she really communes with God?" asked Chretien slyly.

"I have no doubt of it. She is a very saintly person." He adjusted his robe a little and said briskly, "Well, I must go now. Please don't disturb her."

But Chretien, twice as sly as the Father, was not to be put off. "Could it be that she communes with Satan?"

Father Luce looked at him sharply, and as though the future had been opened to him he shuddered and said hastily, "It could be."

"I have wondered about it," said Chretien, his gaze still probing.

"She's very strange," said Father Luce. "After I've heard more of her confessions I can tell you."

He hastened away and Chretien looked after him. Chretien

66

went over to Simone and took one of her hands. "He says she sleeps," he said. "Come." Hah! he thought, glancing in the direction Father Luce had taken, you are a fox if I ever saw one but Satan and I will be too smart for you!

Madelon was unconscious for more than an hour after Father Luce left her. As she came slowly into consciousness her first awareness was of intense pain. She stirred and felt pain and was quiet; she was somewhere in the clouds, floating, high above the earth and there was pain in her and all around her and she felt dizzy and nauseated but sleepy, like one sinking into sleep. She stirred again and the pain was so sharp that it brought a gasp from her and opened her eyes. Her eyes were wide and unseeing but after a little they filled with wondering; and her lips parted and opened, wider and wider until her mouth was grotesquely ajar. So for a minute or more she lay without moving and without blinking and almost without breathing.

Then, almost warily, her right hand, which had been lying on her bosom, began to move downward. Her eyes were still wide and wondering. Her mouth was still open. Her hand crept downward, slowly, to her naval and rested there; and moved again and lay for a few moments on her belly; and then, even more slowly, warily, wonderingly, moved downward to her loins. In her groping half-asleep half-conscious way she was seeking the center of the pain which enveloped her, now more in troubled memory than in fact. Her fingers like quiet strange cautiously alive things explored and found wetness and paused. Her eyes now mirrored the realization that was slowly dawning in her mind. The shadows, the doubts, the wonder, the uncertainty were falling away, as smoke from a choked fire that suddenly overcomes its difficulties and leaps into full blaze.

With a wild movement she came bolt upright. In that moment Madelon realized fully and completely what had happened. She was never to realize it again. The moment of utter horror and shock was more than she could stand, the realization more than she could admit, the incredible truth more than she could ever live with. In that moment, in those few moments, when she sat up, her eyes wild and amazed, she knew the full truth but never in her lifetime would she know it again. She fainted and fell back. She slept in sleep deeper than normal sleep and dreamed and did not wake until morning.

While she slept her unconscious mind did all that it could do to protect her from the shame and the horror. She dreamed that Satan came to her, for it was known to all Christians that the infernal piercing serpent, the prince of devils, did come to mortal women and lie with them. In her dreaming she relived again all the pain of her first sleep. Her dreaming was tortured; she gasped, she feebly struggled, she put hands up to ward him off, she turned her head this way and that to avoid his hot lips; and when at last overcome by his greater strength she was forced to yield she moaned and quietly sobbed; and she was sobbing when she awoke. She was still so vividly living her horrible shameful embrace with Satan that she could feel his presence and thought she could hear him departing. Exhausted and terrified she struggled to a sitting posture, softly sobbing and moaning, and knew as clearly as if the whole thing had happened when she was wide awake that Satan had embraced her. She could feel the wetness and the pain and the pressure of his arms around her and his mouth on her lips.

The full shame and horror of it did not come to her all at once. She sat bowed, her eyes closed, tears falling to her cheeks. She relived the whole experience from the moment when she felt his presence in the room, through his caresses and fondling, through his piercing at her flesh with his teeth or talons. . . . Ah, God's mercy, what was it he had done? Tortured and sobbing she tried to remember but it was only when she moved one of her feet that she knew. Tossing her hair up and back and staring blindly through tears she drew a foot to her lap and tried to examine it. She could not see it and so she felt over it. She felt a sticky wetness and she put it to her nose and lips and knew it was blood. There was some kind of wound on the top of her foot about midway across and an inch or so back from the base of the toes. . . .

It was an hour or more after daylight when the door was softly opened and Richard came in. He was bold this morning because he had bathed and cleansed himself and because Hillel was going to buy his freedom. In his wet garment he came into the first chamber and stood listening.

"Madelon," he said softly.

Madelon heard him but did not understand. Richard then went to the doorway of the other chamber and looked in and saw her sitting on the bed, her hair spilling down over her and her hands clutching her foot.

"Madelon?" he said.

She did not speak. She heard his voice but did not know. Richard went in and stood by the bed and looked at her. He understood after a moment that she was weeping and that there was blood on her foot.

"Madelon, have you hurt yourself?" Then, alarmed, he cried, "Madelon!"

The cry aroused her a little. She looked up at him her eyes brimming and her face stained with the salt of grief.

"Madelon, have you hurt your foot?"

She shook her head, no, like a child. She let the foot slip from her grasp and down and reached to cover it. Richard sat on the bed.

"Madelon, why are you weeping?" That, he thought, was a foolish question: Madelon often wept after one of her religious ecstasies. He supposed that she had seen another vision of the Lord. Still, there was something so sad and shocked and horrified in her face that he knew she was weeping for another reason. Was it Father Luce?

"Madelon darling, I've good news for you. . . . Are you listening?" She gently inclined her head. "I'm to be a free man but please in God's name tell no one. . . . Madelon, do you understand me? *I am to be free!*" He knew that Madelon did not understand. Taking one of her small soft hands he clasped it between his own and stared at her face and wondered about her. She was another Heloise for him; she was a pure and holy girl who communed with God and saw the Lord in visions. He did not want Father Luce to come here any more. He wanted to get his freedom and find a job and marry Madelon and cherish her as Pascal cherished his cats. He wanted to love her deeply and purely, as Abelard in his later years had loved Heloise. But she was such a strange girl that he had never known how to talk to her and elicit her interest.

"Madelon, will you marry me if the baron will let us?"

She glanced at him and shook her head, no.

"Why not? Don't you love me?"

Now she turned her wet eyes full upon him. They were soft melting eyes full of strange pity. She looked into his eyes a moment and then her gaze wandered over his face, not searchingly, no, but as a mother in grief might look at a child, seeing it and not seeing it.

"Madelon, please speak to me."

She continued to look at him and not to look at him at all.

"Madelon," he said, whispering, "I'm going to be free. Then I'm going away a little while, to see Francis maybe or to see if I can find a nice job in Toulouse. It has a great university and I might be able to study there—after we're married. I want you to stay with your parents while I'm gone. Please don't come here any more."

He knew how futile it was to ask her to do things. Her will was not her own but the Lord's will. And how could he, Richard, the son of a serf, circumvent the wishes of a powerful priest like Father Luce? He had felt so bold and free and clean when he came in and now he again felt like the slave that he was. He began to weep.

"Madelon," he whispered, holding her hand, "I love you and we must cherish one another. We must try to make a decent life for ourselves. And we can, we can! But you must help too. We must do it together. We—" He broke off, feeling despair. How could he breach that strange deep quiet and make her understand? How could he get her to speak? "Madelon, do you know what I'm saying? I love you. I want to marry you. Will you wait at your father's a little while?"

Madelon was still looking at him, seeing him and not seeing him, her life sunk to those depths which Richard would never reach. He was looking at her pale wet childlike face when he heard a sound at the door and leapt up. He turned and for a moment listened. He stepped forward and looked into the other chamber and there before him in his priestly robes was Father Luce.

The two men looked at one another, the Father's stare hard and suspicious, Richard's frightened and abashed.

"What," asked the Father, "are you doing here?"

"I—I came to see Madelon."

"Madelon does not wish to see anyone."

"I—I wanted to tell her—"

"What?"

"That I love her!" Richard blurted. "Madelon and I are to marry if—if we can get permission!"

70

"Madelon is married to our Lord. Go now."

God, how Richard hated the man, but more than that how he feared him! His impulse was to slink out, shamed and humiliated, as though he had been found in some sin. But there was another impulse in him, a wish to settle the matter here and now, to learn once and for all if Madelon was to be his wife.

"If," he said, his voice faltering, "if she would—marry me, I mean—"

"She won't."

"But if I could persuade her—"

"I've asked you to go."

"Yes, Father," he said meekly, and would despise himself all the days of his life for having said it. He went to the door and outside, with shame and humiliation and anger burning in him, with hate in him like fury and fear like sickness, with loathing and horror and despair, going blindly, hardly knowing what he did, his manhood outraged and degraded. He went away from the house and stopped and tried to get control of himself; saying, What a coward I am! Asking, Is it always to be this way? Praying, God, our Father, help me, help me to know what to do!

Madelon meanwhile was babbling her dreadful confession to Father Luce. His emotions were mixed and ran deep. Whether Satan had come to her he did not know but at once he perceived that she had no knowledge of his own intimacy with her. He perceived that it would be of great advantage to him to accept her story, no matter whether true or false. He admitted to himself that it might be true. Satan could manifest himself to man in any form that existed in the heavens above, in the earth, in the waters under the earth. He might even show himself as an angel of light, as to Saint Paul.

Patting her hands and trying to hush her hysteria he said, "How did he come? In what form?" Madelon seemed not to understand the question. "Did he come as a man?"

"Yes!" she gasped.

He did not like her answer but he accepted it. Father Luce looked round him and sniffed and thought he detected the odor of sulphur; he searched the room for signs of the Devil's presence. Then he recalled that Satan when he willed could actually appear in the form of Christ or in a Christlike appearance and he asked a question which he was to realize afterward was indiscreet.

71

"Did he by any chance look like our Lord?"

Madelon was so morbidly suggestible that the most casual intimation when it served her emotional need was eagerly seized on and became the structure of fact. In her confused and desperate way she was trying to think of the matter, to remember what Satan's form had been; and it seemed to her that it had been that of her Lord. To think that this might have been so was for Madelon to make it so but she dared not tell Father Luce that. She felt that it was wicked of her to think it but once she had thought it she could never doubt it again.

After a struggle she was able to say only, "I don't know."

"Have you ever seen Satan?" It may be that he meant to ask if she had ever stood near a mustard seed on St. John's Eve at midnight, for it was then that the Devil revealed himself in his own true hellish form to the eyes of man. But Madelon said no, she had never seen him. She was still weeping in an almost soundless way and Father Luce was still looking round him and wondering about her. He was quite sure that he could smell the odor of sulphur, which was the odor of Satan wherever he went and in no matter what form, because his home was the infernal regions. He decided that Satan had indeed come to this girl, and if this was true he could conclude only that there was something very evil in her. He now withdrew his hands from her hands and began to finger the chain of his pectoral cross. He made the sign of the Cross to ward off evil and under his breath he murmured certain holy words that had the power to put Satan to flight.

What should he do with Madelon? Was she a heretic? Was he polluting himself when he visited her? He had believed that there was something extraordinarily pure and holy in this girl and this quality in her had been for him one source of her irresistible appeal. But now he wondered if he had been deceived.

"You had better sleep now," he said. "You're very tired."

"Don't leave me!" she gasped. "I'm afraid."

"You have nothing to fear," he said. "Satan cannot abide where I am."

"But he might come again! O my God, holy Father, protect me!" She gave way to another burst of hysterical weeping. But presently, remembering that it had not been Satan but her Lord who had come to her she felt calmed, she felt almost sly inside, and looking at him through tears she said, "I will be all right."

72

"You will be all right," he said.

"God is with me," she said.

"I am with you," he said. "I'm a holy man."

"Yes, Father."

"You must in all things do what I ask you to do."

"Yes, Father."

"I want you to rest now."

She lay back like the child she was and closed her eyes. Father Luce wished to have his way with her again but her story of the visitation had shocked his emotions and put a blight on his will. He patted her hand and said, "You must sleep now."

He left her then and went to the doorway and looked out, still wondering what he ought to do. One matter he had already determined: whether or not Satan had visited her it would serve his purpose to make her believe that Satan had. He thought this would not be difficult. But he did not know Madelon. He did not know how fully she was possessed with thoughts of her own holiness, or how she would rather have died than believe that it was not her Lord who had come to her. She would become even more pure in her thoughts and more saintly in her appearance, and her desperate clinging to her faith in her holiness would present to Father Luce the most difficult problem he was ever to face.

But this he did not suspect when at last he left the house and stepped out into the sun.

VI

Feeling goaded and desperate Richard was looking for Father Raoul but he could not make up his mind what to say to the priest when he found him. Father Raoul was a wholly different man from Father Luce. Rather short, dark, graying and deeply wrinkled he was a kind and gentle man, a pastor in the sense of that word's Latin meaning, a shepherd, a spiritual overseer, who kept before him always a vision of the humble and patient Jesus. All people who knew him, save those who were evil, loved this man; and he loved all people including the sinners. He was a poor man who had little more than the clothes on his back. When not in prayer or meditation or sleep he spent his time with his sheep, counseling, comforting, and leading them to the green pastures of the Gospel. Unlike many priests he was not an informer; he knew that there were many heretics in the earth but not for the throne of heaven would he have informed on them, hoping to enrich himself with a part of their holdings; and he was so sensitive to suffering and torture and all the miseries that afflicted God's children that he almost rejoiced when a heretic escaped, though he supposed that this feeling in him was wicked. All over the land the gallows was almost as common a sight as the abbey or the castle but Father Raoul would never look at a gallows. He would never be present at the burning of heretics. One of his greatest worries was over the way people of the upper classes fought and pushed and brawled in the churchhouse for precedence in position and seating to manifest their social standing. Sometimes there was such bedlam that Father Raoul in disgust wanted to walk out, leaving the people flushed with their vanities and brilliant in their costly raiment, and go off alone to pray for them.

He was in the chapel kneeling when Richard saw him and Richard waited for him to come out. Father Raoul prayed a long time and Richard became very impatient. He stood, doodling with his toes in the dust and thinking of Father Luce in Madelon's chamber and hating the man and hating his own helplessness. He wanted to tell Father Raoul about it but he knew that he would not dare to. For what had he to tell? Nothing at all but his suspicion and suspicion of a man of the cloth was itself heresy. Besides, Father Luce stood far above Father Raoul in the Church hierarchy.

When Father Raoul came out Richard knelt to kiss his hand. This Father did not like such gestures of reverence; he thought of himself only as a humble servant of his Lord and that all reverence should be offered to the Lord and not to the Lord's servants.

"May God keep you," he said. "How are you this morning, Richard?"

"In trouble, Father. I want your advice."

"Then let us sit here on this bench and you tell me."

When they were sitting Richard said: "First, tell me if bathing is a sin. I went to the river this morning. As you see, my rag is now clean."

Father Raoul did not know what answer to give. Some of the early Fathers had thought bathing a sin and in general the clergy of his time discouraged it, particularly the use of warm water, which was thought to be a sensual indulgence. It was St. Jerome, he thought—Father Raoul was not a learned man—who had said that if a Christian had washed in the blood of the Lamb he need not wash again. The upper classes of Jews had the habit of bathing every Friday, and Father Raoul in his quiet unobtrusive way kept himself rather clean; but what advice should he give?

"If our souls are clean," he said at last, "it doesn't matter much how our bodies are. But I don't think our Lord condemned bathing."

"I've heard that some of the Church leaders do."

"That may be so. But this, Richard, is surely no great problem. You said you are in trouble."

"It's this. I've a friend who will buy my freedom. I need someone to see Baron Guillem. Would you do that and learn how much he wants?"

Father Raoul studied Richard's face. "A rich friend?"

75

"Father, I'd rather not name him."

Father Raoul smiled. "You do not need to, Richard. I know who he must be. I've known for quite a while that you've been seeing Hillel, the doctor. There can be no objection to it, if you are prudent. Still—"

"Oh, I know, I know! The Church does not think we should associate with Jews. But Jesus was a Jew."

"Yes," said Father Raoul softly, "Jesus was a Jew, blessed be Jesus. Now, as for seeing Baron Guillem—"

"Will you? Please, Father, and may our Lord bless your name!"

"What will you do when you are free?"

"I want you to advise me." Without waiting for advice Richard went on impulsively: "I'll go to a city and see if I can find work. Then if I can I want to marry."

It did not occur to Father Raoul that Richard was pretty young for marriage. Girls often married when only eleven or twelve years old, and boys while still boys. It did occur to him to ask: "Would you marry a free woman?"

"No, Madelon."

Father Raoul had been smiling. Now his face became very grave. "But Madelon belongs to our Lord, doesn't she? I don't think she will ever marry mortal man. Has she said she would marry you?"

"No." Richard wanted to ask what Father Raoul thought about Father Luce and Madelon. He wanted to blurt out his ugly suspicions, his jealousy, his hate and despair. But he remembered what Hillel had said. He remembered what his father had said.

There was a long moment of awkward silence. Then Richard said, "Father, I'm very ignorant. I wish you would tell me some things."

"What?" asked Father Raoul, studying his eyes.

"About our Church. Is everything in the holy writings the word of God? Did God say to Matthew that we should gather all things that offend and cast them into fire?"

"Our Father gave that commandment to Matthew."

"Then it means that we should destroy all people who won't belong to our Church?"

Father Raoul hesitated. He did not like the brutalities of the inquisitors, or the torture chambers and the stake. But he knew what he was supposed to say and he said at last, "We must not

76

inquire into our heavenly Father's purpose. We must obey."

"But Abelard—now he was a learned monk, wasn't he? He said that by doubting we are led to inquire, and by inquiring we find the truth. He said all knowledge is good. He said—"

"Abelard in some ways was a wicked man."

"You mean intelligence is wicked? God gave it to us, didn't he?"

"God gave us all things."

"Then if he gave us intelligence he expects us to use it, doesn't he?"

"Right thinking, Richard, leads us to the eternal truth of our Church. Wrong thinking is the work of Satan."

"But how can we know when Satan is guiding our thinking?"

It was not always easy, Father Raoul said, shaking his head sadly. Satan was very cunning and devious in his ways. But with prayer and meditation one could understand God's will.

So many questions were running through Richard's mind. He chose one: "Our Church says the sun moves around the earth and that the stars are the souls of angels. Scientists say that the earth moves around the sun and that stars are only lights. Are scientists guided by Satan?"

"Yes, when they say anything that does not agree with the holy Church's teaching."

"There was a Christian named Eriugena. He said reason is greater than authority. Was Satan in him?"

"Yes, Richard."

"And it is true that when church bells ring they drive away thunder and lightning?"

"Yes."

"And it's true that lightning is the forked tongue of hell's fire? —and that when a house burns it's Satan's work?"

"Yes."

Richard looked away to wood ashes in a field, wondering why Satan had burned the wretched hovel of a serf. Then his gaze turned to the image of St. Christopher on the churchhouse wall. "And if just once when we get up in the morning we look at the face of St. Christopher we'll be protected from disease and death all the rest of the day?"

"Yes."

"Then if all Christians did that they'd never get sick or die, would they?"

"Richard," said the Father gently, "I think Satan is in you a little today. You're filled with doubts and all doubts are his work."

"I'm trying to think," Richard said.

"Doubting is not thinking."

"Does a person doubt if he asks questions?"

"Yes."

"Then we should never ask questions? For instance, if God told Luke that we should go out into the highways and hedges and compel all people to join our Church, and if they won't join should we kill them? Is it Satan in me that asks that question?"

"We must obey our Lord's commandments. The blessed St. Jerome and Leo and others have said that we should destroy those who won't come in."

Richard looked away at the baron's forests. He was thinking of the many crusades to the Holy Land and of the stories that had been told. He asked if Christians fulfilled the Lord's commandment when they cut off the noses and dug out the eyes of infidels and castrated them.

"Such stories are lies. They're the work of Satan."

"But Christians have come back and told these stories."

"They were deceived."

"You mean they lied?"

"They only imagined they saw such things."

For a few moments Richard considered that. He admitted to himself that Satan was in him, for he was full of doubts. Turning to look at Father Raoul he said, "Is the holy sacrament polluted in the hands of a wicked priest?"

No, Father Raoul said, it was not. Mortal things could be polluted but not the things of God.

Richard wondered about that. It seemed to him that a wicked priest would pollute anything he touched. He also wondered about the followers of the man called Waldo, who wished to live humbly in poverty as Jesus had lived. The Church called them heretics but was not Francis teaching the same thing?

Father Raoul did not like such questions. A humble man of poverty himself in his private heart he did not approve the ostentatious wealth and sumptuous living of most of his ecclesiastical superiors. Everywhere in the Christian world there were abbots and bishops, yes, and even monks, who lived the life of nobles—who, armed, spent most of their time drinking and wenching, warring and hunting. Evading the questions Father Raoul asked: "How often do you pray and meditate on holy things?"

"Not as often as I should."

"If you'll only humble yourself and meditate you'll not ask such questions, for they are the tongue of evil."

"But I need to learn. Is it wicked for a Christian to talk to a Jew?"

"All Jews are cast out," the Father said, "except those who come in. If you talk to Jews who won't come in you might as well talk to any infidel."

Richard wanted to say that he did not believe it. He wanted to say that Hillel was a good man and he loved him and wanted him as a friend. He wanted to blurt these things out to the Father but he did not dare to. He wanted to say, I think Hillel is more pleasing in God's sight than Father Luce. He wanted to say, I think God gave us minds to use and that he wants us to use them. Above all else he wanted to say, I must be free, I must study and learn, I must know before I can believe, not believe before I know.

But he said only, "If Satan is in me I should go on a pilgrimage."

"That would be a fine thing, if you can."

"I can't unless I'm free. Will you see Baron Guillem for me?"

Father Raoul looked down into the village and considered the matter. He did not mind asking Guillem if he would sell one of his serfs. That is not what troubled him. He was convinced that the money would come from a Jew and a Jewish doctor of all persons!—and he was not sure that he would not commit a sin if he acted as the agent in such an exchange. But he was a man of deep kindliness, he had always liked Richard, and at last with an effort he said, "I'll talk to him if you wish me to."

"And may God bless you! Then if you wish me to I'll make a pilgrimage or you can give me some other penance, for I do wish to live with the truth."

"You've always been a good boy, Richard. I'll see what I can do."

Faithful to his promise Father Raoul saw Baron Guillem the next day.

"Which one is this?" asked the baron suspiciously. He did not intend to sell a healthy strong man from whom he might expect twenty or thirty years of heavy toil.

Father Raoul said it was the youth Richard, son of Victoir, who was not at all strong but seemed sickly and feeble; and having out of the great goodness of his heart told one small lie he told another. He said that in his opinion Richard could never hope to marry, or if he did marry his wife would be the frail and sickly Madelon, whose children would all die in childbirth. Guillem's cold eyes were studying the priest while his avaricious mind considered what the priest was saying. Neither he nor any other lord liked to have sick slaves; they were not good for much and sometimes they became a nuisance. Still, he suspected that Richard might be able-bodied and he wanted every sou he could get; and after further thought he said he would sell him for fifty livres.

Father Raoul raised a hand in protest. "My lord, your price is too high for a sick boy. And I should have told you that I am sure he is troubled by Satan and may have to go on a long pilgrimage."

"Forty," said the baron, eager to be off to the hunt.

When Father Raoul gave him the message Richard was beside himself with joy. To be free! O God in heaven, to be free! He wanted to rush over at once to Hillel but he knew that Father Raoul would spy on him, to learn if the money actually was coming from a Jew. He dashed out to a field to toil. He labored in the heat and chewed cabbage leaves and dreamed great dreams. For a serf there was on earth no treasure, no glory like freedom. Freedom to do what? Richard in the folly of his enthusiasm thought he would be free to do all things, to go where he pleased, live where he pleased, think what he pleased, worship as he pleased. He knew so little of the world and its people, so little of the vigilance and the immense power of the Church, that he dreamed dreams that could never be. He dreamed of himself as a learned and famous man like Averroes, like Abelard, even like Aristotle whose books the Church was burning. He dreamed of himself as a knight whose sword was truth and of Madelon as his pure and lovely wife and of their children who would be born free and could become merchants or priests, nuns or scientists, doctors or scribes. He dreamed of a clean little cottage somewhere and of good food and of wine to drink on festive days and of the books he would read and the books he might possibly write. Above all he dreamed of the truths which he would discover and make known to men.

Again and again he wanted to rush over to Hillel or to Madelon but he labored until dark, until exhausted, until he could barely stagger, and was then supported not by inner strength, of which he had so little, but by the vision of his future. When he left the field he did not go to his father's hut but to a secluded spot to wait for deeper dark. He was famished but all his life he had known the pangs of hunger; he was athirst but he did not mind. Possibly Hillel would give him a crust of bread.

When at last under cover of darkness he slipped over to Hillel's house he was trembling all over. He knocked softly, the door was opened, swiftly he went in and the door was closed. He sank gasping to a stool, so overcome with emotion that he was afraid he would vomit. Hillel looked at his bloodless face and the glory in his eyes and said, "You must be hungry. I'll bring you something."

With a cry Richard fell to his knees and reached out to grasp Hillel's hand and kiss it.

"No!" Hillel said sharply, drawing back. "Richard, what is the trouble?"

"I love you!" Richard said. He was weeping. He felt that he could endure no more. For forty-eight hours he had had nothing to eat but cabbage leaves and he had labored hard. He hardly knew what he was saying. He was shaking and his teeth were shaking. "I love you!" he babbled. "You're my friend!"

"Come," said Hillel and helped him to rise. "Now sit and tell me."

"He will sell me!" he blurted and he rushed on headlong, "For forty livres, is that too much? oh I know it's a lot—"

"Now, now, get hold of yourself."

"Oh, it's too much!"

"No, it's not too much."

Again Richard slipped to his knees, tears washing down his cheeks. "I want to kiss your hand!" he cried. "I must kiss something!"

Hillel moved quickly. He returned with a folio and held it before Richard, saying, "Kiss this."

Richard kissed a page and spilled tears on it.

"Come, come!" cried Hillel. "You've got to get hold of yourself." He hastened away and returned with a cup of wine. "Drink this."

Blinded by tears but trying to see it Richard said, "Wine?"

"Wine."

"I've never tasted wine! I—" Again he broke down.

81

"Come now, drink the wine!"

"Yes!" he gasped, sobbing. He took the wine and gulped it and at once was strangled and began to cough; but he felt the wine in him, the warmth, the glow. He got to his feet but sank at once to a stool and looking at Hillel said, "Forgive me. I—"

"I know, I know. You don't have to tell me." Hillel went away and returned with bread and a pasty of nuts and figs. Richard began to eat. Never in his life had he eaten such bread. Never had he tasted anything as absolutely delicious as the mixture of fruits and nuts. He ate like a man who had been brought out of a dungeon where he had starved for weeks. He ate every scrap and crumb and drop of juice and licked his fingers and smiled at Hillel and said, "I bathed. I washed myself all over."

A little amused, Hillel said, "I had observed it."

"As soon as I can I'll pay you back the money."

"I'm not worried about it. There are more important things that we must understand. I suppose we should make the pledge of brotherhood."

Vows of eternal brotherhood were common enough, vows between two men never to betray or desert one another, no matter what the provocation or the perils. But such a vow between a Jew and a Christian was very rare, and Richard had been so moved by Hillel's words that he was weeping again. He had never dared hope for such fellowship, for such a friend.

"Before we make the pledge," said Hillel, "let's be sure we both understand what it means." He picked up his badge of infamy, made of yellow felt, and went on: "All over the Christian world my people have to wear this. The reason given is that we are an accursed and outcast people. If we are known by some sign—by something," he said drily, "more dependable than our so-called Jewish nose, then Christian women won't marry us and we won't dare to try to convert Christians to our faith. If you travel you'll find that this badge varies in size, color and character; that it is sometimes worn on the breast, sometimes on the shoulder or back. The women of my people have to wear two blue stripes on their veils or cloaks. You will hear different explanations of what this badge means. Some will tell you that it is in the form of the Host, an emblem which we refuse to accept and so are compelled to wear it. You may hear it said that when in the form of a circle it represents the full moon, which somehow is supposed to manifest contempt for the crescent of Islam. You'll learn that every Jewish boy in some places, such as Marseilles, has to begin wearing the badge at the age of seven, which appears to be," said Hillel, looking into Richard's eyes, "a rather young age for either seduction or marriage. You'll learn that though the color is usually yellow it may be white and red or of several colors. If any Christian informer catches us without this badge, for his vigilance he receives the garment on which it should have been sewn or pinned. And you'll also learn, Richard, that if Jews wish to stoop to such humiliation they can for a sum of money buy an exemption from wearing it. There seems to be nothing that money will not buy among Christians."

Hillel rearranged the candles so that he could see Richard's face more clearly. "Well, we are branded as a pariah class. Our badge invites insult and degradation, from which we have no protection at all. Our lot, God knows, was bad enough before the dreadful edict of your Pope Innocent the Third. It is now ten times worse. Israel is desolate and walks alone in sorrow, wearing a badge of yellow. A pledge of brotherhood must be forever secret between us or we will both suffer horribly."

"I'll keep it secret," Richard said.

"That is so easy to say when you are so young. The pledge you are so willing to make is enough to convict you of heresy. You realize that?"

Hillel had lowered his voice; and in a whisper Richard said, "Yes."

"You realize, then, that from this night you'll be doomed if it becomes known? You know what your fate would be in that case? And do you know that if you are found guilty of heresy, your sin will be visited upon all your people and they will be persecuted?"

"Yes, I know that."

"Are you aware of how many spies and informers your Church has, and how energetic and vigilant they are? Are you aware that many of them are very depraved men? Do you know that if after you become a free man you prosper, no matter what you do, you will be of more and more interest to spies, who will get a part of your goods if you are convicted? I've told you before, Richard," Hillel said solemnly, looking into his eyes, "that as a serf you are safe. I've never heard of an instance in which a serf without property has been accused. There's just no profit in it. You can find vagrant minstrels and beggars all over Europe who make unholy fun of the Church, yet are seldom molested. But you're ambitious to prosper. The more you prosper the more difficult your life will be. Do you know it?"

Richard was aghast. He blurted out, "I, no, I hadn't realized it!"

"There is more than that to realize. You must try to imagine what will happen to you if you are ever accused. I'll try to suggest it. First, you'll never know who your accusers are. They can be liars and thieves and pimps. That'll make no difference. You'll never see them. There'll be no one present at your trial but the inquisitors and clerks. It won't matter at all, if your accusers have lied about you. Even if they should withdraw their testimony against you, they'll be punished for falsehood but their testimony against you will stand. Yes, even if they say it was all lies. Did you know that?"

"God, no," Richard said, astonished.

"No? I do hope that you are trying to grasp the import of these things."

"I am trying."

"Then grasp this. Except in massacres and wholesale slaughters not a great number of heretics are punished with death. But there are other punishments more dreadful. The dungeon, Richard, is worse than fire. Almost as bad as the dungeon is the fate of those who have to wear the cross. Have you ever seen one of them?"

"One, yes."

"Can you imagine how it is with them? If you are accused of heresy and recant and return to your faith you'll have to wear the cross, to indicate your sin to all men. You will suffer the ridicule, the derision, the insults of many people. No one will want to associate with you. No one will dare to give you food, shelter, employment or even a kind word. Under your cross you will wander desolate over the earth, even more of an outcast than I. Your own people won't dare speak to you. And if you happened to be married your wife and children would have to flee from you."

Hillel rose abruptly and went outside. Richard supposed he had been called by his bladder, and while Hillel was outside he stared round him, not without a sense of guilt. Hillel did not have much in the two small rooms: a crude bed, stools, books, papers, a few cooking utensils, a few medicines, a few surgical tools. But it looked like a great deal to Richard and he was ashamed of his envious gawking.

Hillel came in and said quietly, "I wanted to be sure no spy was around."

"Was any?"

"No. Well now, what was I saying? The cross? But what if they threw you into a dungeon? Can you imagine that? There are two degrees of punishment, the murus largus and the murus strictus. In the milder form you have only dark bread and water and solitary confinement. In the worse form you live out the remainder of your life in a tiny dark stinking damp cell overrun with vermin and rats. You might be chained both hands and feet. After a while you would be almost blind. After a while you would lose your powers of speech. And you'd be completely at the mercy of your guards, whose privilege it would be to insult or even torture you. Because they would be paid so much money to feed you it would be to their profit to starve you, so long as they kept you barely alive. For it is papal orders," Hillel said with his dry smile, "that the enormis rigor of your solitary confinement shall not quite extinguish life. Would that be worse than an hour in the flames?"

"God, yes!" Richard whispered, watching with fascination the changes of pity, compassion, scorn, contempt and horror in Hillel's face.

"This also you must never forget, that once an inquisitor lays hands on you he will never let you go. If he were to know that you had made a pledge with a Jew no power under heaven could save you. But no, there is one power, there is one. Now, trying to imagine the horror of these things, are you willing to make the pledge?"

"Yes."

"I must wonder whether you have great courage or great ignorance."

"How could I fail, when you are offering me not only freedom but friendship?"

"Another thing. You have learned to read. Suppose you were fortunate enough to be able to pursue truth; and suppose you found that truth was not in all instances in harmony with the teachings of your Church. Suppose, then, you were put to torture: would you deny the truth or not?"

85

"Never!"

"The young," said Hillel, "can be so sure of things."

"If truth is such an outcast that people are condemned by de-liberate liars—yes, even when it's known they are liars—there must be a few men strong enough to defend it."

"Those are brave words," Hillel said. "If you had the strength to abide by them you would be a great man."

"I'll never be false to what I know is true."

"But how can we know what is true and what is not?"

"We know it isn't true to convict men with lies."

"Yes, we know that."

"We know it isn't truth not to let the accused face his accuser."

"Yes, we know that."

"We know it isn't truth to torture men in the name of God."

"Well, yes, I think we can say that."

"Then if we know some truth, surely there is more."

"No man," said Hillel, as if speaking to himself, "can look into the future. No man can foretell what the fate of my people will be, or of mankind. But I believe deep in my soul that the time must come when all men can believe and speak as they please. I don't have any idea in what land that will be, but in some land, somewhere, some day. It will take a lot of brave men and women to make it possible, a lot of Abelards, yes, a lot of heretics."

"Heretics?" Richard said. He did not understand.

"Today's heresy is tomorrow's dogma. Few people are religious, most of them are ritualistic. Only those can be religious, I some-times think, in whom the faculties of imagination and intelligence are highly cultivated. Do you understand me?"

"I guess not. I hope to some day."

"I mean that this terror upon the earth is not religion. It can never be religion that tortures in the name of love." He was silent a few moments, his eyes studying Richard's face, his mind wondering about him. At last he said, "You really want to make the pledge?"

"Yes!"

"Shouldn't you take a little time to think it over?"

"If I decided no I'd be a coward."

"Would you like to be a martyr to truth?"

"Abelard was. Is there any nobler way to live?"

"None that I know of."

86

"Then I want that way."

"Give me your hands," Hillel said. Richard gave his hands and Hillel looked at him with a wry smile. "Long ago it was the custom to make such a pledge with hands on one another's genitals. God knows why. But people do change in spite of priests, and so we clasp hands and leave our genitals alone. You are sure you want this?"

"Yes."

"Then repeat the words after me. In the name of that God who is the Father of us all, blessed be his name—"

"In the name of that God who is the Father of us all, blessed be his name—"

"—we pledge a bond of brotherhood, neither as Jew nor Christian but as two men—"

"—we pledge a bond of brotherhood, neither as Jew nor Christian but as two men—"

"—and pledge ourselves to be faithful to our pact and our friendship, never to betray one another—"

"—and pledge ourselves to be faithful to our pact and our friendship, never to betray one another—"

"—so help us, God."

"—so help us, God."

"Shall we pledge ourselves to be friends of truth?"

"Yes."

"We pledge our souls to truth, as truth is revealed to us by our Father—" He waited until Richard had repeated the words. Then: "—never to debase or deny it but to be its servants in God's will, serving his infinite purpose—" Then: "—and may our Father protect and keep and guide us and may his light shine upon us to be our blessing."

"—and may our Father protect and keep and guide us and may his light shine upon us to be our blessing!"

Hillel then kissed Richard on his forehead and Richard asked impulsively, "May I kiss you?"

"We are brothers now."

Richard kissed his brother's forehead and felt that if he lived to be as old as a biblical patriarch he would never pay homage to a greater man.

Hillel set two cups on the table and poured wine. He lifted a cup and said, "To truth, Richard. To the truth which our Father reveals to us when we walk in his light."

"To truth!" said Richard and his voice broke. He drank the wine off. Then he slipped downward and put his face in his arms and wept.

VII

The following day was Sunday and more than the usual number of people came to Mass. Richard, who was far back among the common ones, studied as was his habit the aristocrats, whose manners and clothes fascinated him. Those from the upper classes often wore their hawks to church, for these, like their coat-of-arms or their furs, their liveries and swords and purses, indicated their social rank. The knight was privileged to use the gerfalcon; a squire, the kestrel; a yeoman, the goshawk; and a priest the sparrow hawk. Even in hottest weather the lords and ladies sometimes wore their furs, a petty noble clinging to his frayed tippet of lambskin or fox or wolf or civet, while his superiors showed themselves off in marten, black sable or ermine. Such men as Guillem were usually smooth-shaven but allowed their hair to grow long and arranged it in curls. The women of the highest social position applied poultices of crushed beans or of mare's warm milk to their complexions and daubed themselves with vermilion and saffron and drenched themselves with scents.

Baron Guillem had dressed with care. A squire had helped him into his underdrawers and had put on his black or brown stockings, or at most, black with a red stripe, for good taste frowned on more brilliant colors in hosiery. He had then put on his chemise of white linen without cuffs or collar; and next the pelisson, a long fur-edged garment; and over this the bliaut or tunic, fairly loose, which he had pulled over his head like a shirt. It was made of silk. At war or the hunt he wore high leather boots but for church he had put on cloth shoes, embroidered with jewels and worked with gold. On state occasions he would wear a chaplet of flowers or a thin gold wreath; and in bad weather a chaperon, a combination of cap and cape. He wore his sword of course and had a gerfalcon on his wrist. Popes had inveighed against the taking of hawks into church but in such matters the nobility did as they pleased.

The baron's wife Elienor was as resplendent as her lord. Her maid had first robed her with a long white linen chemise, which fell to her knees; and over this she had a pelisson of fine silk with fur edging, which hung to her feet; and over this a tunic fitted tightly with girdles to show off her figure, which was plump but womanly. The tunic had pearl beadwork and golden embroidery, golden buttons, and golden girdles set with agates and sapphires. She wore pointed shoes, which were just coming into style; and from a girdle hung a silken alms purse on a silver chain.

Most of the nobles were invariably impatient with the church services and the sermon: a man on pilgrimage had presented himself for scourging, as he was obliged to do at every shrine and churchhouse along his way. Most of the people were eager to watch the flogging and they poured pellmell out of the building when the services were done. The man was barefooted, in the way of pilgrims, and wore only a simple garment of sackcloth with a diaper under it. He had to wear the diaper because he would be stripped and his private parts had to be hidden. He had brought with him his rod, a stout green gnarled branch of hawthorn; and when, having removed his tunic, he presented the rod to Father Luce, Richard gasped. He had hoped that the scourging would be done by Father Raoul, a gentle and merciful man.

The social elite formed the inner circle and the common people were forced back, where they could barely see. But they could hear. Richard had heard scourgings before, for they were commonplace. He knew that the man was kneeling, with his back bared and his palms on the earth. He heard the first blow and a cry of pain. Shy and afraid, his sister Fleur had come up to him and clasped one of his hands. The second blow fell with terrific force; Father Luce enjoyed these punishments and he was wielding the cudgel with both hands. A third blow fell, a fourth. . . . How many would there be? Sometimes it was ten, or twenty or even fifty, depending on what the offense had been. Sometimes a man sentenced to a long pilgrimage was scourged so many times and so violently that at the end he was only a scarred and crippled creature, with bleak eyes and a dead soul. What horrified Richard most was the delight which many Christians took in these brutal floggings. The baron and his group were shouting and applauding, the women were squealing their approval; and even in the faces of serfs and peasants Richard saw an unholy joy. What, he wondered, was the difference between this and the Roman arenas, which the early Christians had so bitterly condemned? He looked round him and caught the eyes of his father and saw in them fear and pain.

Well, it was over at last and the spectators fell away. The poor wretch, with his back welted and bloody, put on his sackcloth and took up his rod, to continue his journey to the next church or shrine. For twenty days at a time, twice a year, he was to fast, if his health and strength would permit it. He was to hear Mass daily, if possible. Seven times daily he was to recite the canonical hours; ten times daily the Paternoster, and twenty times each night. Never again was he to touch meat, eggs or cheese, except on Easter, Pentecost and Christmas. He was to be continent, humble and when possible silent, and for any infraction of his penance he was to be held as a lapsed heretic and turned over to the secular arm. Such would be his life until a papal legate saw fit to abate or change it.

Though a pilgrimage was thought to be merciful compared to some other forms of punishment, it seemed to Richard to be a dreadful thing. It might fill several years of a man's life and he might return to find his property wasted and his family gone. If he was sent to the Holy Land, as so many were, he could count himself lucky if he got back alive. A pilgrim had to wear the cross: Dominic twelve years earlier had ordered a converted heretic to wear two crosses, as a symbol of his sin and repentance. Those two small pieces of saffron-colored cloth had steadily grown in size until they were now as large as two palms, one on the chest and one on the back. Now and then there was a third cross on the cap. These who wore the cross were like lepers, for nobody dared to speak to them or befriend them.

By the time he saw the poor creature go limping away Richard was sick enough to vomit. All last night sleeping out in a thicket he had dreamed the same horrible dream over and over. He had climbed a very tall ladder to examine a pole, like a flagpole or church spire, that was anchored on top of another very tall pole, set in the earth. When he came to the top of the ladder a deadly black terror seized him, for he was afraid that he would lose his grasp and fall. He had a vision of the awful depth below and of the ladder swaying and his hands clutched more and more feebly, as sweat poured from him and his senses almost blacked out. He did not know what he was supposed to do with the spire on top of the pole and he was not able to think about it or look at it or even touch it. He could think only of what would happen to him if he lost consciousness and fell and desperately he tried to free his feet, which seemed to have been chained, and back down to a more secure foothold. This he was able to do at last sweating, gasping, almost fainting; and he then backed slowly down the ladder and collapsed when his feet touched earth. He then awoke and shivered with the terror of it; and slept at last and dreamed the same dream again. He had no notion at all what the dream meant but memory of it filled his mind and senses when he saw the man go limping away.

He wanted to lose himself in a big city, in Toulouse perhaps, which was only forty or fifty miles distant in the west. When the money was paid and he was a free man he shook all over. "I'm free?" he asked, gasping at Hillel. "Not free," Hillel said. "There are no free men in this part of the world. You're only a little freer than you were." Richard dared not think of himself as a free man at all. Hillel had given him garments, woven of coarse fabrics like his own but clean and whole; and when Richard said he wanted to go away for a little while and think about himself Hillel gave him a parcel of food, bread, salted fish, dried fruits, nuts and cheese.

"Toulouse?" asked Richard, his eyes big and scared in his white face.

"Yes, Toulouse for a while."

Should he slip away without saying goodbye to his family? Should he try to see Madelon? He wanted the tender delicacy of a kiss on her small mouth and a promise to wait for him; but after torturing himself with indecision he remembered that he was now a man dedicated to truth and bound by an oath to loyalty and friendship. Everything that he did now would have to be governed by that, yes, and everything that he said. Hillel encouraged him to go without saying goodbye to anyone. He himself had been thinking of moving to a larger place where he could be more inconspicuous, because, though the baron protected him and depended on him to minister to his physical ills, the baron was fickle and treacherous.

"I may see you in Toulouse," he said.

When Richard at last turned away he felt as if he was departing for the ends of the earth. Not since early childhood had he been more than a mile or two from the village: Toulouse seemed almost as far away as Paris or Rome. He was afraid and he tried to shrug off the fear, telling himself that he would have to be a man now. He knew that outside the villages, towns and cities there was no protection for anyone but those who went with armed bodyguards. Thieves, robbers and brigands roamed the earth and if a man was found plundered and dead nobody thought anything about it. I don't even have a knife, he thought, looking down over himself and feeling as defenseless as the penitent. But he knew that he must go and that he would go.

And at last there he stood at the edge of the village, a youth garbed in a sleeveless sacklike garment that fell to his knees. On his feet was a pair of tough sandals; on his head a small round cap that covered little more than his crown. He was about five feet eight inches in height, and very slender, almost scrawny; with a pale thin sensitive face, soft brown eyes that had seen much suffering and little joy; brown hair falling to his shoulders and a sparse beard. There he stood, deeply afraid of the world and its people, yet fired with a will to raise himself above the level of his origins, to enrich his mind with learning, to open his soul to the light. He was lookng away into the west and wondering if he should not say goodbye to his frail little sister when Chretien came over to him.

Richard looked curiously at the man's face, observing first as all people did the beaked nose that had almost the curve of a crescent moon; and then the eyes that were animal-like in their cunning. But not like the pig's or the cat's or the dog's, not like the cold suspicious eye of the falcon or the wolf; but more like the eyes of the rat, dark, small and bright with intelligence.

"So you're going away," Chretien said. "Will you come back?"

"Yes, some day."

Chretien looked him up and down and then looked into Richard's eyes. "Are you on the side of Satan now?"

Richard was shocked. "Why," he asked angrily, "do you accuse me of that?"

"I'm not accusing you. Some day you'll know what I mean."

"Are you?" asked Richard, looking into the cunning eyes.

Chretien smiled but the only change in his expression was below his nose. "I'm an ignorant man. I know nothing about things."

"Then why accuse me?"

"You've been with a Jew. He gave you that garment and that pouch of food."

"Does that put me with Satan?"

"Asses bray insults at horses. You curry favel, don't you?" Favel was a horse color: those were said to curry favel who sought favors.

"Are you my enemy?" Richard asked, wondering what the man had in mind.

"By God's coif, no. Are you stupid? It's said that some love Satan's ass better than many love God's face."

"I don't know what you mean."

"It's said some prefer Satan's turd to the wafer."

"I say I don't know what you mean," Richard said, looking at Chretien's eyes.

"Did you know the Lord visited Madelon?"

Richard supposed the question was a trap. He looked at the man's eyes and at his mouth and again at his eyes.

"You still wish to marry Madelon?"

"Yes."

"Then why are you going away? You think she'll be here when you come back?"

"I think God will care for her."

"Father Luce is caring for her."

In heaven's name what was he driving at? Richard wanted to be off. He did not want to talk to this strange man whom he had never understood or liked and whom he had suspected of abominable evils. He knew that Chretien's questions were sinister. "I must be going now," he said and moved to go.

"Wait," said Chretien. "You should understand one thing. You're not full of godbelly like a priest. I know why you're running away and if you're smart you'll never come back. I tell you that because I like you. As for Madelon, you can find a better wife. Now go—and farewell."

Chretien turned away. Richard said, "I don't know what you mean. Why shouldn't I come back?"

"You'll understand some day. Now farewell."

94

Chretien went away and for a little while Richard stood undecided looking after him. Then he turned and looked south and slowly he began to walk, following the ruts and dust of the road until he came to the point where it turned west, past the baron's castle and moats and stables and mews. Chretien's words had made him more deeply afraid and uncertain, more lonely and alone. Richard the son of Victoir and Elise, born a serf but now free by the grace of God and the compassion of a Jew, followed the road west, trudging with slow reluctant steps, leaving behind him parents, brother, sister, Father Raoul, Hillel and the girl he loved. The father of that girl—or *was* he the father?—had told him that he was now on Satan's side. He did not know what the man had meant but the words troubled him and he felt a need to weep, though he had told himself that he would be a man now and weep no more. The things that he was leaving seemed dearer now— his father's quiet eyes and his sad little sister and the gentleness of Father Raoul and the friendship of Hillel. He even felt tearful about the ugly little village and the fields where he had labored and he would have turned back but for the look which would be in Hillel's eyes. No, he would have to go on, even if it broke his heart. He would go on but God knew where or why. He could not put away the memory of Pascal sitting and fondling his scrawny cats or of his mother staring with wild suffering eyes at his father. But he must put them away.

He must go on, he must try to be a man. He must get away for a little while from these things that he feared and loathed or he could never determine what he felt or what he was. Hot tears were falling to his cheeks now and he was despising himself for his weakness. In an effort to gather strength and force the grief back and down he recalled Hillel's words: "God reveals his purpose to each of us to the extent of our understanding, and our capacity to understand his will is the measure of our godliness." Hillel had said, "I'll pray for you and ask God to bless you. Come back if you must but if you do not have to don't come back. May your light shine on." Richard had been deeply moved by many things that Hillel had said; he admired the way Hillel expressed himself and he said some of the words over and over and found in them a little strength and calm. "I think your capacity will be great," Hillel had said—meaning his capacity to understand God. What sweeter thing could man say to man? One's capacity to understand his will was one's measure of godliness: how beautifully he had said it! What a remarkable man he was! Richard no longer thought of him as a Jew and would never again think of him as a Jew, but only as a man and a brother. It occurred to him then in a flash of illumination that this is what Hillel had meant: in thinking of him not as a Jew but as a man and brother, Richard —but dared he believe it?—was revealing his capacity to understand the will of their Father. Yes, he liked to think that that was what Hillel had meant, that and much more, that and all the things that Richard must learn, until he could really be Hillel's brother. How fine he had been to offer him his help and his friendship!—for who among all the followers of the Jew of Nazareth would do that for a Jew?

I must not think such thoughts, Richard told himself, and again the hot tears fell. I must think thoughts true and strong and I must be strong and true, so that my friend will not be ashamed of me. I must be alert to enemies. I must be cunning and prudent. I must not be afraid. I must walk strong under the heaven of God, keeping Hillel's advice always in my thoughts—yes, but he was stumbling, he was barely able to see the road, he was not alert to danger, for suddenly he became aware of a sound that was close. He swung and there on the road behind him, astride a palfrey with a hawk on her wrist, was the Baroness Elienor. He now sensed how unaware he had been of the world around him.

She cantered up, sitting with both legs on the right of the saddle, in the manner of highborn ladies, and drew her horse in. He had seen her many times when her face was smiling but now her face was suspicious.

"Where are you going?" she said.

"You mean me?" asked Richard, shamefacedly trying to rub the signs of grief from his cheeks.

"Who are you?"

"Richard, the son of Victoir."

"Are you sent on a pilgrimage? But no, you have no cudgel."

"No, my lady. I'm guilty of no sin."

"Really?" she said, and laughed. "If so, is there another man in the world like you?"

"My lady—"

"Do you know who I am?"

"Yes, my lady."

"You're very polite, aren't you?—and would be handsome with more meat on your bones. Were you at the services last Sunday?"

"Yes, my lady," he said, his gaze sweeping her fair face and noting its mirth.

"Did you see the man scourged?"

"Yes, my lady."

"Did you enjoy it?"

"No, my lady."

"No?" For a few moments she looked at him with womanly interest. Then, impatiently, "Surely you know where you're going."

"I—I want to go to Toulouse. I'd like to be a student there."

"Have you money?"

"No, my lady."

"No money? . . . None?" She drew her silken purse up and held it and looked at him. She reached into it. "Come over," she said.

Richard flushed. "My lady—"

"Did you hear me? Come over!"

He moved over awkwardly and stood before her but he did not look up at her.

"Look at me," she said.

"Yes, my lady," he said and with an effort met her eyes.

"How can you travel without money?"

"Many people do."

"Pilgrims?—but they eat at the convents. Where'll you eat?"

"I have some food," he said and dropped his gaze.

"Look at me," she said and again he met her eyes. "You have nice eyes. You have a nice mouth and a strong nose." His gaze fell. "Can't you look at me? An ass can look at a king, you know."

"Yes, my lady," he said and flushed again.

She drew forth a few coins and looked at them, considering, and then laughed gaily. "Why should I be so damned stingy?" she said. "What will you study?"

"My lady—"

"Latin?"

"I hope to."

"And when you come back will you teach me?"

"My lady, I—"

"If I command you to?"

"Yes, my lady."

"Then here." She drew forth more coins, some gold and some

97

silver, and proffered them. When he moved to back off she cried, "Richard, don't be a damned fool! Here."

"But, my lady—"

"Come, come, don't be so proud and silly." She held the coins out and Richard advanced to accept them. There were so many that they spilled from his hand and he knelt to recover those that fell. Then with the coins in both hands he stared at them. "You know what they are?"

"My lady, I've never seen coins before."

"Now don't let some brigand get them. Where can you hide them?" He looked down over his garment. "Have you a secert pocket?"

"No, my lady."

"Have you a purse?"

"No."

She searched in her big purse. "Here," she said and drew forth a small silken pouch that tied at the mouth with strings. "Come close and turn your back," she said. Richard moved over, still awkward, confused, shamed, and turned his back to her and felt her warm hands under his hair at the nape, concealing the purse and tying the strings to a strand of hair. "There!" she cried and patted his head. "Now look at me." When he turned and looked up at her she asked: "Would you like to be a knight?"

"I'd rather be a scholar," he said.

"Can you read?"

"Some, my lady, but not well."

"Why do you want to be a scholar?"

"To know the truth."

"But all truth is in our Church."

"Yes, my lady."

"You don't believe it? Well, by God's eyes I don't either. But you must never say that. Always be prudent, Richard, for you are good-looking and I may make you a knight. When are you coming back?"

"My lady, I don't know."

"You must come back soon. I command it. And when you return come and see me. I shall have something for you—and you are to teach me Latin." She looked at him, her eyes and her rich mouth smiling, and then abruptly swung her horse and galloped away.

Richard stared after her until she had vanished and then, as if doubting his senses, put a hand to his nape to feel the pouch. It seemed to him that she had given him a great deal of money, for some of the coins were of gold. He tugged a little at the pouch to see if it was secure, thinking meanwhile of her fair face and laughing eyes and full womanly mouth. She had asked him to come see her but what had she meant by that? Richard was an intuitive youth and he thought he knew what she meant and he thought it very foolish of him to think it. Highborn ladies, he had heard, had many lovers, or those had whose husbands did not lock them up or put dreadful diapers on them to keep them chaste.

He trudged down the road, thinking of her warm smiling face, putting a hand back now and then to see if the pouch was there. He thought her very alluring, very gracious and charming, very spirited, yes, and very worldly. He had been thrilled by the way she had looked at him and by her hands in his hair. He had met her eyes only a few times but every time he had seen in them the meanings that a man can read. He liked to think of himself as her lover, teaching her Latin, though the thought paralyzed him with anxieties, with a sense of shame for his uncouthness and his ignorance of the ways of love. Highborn ladies, he had heard, were adept at wanton dalliance; they were specialists in the cultivation of erotic raptures. I shall have something for you, she had said. What had she meant?

He tried to put her out of his thoughts but she would not be put out. She was there, snug and smiling and colorful and intimate, with that light in her eyes which a man knew the secret of. Richard had never dreamed of himself as a ladies' man. He imagined there was in him none of Baron Laurent's impetuous headstrong ardor, when, enamored of a lady, he mounted his horse and pursued her into a church building on a Sunday, to the consternation of the priest and the worshipers. All highborn men, it was said, gave a good part of their time to their amours, and a knight worthy of his blade preferred above all to engage in battle the most amorous knights, that is, those most pugnaciously devoted to women. The more timid ones pointed their weapons for the joute à plaisance but the bolder ones insisted on the joute a l'outrance, when they fought for real blood. One of the hot-blooded gallants had had his helmet so dented and jammed about his face that a blacksmith had had to hack it off with chisel and mallet. Baroness

Elienor had asked him if he wanted to be a knight but Richard had thought of knights as rather ridiculous fellows; with their coif thrown back they would try to dance in their heavy armor but, barely able to move, were like a beast weighted down with fat and blubber; or in their armor they would practice lifting weights, jumping fosses, and climbing, looking for all the world like ungainly and mindless creatures. One eye covered with a red cloth as a sign that they would perform some mighty feat of valor they would ride forth, their horse covered with little bells, the sound of which, it was said, gave them courage; or they would fix their shield on a tree or bridge or paling, to give notice that they would contest the passage of anyone who dared to go that way.

No, he did not want to be a knight. He did not know much about knights he now realized while trudging along the road, one hand rising again and again to feel for the purse. He had seen them many times in their chausses of chainmail, worn to their knees or to their feet, their hands covered by the hauberk that ran up their arms. He had seen them in their brilliant surcoat, charged with heraldic emblems; and their gilded spurs; and coif and chapelle de fer. He had seen their big flat shields, two feet wide and four feet long, covered on both sides with leather; and their horses, heavily armored, the headpiece of the destrier blazing with jewels; and the gay colors of their ladylove. He had heard that everything they wore was symbolic: the sword was in the form of the Cross, to indicate that it was to be used in defense of the Lord; their spear was straight because truth was so; their pennon must be visible from afar because it was for courage. The steel helmet was for modesty, the hauberk for a fortress against evil, the spurs for swiftness in the service of virtue, the gorget for obedience, the gauntlets for prayer, the saddle for safety.

He knew that not all knights were bold and impetuously amorous and he had seen Baron Guillem deknight one who had been false to his vows. A herald-at-arms had asked thrice, Who is there? and three times in a loud voice had come the name of the knight to be degraded. Three times the herald replied, It is not so, I see no knight here, but only a craven and a coward who has been false to his vows! The miserable creature, exposed on a scaffold in nothing but his shirt, was stripped of his armor which was then broken at his feet. His spurs were thrown into a pile of dung. His charger's tail was cut off. His shield was dragged through the

100

dust and dung of the village streets. Then the sweating wretch had been borne on a litter like a corpse to the churchhouse and forced to listen to a burial service read over him. Remembering what a shameful ordeal it had been Richard recalled how the poor devil had groaned and supplicated while his spurs were hacked off with a cook's axe.

Lord no, he did not want to be a knight! He did not have for knighthood either the courage or the folly. He did like to think of himself in a modest and humble way as one delighting in the favors of beautiful ladies. Physical love among the kind of people he came from was a matter to think of with shame: too often a man would take his woman with a blow and cover her and with a blow release her. Because it was regarded as incest to marry a cousin even at the sixth remove and because the lord of a manor would not allow his slave to marry the fief of a neighboring lord it was difficult for a man to get married at all. And if you did marry a girl from another village, as likely as not she would drive her mother-in-law out of the hovel and leave the poor woman to starve. Among Richard's kind the son succeeded on marriage to his father's rights, including possession of the mother, whom he could flog or lie with or drive from him. Richard's father had known a son who was first intimate with his mother and then beat her to death. In another instance the son had made his mother his mistress but had abandoned her after she became too old and unattractive. Incest among the poor was so common that Richard had thought little about it, until that day in the field when his father had said, "I want you to know that there has been no incest in our house."

Thinking of these matters, while keeping an eye out for enemies or approaching horsemen or carts, Richard wondered what virtue really was for Christians. Hillel had told him in his dry urbane way that two Christians once went to the tomb of Ovid to ask him which was the greatest line he had ever written; and out of sepulchral gloom a voice had replied, Virtue is to abstain even from that which is lawful. They had then asked him which was his poorest line: Whatsoever delights is accounted by Jove to be righteous. Hugely edified the Christians began to chant paternosters and aves, when a third time the voice spoke, saying: I like not your paternosters and aves; fools, be on your way! Richard had perceived that the story amused Hillel but for the life of him

101

he could not imagine why. It's because I am ignorant, he thought, and looked up through shimmering leaves at an afternoon sun.

Then he felt again for the purse and turned a wary eye all around him. A little before sunset he came to a deep hedge by the wayside and crawled into it and sat. The thicket was so dense that he did not believe anyone could find him, unless he had a dog. Beyond him on both sides was deep forest, in which were bears and wild boars but he was not afraid of them. His only fear was of man. He was not sure that if a brigand examined him he would not discover the purse and he wondered on what part of his body he might more safely conceal it. He thought of his mouth, his ears, and at last with a faint blush of his anus. He stroked down over his hair to see if he could feel the purse at his nape and he could feel it when he bore down with enough pressure. If a robber met him he would take his garment and his sandals and his packet of food; and if he failed to find the purse he would leave him standing stark naked on the road. If he found the purse he might flog him just for the hell of it.

He opened the parcel and began to eat, smelling around him mimosa and thyme and the dark heavy smells of wild life out in the forests. He needed water and listened but could hear none. Choking the dry food down he felt a warmth rise in him for Hillel, a warmth that drew so deeply on everything in him that tears were forced to his eyes. As though he were counting priceless treasures he put a hand into the knapsack and felt of the items of food one by one. He carefully broke off a piece of bread and a piece of cheese and put the bread and cheese together and ate, murmuring under his breath, God bless Hillel! promising in a whisper, I will never betray you! Having eaten sparingly he gently set the parcel aside and on hands and knees examined his position, raking old leafdepth into a pile for a bed. Then he tried to peer out and he listened but the only sound was of fluttering birds. He thought that perhaps he should pray but it then occurred to him that nearly everything that he thought and felt was a kind of prayer, a praying all through him, a tenderness of yearning, a wish to be good and brave and noble, a hope that he was in the eye of God. He buried the food packet under leaves and stretched out on his bed and closed his eyes, murmuring, "God bless Hillel and keep him—and keep him!"

VIII

He took the road at daylight, looking round him as he walked, for he was now in a strange world. It was a world with wide tracts of primeval forest, wild and unfenced moors and commons, marches and meres; and scattered villages with narrow dirty streets and gabled timber houses, surrounded by walls and towers, with the steeples of churches and abbeys on the highest hill. If very small the village was little besides hovels, before each of which stood a tub of water in case of fire. Always in the middle of the village was a cross; and not far distant there might be a manor house, moated, or the house of a bailiff. The commonest trees along his way were linden, oak, beech, hazel, fir, elm, willow, walnut, pear, apple and one called the red tree. In wintertime the sweet briar was in bloom far and wide, and the wild thyme; in summertime the countryside looked burnt up and lay naked and hot under the furnace of the sun.

It was early September and Richard was walking on a dusty path called a road, with forest all around him, when suddenly he emerged and saw before him a town—a city, he would have called it, who had lived all his life in a village. He entered the town, hesitant and fearful, and the first person he saw was a leper in his gray coat and scarlet hat, holding in his hands two bones to warn people of his presence. He next saw a man with a donkey and a cart, laden with straw. He came to a row of squat ugly shops called the Tin Pot, the Crunching Hat and the Silver Fish; and saw leading off to the right various crooked streets, Tanners Row, Butchers Way, Cobblers Alley and Goldsmiths Lane. It was in Tanners Row that he saw a terrible thing.

103

First there was an immense cloud of dust. Out of the cloud emerged a team of asses, driven by a tall man in a black coat. The team was hitched to a chain, and the chain, attached to the neck, was dragging the skeleton of a human being. Behind the skeleton came a shouting mob. Richard slunk back close to a building and the man in the black coat drove the team past him and he then had a good view of the skeleton, bobbing and twisting grotesquely, rolling and tumbling and making bone-sounds, for there were only bones, with no meat on them. In one moment the face was up, the empty sockets staring at the sky; in the next the face was down and a mane of matted hair looking gray with dust concealed the skull. The torso and leg bones were jerked into one ghastly posture after another, as the skull hit obstructions in the road and the chain tightened and then yanked the skeleton forward, when it wildly crawled again. The mob followed and Richard followed the mob; and from the words being shouted he made out that this was the exhumed corpse of a heretic that was to be publicly degraded. The skeleton was dragged down Tanners Row. It then vanished into another street, with the mob after it, and Richard for a few moments stood alone. Then he entered the street and followed the path in the dust that the bones had made, wondering what this man's sin had been, wondering why vengeance had to follow the sinner beyond the grave. When he came up with the mob he saw the skeleton lying before a house and he saw the people tearing the house down. The frenzy was now dreadful. With crude tools or with only their hands men, with a few women assisting, were dragging the structure down timber by timber. They were making a pile of the timbers and they then threw the skeleton upon the pile and set the pile afire. Richard now heard the sound of bells and listened to their sweet sad music while looking at the Christians before him.

When the flames had burned the pile low men moved in to see if the corpse had been consumed and Richard moved in too, looking at the fierce emotions in the faces or at the gray mass of glowing embers and the ash. He saw the skull. There was fire under it or inside it, he could not tell which, and flames like pieces of yellow lightning were shooting out of the eye sockets and the mouth. The bone of the skull was white and looked as if it would crumble at a touch. The whole skeleton was dimly visible in flame and smoke and ash, the arms and legs in postures of agony, as though a live person had been burned and in the throes of death had distorted the frame. A man seized a pole and thrust at the skeleton, jabbing at it, smiting it, and it began to break apart and crumble. He jabbed at the skull and it sank out of sight. He kept jabbing and thrusting until nothing was visible, all of it having crumbled and sunk into the bed of ashes.

An hour later, hiding in a latrine behind a tanner's shop, Richard extracted a coin from his hoard and bought a small water-pouch and filled it and went on his way. He was now on the main thoroughfare lying between Avignon and Nimes to the east and Toulouse to the west. In this time there were tremendous movements of people all over Europe, of merchants, pilgrims, troubadours, singers, players, acrobats, dancers, highwaymen. He had gone a few miles when he saw ensconced under a grove of trees a group of people and heard voices and music. He thought at first that it was some kind of religious service but as he approached he realized that two vagrant entertainers had taken up their stand here and that people had come out from a village near by. One of the men was playing a flute and the other was haranguing his audience. On seeing Richard the speaker cried, "Come on over!" and beckoned. Richard wanted to back away for he had no money for flute-players or strange tales of far places. But there was no escape now. All the people had turned to look at him and the man was calling, "Come, your highness, and listen to our song! Do you want music and singing?—or juggling with knives?—or dancing?—or tales to make your hair stand up? Sir, state your choice and you shall have it!" In one hand Richard clutched several cheap coins that had been given in change when he bought the pouch. This would cost him money, he thought. Lord, what a fool he was! The flute-player had now rushed over and bowing low said, "Sir, come over and let us entertain you." He looked like a crafty rogue. He now began to blow on his flute and the other man shouted: "We have here some distinguished traveler who pauses for a moment of rest and joy! Great and famous gentleman, what will you have? Will you hear a tale of Priam and Pyramus, or of the beautiful Helen, or of Aeneas weeping over Dido, or of Jason or Narcissus or Leander or Daedalus or Icarus? Do you wish Charlemagne's Round Table or what Delilah did to Samson?"

Seizing Richard's arm the flute-player led him forward and

then hastened over to his companion; and while the one played the other sang:

> If you brought Hippolytus
> to Pavia Sunday
> He'd not be Hippolytus
> the following Monday!

There was wicked laughter. The singer was staring hard at Richard, looking him up and down. "We have here," he said, "a Signor from Venice, proudest city on earth. I now recognize this gentleman. He's a trader in the stone counting-houses, washed by the canals; there I have seen him checking his bags of cloves, nutmeg, mace, ginger and cinnamon from the Indies; and his ebony chessmen from China; and his ambergris from Madagascar and his musk from Tibet; and his diamonds from Golconda and rubies from Badakhshan and pearls from Ceylon. I've seen him with his bales of silk and muslin and brocade from Bagdad and Yezd and Malabar. In the evenings he takes to his gondola draped with silk and dallies with red-haired women and salutes the morning sun."

All the eyes were now staring at Richard and he was feeling more and more foolish.

"I've seen him," the rascal went on, his eyes glowing, his hands gesturing toward Italy, "marching in the gilds. Shall I tell you how it is?" His companion blew furiously on the flute and then yanking his cap off went through the crowd, trying to collect coins. "First the master smiths with garlands on their heads, banners and trumpets, oh the trumpets! And then the furriers, robed in samite and scarlet silk and mantles of ermine and vair; and then the weavers and the ten master tailors all in white with crimson stars; and then the master clothesworkers carrying boughs of olive with olive crowns on their heads. Ah, the crowns!" The flutist blew shrilly. "Then the fustian-makers in furred robes and the quilt-makers with garlands of gilt beads and white cloaks with the fleur-de-lis. Then the makers of cloth of gold robed in nothing but cloth of gold! The gospel of Goldmark!" The flutist made furious impudent sounds. "The mercers in silk and the butchers in scarlet, the glassmakers with gold-fringed hoods and garlands of pearls and Venetian goblets; and the goldsmiths glittering with sapphires and emeralds and diamonds and topazes and jacinths and rubies—

106

every one of them drinking flagons of old wine, while our master here before us shouts, Long live our Lord, the noble Doge!" He bent forward, peering intently. "Noble master, what is your name?"

When Richard hesitated the flutist rushed over and rubbed swift fingers over his ribs, whispering, "Your name, your name?"

"Richard," Richard said.

"Richard of what, whom, where?"

Again the flutist urged him. "My father's name is Victoir."

"Long live our lord, the noble Doge Richard of Victoir!"

There was laughter.

"Those who are rich, says Richard, don't have the itch, says Itchard!"

The laughter was lewd and explosive.

"Doge Richard, what song will you have?"

"Name one, name one!" said the flutist, busy with his fingers and whispering.

Take the good and cast the evil,
listen, people, to my song!
For 'tis God for whom I'm speaking,
ye, the valiant and strong!
Take the cross, the cross he died on,
O repay him as ye may,
for in dying he redeemed us,
Can we give him less today?

The flute-player now stood before Richard, bowing, holding his upturned cap with both hands, his small black crafty eyes looking at Richard's eyes. Richard put a sou into the cap and the rogue first peered in as though doubting his senses and then took the coin out, the cheapest of all coins, and gazed at it as if incredulous and amazed and held it up with a great flourish for the people to see. "Fifty livres Tournois!" he shouted. There were squeals of laughter. Richard flushed and backed away.

"No, no!" cried the speaker-singer, and the flutist seized Richard by the arm to hold him. "If you don't like our singing," said the other, "I'll tell you a tale. Silence!" he thundered, though everyone was silent. "You," he said, pointing to an inoffensive little man, "stop making sounds like a boar! Or are you muttering your paternosters? Our distinguished guest," he went on, turning his gaze to Richard, "the noble Doge Richard of Itchard, doesn't like our music. All right, I'll tell him a story. Have you ceased your mutterings?" he asked, bending forward to glower at the little man. "Your lips are still moving, like an ass's over his oats." There were ribald snorts of joy. The flutist was now playing soft music.

"This, then, is my story," the rogue said, looking with intent interest from face to face. "Are you all Christians? If not I'll not tell it. Are any heretics present?" he asked fiercely, and scowled at the little man. "Very well. In those days the Pope spake unto the Romans, When the son of man cometh to the east of our majesty, first say unto him, Friend, wherefore art thou come? But if he shall continue knocking and giving nothing unto you, cast him forth into the outer darkness. And it came to pass that a certain poor clerk came to the curia of the Lord Pope—" the flutist was now making appropriate sounds of exclamation, wonder, derision, scorn, incredulity, depending on what the other said "— and cried, saying, Have mercy on me, ye doorkeepers of the Pope, for the hand of poverty hath touched me." With comical earnestness he looked down at his own garments, at Richard's, at the people's, and then up at the sky, his mouth opening, as though his soul were filling with revelation. "For I am poor and needy—" his forehead puckered, his eyes peering he was again looking from person to person, his face registering in turn alarm, astonishment, pity "—and I pray you that ye shall have compassion upon my great woe! And they, hearing him, had indignation among themselves and said, Friend, thy poverty go with thee to perdition! Get behind me, Satan, for thou savorest not the things that be of pelf." He leaned forward, gazing hard at Richard as though something about the man troubled him. "Verily, verily, I say unto thee, thou shalt not enter into the kingdom until thou hast given your last sou." The flutist hastened over to Richard and, cursing himself for a fool, he gave another coin. "And the poor man went away and sold his cloak and his tunic and all that he had, and gave to the cardinals and the chamberlains and the bishops. They said, What is this among so many?" The flutist held the coin up, shaking his head sadly from side to side. "And they cast him out, and going out he wept bitterly and could not be comforted. And thereafter came to the curia a certain rich clerk, fat and well-fed and puffed up, like a priest in full fig; and this clerk had committed

108

murder. He first gave to the doorkeeper and then to the chamberlains and then to the cardinals. And they took counsel among
themselves, which of them should have received the most. But
the Lord Pope, hearing that his cardinals and servants had received
so many gifts from the clerk, fell sick nigh unto death. Then sent
unto him the rich clerk an electuary of gold, and straightway the
Pope recovered. Then the Lord Pope called unto him his cardinals
and servants and said unto them, Brethren, see to it that no man
seduce you with vain words and humble yourselves; for I have
given you an example, that even as much as I take, ye should take
also!"

The flutist struck in with high insolent notes and there was
some laughter. Richard felt ashamed and afraid, for if this was
not heresy, then what under heaven was?

The tale-teller, whether heretic or not, was hugely enjoying himself. The flutist hastened to Richard and again he gave a sou;
and as before the man peered into the cap as if he were seeing a
pile of diamonds and then triumphantly held it aloft, crying,
"Forty solidi, all in gold!" He stepped up close, his small black
cynical eyes looking with bright insolence into Richard's eyes;
and then bowed low in humble thanksgiving and trotted back to
the speaker.

"Did our honorable Doge from Venice like the story of Silver-
mark? Would he like to hear of Pomilli of Narbonne for another forty solidi?"

Richard moved to go but the flutist captured him and held his
arm while looking into his eyes, his own eyes staring out of feigned
innocence.

"Benoit tells the story, that the cross which our Lord carried
was so heavy that not ten men in the world today could lift it; and
when the Virgin, our holy Mother, stood at the foot of the cross it
bent forward so that she could kiss our Lord's hand."

"Hear, hear!" cried the flutist.

"Does our distinguished visitor know that at Autan is a golden
vase in which are the tears Jesus wept over Lazarus? Let no man
doubt it. Does he know that the dove has two wings, not to fly with
—it could fly just as well with none—but because man needs the
two wings of meditation and action?—to meditate where to burn
the heretic and then to burn him. Its eyes are of the color of ripe
grain because the Church is full of matured wisdom."

"Hear, hear!" cried the flutist, looking with bland insolence into Richard's eyes.

"Has he heard the story of Bishop Ursin of Paris? A mother had her infant in a bath set above a fire and when she heard that Bishop Ursin was passing she went out to look at the holy man; and the fire burned hot and the water boiled and walloped but there was no harm to the child. As the water boiled and the fire roared he played with the bubbles and crooned and splashed and gurgled. Returning and finding her babe unharmed the mother rushed outside with it, crying, Behold, another miracle! I went out to look at the holy bishop of our Lord and my child was in boiling water yet was not harmed. So do the miracles multiply as testimony that Christians are the chosen people of God. Let no man doubt it."

Richard again tried to get away and at once the flutist offered his cap and bowed and Richard gave another coin. Then he went back to the road for it seemed to him that these people were heretics and he was afraid of them. Why were such men allowed to go free, while others, who taught only the poverty and humility of Jesus, were taken to the torture chambers? Richard failed to perceive that the sly rogue had said nothing that could be turned against him. He had not denied that the Virgin's tunic was at Chartres, her tears at Autan, or that the child in boiling water had not been harmed. The man promised him greater miracles and holier bishops but Richard had heard more than he would dare to remember.

Two days later while wandering off the road to find a safe spot for the night he heard a man talking and he drew near to listen. Richard had heard from Hillel that there were teachers so popular, in the way of Abelard before them, that their devoted students built huts around them, of mud and straw, and lived for some time in their small community while feeding at the lips of their master. He saw huts here and men sitting around one who was talking. The speaker was a small thin man in his middle years, his beard gray and his wrinkled countenance sad but his eyes flashed over his words and his voice was strong. Richard was wondering about him and his group when one of those sitting looked around him and then leapt to his feet, his face hostile.

He rushed over to Richard and asked angrily, "What are you doing here?"

"I—I heard voices. I—"

"Who are you?"

"My name—"

"Are you a spy?"

"No."

"I think we have a spy here," the man said.

The teacher came over and fixed Richard with grave searching eyes. "Who are you?"

"My name is Richard. I was looking for a place to sleep when I heard voices." He was silent and when neither man spoke he asked: "Are you one of the university teachers?"

"No. My name is Gerart."

"But you are a teacher?"

"Yes."

"May I listen to you?"

Not tonight, the man said. Tomorrow Richard could come if he wished and be questioned.

Were these persons heretics? If so, what an idiot he was!—for he walked from one group that scoffed at the holy Church to another that eyed him with hostility and suspicion. Richard felt that he ought to go on about his business but the next day against his better judgment he returned and the students eyed him like alert watchdogs while Gerart asked questions.

"Why do you wish to hear me teach?"

"Because I'm ignorant and wish to learn."

"To learn what?"

"The truth."

"The truth about what?"

"Everything."

"Can you read?"

"Some."

"Who taught you?"

"My mother a little and a friend."

"Who is this friend?"

"I must not tell his name."

Gerart's face softened. "I think we can trust you," he said.

But one standing close to the master now spoke up, saying, "We do not know this man. He is secretive and evasive—"

"Spies," said Gerart, "have answers to all questions. This one is too young and innocent."

And so it was that Richard sat with the group and heard Gerart teach. The master sat in the doorway of his hut and in a half-circle the students faced him; and after they had all bowed in a few moments of meditation and prayer Gerart said: "Shall we let our new friend suggest the subject?"

Eyes turned to Richard. He was sitting at one end of the circle, at the corner of the hut. He had counted the students—there were twelve; and he had been wondering if Gerart had chosen this number for that greater Master, and if so, which among them was Judas. Now, with all eyes on him, he felt shamefully out of place and wretchedly self-conscious.

"I don't know that subject—" he began and broke off and then blurted: "I'd rather ask questions."

"Very well," said Gerart.

Richard's discomfiture deepened. Some of the faces seemed not to be friendly but still suspicious and hostile. Be prudent, he told himself; these may not be friends at all. With an effort he asked: "Was Abelard a great teacher?"

"A very great teacher," said Gerart. "He was a very learned man, while I have only a little learning. Have you read him?"

"No, master. I've heard some things he wrote. Did he say that by doubting we are led to inquire and by inquiring we arrive at truth?"

"He wrote that, in *Sic et Non,* I believe it was, or possibly it was in *Scito te ipsum.* Gui," he said, turning to one of the group, "remind me to check on that."

"Is it true? I mean what he said. For if it's true—well, our Church doesn't look with favor on inquiry, does it?"

Gerart looked into his eyes and said, "No."

"If to discover truth we have to inquire why does our Church oppose it?"

"Our Church thinks all truth has been revealed, through the sacred writings and the Fathers."

"But has it?" said Richard, looking at Gerart's brilliant eyes.

"I would answer you this way. Why has our Church borrowed so many pagan titles for Mary?—for she is the Mystical Rose, the Tower of David, the Ark of the Covenant, the Lily of the Valley, the Cedar of Lebanon. March 25th is called her day but it is the day of the miraculous conception of the virgin Juno. Who is Saint Veronica?—for does the word not come from two words,

112

vera and icon, meaning the true image?—that is, the image of Christ impressed on the cloth when he wiped his face. Sic et non, said Abelard, but what man knows how much is sic and how much is non?"

Richard had never heard these things and he was confused. Was Gerart rebuking him with parables? Returning to simpler ground he said, "But if we should inquire, should we also believe the Bible where it says that in much wisdom is much grief and he who increases his knowledge adds to his sorrow?"

"Is the wise man happier than the fool? Was Abelard happier than the peasant who was drunk last night in the tavern?"

"I don't know," Richard said. "Was he?"

"What is happiness? In many churches on Christmas day Jews are compelled to attend the services, in the hope that the sermon and the drama of Jesus and the tree standing in the loins of Jesse will persuade them to turn from their old ways. Before they enter their ears are examined, to be sure they were not plugged with cloth or wax; and during the services a proctor walks up and down, to be sure that no Jew sleeps. 'You, O Jews,' the preacher cries, 'who have been summoned here have to this day denied the Son of God! Do you wish a witness to this Christ? It is written in your own Law that the truth will be established by the mouths of two witnesses; let, then, the men of your Law stand forth. Speak, Isaiah.' And one who represents Isaiah cries in a loud voice, 'Behold, a virgin shall conceive and bear a son, and his name shall be called Emanuel!' But the Jewish word is not virgin, but girl or woman. Does Isaiah, then, bear witness? Does this knowledge make us happier?—for knowing this we can apologize to Jews, for these twelve centuries of misinterpreting their books. But in ignorance will we not continue to insult and hate and degrade them?"

Richard felt more and more unhappy, for he was convinced that he was in the company of heretics. What would Hillel think of him now!

"One of our Christian dramas," Gerart was saying, "shows Mary being carried to the grave, while Jews led by the high priest try to seize her body and burn it; and the moment his hands touch the coffin they are withered and made fast and he is unable to loosen his grasp. In great agony he calls upon Saint Peter, and Peter says, 'You cannot be healed until you believe in Jesus the

Christ, and in her who is being carried here.' Then the high priest is made to say, 'I believe that Jesus was the true son of God and that Mary was his mother.' He is then released, but not his hands, which are torn from his arms and left attached to the coffin. Then Peter says to him, 'Say you believe in Jesus Christ and in Mary who remained a virgin after having borne a son.' When the priest repeats these words his hands are given back to him and he is well.''

Gerart looked at the faces of his students and then at Richard. "You say you wish to learn. Do you seek knowledge or happiness?"

"You mean a man can't have both?"

"You will be more and more saddened as you learn more and more of the record of human bigotry and folly. Only a few have the strength for learning. If you have it, surely you will find some joy in helping to right old wrongs. If you do not have it, learning can only multiply your confusions and fatten your misfortunes, until you will cry out and flee deeper into error. God reveals himself to those who inquire, and those afraid to inquire he leaves to their folly. Before a man sets out on the path of learning he ought to be sure that he has the strength to face what he may meet, including the inquisitors. Do you have that strength?"

"I hope I have," Richard said.

"Has your courage ever been tested?"

"No."

"Have you faced the probability that it may be tested?"

"Yes."

"And you still wish to follow the light set in the sky by the Abelards?"

"Yes."

"'This man," said Gerart, turning to his students, "may indeed be one of us. He is young but there seems to burn in him a great yearning. Shall we ask him to remain with us?"

"He will make an odd number."

"For shame, Fabre. Until the twelve make room for the thirteenth our Lord will never come again."

114

IX

Father Luce meanwhile was a worried priest, but anxiety instead of abating his lust seemed only to inflame it. When Madelon insisted that God or one of his angels visited her, he tried to convince her, at first gently and patiently, that she had been deceived by Satan. She would move her head slowly from side to side, telling him no, no, it was not that. She would give him a soft sweet smile, half in pity for his obtuseness, half in wonder for his failure to understand that all her life she had been too pure to succumb to the lures of the Devil.

"These things, dear child," he said to her, "I understand and you do not. I know all the tricks and stratagems of the Prince of Evil. He can deceive all but those who walk daily in the way of our Lord and know his purpose. Satan can show himself in any form, including that of angels; and if he came to you would he appear in his own form, do you think, so that you would recognize him, or would he take some form to deceive you?"

But she was shaking her head and looking at him.

"Child, listen to me. I'm your master, your God. I—"

"I *know*," Madelon whispered.

"You know what?"

"That our Father sent an angel to me."

"Do you know how wicked your words are? Don't you understand that there is in you some awful evil? You must confess to me your sins and cleanse your soul—"

"I have not sinned."

"Are you the judge of that, or I, a holy man?" He was fingering his pectoral cross and he now leaned forward to look into her eyes. Her eyes closed, and when he clasped her arms she sank at once into unconsciousness. In that first and only moment of realization and shock her unconscious mind had built a defense against him, against knowledge of his evil and of her own sin; and in subsequent days and weeks that defense had been so superbly perfected that at the slightest hint of his lust she sank swiftly into her own dark chamber, as though her soul deserted its body, leaving it to be degraded while itself drawing into deeper holiness, beyond mortal knowledge and memory. So long as he did not touch her she saw him as her conscious eyes and mind had always seen him, as a blessed and holy man of God, whose great compassion sheltered and protected her; but when he moved to seize her then her mind instantly blacked out and she was buried deep beyond knowledge of his will and acts. Her unwitting custody of her own notions of her purity and goodness was so marvelous, so alert and responsive, that she remained unconscious an hour or more after he had had his way with her; and when she came back to her senses she had neither memory nor realization of what he had done.

Her unknowing about him delighted Father Luce, for he could indulge his lust as often as he pleased. When unconscious she was so utterly helpless and white and still that he was not able to resist her. Passion was such an unleashed force in him that he wanted to destroy her, not consciously, for he had no conscious knowledge of his purpose and impulses, but deeply, under consciousness, where his passions possessed his soul. Sometimes he was brutal with her and would gouge her flesh and try to wreak on her body the holy stigmata; or he would bite into her neck or her soft lips; or he would try to crush her in the embrace, and when he heard her moans or heard her gasp as though struggling for breath the wish in him to destroy was an almost overmastering urge.

This wish seemed to grow in him. For one thing, Madelon's conscious acts were largely determined by the knowledge in her buried mind. In that mind there was knowledge of the pain and violence and degradation; and so it was that she began to crave pain. So it was that she came to believe that God was calling on her for an immolation, a sacrifice, a martyrdom, in which she would spill her blood, as Jesus had spilled his. She was convinced that she would soon die and she wanted to die. Her buried mind compelled her to this longing, for death was the only way out of her misery and sorrow. She prayed to God to take her away.

For another thing, Father Luce was haunted by the fear that he would find her pregnant. He thought he had seen signs. There

116

was no visible swelling yet but Madelon was sometimes so sick that she vomited. If he found her pregnant what would he do?—and what would Chretien do? As a subtle and crafty man who in erotic pursuits had extricated himself from more than one grievous predicament he tried to foresee events and be prepared to meet them. If Madelon were in a convent—in the convent of Patres—Well, the abbess there was in his power and did his will. He thought he should delay no longer but arrange with Chretien to have her moved to the convent: once there, if pregnant, she could be hidden from sight, and the child when born could be got rid of. But he hesitated to make his move; there were three nuns in the convent whom he had betrayed, and one who hated him with implacable hatred. And there was Chretien, whose sly eyes looked at him with more than human knowledge.

While he delayed and plotted her destruction, Madelon, when conscious, continued to revere, indeed, almost to worship him, as one who took time from his many duties to instruct and comfort her. She told him one day that she had in a vision seen her name in heaven, united with his in the Book of Life. She had gone to heaven and an angel had opened the book, which was all of gold and shone like the sun; and there upon one of the golden pages was the name of Father Luce in beautiful script, for an angel had written it, and under it was her own name. The names of the two, she said, had been set apart on the page from all other names, as on earth she and Father Luce were set apart in holiness.

Since she was not able to read it might have occurred to him to ask how she had known what the names were. He was too confused and baffled and sometimes too frightened, for he failed completely to understand her. He had at first believed that she had visions, that her soul in sleep wandered to holy places; but as the weeks passed he became more and more certain that she was an instrument of Satan. If that were so, then she should be destroyed. Still, he could not deny the look of utter innocence on her face and in her eyes, or the pure angelic way in which she talked. The bells were ringing for Vespers and as she listened her white face was illumined with gentle ecstasy.

She whispered, "Father, the bells! What do they mean?"

He told her, meanwhile studying her face, that the golden solemn music of church bells was of all sounds on earth the most abhorrent to fiends and goblins and devils. When the bells rang to summon Christians to prayer, demons departed in terror and the evils in the sky and the storm and the elements were abashed. Even the specters of the dead vanished when the bells pealed forth. On hearing the trumpets of the church militant the forces of evil cowered in fear, as tyrants cowered when they heard the trumpets of their foe. When a person was dying evil spirits always stood at the foot of the bed, ready to seize if possible the departing soul; but if bells were rung the spirits fled.

"Let us pray!" she whispered. She closed her eyes and her lips began to move. Father Luce, his black eyes intent and unblinking, stared at her and wondered what words her lips were saying.

When Madelon lived with her parents, as part of the time she did, her sleep was deeply troubled and she would cry out. Her commonest cry was the words, "Leave me! Leave me!" Chretien sometimes sat to observe her while she slept and one night he put an ear to her belly and heard the beating of an infant heart. He knew that his daughter was pregnant a full month before Father Luce was to know it. He knew who the father was. He could not understand why Madelon did not know what had happened to her.

He tried one day to lead her out. "Madelon," he said, sitting by her, "do you hear me?"

"Yes."

"When you're alone with Father Luce what does he do?"

"He teaches me."

"What?"

"Many things. He has told me what it is like in heaven, but I knew that for I have been to heaven. He has told me how wonderful life is in a convent. He has told me the meaning of bells. He has told me that our Lord will come again when all men are as holy as he is."

"Did he tell you that our Lord came again?—that he came and looked and went away?"

"No, for that isn't true." She was not looking at her father's sly face.

"When he's not teaching you then what do you do?"

"We pray."

"And after you pray what do you do?"

"I sleep."

Simone had come over silently to stand by her father and listen.

"Madelon, I want you to tell me something. Will you?"

118

"Yes," she said without looking at him. Her eyes were closed. "Are you still a virgin?" She was silent but there was no change at all in her face. "Are you?"

"God sent an angel to lie with me."

Her words so shocked him that for a few moments he could only look at her. "An angel, my daughter? Do you know what you're saying?"

"Yes."

"Did you see this angel?"

"Yes."

"Did he have the form of Father Luce?"

He thought the question would trick her but there was no question on earth that could have caught her in its snare. Her father did not know and was never to know how beautifully and perfectly she had established herself in holiness beyond the reach of evil.

She said, still speaking in her soft childlike way: "The angel was nicer than any man. He had a light all around him and he smelled like the incense on the altar."

"And this angel lay with you?"

"Yes."

"Are you now with child?"

"I will die soon," she said.

"Are you with child?"

"If that is God's will."

"Why do you say you'll die soon?"

"Because our Father has called me. He will take me away."

Again Chretien was silent, baffled. "Sometimes you cry out in your sleep. You say, Leave me. Who is it you want to leave you?"

Madelon was silent.

Her father persisted. "Who is it you want to leave you? Does some one visit you while you sleep?"

"It is Satan," she said.

"Satan?" he said, and turned for a moment to look into Simone's brown eyes. "What does he look like?"

"Like a serpent."

"Does he look like Father Luce?"

"No. He looks like a serpent and he bites me."

"You mean he bit you there on the neck?"

"He bites me and he almost smothers me. But it doesn't matter. God will take me away soon."

Chretien turned again to look into the eyes of Simone, his own eyes shining with devilish things. Her eyes were round and full of solemn wonder.

"Madelon, you're going to have a baby. Do you know that? Do you know what people will say if it has no father?"

"All babies," she said quietly, "have fathers."

"Well," he said, "and so they do. But who is its earthly father?"

"Not all children have earthly fathers."

"Madelon!" he cried impatiently. "Do you realize that if you say the child has no earthly father you'll be charged with heresy?"

"I don't care," she said. "Jesus wants me to suffer. I'll suffer for him."

Baffled but full of sly designs Chretien turned away.

Sometimes in her sleep Madelon became violent. When in her dreaming she cried out, "Leave me!" her voice expressed strong distaste, contempt and weariness of soul. In her violent moments she wildly supplicated the return of someone, whom she never named. She would start up in her sleep like one abandoned and cry, "Why has he left me?" She would then stare into darkness and moan, while grief and loss gathered their forces within her. She would sit like one waiting and expecting, mumbling words which Chretien could not catch, as tears welled to her eyes and rolled down her cheeks. Then, as though she heard retreating footsteps, she would be shrill and frantic, crying, "Bring him to me! Bring him back, please!" If not restrained she would then stagger from her bed and go stumbling off into the darkness, her hands outstretched, her eyes filled with anxiety and terror. When Chretien forced her back to the bed and held her there and murmured comfortingly he knew that she was not awake, that she was aware of nothing around her.

He was holding her one night in her trembling terror when Old Noelle said: "Who is it she wants?"

"I don't know," Chretien said but he thought he knew.

"Is it Richard?"

"I don't know."

He was convinced that she wanted Father Luce. Who else could it be? While he held her she would mumble strange mystical jargon and weep and breathe in long deep sighs. Was it God or

120

Satan in her? Chretien thought it was not Satan, for Satan's way was the serio-comic, the sublimely ridiculous, the droll farce, the extravagant burlesque, the bizarre, the fantastic, the ironic. Satan was hugely amused by human beings whose devotion to God—which in his view meant to darkness—plunged them into almost continuous sorrow and pious sighs and frantic prayers, as though in all the world there was neither light nor joy but only the funereal gloom and sepulchral moods of a people who felt themselves doomed. Chretien was a philosopher in his own way. He believed that Satan with the aid of alcohol and the ironic muse might some day lift Christians from their self-imposed degradation and fear and perpetual moaning and turn them away from the dreadful imprecations and thunderous threats of God, as these had come from the tongues of the prophets. He held his daughter and felt that she belonged to God. He felt that Father Luce was a man of God. He pitied the one because she was so frail in her saintliness, despised the other because he was so stupid.

Madelon so completely exhausted herself in her trances that she would sleep for a long time, lying as white and still as one in death. When at last she awoke she would not move at once but would stare up at the roof, like one unable to wake or sleep. For her pert and roguish sister she was a very tiresome riddle. For her mother. . . . What did Old Noelle think of all this? Not much at all. She was too tired and weary and scared to think. Many years ago she had seen one of her sisters die. It had been a difficult childbirth and in this case as in most cases like it the unborn child had been baptized and both mother and child had been left to die. Chretien had once aborted his wife and Old Noelle knew that the punishment for abortion was eternal damnation. She was doomed and she knew it. She had nothing to live for and nothing to die for but eternal torment.

The only woman in the village who could in any sense have been called her friend was Elise. If she had a few idle minutes Old Noelle would go over to see what Elise was doing and she was always fascinated in a tired stuporous way, because Elise did the most extraordinary things. On retiring and before making her prayer to the Virgin Elise would put out a few drops of milk for the ghosts of her dead children, or water, if she had no milk; and sometimes at night she built a little bonfire for the fairies, or by day gathered a bunch of wild flowers for some saint. All this for

Old Noelle was the more strange because Elise had come to be a woman with a murderous temper and a profane tongue. In one mood she would say, "To hell with the highborn ladies! They wear girdles and they say a peasant woman has her gall to wear a girdle but I wear one and they can go fart at it!" In the next mood she would be mumbling over a penitential and trying to figure out if she was guilty of pollution because of erotic assaults on her imagination, or if she had fouled her lips by cursing the Baroness Elienor, or if she had sinned the hopeless sin for having married a man as dull and ineffectual as Victoir. "Victoir!" she would shout. "The fool's name means victory and a hell of a victory he has had, the short-peckered hog-gelder!"

Elise had once been a very handsome woman. Her face was square and strong—too large to be lovely but with no weak feature: she had a fine chin, a fine straight nose, a broad forehead, and dark eyes that when not flashing were filled with a brooding somber glow. Her teeth had been perfect and unlike most peasants of her age she still had all of them. Her voice was throaty and deep as though it came out of deep resonant chambers; and her laugh like her voice seemed to rise from muffled depths. Her son Richard hated her but it was from his mother that he had got his strength and his courage.

Elise spent much of her time in her devotionals or in furious rages. She had only to look at Victoir's abject and defeated and unmanly face to be off in a towering fury: then her whole strong being was filled with hellish vapors and energies and impulses and she wanted to take him by the heels and knock his brains out. "Except that he has no brains," she said. "He has only a cabbage in his skull." Her appalling evil moods, as though Satan had passed through her and left his fires burning to inflame her emotions, exhausted her almost daily; and she would then punish herself by assuming some grotesque posture, such as resting on her shoulders with her legs in the air and her arms extended in the form of the cross. Or she would rub the stinging and caustic juice of some plant over her sagging breasts and her belly and loins. Or she would shove her head into the tub of water before her hovel and hold it there until she almost drowned. Such punishments cooled her fires and restored her momentarily to sanity and calm.

Her trouble was that she hated men, all men. In the horrible massacre of Beziers she had been raped, not once or twice but so many times that she had fainted. After that she had decided that all men were fiends from hell let loose on earth and by merely thinking about them she would arouse herself to such insane rage that she would swoon and almost fall, as her senses darkened and her eyes turned blind. "They talk about the lust of the goat!" she said to Old Noelle, her throaty voice almost unintelligible with contempt. "Who has ever seen fifty goats rape one nanny? They talk about the lust of the ram, but when has one ever rammed as hard as a man killing and raping in the name of God?" Then, appalled by her wicked tongue, she would begin to mumble holy verses and would cast wildly around her for some way to atone for her sins.

Elise was intelligent; she had taught herself to read and she had memorized many things that she had heard in church. In her way she had been proud of Richard. But being so head-strong and violent she was a woman with favorites and Pascal had alway been her favorite. She did not think of him as a man. She thought of him as an infant, a helpless babe. Her aggressive unbridled nature had made him what he was. She had shared her bed with him until he was almost grown. Had she been incestuous with him? Victoir did not know and he refused to think about it, for he did not greatly care. Richard did not know but he had felt for years that the relationship between mother and son was in some ways unclean and he had despised his mother for it. He despised her because she had made a whining, mewling weakling of Pascal and driven him into such idiocy with self-pity that he could think only of stray cats. "My poor baby!" Elise would say, and her eyes looking at Pascal would turn gentle and fill with tears. "My poor little Easter egg!"

It was the astounding ambivalence in Elise that fascinated people. She was such a good woman when praying to the Virgin, such a hellcat when cursing her man, as though both God and Satan occupied her and struggled for mastery. "All men are worse than dogs," she would say grimly, her eyes daring those who heard her to utter a word. "They're nothing but boars full of godbelly." Somewhere she had picked up a Latin phrase that had become a favorite with her and she always used it when, other words failing her, she wished to express contempt. "Qui semen in os miserit!" Old Noelle had no idea what the words meant but she loved to hear them roll off Elise's tongue, round and fat and bloated with contempt. But a few moments later Elise would be saying, "Blessed are the undefiled in the way, who walk in the way of our Lord. Blessed are they that keep his testimonies and seek him with the whole heart. I will keep your commandments: O forsake me not utterly!"

O forsake me not utterly! It was a terrible cry of anguish that came straight from her heart. It was so wholly sincere that Old Noelle was always deeply moved by it and felt that she was in the presence of something holy; but even while she was looking at the somber glowing in Elise's eyes and observing the trembling of her full ripe lips, Elise would fling an arm out, as though to dislodge a mountain or hurl a man into hell; and she would shout: "And he, as a rotten thing, consumes, as a garment that is moth eaten! Should a wise man utter vain knowledge and fill his belly with the east wind? Hah, great God, with the east wind! What else are men filled with, with their pious farting while they rape a woman? Qui semen in os miserit!"

One day Old Noelle was sitting in her tragic silence and listening to Elise and watching the awful lights in her eyes when Elise said: "What's wrong with your daughter Madelon? Is a demon in her?"

"Why do you say that?"

"Then why does the priest spend so much time with her? You'd think he must be her lover, if she wasn't such a scrawny little bitch. For where is her hindend, I'd like to know! Has she any breasts?"

"Le sainct homme!" murmured Old Noelle.

"Le sainct homme!" snorted Elise. "Have you heard what happens in the convents? Do you know how many piles of baby bones they have hidden away?"

"Oh no," said Old Noelle piously.

Elise liked to shock this sad tragic stupid woman, with profanity or lewd stories. She now told her the tale, which had been widely told and was in the repertoire of wandering tale-tellers, of an archbishop who lived in a castle, to which a rival archbishop, waging war against him, laid siege. The castle with its moats and gates proved impregnable until an archer contrived to get inside the defenses. Like most castles this one had a privy at the end of a hall, a small chamber where a person could sit on a stool, rounded to fit the buttocks, his excrement dropping fifty feet down a shaft to the moat below. The archer managed to get into the bottom of this shaft and on looking up saw the round white bottom of the archbishop; and taking careful aim he drove an arrow deep into the rump. With an infernal howl the archbishop had rushed out of the castle, his garments falling off, the arrowhead imbedded in him, and had surrendered. When Elise told this story she always laughed until she thought she would die.

"No, no!" gasped Old Noelle, horrified, looking at the hellish mirth in Elise's convulsed face.

"Yes, yes!"

"If you say such things you'll be accused."

"Me?" asked Elise, sobering. "Listen, you fool. I'm only a slave. I own nothing but the lice in my rags. Do they accuse those who have nothing to steal? Never! Besides, I say my aves and paternosters. Who says them as many times every day as I do? Who lies for hours in the sign of the cross? Who feeds the ghosts and the fairies? God protects me, Old Noelle, but you're a belled cow."

"What do you mean?" asked Old Noelle miserably.

"As a man bells his cow so the Devil has belled you. No matter where you go or what you do—"

"No, no!" cried Old Noelle, suffering.

"Then tell me, is your daughter with child?"

"God forbid."

"Who is the man?"

"There is no man."

"Is it Richard? If it isn't Richard why did he run away?"

"He's your son. You should know."

"Did he visit Madelon before he went?"

"I—I think he did."

"If it isn't Richard is it that godbelly Luce?"

"Mercy, mercy!"

"Does your daughter have a baby in her?" asked Elise, her eyes merciless.

"Oh, I don't know!"

"Won't she tell you?"

"I've not asked her."

"Don't you care if bastards fill your house?"

"Yes."

"She looks too scrawny to hold a child but you can't tell. Maybe you want to put her in a convent, huh?"

"I don't know."

"Then what happened to the child you'd never know. If you don't do that and a child is born and it's Richard's, that won't matter. But listen—"

"No!"

"Listen! If the father is that priest do you know what he'll do?"

"Oh, please, please!" cried Old Noelle, shuddering and bursting into tears.

X

What he would do was precisely the problem that was occupying Father Luce's thoughts. Since he lived by craft and stealth he was considering the possibilities and calculating the risks. Of possibilities he had thought of three: he could persuade Madelon to enter a convent; he could induce her to imagine that the father was Richard and force Richard to marry her; or he could say that the father of the child was Satan and have her summoned for heresy.

Trying to decide which course to pursue he was wholly guided by a sense of his own security and welfare. The question was, which of the three possible courses would cause him the least trouble? With the cunning and thoroughness that characterized his deliberations he turned over and over in his mind each of the three, trying to anticipate the developments, the dangers and the conclusions.

If he prevailed on Madelon to enter a convent it would be known by the sisters that she was pregnant and it would be suspected that he was the child's father. The abbess would give him no trouble; he had seduced her long ago and she was afraid of him. She would obey his will, even if he asked to have the child destroyed. The great advantage, as he saw it, in having Madelon in a convent was that, once immured, she would be hidden from all eyes and her people would never know the truth. More than that, he could visit her there until he tired of her. He did not imagine that she would live long; she was too enfeebled and sickly and too indifferent to food.

The great disadvantage in this instance was the presence of Sister Ruth. Ruth eight years ago had been an innocent girl like

Madelon; he had had his way with her and had got her into the convent when pregnant, and there her child had been born and had died. But the Devil had got into Ruth: she had turned on him with the most murderous hate and had threatened to expose him. She was a woman of strong temper and strong will; her passions were like leaping fires and her tongue was like the lightning out of hell. She had become such a model nun, so devoted to God and holiness and so kind and sweet to the other sisters, that every nun in the convent was her loyal friend. This raised a problem which Father Luce could not see his way around. He would not dare to accuse Ruth of heresy; the other sisters would rise like hornets around him and send for a bishop or a papel legate to investigate the matter. An investigation of his life was the last thing on earth that Father Luce wanted. It seemed to him that he had been reasonably prudent so far and he did not intend to risk any course that would expose him and open him wide to scandal and outcry. He abandoned, at least for the moment, the idea of prevailing on Madelon to enter the convent.

Whether he could make her believe that Richard was the father he did not know. He hoped that Richard had lain with her but he doubted it. If Richard had done so he could easily get out of this nasty predicament by blackmailing him; for he was aware that Richard had consorted with a Jew and he believed that under torture confessions could be wrung from him that would send him if not to the stake at least to a dungeon for life. Surely such a headstrong and freethinking youth had made statements that were heretical. Possibly Victoir would reveal them, if Father Luce were to confess him. Still, Victoir always confessed to Father Raoul. If Richard were innocent he might decide to make a fight of it; Father Luce could not foresee the developments in this case and he shuddered to think what they might be. He knew as well as any man that Hillel was protected by Baron Guillem and that Hillel was fond of Richard. And besides, there was Chretien, a strange and unpredictable rogue whose eyes looked at Father Luce in a way that chilled him. How much, he wondered, did Chretien suspect, how much did he know?

One day Father Luce was comforting Madelon. He was, that is, uttering pious thoughts and asking her to pray and meditate with him, all in preparation for an embrace, for he found her most irresistible when her face was angelic in its sweetness. He heard

128

a slight sound and turned to find Chretien looking at him. Chretien had entered the house and tip-toed over to look into the bed chamber.

Father Luce arose swiftly to face him. "What do you want?" he asked angrily. "Why are you here?"

Chretien looking him straight in the eye said blandly, "Should I not be where God is?—and isn't God where his holy men are?"

The two men looked into the eyes of one another and their looks were evil, like those of two villains taking the measure of one another's powers and will. It was Father Luce's stare that faltered. He turned back to Madelon, saying, "I am confessing her. You will please go outside."

Chretien sniffed. "Yes, father," he said with the same bland insolence and left the house.

In looking back on the incident Father Luce saw nothing to worry about. He had been sitting on the edge of the bed and had been reciting the nineteenth psalm and he had not been touching her and she had been lying white and still with her eyes closed. But the priest now knew that Chretien's suspicions were strong. That in itself would be no great problem if Chretien were an ordinary man. But he was by no means an ordinary man. Father Luce sensed in him a prodigious capacity for craftiness and violence that made him feel almost impotent by comparison. It was not alone, then, in this second course, that he might have Richard to contend with, but that he might have a most formidable and dangerous adversary in Madelon's father. Chretien, he felt, could kill while smiling, and would, if provoked beyond that barrier that corraled his passions.

The possibility that in the second course he might find himself in a desperate struggle not only against Richard and Chretien but the baron also made him abandon, at least for the time being, and until he was more certain of the intentions of these men, the notion of inducing Madelon to accept Richard as the father. Still, there was gossip in the village about Richard and his strange and sudden flight, and Father Luce heard one day that Richard's own mother had asked Old Noelle if her son had lain with Madelon. Sensing an opportunity here the priest went to see Elise.

She was not in the shack. He looked in and saw the loutish Pascal sitting with a cat held up against his throat. He next saw

Fleur, her hands piously clasped and her eyes looking at him fearfully. Staring at her he sniffed the stink of the place.

"Where's your mother?" he asked.

Fleur arose and made an obeisance of reverence. "Father, she is outside somewhere."

"When will she be back?"

"Father, I don't know."

A very polite child, he thought, looking at her more closely. "My dear," he said, "come over to the light." In her unclean rag and on bare feet Fleur came over and stood timidly with bowed head. "Look up at me," said Father Luce. She looked up and her white face colored a little. "How old are you, child?"

"Father, I am ten."

"You're a pretty girl."

"Thanks," she faltered and dropped her gaze.

"Child, do you know why your brother Richard went away?"

"Father, I do not."

"Are you sure? Remember, my dear, that you are talking to a holy man of God and that our Father in heaven is listening."

"Yes."

"Now tell me why he went away."

"He—"

"Yes?" said Father Luce gently.

"He—he spoke about going to a university."

"Oh, he did? To which one?"

"Father, I think he said in Toulouse."

"Toulouse," said the priest softly. In his opinion the university at Toulouse was full of heretics. He found the scent exciting. "But did your brother have the money to go away to school?"

"I—I don't know."

"Did the Jew Hillel give him money?"

"Father, I don't know."

"You must not lie, child, for God is listening to you. Now tell me, has your brother sometimes been—well, I mean a little unhappy in our blessed faith? That is, a lot of people, you know, don't find it easy to believe all the things that our holy Father in his infinite wisdom has revealed to us. Your brother, my dear child, sometimes went to the house of this Jew. Jews, you know, are an accursed people. For instance, they like to marry very young, for they say that the messianic age cannot come until all souls have bodies and they marry young to multiply offspring. And you know—" He now put a finger under her chin to tip up her shy frightened face. "Jews say that sexual intimacy is communion with the spirit of life. That is horrible blasphemy," he said, looking into her lovely eyes. "So why should your brother go to see a Jew?"

"Father, I—I don't know."

He was still tilting her chin and forcing her to look into his piercing and hypnotic eyes. "I've said that some people can't believe all the holy things in our faith. For instance, some of them say that the holy sacraments are polluted if touched by a wicked priest. I suppose maybe your brother has felt that way about it. Hasn't he, my child?"

"I—I suppose!" she gasped and swallowed hard.

"Well, that is not so strange, is it? There are other people who feel that way. There are people who think that if his Holiness the Pope is a wicked man he does not speak for God. Would your brother feel that way about it? . . . My child, would he?"

"I—" There was such a strain on her neck that she found it hard to speak.

"Would he?"

She struggled a moment in the torture and gasped, "I suppose!"

"Well, now, you're a truthful child and God loves the truth. He will bless you for telling it and appoint you for great rewards. I feel very sorry as a priest that your brother feels the way he does and I will pray for him. Of course he is very young and the young sometimes have foolish notions. Have you heard him question any of the things in our holy faith? But of course you have," said the wily inquisitor, "for you have just told me so."

Tortured, with her chin still held in his clasp, and almost swooning she said in an anguished whisper, "He confesses to Father Raoul."

"Yes, dear, I know that. And do you?"

"Yes." She would not meet his eyes but looked away at the sky, save when he clasped her chin harder and shook her gently. Then she would meet his gaze a moment and again look away.

"Sometimes you question things, do you? Truth is a jewel, dear child. If his Holiness the Pope is wicked you don't think he speaks for God? I'll talk to you about that some day and meanwhile you

131

pray to our Father and ask him to guide you and lead you to the light. Will you do that?"

"Yes!"

He released her chin and drew her outside into the full light. Looking round him he saw a wooden bench at a little distance and he took one of her small white hands and led her to the bench. He sat and drew her down at his side. He framed her face between his soft moist palms and looked into her eyes, his own eyes so hypnotically intent as they searched out her soul that tremors ran through her frame. Still holding her with his piercing gaze he said: "My child, you must put yourself in my care and do what I ask you to do. Will you promise me that?"

"Yes!" she whispered and turned rigid.

He then released her but his moist palms did not leave her cheeks at once but withdrew from them slowly and caressingly. He clasped her two hands and squeezed them and lingeringly took his hands from hers and raised them to his cross. Fleur gasped again and looked away, for she could not endure his deep fixed and unblinking stare.

"You remind me of Madelon," he said softly. "She has placed her trust in me, as you will. Now say after me, I vow and promise by the God omnipotent and by his sweet Mother—"

Fleur tried to say the words but was so stricken with fear that she was trembling all over.

"Say after me—"

"I can't!" she gasped, looking round her for succor.

"Say, I vow to God—"

She moved, intending to flee but at once fell back, shuddering. "Please!" she said. "May I go?"

"You may go," he said.

She fled from him and into the hovel. In such moments as this he reminded himself to be prudent and now slowly and cautiously he looked round him to see if anyone had been watching. Then with great dignity he arose and walked away, fingering his pectoral cross and murmuring a paternoster.

A few days later he was passing by when he saw Elise outside. He stopped and indicated the bench and said, "My good woman, come over here. I want to talk to you."

"About what?" asked Elise, who despised him.

"About a matter of importance to you."

132

Reluctantly she went over and he sat but she did not sit. She stood, looking at him, and every thought she had ever had about him was in her eyes.

"Sit down," he said.

"I can hear just as well if I stand. What is it you have to say?"

"It's about your son Richard."

"Oh, Richard. Well, what about him?"

"Why did he go away?"

"I don't know."

"Is it true that he got himself into some difficulty and fled?"

Elise looked at him a long hard moment before she said: "You mean about Madelon?"

"Yes, Madelon."

"You mean she's with child?" said Elise, who had no power to dissemble or to feign what she did not feel.

"I'm afraid the poor child is—uh, that way."

"You think the father is Richard?"

"Richard was with her before he left."

"Well, if it's Richard I guess he'll marry her. But if it is or isn't what has it got to do with me?"

"It's not just a simple matter of marriage," said the priest, choosing his words with care, uttering them softly, while he looked steadily into her eyes. "It is told that your son has questioned some of the truths in our holy faith."

"Who told you that?"

"It doesn't matter where I heard it. It's also well known that he visited the Jew Hillel. Did you know that?"

"I had heard it."

"Why does your son associate with such people? You must understand," he said, holding her eyes, his own unwinking, "that such things may arouse suspicion of your son, whether he abides in the faith and holy truths of our Church or whether he is getting false and heretical notions. I don't wish to alarm you. If he'll return and marry this girl—"

"What if he isn't the father?"

He did not like her arrogant spirit and the way she looked at him with contempt. He wondered how he could humble her. "Your other son, I have heard, is very devoted to cats. I've heard it said that he won't kill any animal, not even a mouse. Is that so?"

"He doesn't like to kill things. Does that make him wicked?"

133

"Well, you don't seem to understand. There are persons who won't kill animals because they believe in reincarnation. Such a belief is heresy."

Anger came up in Elise and dyed her whole face. "Are you accusing my son Pascal of heresy?"

"No, no," he said, realizing that he had gone too far. "I only pointed out that it is strange—"

"There's nothing strange about it. I don't kill things either. But where do you know a woman more devoted to our Lord?"

"My dear woman, I was not accusing you. Your devotion is well known. I was only pointing out—"

"You're accusing both of my sons!"

"Oh no, I was only saying—"

"Show me a man anywhere more God-fearing than my son Pascal. As for Richard, if you want to know what he thinks why don't you ask him?"

"Then you admit you have some doubt about him? Your little daughter Fleur told me the other day—"

Her voice now was deeper in its throatiness because of her rage. "Have you been questioning my daughter?"

"The shepherd watches over his flock," he said sharply. "It is my duty—"

"It's not your duty to snoop around and question little children."

If she had been observing closely she would have seen the danger signals in his eyes but she was hating him too deeply to see anything but the evil in him.

"As for children," he said, "you know very well it's their duty to accuse their parents if they suspect them of waywardness. Your daughter—"

She moved a little closer to him, bending forward a little, and asked biterly: "Why would you accuse any of us? We have no property. If we were all burned or thrown into dungeons what would you get but filthy rags, broken pots, stinking bedmats? Who is ever accused except those who can be plundered?"

"Woman," he said, "watch your tongue. The words you have just uttered—"

"Oh, to hell with it! And by the living God you'd better watch your tongue! Don't you ever come to my face and accuse me or my son Pascal! Don't you ever—"

"Now wait a minute! After all, I came about your son Richard."

"If Richard is the one you want then go find him."

"I intend to," he said.

"But how do you know Richard is the father?"

"If not Richard, then who?"

The words were deep in her throat and bitter: "Yes, who! Some priest!"

He stood up abruptly and he was very angry. "Woman, there's a limit to the things I will hear from your mouth! These things you are saying—"

She was facing him and looking deep in the eyes that paralyzed others but not her. "Oh, to hell with your godbelly airs! I'll tell you this, Father Luce, that I'm one person in the world who isn't **afraid** of you. You're not going to scare me. If you want to accuse me then accuse me and summon me for trial; but let me warn you that when you do that I'll have some things to tell—and I mean some things about you. I'm not blind and I'm not deaf and I'm not stupid. I know about some things that have been going on here for years. I haven't talked about them but if you're going to come to my face and accuse me and Pascal and snoop around to pry information out of my girl, then by the God of heaven and earth—"

"No, no!" he cried. His anger had cooled. This woman like Chretien was too much for him. He was afraid of her. He saw in her eyes, in her face, in her whole furious body a wild and fool-hardy courage that would stop at nothing if aroused. "I never came to accuse you," he said, again speaking softly. "I only came about Richard, who is a fine young man. The poor child Madelon—"

"Why don't you ask *her* who the father is?"

That dashed him for a moment. "Well," he said, recovering, "she doesn't seem to know. Madelon is a strange girl. She sees visions and lives in a state of almost continuous ecstasy. She doesn't know much about what goes on around her."

"If some man seduced her I guess she'd know about that."

"As a matter of fact she doesn't seem to. She has the strange and awful notion that God sent an angel to lie with her. But if she was visited by a supernatural being I would think it must have been Satan."

"Satan? What are you saying?"

"Satan does lie with women, you know."

Elise did not question that. Doubt of that was heresy. She said: "Well, if it was God or Satan why blame Richard?"

"When you imply that it could have been God do you know how horrible your blasphemy is?"

"Why blame Richard?" she said.

"But if Madelon does not know how am I to know?"

"I supposed," she said maliciously, "that God guides you in such things. Do you tell me that you, a holy man, don't know who the father is? How could that be!"

"God doesn't reveal all things to me. He has never revealed all things to any man, not even to his Son."

"I'd think that's one thing he would reveal. Besides, you've been Madelon's confessor for quite a while now. Surely she has told you. She must have told you soon after it happend. Has she ever mentioned Richard to you?"

"Oh yes," said the sly rogue. "Many times, in fact. You know of course that Richard is in love with her and wants to marry her. You also know that before he went away he spent quite a bit of time with her. Alone, I mean."

"I didn't know it."

"Her father knew it. Old Noelle knew it."

"Well," she said, impatient to be rid of him, "it's something for you to figure out. I have work to do."

She went away from him and Father Luce stared after her, looking her up and down from her strong shoulders to her large buttocks. You wicked woman, he thought, God will humble you. You will not be so arrogant before this matter is settled. But he did not know how to settle it. He did not know where Richard was or if he would ever return to the village.

Then, while walking away, he thought of abortion. Unwedded girls were sometimes aborted by their lovers, with the use of poisons or drugs. More commonly than not they died in the ordeal and if Madelon died, Father Luce reflected, the problem would be settled once and for all, so far as they were both concerned. Death was more commonplace than marriage. From famine and war and from a host of pestilential diseases, including smallpox, typhoid and diphtheria, most people died before they were thirty and many before they were grown. Disease was punishment from God for sin.

Hidden away Father Luce had a few drugs that were the most powerful abortifacients he knew of. He decided to mix two or three of them in wine and give the potion to Madelon, telling her that it was a theriac against mosquitoes and lice and all stinging and biting creatures. She had skin eruptions which itched intolerably and she scratched herself untl she bled. He would tell her that the medicine would cure her sores.

Madelon did not doubt him. Like the child she was she looked a moment at the dark red liquid and drank it off. She lay back and smiled up at him. "It burns," she said.

"It will make you feel better," he said.

"I can feel it all through me," she said.

"It will purify your blood," Father Luce said. "It was a little wine and the juice of herbs. I take it now and then and that's why I'm so healthy."

"It doesn't matter for me," she said. "I'll die soon."

Then they were silent. She had closed her eyes, and Father Luce sitting by her was studying her face. After a minute or two he saw tremors in her body and in a few moments she struggled up and collapsed forward, convulsed and trying to vomit. She gagged horribly and seemed to be gasping for breath; and with cool professional calm he looked at her and wondered if he had given her a sufficiently potent dose.

"I'm sick!" she gasped.

"You'll be all right soon," he said.

"Father, oh, I'm sick!"

She began to writhe like one in agony and to bubble and froth a little at the mouth. She was choking for breath. He went into the other room and stood by the door, listening. He opened the door a little and peered out but he saw no one. He went back to the bedchamber and saw Madelon convulsed on the bed and choking and feebly struggling. He returned to the front door and quickly let himself out and hastened away.

XI

Richard spent two months learning from the tongue of Gerart, when, having most of the money Elienor had given him, he struck out to see more of the world; and the more he saw the more he marveled and the more he questioned the Christian faith.

Nothing disturbed him so much as the widespread use of phallic symbols in the worship of God. He found them everywhere, for representations of the genitals, male and female, were all over Europe—above gateways, over the doors of churches and public buildings, and in sculpture and painting. He would not have understood these things but for Gerart. Now he recognized the exaggerated pudenda on sacred lamps and other Church utensils and the exaggerated penis reddened by the many libations of wine which devout women poured over it. After a while he understood that the windows and doors of all the sacred buildings were in the form of the door of life. Gerart had explained that the *pallium* worn by the priest was an ancient pagan symbol which represented the female part; and that confessors of the Church wore the *crux ansata* over their necks and hanging down their fronts, an Egyptian emblem that combined the male and female genitals, the female being around the priest's neck and the male hanging down his chest. He had at first doubted that this was true but after seeing so many symbols and studying them and thinking about them he supposed that Gerart was right. He was forced to admit that the *chasuble* seemed to be no more than the *vesica piscis,* a common emblem of the female. Why, he wondered again and again, was the symbolism of the Christian faith so saturated with paganism? And why, since the Church thought sexual intimacy a sin or at best a necessary indulgence, were so many holy matters represented by sexual symbols? He would ask Hillel.

Everywhere he went, south from Toulouse and then east and then north, he saw penitents on pilgrimage, wearing their huge crosses, some with one cross, some with the two of Dominic and some, the perfected heretic, with three, the third being on their cap. He saw these unfortunate wretches exposed to derision and ridicule, too ashamed almost to lift their heads to the stranger's gaze, each with his robe, staff, cap and script, the robe usually of coarse shaggy wool in imitation of John the Baptist's camel-hair. He knew that there were spies ready to inform and share in the plunder and once in a while he thought he recognized one, by his furtive appearance and his sly way of looking Richard over, as though speculating on his riches.

Everywhere too he saw the great estates of the nobles, both secular and ecclesiastic; the castle with pennon flying, usually built on a hill surrounded by a wide deep fosse, on the inside of which was sometimes set a palisade of squared logs with towers along it. The door of the citadel could be reached only by way of a bridge across the fosse. In the huge enclosure was a second building or palais, the home of the lord and his family, with a second enclosure for the lord's chief dependents. He saw castles that looked more magnificent by far than Guillem's. It was a world of appalling contrasts: the resplendent clothes and livery and trappings of the lords when they rode abroad—and at the roadside filthy naked beggars, dying. He saw the poor everywhere, the serfs, like his own people; the hordes of diseased vagrants; the homeless and the outcast. It was a Christian world that ranged from the most unspeakable poverty to the most luxurious idleness, from the leper in the gutter to the bishop in silks and velvets officiating at Mass, from the lord with a thousand retainers waging war in the hope of extending his barony to the fugitives living like beasts in the forests. It was a world whose contrasts spanned the distance between hovel and cathedral.

It was a time of cathedral building: Chartres had been rebuilt after fire destroyed it in 1194; Rheims in 1210; and Amiens was building now. He had wanted to see Chartres and Rheims but the distance was too great. Gerart had talked one evening about the ineffable beauty of the south porch of Chartres and the great portal at Rheims. On the north side of one were Old Testament scenes, where the sun of revelation shone no more; on the south side were New Testament scenes, in revelation's full sun and glory; and on the west wall was the Last Judgment, where the sun would shine for the last time. Within these cathedrals, Gerart had said, the symbolic plans were so vast that the human mind could hardly grasp them: at Chartres alone there were over six thousand painted and sculptured figures. Much of this beauty, Gerart had told his students, had been built with slave labor, the poor wretches being driven to their toil under the rod and the lash. That, Richard thought, was shameful enough, but still more shameful, if what Gerart said was true, was the way hundreds of pagan symbols had been wrought into the magnificence of the ceilings and walls, the windows and doors. The Church dreamed and saw visions and spoke to the world but the dreams and visions troubled Richard, for he was not sure that they were the house of truth.

He had also wanted to see Paris. Gerart, who seemed to have been everywhere, told his students about it: how it was an assemblage of castles each fortified and each with its own gardens and dependencies; and of the churches and monasteries, all within walls. Each trade had its quarter: the apothecaries were in the Cité; the parchment-sellers, scribes and booksellers were in the Latin quarter; the money-changers and goldsmiths were on the Grand Pont; the butchers were near the Grand Châtelet; the mercers near the Rue St. Denis. You went to the Place Maubert for bread, to the Grand Châtelet for meat, to the Petit Pont for flowers and eggs, and for herbs to the quayside of the Ile de la Cité. Every level of human life was to be found there: beggars sitting by church doors or by bridges; artisans and craftsmen in their open shops; jongleurs and moutebanks, monks and canons of the cathedral and professors of the university; couriers with their white wands, heralds in tabards, knights in armor; nobles riding out to hunt or hawk, women in their glittering litters; judges in scarlet riding to law court and pilgrims going to St. Genevieve; prisoners gyved and bound on their way to the Grand Châtelet; and within his turreted fortifications the king in the Louvre. If he were to go there as a student, Richard had learned, he would hear lectures only in Latin; and he would be initiated as a freshman by being treated as a fool, driven through the streets like a wild donkey, and then purged and almost drowned.

Gerart had told them that all over Europe warfare, among

140

Christians, was almost as common as hunting. He had told them how war was waged. When siege was laid to a castle by a lord who envied and coveted another lord's possessions, the first task was to destroy the outworks, the posterns, barbicans and other barriers. Most of these were of wood; they were hacked to pieces or fired with burning arrows steeped in sulphur. Moats were filled and ladders were then reared against the ramparts. The attackers would dig under a wall and prop it with timbers and then fire the timbers. They used huge battering rams covered with an iron head, and from huge catapults projected stones and dead horses and cats and dogs, or fireballs of inflammable materials. For weapons in hand-to-hand combat they used hammer-axes; sticks fitted with iron hooks; the guisarme, a weapon like a scythe with which they cut legs off, or the fauchard, a scythelike instrument that opened ghastly wounds; the espadon, a two-handed sword; the espringale, a contraption mounted on wheels that hurled arrows and javelins; and a ball of iron or of lead attached to an iron chain. They fought for conquest, for loot and plunder and rape. They fought, Gerart said, because they were so damned bored with living and had nothing else to do.

From Toulouse Richard went south to Narbonne on the sea, thence up the coast and inland to Nimes and overland to Avignon; and along the Rhone River a two days' journey before turning west and south and back to Patres. In all his wanderings he covered a distance of only three hundred miles. Paris was many hundred miles to the north, too far for his time and his purse. He had put on twenty pounds of weight and looked muscular and fit. He had seen only a tiny part of the world and had heard only one teacher but he had learned many things and he was all the more eager to become a scholar and a philosopher. He was eager to talk to Hillel.

He also wanted to see Madelon. He had thought about her and had dreamed about her but absence and wandering had taken the bloom off his youthful infatuation and turned his fancy elsewhere in search of a Heloise. He had dreamed about the Baroness Elienor. He wanted to see his people, for he worried about them and now felt it to be his duty to labor and save money and buy their freedom, or at least to see that they were clothed and fed.

On the day after Christmas he came down the road from the east, which led to the village, and stood for a little while looking

141

at the place where he had spent most of his life. He wore leather boots and a tunic of strong fabric that fell to his knees. He was a handsome youth, standing there on a hill against a pale sky, the captive of emotions that had risen to confuse him. He had hated this place and his miserable life here; but everything that he had loved was here—his frail little sister, his sad and silenced father, Hillel and Madelon and Father Raoul—these and the flowering plants and the church bells. Everything that he had hated was here—the stinking hut, the hot fields where he had toiled, his dullwitted brother, his violent mother and Father Luce. On a hill he could see the church and, dimly, the huge likeness of Saint Christopher on the wall. He could see the filthy ugly winding street and the alleys leading off from it and the shabby shops each with its tub of water out front; and beyond all these the baron's castle with its red pennon flying.

What were the people doing at this moment? The harvesting was over; his father would be out in the woods gathering timbers for the baron's fires or over at the baron's mill grinding his corn; or he would be gathering forage for the baron's stunted beasts, most of which by the time grass grew again would be so weak that they would have to be dragged out to pasture on sleds. Or maybe he would be repairing the yokes and the tools. His mother might be patching a ragged garment or trying to find a bone from the head of a mare to put into the soil next spring to drive pests away or a small candle which Victoir would light and carry three times around the plough before using it again; or she might be sitting before a small fire and rubbing her eyes in the smoke and muttering; or she might be on one of her mysterious errands into the woods. Pascal, the dimwit, would be sitting with a starved and lousy cat thinking God knew what thoughts; and Fleur like a pale little image with hands clasped would be silent and waiting. Hillel would be bent over his studies or at the risk of his life he would be purging the gluttonous Guillem.

Madelon, where was she? Was she in the house of her father or the house of the priest? The pain when he thought of her was too deep and he put her out of mind.

He now took the road down the hill and stopped at the hovel of his parents to look in. At once Fleur leapt up like a shadow out of deeper darkness and fled to him, her arms outstretched and her

142

voice crying his name. He knelt and enfolded her, with her face against his cheek and her thin body trembling against him.

"Now, now, little sister, why do you weep?"

"To—to see you!"

"You are so happy to see me?"

"Yes. Oh, you've been gone so long!"

Richard felt tears flood his eyes and he bowed his head to hide them as they fell. "Poor dear little sister. You haven't grown at all since I left."

"Not much."

"Poor scrawny little Fleur. I'll buy you something to eat. I'll buy you something to wear."

"Richard?" she breathed against his face.

"Yes, dear."

"You won't go away again?"

"Well, not for a while, I guess." He drew back and framed her face and kissed both her cheeks. "Where is father?"

"I—I don't know."

"Where is mother?"

"I don't know. Richard, please hold me."

"Yes," he said and held her close and felt her tremble. In all her ten years what of love had this child had?

Pascal was in the hovel but Richard did not speak to him and would have received no reply if he had spoken. When Richard turned away from her Fleur clutched frantically at his hands and he again held her and she trembled so violently that he sank back and drew her to his lap, marveling how thin she was, for she seemed to be only hide and bones. Her head was against his left shoulder and her arms were around his neck. Shyly, softly she kissed his throat and nestled against him, her arms tightening. Again it occurred to him that in all her years this child had had no tenderness, no love. Poor little waif! he thought. Poor sad frightened lonely little thing!

He went to a shop and bought food and gave it to her and told her to eat. He said he would be back soon.

"Don't go!" she whispered.

"Why?"

"Because." She began to sob. "Where you going?"

"To see Madelon."

"Don't go!"

143

"Poor little sister, what is it?"

"Don't go!"

He released her clinging hands and looked round him, knowing well that there was some terrible meaning in her words. "I want to see her," he said. "I'll be back soon." As he walked away she clung to him and he turned to look at her; her face was distorted with anguish and fear and her whole body was supplicating him not to go. What could it be? he wondered. Something dreadful had happened. "Don't worry," he said, "I'll be back soon."

She let him go now but looked at him, her eyes filled with tears.

"I'll be back soon," he said. "I promise."

Should he see Father Raoul first? He went to the priest's house but he was not there. He stood in thought, hesitating, wondering what Fleur could have meant and sensing at last that she had wished to spare him some grief. Was Madelon dead? Did she have a child? He then turned to Chretien's shack and saw Chretien with his back to a wall, his lean strong hairy hands hanging from his knees. Richard went over and Chretien seemed not to recognize him.

"I'm Richard."

"Richard?" said Chretien, looking up at him. He then looked at the tunic and the boots and again at Richard's eyes. "So you have come back."

"I said I would come back."

"You seem to have money. Such clothes are not bought for a sou."

"Where is Madelon?"

"I told you never to come back."

"I remember it. Where is Madelon? Has something happened to her?"

"I told you never to come back. I said that some day you would understand."

"Is she in there?"

"Does the soul linger on earth?"

"What do you mean? Is she—is she dead?"

"Did you know that looking at altar lights will strengthen your eyes? But looking in a mirror is better."

"Are you going to tell me where Madelon is?"

"Why don't you ask where is Father Luce?"

144

"Is she with him?" Richard heard footsteps and turned to see Simone. She stared at him gravely with her round brown eyes.

Then she asked: "Are you Richard?"

"Yes." She had grown. Looking at her he said: "You're almost a woman now."

"She has all a woman needs," said Chretien. "Why don't you marry her?"

Richard looked at Chretien and at Simone, back and forth, and said to Simone: "Where is your sister?"

Simone looked at her father. "Shall I tell him?"

Chretien shrugged. "Let him see her if he wants to. He has no sense."

"She's in the house," said Simone.

Richard walked over to the doorway and looked in and Simone came up and stood behind him. At first he could see nothing in the gloom. "Madelon, are you there?"

"She's there," Simone said.

He could now see in a far corner what he took to be a person lying on a mat. Softly he stepped inside and went forward and looked down at the figure. He stepped aside to allow light from the doorway to fall and then knelt, slowly, like one preparing to look at a dead face. At first he thought the face was dead, even though the eyes were open. It was Madelon but he barely recognized her, she was so thin and white and still. He did not know if she was alive or dead.

"Madelon!" he whispered. There was no response. Her eyes were open and staring but there was nothing in them to suggest that she was alive. He had seen dead eyes that looked like that. "Madelon?" He was beginning to feel horror. He was beginning to feel that she was neither alive nor dead but suspended between death and life, breathing feebly but unable to move. Gently he placed a hand above her heart but could feel no heartbeat. He bent forward and lowered an ear. He listened, with his ear to her breast. Yes, the heart was beating feebly but there was no other sign of life in this frame, no sign that she was breathing, no sign that she could see or hear. Horror gave way to rage as he got to his feet. He went over to the doorway where Simone was waiting.

"What has happened?" he said. Simone did not speak. He looked back at Madelon and at Simone. "How long has she been like this? She seems to be dying." He looked into Simone's eyes

145

and cried, "Why don't you speak?" His voice had risen in anger. He turned to Chretien and looked down at him. "What has happened?"

"I told you not to come back."

"I'm tired of hearing that. What has happened to her? Is she dying?"

"The Lord gives and the Lord takes away."

Richard sucked in a furious breath. "Did Father Luce do this to her?"

"Richard, do you have to talk like a fool? I'm only a poor ignorant man. Do you expect me to know the purpose of God and the holy fathers?"

"Where is he?"

"You'd better listen to some sense."

"Where is he?"

"Are you an absolute fool? You're young and you have most of your life before you. You're a Christian. As a Christian you must not only accept the faith but believe that the holy men of the Church can do no wrong."

"To hell with all that!"

"There you go, acting like an idiot. That's what I mean. You certainly won't have a happy and fruitful life if the inquisitors hear you say such things. Do I have to tell you that? Does Hillel the Jew have to tell you that? You're angry. That's your fault. I told you not to come back. If you hadn't come back you wouldn't be angry. No matter what has been done, no matter who did it, it's a part of God's inscrutable plan and there is nothing you can do to undo it. You can make a lot of trouble for yourself and you seem determined to do it. Why don't you marry Simone?"

"And take her to Guillem for the first night?" He was looking down at Chretien and thinking about him. As a child he had been afraid of this man. He had always felt in him something sinister or a deep gloating or a subtle knowledge. Or what was it? It had been Chretien's way to talk in riddles and parables and Richard felt that he was talking in riddles now.

"I ask again, why don't you marry Simone?"

Richard turned to look at her round roguish eyes and she gave him a small quick mechanical smile. "I don't want a wife," he said.

"Every man wants a wife, though only God knows why. You

146

thought you were in love with Madelon. You weren't. If you'll put your anger away I'll tell you something else."

"All right, what?"

"You haven't put your anger away."

"Do you expect me to look at that girl and feel all right about it? Is there no pity in you, her father?"

"Am I fool enough to waste pity on God's fulfillment of his plan? Should I be stupid enough to find fault with the divine purpose merely because I can't understand it? Sickness and suffering, our Church says, are punishments from God. Should I grieve when our Father punishes?"

Richard knew that there was much more in Chretien's words than there seemed to be. The man was talking in parables.

"What do you want to tell me?"

"You've come back. You should know that it has been told around here that you seduced my daughter and got her with child and fled."

"Who told that lie?"

"I haven't said it is not a lie. But the story has been told. Now if you go around in anger accusing people—"

"I tell you it is a foul stinking lie!"

"All right. Now you're angry again. Anger does you no good in this world if you're neither baron nor bishop. It would be a very fine thing for you if you could keep your mouth shut."

"You mean," said Richard, "you mean I'm not to deny it? You mean that I'm to pretend that this lie is the truth?"

"There is another thing," said Chretien. "It is also being told that you have questioned some things in our holy faith."

"Who has said that?"

"Does it matter? The story has been told."

"It matters to me who told it."

"Should we tell him?" Chretien asked, looking at Simone.

"I don't know," Simone said and shrugged.

"He will be angry again, for the man is a fool, but we may as well tell him." Glancing up at Richard he said: "Your sister."

"My sister! No! You mean Fleur?"

"Do you have any other sister?"

"Fleur told that about me?"

"Possibly Father Luce talked to her."

"That nasty contemptible—"

147

"Silence, you fool. In my presence today you've already said enough to put you in a dungeon. Are you a complete idiot? Will nothing satisfy you but to be dragged into the torture chamber? I tell you that you must accept the faith and believe that our holy men can do no wrong. Haven't you gumption enough to know that?"

Suddenly Richard bent down and looked hard into Chretien's eyes. He was sure that he saw mirth there, mirth that was sly and sardonic, that was laughing inside. He said: "Are you making a jest of all this?"

"No, Richard. I'm trying to get some sense into your thick head. Believe it or not I'm your friend. We're on the same side."

"The same side of what?"

"There are two sides, aren't there? God's and Satan's. Which side are you on?"

Again Richard looked deep into the small close-together cunning eyes and he was sure that behind the eyes was laughter. "Which side are you on?"

"Your side," said Chretien. "And now for the health if not of your soul then your body go away and do a little thinking and don't get irons on your arms and legs before tomorrow's sun goes down. Playing the fool is a luxury that only the powerful can afford in this world."

XII

Richard turned away and left Chretien sitting by the wall. He was so enraged and sickened by his vision of Madelon that he did not know where he was going or what he would do. Should he talk to Hillel first?—or to Father Raoul?—or to Fleur? He would talk to all of them but to which one first? He was trying to decide the matter, trying to cool his anger and be prudent, when he saw Father Raoul climbing the hill to the church and he hastened to overtake him.

"Father Raoul," he said, coming up, "I must talk to you."

The priest turned and looked at him. "Is it you, Richard? I hardly knew you."

"I'm a little bigger than I was," Richard said. "I want to talk to you, alone, if you will."

"We can sit here," said the priest, indicating a bench. "When did you come back?"

"Today." They sat on the bench and Richard said impulsively, "Have you seen Madelon?"

"No, not for quite a while. How is she?"

"I think she's dying. What happened to her while I was gone?"

Father Raoul looked off at the December sky and for a few moments did not speak. "I don't know," he said at last. "I've heard that she was visited by Satan."

"Satan! But you don't believe that. She was one of the purest and noblest souls that ever lived. Now she's over there in her father's house, a ghastly little thing of skin and bones, hardly more than a corpse and that's what she looks like, a corpse. Something terrible has happened to her."

"Do you know the story of Theophilus?"

149

"No."

Theophilus, Father Raoul said, lived many centuries ago. He was a bishop's vice-dominus and such a good and worthy man that on the death of the bishop the people wanted to raise him to that high position. Out of modesty he declined. The new bishop, because he had been second choice, felt vengeful toward Theophilus and persecuted him, until at last in desperation Theophilus went to a Jewish magician and through him got an appointment with Satan. Theophilus made a pact with the Devil to deliver to him his soul and to deny Christ and the Virgin. Satan then gave him great powers and riches and for years Theophilus lived a sinful and scandalous life, until, with death near, he repented and fasted and prayed to the Virgin for forty days and nights. The Mother of Mercies at first would have nothing to do with him. But one midnight while he lay at the foot of her altar supplicating her mercy and forgiveness she came down from heaven and said that she would forgive him if he would deny Satan and return to Christ. He did so, and ever since that day he had been known as Theophilus the Penitent.

"But why do you tell me this? Does it have something to do with Madelon?"

"I'm telling you because you seem not to believe in the powers of Satan and his imps. The blessed Augustine tells us of many known instances of sylvans and fauns, usually called incubi, assaulting women and working their lust on them. He tells us that the minor devils are forever busy trying to seduce women. Do you know what incubus means?"

"No," said Richard, staring at Father Raoul's face.

"It means to lie on. Female imps assault men. They are called succubi and this means to lie under. Do you question these things that so many times have been proved?"

"I—" Richard broke off, thinking, Be prudent, be prudent! "No," he said.

"You don't doubt that Satan begets children by virgins?"

"I—I guess not."

"Do you doubt that witches conspire with Satan? I'll tell you how the witch does," said the priest gravely. "First she takes off all her clothing. Then she sits on a broomstick and drinks three swallows of something from a black bottle and flies up into the air and is gone. If she rides a goat instead of a broomstick she a-

150

noints her body with some oil and this gives her the power to fly through the air with the speed of lightning. Do you know Ambre out in the woods?"

"Yes."

"She has trysts with Satan. Richard, you must never question these things, which the blessed Augustine told us have been proved again and again."

"But does this have something to do with Madelon?"

"Doesn't it? It is said that she was visited by Satan."

"Who said it?" asked Richard bitterly. "Father Luce?"

"I've heard it from many people."

"In my wanderings," said Richard, "I heard things too. I heard that most priests have concubines but call them priestesses. I heard that most Christians would rather be called a thief or a dog than a priest or a monk. I myself have seen them cross themselves on seeing a priest."

"Yes, Richard," said Father Raoul, "you have heard things but they come from Satan."

"Father, you don't think any priest has a mistress? You don't believe the stories told about the convents?"

"Satan's evil words are everywhere. I don't know about all the priests but I do know that Satan is very crafty and wicked and delights in nothing more than to confuse people and lead them into error."

"And you actually think this of Madelon?" asked Richard, choking up.

"We know that Satan does these things and that he prefers virgins. If you doubt that then you doubt what the holy Fathers have said."

Richard was silent, brooding, doubting, hating. "Father Raoul, have you heard of Averroes?"

"I think I have, yes."

"He says women should be emancipated. Why do Christian men regard women as a lower order of creation?"

"Mercy on us, Richard, they are. If woman was not to be inferior would our Father not have created her from man's head instead of his rib?"

Richard stared at him, remembering the biting words of Gerart. "You think Madelon is a lower order of creation than Father Luce?"

151

"I believe," said Father Raoul with a touch of impatience, "what the holy Fathers have told us, for when they spoke, our Father in heaven inspired them to speak the truth. I don't know about Madelon. If the Devil visited her I don't know what evil was in her, for she has always seemed to be, as you say, a good girl, pure and sweet. But we can't always know by looking at the surface what is under it. We are sometimes deceived by appearances."

"You don't think—" He was going to say, You don't think Father Luce seduced her? but broke off, for he dared not say that. He said, to cover his confusion, "Jewish women don't have equal rights with Jewish men but Jews have a tender regard for women. They don't believe that men today would be more godlike if it hadn't been for Eve."

"Let us not talk about them," said Father Raoul. "You know very well that when they rejected—"

"I don't believe it!" Richard cried.

"You don't?" said the priest, turning to look at him. "Richard, I think Satan must be in you today."

"Father, maybe he is. But I can't think and I can't believe that some of these things are right." There came to him in a flash the last words that he and Chretien had spoken. Which side are you on? Richard had asked; and Chretien had replied, Your side. Is this what he had meant?

"You're upset," said Father Raoul and for a moment clasped one of Richard's hands. "You don't really mean these things. I might almost doubt your faith if I had not known you all these years and known what a good boy you have been. You're feeling unhappy because of Madelon; but Richard, my son, it is not ours to question but ours to obey. The will of our Father is our task, and though sometimes we may not understand that will we must never doubt it, but place our souls in his bosom and abide and pray and have faith. I'm going in now to pray. Will you go with me?"

"Father, not now. Tomorrow or any other time. Right now I'm—well, I'm too deeply upset. I think I'll go off alone."

"Not alone, my son, but with God. He will answer your questions and your doubts."

Richard left the priest and went down the hill. He thought he would go to Hillel and bare his soul to him but then he thought of Fleur; and recalling that Father Luce had gone to this child, perhaps to question her, perhaps to lead the innocent little thing into damning confessions, he headed for his father's house. It was late afternoon and Victoir was still away, toiling for the baron; but his mother was there. She was kneeling before the stones, preparing to kindle a fire, when Richard darkened the doorway, and she looked up. In the gloom she did not recognize him.

Sharply she said: "Who are you and what do you want?"

"I'm Richard, your son."

She arose and came over and put a hand against him to push him out of the doorway. She then went outside and stood before him, looking him up and down. "Well!" she said. "Leather boots and nice clothes! Are you now a thief?"

"No, mother."

"Where did you get these things?"

"I didn't steal them."

"You now have the fine airs of the highborn, now you're a free man. Go away. We're still slaves here. . . . Did you hear me?" she shrieked. "Go away!"

"I want to see Fleur."

"No. She doesn't want to see you."

But Fleur had come out and had sidled up to him and had clasped his hand. "Come," he said and turned to lead her away when, spitting with fury, Elise rushed at him.

"What do you intend to do with your sister?"

For a moment Richard did not know what she meant. Then he read her meaning in her eyes and in her whole face and such fury seized him that he turned pale and trembled. He released Fleur's hand and shoved her back and turned to face his mother.

"What do you mean?"

"Oh, don't put on your high airs with me! If you ever touch your sister—"

"If you were a man I'd break your neck!"

"If I were a man," said Elise, sneering at him, "I'd not take a sister out to the woods. I could find women not of my own house."

Richard choked the hot words back. He called to Fleur and they went over to the bench and sat there. Richard was so hurt by his mother's suspicion that for a little while he was not able to speak but stared over at her, for she stood in the doorway, looking at him. Then with deliberate insult she made the sign of the cross

153

to tell him that he was evil and that she needed protection against him. Then she entered the hovel. Fleur was looking up at Richard's white face and patting one of his hands.

"Fleur?" he said.

"Yes, Richard."

"You sat on this bench one day with Father Luce."

"Yes."

"He asked you questions."

"Yes."

"About me?"

"Some," she said.

"Tell me what he said."

"He—he said I was a pretty girl."

"Oh, he did?" Richard squeezed her hand. "Being a woman you'd remember that above all, wouldn't you? You are a pretty girl. What else did he say?"

"He said I was talking to a holy man and must tell the truth."

"Yes, go on."

"Let me think. Oh, he wanted to know why you went away. I said you wanted to go to a university."

"Yes, go on."

"He—he asked if Hillel gave you money. I said I didn't know."

"And what else?"

"He wanted to know why you visit a Jew."

"He did? And what did you tell him?"

"I said I didn't know."

"What else did he ask you?"

"Richard, did I do wrong?"

"No, little sister. Just tell me what he asked you and what you told him."

Fleur drew a sharp breath. "Well, he wanted to know if—if you ever doubt our faith. He wanted to know if you think—that is, if a priest—What is the word, Richard?"

"Pollutes?"

"Yes, if a priest pollutes—"

"—the sacrament if he is wicked?"

"He asked if you thought that."

"And what did you tell him?"

"I—I said I guessed you did."

"You told him that?"

154

"O Richard!" she gasped, tears coming to her eyes. "He said God was listening and I must tell the truth!"

"Yes dear, I know. Don't cry. Just tell me what else happened."

Fleur was silent, trying to remember. "He asked did you think the Pope—that is, if he speaks for God—"

"If he is a wicked man?"

"Y-yes!"

"There now, don't cry. It is all right."

"No it isn't!" she gasped. "I can tell by your voice!"

"It's all right," he said, patting her. "And you told him I thought the Pope did not speak for God if he is wicked?"

With a terrible effort she forced the word out: "Yes!"

"Little sister, why did you tell him such things?"

"Because God was listening. Because I heard you say them."

They were silent. Richard was thinking, He already knows enough to have me up for heresy, he already has me in his power. Gently he asked: "Is that all?"

"He—he told me to put myself—I mean, to trust him and do what he asks me to do."

"He—he told you that?" For a moment Richard closed his eyes. He then turned to her and said: "Did you promise to?"

"I—"

"Fleur, did you?"

"Yes, Richard. He said I remind him of Madelon."

Richard was too amazed to speak. A deep quiet ugly fury was taking possession of him and he had difficulty breathing. Curiously he looked at Fleur, he looked her up and down, and he saw for the first time in his life that she was much like Madelon.

"Richard, why do you look at me like that?"

"You'll never know," he said. "May God in his mercy grant that you never know." He took one of her hands. "Fleur, pay very close attention now to what I say. If Father Luce ever comes to you again answer no questions. None. Do you understand?"

"But if he says God is listening?"

"I'm not asking you to lie. Just don't answer his questions. Tell him nothing, absolutely nothing. If he asks questions about me tell him to ask me."

"But Father Raoul, should I confess to him?"

Richard was silent. Could he trust Father Raoul? Well, even though Father Raoul was a gentle priest and a fine and compassionate man, Richard knew that he could not trust him. What man could a heretic trust but another heretic?

"Fleur, do you love me?"

"You know I do."

"When you confess to Father Raoul—but what would you have to confess at your age?"

"I sometimes have wicked thoughts," she said, for she was older than her ten years.

"Such as what?"

"I won't tell you. I shouldn't."

"That's right. But don't tell anything about me. After all, you know almost nothing about what I think or believe."

"I heard you talk to father."

"That was only talk. If asked anything about me always say you don't know. You'll not have to lie for you don't know."

"I'll say I don't know."

"If Father Luce comes to see you again tell me as soon as you can."

"Richard, don't you like him?"

Richard hesitated, thinking bitterly, I'll now become a liar to save my neck! He said, "Why, of course, sister, I like him."

"I don't think you do," Fleur said. "I don't. He said I must trust him as Madelon trusted him. Does Madelon like him?"

"I don't know."

"You mean," she said, wise for her years, "that you don't want to tell me."

"Fleur, look, I simply don't know what Madelon thinks. She seems to be dying."

"Is what they say about her true?"

"What do they say?"

"You know. They say that she will have a baby and it's Satan's."

"Then you had heard it. I guess everybody has heard it."

"Is it true?"

"I don't know."

"After this will you and I always say to one another, I don't know?"

Richard was stung. "I'm only an ignorant peasant," he said. "I know nothing. Some day I may know things." O God, he thought, to be forced to lie and pretend to his own sister, to his own people!

156

"Are you going to stay here now?"

"I don't know. Honestly, Fleur, I don't know what I'll do."

"If you go away again will you take me?"

"Well, if I can."

"I wouldn't be much bother. I could keep your house if you had a house."

"Yes," he said, patting her. "I don't know what I'll do. We'll see."

"Will you marry Madelon?"

"I told you Madelon is dying."

"Maybe not," said Fleur. "She's always been funny like a saint."

Funny like a saint! In spite of himself Richard smiled.

"Richard, why do you visit a Jew?"

Before he could remember to be prudent Richard said, "I like him and he is my brother."

"Your brother? Oh no. Isn't it wicked?"

"That is what—" he was about to say *our* Church says but hesitated and said, "—the Church says."

"Why are Jews wicked?"

God, O God! He wanted to rise and shout, They're not wicked! But he said, "Let's not talk about that."

"Did you know father is sick?"

"He hasn't been well for a long time."

"What will we do when he can't work?"

"I'll try to take care of you."

"You mean Pascal and mother and all of us?"

"No, just you."

They were silent. Then Fleur said, touching his hand, "Richard, I love you very much. I want to be with you always."

"I hope you can be."

"But if you marry your wife won't like me."

"I'm not planning to marry," he said, and thought of Simone.

"I don't want to either," said Fleur. "I'd just like to keep house for you."

"We'll see."

After a few thoughtful moments Fleur said, "When they take the ass into church and the people shout, He haw, sire ass! does God like it?"

Again Richard smiled. "I don't know," he said. Fleur had in mind a Christian custom of celebrating on a certain Sunday the

157

virtues of the ass: the choicest one in the neighborhood was caparisoned in bright colors and led through the streets and then into the church and up to the chancel, where it was tethered to the altar rail. While someone chanted the virtues of the beast on which Jesus rode the congregation brayed in loud voices, He haw, sire ass. . . . He recalled having seen the Baroness Elienor's flushed face while she brayed as loud as any other. Some of the Christian customs seemed pretty foolish to Richard, as when on Noel eve a heifer, an ox and an ass were installed in the church where it was pretended that they breathed on the holy babe to keep it warm. There was another custom—

"Richard, what are you thinking?"

"That I must buy you some food and then look around."

"That wasn't it," she said, her eyes gravely searching his face.

"That was part of it. Now come along, for I have a little money. What would you like to eat? Some Christmas bread?"

Christmas bread! It was made of the finest flour and eggs and milk; in all her life she had never tasted anything like that, nor simnel and manchet, nor even wassel or cocket, but only muslin, made of coarse meal from barley and oats.

She walked at his side, clasping his hand and said simply, "It would be nice to taste it once."

XIII

Of course he would see Hillel, he was thinking, after he had bought a little food for Fleur and sent her home. Jews, it now seemed to him, were a strange people. There had been a Jew in Gerart's group and from him Richard had learned that kissing of man and woman was not looked on with favor, and kissing of the lips by betrothed couples was not approved at all. Brothers kissed one another on their lips but their sisters they kissed only on their hand. Richard was wondering if Hillel would kiss him and if so, where, when he presented himself at the door.

The door was opened a little and Hillel peered out and for a moment the two men looked into one another's eyes.

"Is it you, Richard?"

"Yes."

The door was opened and Richard stepped inside. He felt ill at ease and ashamed and mean, for in spite of Hillel's sage advice he had been imprudent and now had confessions to make. Hillel, he perceived, had been interrupted in his studies, for a table was covered with parchment and notes and on it burned a light. Since artificial light was very expensive the cresset of oil marked Hillel as a man of means. So did the garments he had on: for a cultured Jew dress was more important than food.

Hillel also seemed to be ill at ease. He brought forth a stool and said, "Will you sit?" but he had not offered to kiss Richard or made any gesture of brotherly affection.

Richard sat and Hillel returned to his table and sat there in the light. "If you are busy," Richard said, "I'll come another time."

"Oh no, it's all right. I'm always busy, so one time is as good as another. Tell me about yourself, where you have been, all of it."

159

"Over to Toulouse and other places." The silence then was strained and Richard blurted: "I may as well confess and get it over with. I'm sure I'm already in trouble."

"Trouble? What kind, Richard?"

"I've talked too much."

"I thought you would."

"Shall I tell you all about it?"

"Of course. We're brothers, you know."

"That's what bothers me. For you, I mean."

"And for yourself too. Go ahead."

"I found a teacher at Toulouse," Richard said, now and then meeting Hillel's eyes. "He had a group of students and for weeks I was one of them and I guess I learned a few things. . . . Well," he said, speaking with an effort, "I guess I'm a heretic."

"I'm not surprised," Hillel said quietly, "but what makes you think you are?"

"I just can't believe all the things my Church expects me to."

"What, for example?"

Speaking as though he had to face each word and drag it out, word by word, he said: "I've heard that some priests tell women it's no sin to copulate with them. I've heard that the right to sin can be bought. I've heard that for enough money any Church office can be bought, even the papacy. I've heard that the Church forges documents to add to its dominions and make itself secure in its great powers. And then there's another thing."

"What is that?" asked Hillel, watching his face.

"The Church says sexual intimacy is evil but if so, why has it used so many sexual symbols in its ritual and worship?"

"I suppose most churches do."

Richard thought of that and became aware of a wind outside, a tormented and complaining wind, a wandering and knowing and unhappy wind. It recalled to him another matter. He said, glancing at Hillel: "Augustine—well, he seems to be regarded as the greatest of the Fathers—he said we should not think that God detests the things in us that make us superior to other animals. He said faith does not dispense us from accepting and demanding proof. If that is so, why does the Church teach that we should question nothing but just believe, not inquire but have faith? When I left here I thought I'd try to see Francis but then I learned

160

that he said it isn't good for people to know how to read. Now either Augustine or Francis is wrong."

"Which?—do you think."

"I think Francis. I think Augustine was right when he said that God gave us intelligence to use, that pure faith is not enough but we should demand proof. But if we demand proof we're heretics. It's just as Abelard said. He said the Christian religion has become hypocrisy."

"Who told you all these things?"

"The teacher at Toulouse."

"All right, go on, get it all out of you."

"I heard that a Christian was tried and put in a dungeon because he said love between man and woman can be good and beautiful. He said the word woman is a higher and nobler word than lady. He said the Pope has no power to forgive sins. And that reminds me," said Richard, turning his hands over and over, one over the other. "I heard that some of the popes have been criminals. One had children by his sister Tropea—and this wasn't so very long ago. And some must be heretics, because they contradict previous popes. Some pope said Jesus and the apostles lived in poverty and some other pope says that isn't true.

"There're still other things," he said, wondering what Hillel was thinking. "An abbot-elect had seventeen bastard children in a single village and another had seventy concubines. Are these just the wicked exceptions? Maybe, but it is said that stealing in abbies is so common that monks have to keep their cupboards locked. It's said that the right to squeeze the poor and to despoil and torture is sold to the highest bidder. It's said that litigation is so profitable that some priests when inducted are made to swear that they will settle no quarrel without profit. It's said that criminals escape punishment by becoming monks. And this teacher told us that when Pope Innocent the Third was asked if a member of the clergy could be arrested if caught redhanded in crime he said no, only with the consent of a prelate, which means he couldn't be arrested at all. It means," Richard said, looking at Hillel, "that Father Luce couldn't be arrested. So I have to ask, what is the Church like?"

He was silent, listening to the wind, thinking of his own inner torments, until Hillel said: "Is that all?"

"Oh," said Richard, catching himself up with a sharp breath,

"I could tell you more. I could talk all night about it. About what the teacher told us. He said the Church has become a scandal and a shame on earth, yet its leaders have the gall to say that Jews are an accursed people."

"Pope Innocent said that."

"Yes, he said it and others said it."

"This teacher must be a very bold man."

"He is, I guess. But he takes only a few students he can trust. I told him maybe I would see Dominic and he told what Dominic did. Dominic, he said, was disturbed by a sparrow that interrupted his meditations. He thought he saw Satan in it. So he caught the sparrow and pulled every feather out of it and was pleased by its screams. So why should I see him? They say he loves to see heretics burned alive. They say he flogs himself until he is almost dead. What kind of man is that?

"In fact," said Richard, "what is a Christian anyhow? Most of the clergy seems to be so vile and the people hate it so that the word of contempt is not now, I'd rather be a Jew but I'd rather be a priest. My teacher said, What part of speech is peasant? A noun. What sort of noun? Jewish. Why? Because the peasant is as silly as a Jew. But Christians now say he's as silly as a priest. Does God reveal his purpose through such men?"

"What do you think?"

"Our teacher said the monk is not proud because he's a good man. He's proud because he has two teeth from the prophet Amos, or a part of St. Martin's beard, or a fingernail from John the Baptist, or a toe-bone from St. Helena, or the jawbone of St. Sixtus, or a handful of hay from the manger, or a splinter from the cross, or a pint of milk from the breasts of the Virgin, or a few ashes—"

"Enough," said Hillel. "Such a list can become pretty tiresome to a doctor. Have you finished?"

"No. I'm thinking now about the seduction of women in the confessional. What can be lower than a priest who uses a woman's confessions to seduce her? And what does the Church say? Why, it says that a woman must be very careful in the language she uses, so she won't arouse the lust of her confessor! And what do the Dominicans and Franciscans say? Why, that the woman if seduced should not confess to her lover, but that if she does confess to him then he has power to absolve both her and him!"

Hillel smiled. He had been closely observing Richard. He now said, "Wait till I bring us some wine." He went into the other small room and returned with a jug and two cups. He poured wine into the cups and said, "I don't usually indulge myself in wine as good as this. Here, let us drink."

Richard drank and wiped his mouth with the back of his hand. He coughed a little and said, "I don't know anything about wines or about anything. I'm an awfully ignorant person."

"You seem to be learning fast. Have you any more you want to tell?"

"I had heard that bishops, these holy men of God, wage war on one another. Not long ago—it was since my father was born—the abbey of St. Tron was attacked by the bishops of Metz and Liège and every person there was butchered. Are these Christians? And our teacher said that every discovery of science, every invention, even this light on your table is the work of the Devil. The Church says so."

"Medicine above all," said Hillel.

"Yes. Well, the Church says disease comes from God and it's a sin to do anything about it."

"You seem to have had quite a teacher at Toulouse."

"A heretic," Richard said.

"I had come to that conclusion," said Hillel drily. "Did he tell you that every new truth is heresy in its time?"

"Is it?"

"What do you think?"

"I guess it is. Then there can't be progress without heresy."

"As long as there are men who dare to be heretics and are willing to pay the price. But are you willing?"

"Yes, but if a man pays the price he should leave something, shouldn't he? It would be stupid to rot in a dungeon or burn at the stake if you leave nothing behind that will help destroy the stake and the dungeon."

"That's true."

"I'd like to leave something but what could I leave?"

"We don't yet know, Richard. Now you said that you had been imprudent. What is that story?"

Richard emptied his cup and Hillel leaned forward to fill it. Then Richard met his eyes and said with a shudder, "That's the hard part to tell. I talk too damned much. It takes time to learn what not to say."

163

"Or to whom."

"Yes. Well, there's Madelon. I guess she's dying. I don't know why. They say around here that Satan came and seduced her. I don't believe it. I think Father Luce has done something to her. And there she is, like a corpse, unable to speak or move and when I saw her—well, I said some things. I said them to her father."

"All right, tell me what you said."

"I don't remember very well. I called Father Luce some terrible thing. And when her father said that I must accept the faith and believe that the holy men of the Church can do no wrong I said to hell with it."

"You did? To Madelon's father?"

"But that's not all. I have to tell you the whole truth. My sister. . . . Well, some time somewhere my sister heard me say things to my father. Father Luce came to see her and he dragged confessions out of her. She told him I had said that a wicked priest pollutes the sacrament. She told him I had said that a wicked pope does not speak for God. She told him—"

Hillel raised a hand. "That's enough, Richard. That's more than enough. My God, man, that's enough to get you burned twice over." Hillel had been very quiet but he now seemed agitated. He filled his cup and drank it off.

"Richard, you've been very imprudent. Now I must say some things."

"Tell me what a fool I am," Richard said.

"I'll do that. Your confessions don't surprise me at all, for I knew you were hot-headed and I doubted that prudence was in you. But you ought to have sense enough to know that if you want to become a learned man and leave behind you some benefit to mankind, that will be the light you die with, if you should die a terrible death, you have at least to be circumspect until your work is done. If at your age, before your work is begun, you go around spouting heretical notions you'll have the inquisitors on your neck before you have even made a start. Don't you understand that?"

"By the merciful God, yes, I do."

"But apparently not well enough. Can't you control your tongue?"

"When I saw her lying there—"

164

"Yes, yes, I know. I know how you felt. But you may see a lot of things that will sicken and anger you. How long—"

"I'm awfully sorry," Richard said and his shame was deep.

"But you'll say such things again. You may hear that Pope Gregory said that ignorance is the mother of devotion. Then—"

"Isn't it?" Richard asked.

"There you go!"

"To you I say such things. Not to anybody else."

"No, Richard. You've just admitted that you talk too much. You seem not to realize that Jews have a hard enough time at best."

"I know that," said Richard contritely. "But I'll never betray you, never."

"Not willingly. I believe that. But when your emotions are hot nobody can predict what you'll say. You simply have to learn to control your tongue."

"I'll never betray you," Richard muttered, feeling unspeakably worthless. "Not even torture can make me do that."

"Further," said Hillel, "you don't seem to understand that there are good things in your religion—very possibly in any religion. It's foolish to condemn your Church merely because there are evil men in it."

"But what is it? It's not what Jesus taught, is it? Jesus taught love and brotherhood, didn't he? What would he think of bishops who butcher all the people in an abbey? What would he think of Father Luce?" He looked at his empty cup.

"Are you going to get drunk? Wine, you know, hinges the tongue at both ends. You're welcome to it but if you drink any more you'd better spend the night here."

"I'd like to. Spend the night here, I mean."

Hillel filled the cup. "Before you drink again listen a moment. Does Father Luce now have you in his power?"

"I suppose he has."

"Your sister could be put to torture, you know."

"I know it."

"And your father."

"Yes."

"Does Father Luce have some reason to hate or fear you?"

"None that I know of. Oh, there's another thing I haven't told you. I'm sure he seduced Madelon. Isn't that what these foul priests—"

165

"Now wait a minute! The priests have something on their side, haven't they? It's really too much to expect a healthy man to be celibate. It may be that your Church made a grave mistake when it demanded celibacy in its clergy."

"But do they have to choose helpless girls? Does he now have to fix his damned lustful eyes on my sister?"

"Oh?" said Hillel. "Is that it?"

"I'm sure that's it. He asked her to put herself under his guidance and trust him. That's the way he started with Madelon."

"Well, if it is his wish to seduce your sister I don't suppose he would bring any charges against you."

Choking, Richard said: "He'll never seduce her as long as I live!"

"I know how you feel about it. But if it's to be a fight between you and Father Luce—after all, isn't he one of the inquisitors in this area?"

"I guess so."

"In a struggle against him what advantages would you have?"

"I could kill him. Better that than to rot in a dungeon or burn at a stake."

"But what about this legacy you wish to leave to mankind? Don't you see how you're in the power of emotions that will defeat you?"

"You mean I should let him have my sister?"

"I mean, Richard, you obstinate jackass, that you don't have anything to fight with. Your concern about your sister is one thing. Your helplessness in a situation is another."

"I could take her away."

"Not until she's free."

"I could work and earn money and buy her freedom."

Richard drank again and they were silent. He could hear the damned moaning melancholy of the wind and he hated it and he thought of Madelon lying over in the hut and he hated and above all he hated his own helplessness. He knew that Hillel was right: there was nothing he could do.

Hillel said: "You tell me people are saying that Madelon was visited by Satan. What do you suppose is the origin of the story? I sometimes think that so many Christian women turn to Satan because he gives them a higher social position and more dignity and pride and sense of meaning. After all, if they plunged men into mortal sin, from which they must clamber out like beasts from a pit to save themselves, it was quite an achievement and it gives them quite a distinction, doesn't it? And what does Satan think of the whole thing?"

Sensing that Hillel was amused Richard looked at him. "You seem to think it's all pretty funny."

"Or tragic, depending on how you look at it. I've heard that Satan's power of impersonation is so extraordinary that women sometimes give birth to children that have a remarkable likeness to the parish priest."

Richard was staring at him. It took him a few moments to grasp Hillel's dry irony. Then he smiled. "Remarkable," he said.

"And isn't it strange that if the sign of the cross can put him to flight he is not forever fleeing?—for it takes so little effort to make that sign."

"Remarkable!" Richard said.

"Another thing that occurs to me," said Hillel, his face touched, but only faintly, with humor, "is that neither your people nor mine are very decent to women—but mine I sometimes think more than yours, for the sexual embrace is no sin with us and we do believe in tenderness between husband and wife. Christian chivalry looks to me like an enormous system of bigamy. Do you know what the life of a highborn lady is like? Why, she must forever feign the most ardent feelings toward all the silly parasites who pretend they're eager to go out and die for her. Is it any wonder that many Christian women want to be brides of Christ or that languishing with desire they lie month after month, year after year on their beds, too weak to rise? Was that perhaps Madelon's case?"

"I don't know. Would you see her?"

"You know the risk a Jewish doctor takes when he sees a Christian?"

"Forgive me. It doesn't matter, she'll die anyway."

"It probably doesn't matter, Richard, in this awful world where death is as common as diarrhea. We doctors know how little it matters. But it matters to you if you really love her, though I would tell you this, that if you expect to become a learned man and a scholar you'll find little time for a wife and family. Learning is not tolerant of rivals."

"Is that," asked Richard, looking at him, "the reason you never married?"

"One. There are others. Now tell me before you drink any more what you intend to do."

"I don't know."

"Have you learned to write?"

"No."

"Are you willing to learn?"

"Can a man be a scholar and not know how to write?"

"Will you learn Latin?"

"I'll learn anything anyone will teach me."

Hillel brought his long slender hands up and clasped his beard and was thoughtful. "I need an assistant," he said at last. "Would you like that?"

"Would I! How in the world can you ask? What would I rather be than your assistant?"

"I'm a Jew, remember."

"I wish I was," Richard said.

"I don't think association with a Jew is grounds for heresy but I'm not sure. You'd better ask Father Raoul. And if he says it's all right then it might be best for you to live with me. I can arrange for two beds. You can eat with me. I can't pay you anything until you have learned to write. You—" Hillel broke off and leaned forward. "Richard, what is the trouble?"

Richard had burst into tears. He now sank to his knees and groped toward Hillel and rested his head against him.

"Come, come, Richard, be a man."

"I—I can't help it!"

Hillel helped him back to his stool and said, "Here, another cup of wine." He poured the cup full. He then took Richard's right forefinger and placed it against his left wrist. "Can you feel anything?"

"A little," Richard said.

"What is it like?"

"It—it beats."

"You know," said Hillel, sitting back, "I have an idea that blood flows through the whole body. If not, why does the heart beat? It's only an idea I have and you'll say nothing about it. I've a number of ideas but I can't prove them." He turned to papers on the table and picked up one. "Come over here to the light."

168

Richard moved over and Hillel held the paper by the candle and indicated a number of words. "Do those mean anything to you?"

"No," Richard said.

"The words say, If the beating of the heart drives blood all through the body we will have to change our notions about the causes of disease. That's what the words say. When you have learned to write you will be my scribe and words will mean something to you."

Richard stared at the words that Hillel had read. He was not thinking about blood flowing through the body but about words and about how wonderful it would be when he could write as well as read and be Hillel's scribe and copy Hillel's thoughts for men of the future. He turned impulsively and clasped Hillel's face and kissed his forehead.

"You're a little drunk," Hillel said. "Here, sit."

Richard struggled back to the stool and wiped shamefully at his eyes.

"I'll see about another bed now," Hillel said and went into the other room.

Left alone, Richard stood up and moved softly to the table and bent forward under the light to look at the papers on which Hillel had written. He touched them as he might have touched Madelon's cheek or the bones of Abelard or the robe of Gerart. For him the presence of God filled this room.

XIV

Richard had spirit because he had intelligence, and pride because he had both. He had little sense of irony because he was too young and too intense, but a great sense of dedication because he was unwilling to die. With the devotion that Hillel had sensed in him but had never seen in another man he gave himself to his mentor and would have worked day and night if he had been allowed to do so. His first task was to learn to write in his native tongue and to read Latin, for until he had mastered these two accomplishments he would be pupil instead of scribe. He was to discover what he had already suspected, that Hillel was a learned man, and Richard fed eagerly at his mouth, as one whose hunger to know had for years been deeper in him than his hunger for food. And as he learned it was inevitable that his heresy should take on breadth and depth of meaning.

He soon rejected Pope Gregory's statement that the Christian Church had never erred and would never err to the end of time. He hugged to him Augustine's word, that God had given intelligence to man that he might not need to assent in pure faith but would demand proof of what he believed; and Abelard's words that through doubt a man was led to investigate and through investigation perceived truth; and Hillel's words that God's revelation to any man was measured by his power to understand. He saw new meaning in an old song: God be in my head and in my understanding; God be in mine eyes and in my looking; God be in my mouth and in my speaking; God be in my heart and in my thinking; God be at my end and at my departing. He decided to learn write Latin as well as to read it and one day formed the words: in antiquis est scientia. How true that was! But his

Church, it seemed, had destroyed all the pagan books it could get its hands on and might have obliterated the ancient learning from the face of the earth, or most of it, if it had not fallen into the keeping of the Arabs, who had brought it to Europe. Some of the Romans, he began to understand, had been great thinkers: vincit omnia veritas—truth conquers all things; orator fit, poeta nascitur—an orator is made, the poet is born. Windows were opened to him on the deeper truths of human nature: est quaedam fiere voluptas—there is a certain pleasure in weeping; igran dolori sono muti—great griefs are mute. There was revealed to him an ancient compassion for the common people which his Church seemed not to have at all: vox populi, vox Dei—the voice of the people is the voice of God; salus populi suprema lex esto—let the welfare of the people be the supreme law. There grew in him the notion that he ought to have a motto, a star to steer by, and for days he gave his heart to one and another. Should it be in vino veritas?—which he translated, One talks too much when drunk. Or should it be amicus humani generis?—a friend of mankind. Or fide, sed cui vide?—trust, but take care whom. Or vitam impendere vero?—to devote one's life to truth. At last he settled on two simple words: Fiat lux! Let there be light!

Fiat lux! A whole world, a whole universe, was opening to him, the existence of which he had only dimly suspected, and knowledge of which his Church would have concealed from him and all people like him forever. When not busy with his studies or his writing or the baron Hillel would talk to him, sometimes dropping a casual remark and turning back to his table. "Are you beginning to understand why your Church is burning the works of Aristotle?" Or he would hand him a scrap of parchment, saying, "Here are two lines of poetry you may like."

Richard would read:

> The written word alone flouts destiny,
> revives the past and gives the lie to death.

Or Hillel would say, "Here's a line I like from Virgil's Georgics." Richard read:

> A crimson sky at dawn; and rain; at evening, light.

He liked it. It went into him like love.

Or, smiling in his faint enigmatic way, Hillel would observe:

171

"At the university in Paris they specialize in logic. The story is told of a young man who spent three years there and came home and said to his father, You think there are only three eggs on the table but I can prove there are six. The father ate the three eggs and told his son to eat the other three."

Richard would then wonder about Hillel and the sly things he said; and he would wonder about him when with dry humor Hillel adverted upon his own people. "Mazol tov, said Abraham to Isaac. In our language that means good luck. Isaac, you see, had just copulated with his wife and Abraham was hoping that he had not wasted his seed."

Richard sometimes wondered if he was being rebuked. "Am I Isaac?" he said.

"You don't waste your seed, do you?"

Richard flushed. Burning with shame he glanced over at his bed in a corner, knowing that Hillel had seen something there.

"Where there is no mikva," said Hillel, bending over his papers, "bathe in the icy waters of the river."

Richard's confusion and shame deepened. An hour later he slipped away and went to the river to bathe.

One day Hillel rested from his labors and said: "My people are absurd the way they multiply sophistries out of ancient primitive meanings. But the Christians! Do you know the story of David and Bathsheba?"

"I guess not," said Richard, wondering what was coming.

"It's a simple story. The lecherous David, seeing the beautiful woman naked, sent for her and put her to bed at once. As king in those times that was his privilege. It was also his privilege to have her poor stupid husband shoved into the front line of battle where he would get a lance through his guts. Augustine, who in his early years wenched as much as any man on earth but who in his later years decided that wenching is a dreadful sin, made a wonderful conversion of David's lust.

"According to him David didn't use his staff on her at all. David simply means strong of hand—not of penis—and Bathsheba means the seventh well, for is not the Church the well of living waters? So Augustine comes up with a spiritual consummation in seven times seven. As for the stupid Uriah, he is nothing more than the evil principle. The Church without spot or wrinkle, wen or wart is wedded to her holy savior, and since Hit-

172

tite means cut off—according to Augustine—and since Uriah was a Hittite, what can it mean except that he was cut off from the light of God? The poor devil didn't get a lance run through him after all. David was simply enamored of the Church bathing upon the roof and he killed the devil and married the Church. In such nonsense men waste their intelligence while trying to deny their staff and stones."

Gazing benignly at Richard for a moment he said: "If Augustine could see so much in so little, dare any man doubt that Christians can excommunicate the fish in the river? For they do resemble the penis, through no fault of their own. Why do you suppose the early Christians called Jesus the Big Fish and themselves the little fishes and why do you suppose they eat fish on Friday?"

"Don't ask me," said Richard. "I haven't any idea."

"Don't you ever think about such things? Isn't Jesus supposed to have been crucified on Friday? What better thing to eat on that day of death than a symbol of the fructifying powers?"

Such exercitations bewildered Richard. He could never tell when Hillel was gently scoffing and when he was in dead earnest. He found the man very exciting, like a line of great poetry, but terrifying too, like an image hovering above him in the dark; and often when thinking about Hillel he recalled the Roman statement that the eagle did not eat flies.

"Did you know that Christians think and live almost entirely in symbols?"

"No," Richard said and got ready for another parable.

"Do you understand the Mass?"

"No."

"Would you like to?"

"Of course," said Richard, wondering how Hillel knew so much about Christian things.

"The antiphonal chanting stands for the aspirations and deeds and prayers of the ancient patriarchs and prophets who were looking for the coming of the son of God—but who in fact were looking for nothing of the sort. The chanting of the clergy is supposed to convey the yearning of the saints of the ancient law—that is, of the Hebrew Law. The bishop in his sacred robes coming out of the sacristy and walking to the altar represents Jesus emerging from the Virgin's womb, but Jesus never robed himself in velvet and jewels and physiology raises some doubt that his mother was a virgin. The seven lights are intended to be the gifts of the holy spirit descending upon Jesus. The two acolytes who precede him are the Law and the Prophets—both Jewish unfortunately. The four upholding the canopy are Matthew, Mark, Luke and John carrying the gospels. The bishop sits and puts aside his mitre and is silent, because Jesus is supposed to have been silent for thirty years. When the epistle is read the reader turns to the north, for John the Baptist is preaching to the Jews, and in the north the sun of the ancient Law shines no more. When he is done he bows to the bishop, as John is supposed to have bowed to Jesus.

"In the responsorium," Hillel went on, speaking slowly and quietly, "John is still the main person until the gospel is read, which indicates the beginning of the ministry of Jesus. The twelve parts of the creed are the twelve apostles. Qui nimium probat nihil probat. I'll not weary you with all of it. But I think it strange that so many persons go to the Mass so many times without understanding it. I wish I had Abelard's Historia calamitatum. You ought to read it."

"I hope to," said Richard fervently.

"But knowledge adds to sorrow?"

"I've thought about that. It's the kind of sorrow a man can bear."

"Fine," said Hillel. "You're a good student."

One morning Hillel put on his yellow badge of infamy and slipped out, leaving Richard struggling with a Latin text. Hillel had decided to see Madelon. He saw Chretien first and went up to him and said, "May I see your daughter?"

"If you want to," said Chretien and led Hillel to the house.

Hillel looked in and sniffed the evil smells and thought he detected among them the odor of death. After a while he made out Madelon's form in a far corner and stepped inside and, bent over, approached her. When Chretien darkened the doorway Hillel turned to say, "Let me have light, please." Chretien stepped inside and stood by a wall. Hillel knelt by Madelon and looked at her ghastly wasted face and open staring eyes. He moved a hand before her eyes and she did not blink. He took one of her hands to feel her pulse but it was so feeble that he could feel nothing there; and then he bowed and put an ear to her breast. He thought he could hear very faint movement of the heart.

He arose and went outside and Chretien followed him out.

"Do you give her food and drink?"

"We have to force it down her," Chretien said.

"Does she swallow?"

"When I rub up and down her throat."

"How long since she has spoken or made a sound?"

"Quite a while."

"Does she ever move?"

"No."

"Not even a hand or her eyelids?"

"No."

Simone had come up and Hillel looked at her. "You're getting to be a young woman," he said. "Will you be marrying soon?"

"Richard should marry her," Chretien said.

"Why?"

"She's as good as he can do."

"Well, maybe he will."

As Hillel turned away Chretien said: "Is there anything you can do for her?"

"I don't think so."

"Is she dying?"

"All people are dying. We are a day nearer death for every day we live." He then looked at Chretien's eyes and saw something strange there, as if the man had sly and malign knowledge of things.

"My daughter will be a saint," said Chretien.

"A saint?" said Hillel, startled.

"A saint," said Chretien, and Hillel thought one sinister eyelid winked.

Deep in thought Hillel returned to his house and took off his badge. He sat at the table and bent to his studies but that evening he said to Richard: "I went over to have a look at Madelon." At once Richard began to shiver and Hillel fetched a coarse blanket and draped it around him. "It has turned colder," Hillel said.

Suspecting another parable Richard said: "You mean for Madelon?"

"I don't know what's wrong with her, Richard. It looks like poison."

"Poison! You mean Father Luce—"

"Fide, sed cui vide."

"Yes," said Richard and swallowed hard.

175

"I don't think she is suffering. I think she'll be dead soon."

A few days later Madelon died but Richard did not go to see her corpse or to see her buried. He did go once to her grave. The cemetery outside Patres, like most Christian cemeteries, was an unsightly wilderness of dung heaps and of holes where pigs had rooted, for beasts both tame and wild prowled as scavengers through graveyards. There was no headstone nor anything to mark the spot where the gentle Madelon lay but he knew the spot by the freshness of its earth and he sat by the grave and let his tears fall. Est quaedam fiere voluptas! he thought fiercely, bitterly but he could not hold the tears back. He had loved her, it seemed to him now, more deeply than he had known, but he had loved her, he now understood in the light of Hillel's wisdom, as a symbol, as a symbol of what was most pure and holy in life. She had been his Heloise and now the poor sad thing lay in the earth and would never know that he had loved her, would never know how vilely she had been used. "Poor sweet Madelon!" he murmured, his tears falling. "Poor tired little Madelon whose heart was with God! You'll never know, not now, not ever! If somewhere your soul hears me then listen to my promise, that all my life, all my life I will fight to destroy the ignorance that makes wicked men and the wickedness that destroyed you! If I can leave something behind me—Madelon, do you hear and understand? . . . Madelon, now farewell!"

But he could not rise and leave her. He could not put away from him an image of her thin little face down there in the earth, in the dark, alone. He tried to rise but remained here, sitting by the grave, clasping a little of its earth in his hands; hating, cursing, despairing, yet under all his dreadful bitterness feeling an angry and invincible strength, feeling that he would, that he must, leave some goodness to mark his spot, some noble legacy to mankind. . . .

He was still there when darkness came, and Hillel. Hillel put arms around him and helped him to his feet and led him back to the house; and on the way they passed Father Luce and Hillel knew it but Richard did not know it.

A week later Richard's father died. As was the custom, his body was borne to the church on a litter. As was the custom, a member of the Church came to claim the monastic hariot, that is, to take the best beast or chattel, left on the death of a husband, no matter how poor the family was. Victoir had had no beasts. Father Luce came to the hovel at a moment when Richard was there and he stood looking at Richard, with his black too-close-together hypnotic eyes. Then he entered the shack and examined its furnishings but could find nothing of value. He came out and looked down at Richard's fine leather boots.

Believing that the priest would again meet his eyes after the appraisal was done Richard got ready for him but when at last the eyes turned on him he was not prepared for what he saw. It was something that he could not define, a sort of bright canny knowledge of him that was almost like a light in the black depths. For a moment they stood thus, each trying to take the measure of the other.

"Are the boots yours?" Father Luce asked.

"Yes."

"Did you earn the money to buy them?"

"A lady gave them to me."

"A lady?"

At this moment Fleur came up and stood by Richard and slipped a hand into his palm. Father Luce saw the gesture. He met Richard's eyes again and then looked at Fleur. As he stared at the girl his eyes changed or perhaps the change was not so much in his eyes as in his face. He smiled and he intended his smile to be warm and fatherly.

He said to Fleur: "My child, come over here. I want to talk to you."

"Oh no you don't!" said Richard and tightened his clasp on Fleur's hand.

Again Father Luce met Richard's gaze. "What do you mean?" There was nothing warm and fatherly in his face now.

Fide, sed cui vide! Richard knew that he had gone too far. "She's very upset," he said. "I don't think she wants to talk to anyone."

"She needs comforting," said Father Luce. "Child, come with me."

Fleur looked up at Richard. "Go over to the bench with him," Richard said. "I'll wait."

Father Luce went to the bench with Fleur and they sat there and he talked to her. Richard stood where he was and looked at them and listened but the priest was talking in a low voice and Richard could not hear what he said. He sensed that a desperate struggle was shaping up between him and Father Luce and he felt miserably helpless, for what powers did he have on his side? The priest had on his side all the might of the Church, all the powers of an inquisitor, and his own ruthless nature that would stop at nothing. Richard was frightened but he was determined that Fleur would not be another Madelon, even if it were to cost him his life. Yet what could he do? If he resisted the priest's will he would be summoned for heresy, and Gerart had told his students that no person summoned for heresy ever escaped. If he were to kill he would then be killed, and gone would be his dream of himself as a scholar devoted to truth. Gone would be Fleur. If he resisted, they were both doomed; if he did not resist she was doomed and he would be safe with his shame and his cowardice.

"What in the world can I do?" he asked Hillel later. "I've about as much chance as a rabbit when Baron Guillem goes out with his dogs."

"Are you sure this man wants your sister that way?"

"I can't doubt it at all."

"It couldn't be that you're attracted to her yourself and so imagine things?"

Richard looked at Hillel. What did the man mean? This sounded like an echo of what his own mother had said.

"Did your sister tell you what the priest said to her?"

"He pledged her to secrecy. She told me a little but only a little, for he has her scared."

"What did she tell you?"

"Oh—only that he's a holy man and she must trust him and all that stuff. By God, I'll not believe in a religion that gives men such power over women! There's something rotten in a religion—"

"There you go again. Don't you realize that there are men whom no religion could save? If this man were a Muslim or a Jew I suppose he'd be about what he is now. Don't confuse religious principles with the men who debauch them."

"You think there are men who are born evil?"

"I don't think we are born either evil or good but some have greater capacity for evil. Could Father Raoul help you?"

"He'd be afraid to try."

"Isn't there some man Fleur could marry?"

"She's only ten."

"Surely Father Luce wouldn't want to lie with her before she's nubile, would he? And the moment she's nubile she can marry."

"I don't think he'll wait for that."

"Well, don't worry about it now. I'll see if there's anything I can do."

Hillel had in mind that he could speak to Baron Guillem but he doubted that that would be wise. After all, he had gone a long way for a Jew, whose own life was precarious enough, when he took Richard in and gave him food and friendship. He could not save every person threatened by evil or even try to, without bringing dreadful things upon his own head; but he decided nevertheless to talk to Baron Guillem to see if something might be done.

XV

Most people in the area roundabout and the poorer people above all envied Baron Guillem, whose gay pennon fluttered from a lofty staff atop a castle tower; who lived in a big fortified castle with knights and squires to serve him; who had profited enormously and was still profiting from the Church's persecution and destruction of the most cultured and civilized group of people in southern France; who had broad acres and pasturelands, hay granaries, stacks of wheat, barley and oats, many storehouses, mills, cattle byres, slaughter and salting houses, gardens, hunting steeds and dogs, costly garments and scents and foods and wines, and his own chapel, completely furnished, in which Mass was said every day. He spent his time in hawking and hunting, gluttony and drink and lechery.

But these people who saw the great walls of his castle and heard the neighing of his many horses and the baying of his many hounds and the clear call of his horns, these people did not know that the interior of the castle was dank, gloomy and depressing and in its atmosphere more like a dungeon than a house of revelry; with dark and narrow halls and drafty rooms in wintertime; with chickens and small beasts running everywhere and with a sickening odor of human and beast filling it from cellars to attics. In this time there were no brilliant tapestries hung up to cover the ugly stone walls from which the mortar was crumbling; no deep carpeting on stone floors but only rushes and straw mats and a stinking depth of hay and straw and old dead plants and flowers in which there was a long accumulation of filth—of excrement and vomit, of snot blown from noses and bones thrown to dogs, of chicken and dog droppings, of vermin and insects and old decay.

The windows were only small holes unglazed, which were sometimes covered with wooden shutters or oiled paper but most commonly with nothing at all; the tables were of ordinary plank; and only a few of the stools and settees were upholstered and the upholstery on these was teeming with lice.

The poor people heard that his life was more sumptuous and magnificent than that of any Roman emperor. They did not know that the lords and ladies usually slept with most and in wintertime all their clothes on, on beds that lacked springs and at best had only a mattress stuffed with straw or wool. The bed of Guillem and Elienor—though of late he had refused to let her share it—was under a great canopy of heavy curtains, set upon a platform. After Guillem retired, servants drew the heavy curtains together and he was a prisoner without a breath of fresh air, fighting the mosquitoes that bred by the millions in his foul moats and poured through the open windows; fighting vermin in a mass of bedding that was almost never cleaned or even hung outside to ventilate; scratching himself until he was raw and bleeding; cursing, tossing all night, until at the ringing of the morning bells he arose for another day. Having been dressed by his servants, who had slept on straw pallets, he would walk across a floor recently strewn with lilies, flags, mint, thyme, roses, all now mixed with the offal of dogs, cats, chickens and children.

The poor people heard him singing when he set off to hawk or hunt and they thought he was a happy man—

> By day mine eyes, by night my soul desires you!
> Still let me love, thought I may not possess. . . .

They were thrilled by his deep voice when he went thundering forth:

> Peace delights me not!
> War—be thou my lot!
> Law—I do not know
> save a right good blow. . . .

There were tales told of his nightlong, sometimes his weeklong, carnal carousals but Guillem had never been a very erotic man, nor a gallant man. In his younger years he had no taste, as some knights had, for the great risk of dashing into the brothels, which some of the nunneries had become, to carry the virgins of noble

181

birth away to safety. In trying to nourish and cultivate such amorous desires as he had he had devoured every aphrodisiac known to man, including hot spices and strange herbs imported from the East, with the result that he had ruined his stomach and practically his whole alimentary tract, and now suffered from horrible cramps and bellyaches and excruciating vomitings, as well as from skin rashes and diseases and open sores that baffled all of Hillel's medical skill. People had a picture of him as a glutton drinking huge quantities of rare wines and engorging tableloads of sausages and venison and beef and boar and stag and pottages and sauces and sweetmeats; and it was true that in his prime he had been able to drink or eat almost any man under the table. But now he was sick from too many rich sauces, too many strong spices. Because there was no way to keep meat fresh Guillem like other nobles often ate it when it was half-decayed, trying to hide its nauseating flavor and make it more palatable by drenching it with strong sauces and highly seasoned gravies; and many a time Guillem had bent double and discharged the contents of his outraged stomach into the depths of the filth that covered his dining floor. Many a time he had hoped to God he might die.

It was told among the common people that he not only had lackeys everywhere to applaud his feats or his efforts to make music with the gigue and the gittern but that beautiful women also waited on him adoringly, washing his tired feet and digging wax out of his ears and lice out of his hair; but Elienor had never been that kind of wife. She despised the fat round-gutted glutton and hoped he would die. It is true that when he gave a big supper the guests smacked loudly over roast crane and stag-in-sauce and dripping puddings and loudly applauded his boasting or his singing; but they despised him too.

He itched intolerably even while singing and boasting, for under the sheets of iron which he wore when boar-hunting or jousting he had a thick heavy stuffing of cloth sewn, to keep his flesh from chafing; but in the heat and sweat his flesh became red and raw and swollen and tortured him day and night and his scrotum nearly drove him mad with an itching rash. His banal and obscene verses which he composed and sang; his knights around him in burnished armor and emblazoned surcoat; his pages in silk and gold; and his own doublet of silk drawn tight over his paunch, his tight hose on his itching legs, his cloak of

182

heavy velvet and fur, which made the sweat pour from his tormented and despairing frame, as well as his tuneless twanging on viol or harp—all these and more were a part of the kind of life the idle rich had got themselves into and which they hated even more than the poor envied it. Not all of them were as suffering and tortured, as bored and weary, as obsessed and goaded and stung as Baron Guillem; but even a young knight, when at a feast he stood up to recite his boastful lays, was seen to dig under his garments and scratch, while he sang of peerless charms and ripe red lips and of himself as the flower of chivalry upon whose sword a thousand ladies were laying their hearts. And Baron Guillem with a snort that would have blown a child down loved to tell about the more elderly warriors who, when encased in their paddings and metal, had to piss down their legs for the reason that they couldn't get their penis out. Lord, how he would snort over that. "And sometimes," he would say in an aside to a lady, staring at him like an owl in daylight, "they shit down their legs too."

Hillel, who had been Guillem's physician for years, and who because of this had been shielded against persecution and abuse, knew the story of the idle rich, for he had been at the feasting and drinking and had seen the pathetic buffoonery and heard the loud boasting. He had seen the skin diseases under the velvets and silks. He had smelled the sickening stink of the castle chambers and of its people who, to conceal their odors, drenched themselves with more and more scents. He did not think that Guillem had ever taken a bath and he would not have bet a sou on Elienor. Her face sometimes looked to him as though she had put on one layer after another of mare's milk paste, without ever washing a layer off. It was little wonder that the highborn when they went strolling or hawking broke off boughs of hawthorn or other sweet plants in which to bury their faces. Every peasant in all the broad lands of Europe had heard the story that the first thing a knight and his lady-love did when they met at a tryst was to strip off their clothes and bathe. Many a peasant wondered why they did that.

Highborn life amused Hillel, a fastidious man who put on a clean garment before sitting to his studies and who washed his hands and dipped his fingers in rose-water before touching the pages of a great poet. And he despaired of ever getting any sense into the head of Baron Guillem.

The baron had a round moon of a face, heavy lips that looked saturated with sensuality, a short beard but no mustaches, silken brown hair, and dark gray eyes in which the only or at least the habitual emotion was cruelty. One day his steed had got frightened and thrown him off and in dreadful wrath he had hacked the beast to death with his weapons. He thought no more of running over a peasant child than of spearing a boar. He was lord of his manor and the only power on earth he was afraid of was the Church in Rome. And he was not much afraid of that: the hierarchs needed the barons as much as the barons needed them. It was as though they had united to decimate and exploit the earth for their own enrichment: the Church owned most of the wealth of Europe but the secular lords also had great holdings and titles and annuities and Guillem had dreamed of being a king before disease and itching laid him low.

Hillel had begged him to keep himself clean but Guillem had snorted and said, "Who bathes except Arabs and Jews? Water is for those who indulge their baser passions."

Hillel had not disputed with him. Nobody dared to dispute with Guillem. Hillel had applied ointments and salves to the baron's sores and itching spots and because these always soothed him Guillem thought Hillel a doctor of extraordinary genius and bestowed upon him extraordinary emolument. Hillel was very shrewd in his anointing and massaging, in his choice of poultices and physics and painkillers. He kept the baron's bowels open and as well as he was able his stomach cleaned out. He gave him mild drugs to induce sleep. He flattered and soothed him and lulled his suspicions. And though the baron in his heart despised Hillel because he was a Jew the two men had a kind of friendship or in any case a mutual dependence on one another, which they took for granted and not for all the world would have discussed.

The moment that Hillel decided to talk to Guillem about Richard's problem he knew that he was foolish. The baron would care no more about Richard and his problems than he would care about the death of Victoir or a leper in a gutter or a sick serf dying after huntsmen had run over him. Because Guillem was an inordinately suspicious man Hillel knew that it would be imprudent to mention the matter to him at all. I counsel prudence, Hillel thought, yet what a fool I can be!—to imagine that Guillem can be appealed to in any terms but his itching and pain. It would

184

be stupid to entreat the man. Nevertheless he would go see him, for now that his physical woes were multiplying the baron expected him to come almost daily.

Hillel took a roundabout course, as he usually did, to gather certain herbs by the way, which he crushed or steeped to extract their juices; and while following one of the river paths he saw the Baroness Elienor. She was out strolling, with her hawk on her wrist. Hillel thought her a very vain woman though not so vain as she had been before she got stout. She was a blonde and blondness in this area was the first and highest mark of feminine beauty and she had a blonde's contempt for brunettes. To be among the loveliest of lovely women she would have needed lips as small as a babe's but hers were full and ripe like the baron's; cheeks like peach bloom and she did have a fair skin which she abused with pastes; and a breath as sweet as the censer on the church altar. She chewed aniseed and fennel before breakfast and during the day. The knights, singing to her beauty, said that she was so lovely that her beauty illuminated the castle and no lights were needed. She delighted in such flattery while knowing that it was an empty formula. In earlier years to prove great capacity for love she had, like some other ladies, braved extremes of weather, wearing heavy garments in the hottest months and thin garments in the coldest. She was older now and cynical and dreadfully bored.

"Good morning, my lady," he said and gave her a courtly bow. He was about to pass on when she stopped him.

"In a hurry?"

"My lady, I'm on my way to see his highness." Hillel knew that Guillem was not his highness but he had learned the value of flattery, had learned indeed that no flattery was too extreme. "I hope he feels well this morning."

Elienor unhooded the hawk and said, "Scoot! Go off and kill a duck." The bird flew away and she turned to Hillel. "He grumbles and groans and pukes, if that's what you mean."

"I'm sorry to hear that."

"Oh, hell, you're no more sorry than I am," said Elienor, whose speech was blunt. She looked round her for a place to sit and sank to a grassy hillock and composed herself. "Come sit by me. I want to talk to you."

"Yes, my lady," said Hillel and sat at a respectful distance.

"What do you have there?"

"Some herbs," he said, glancing at the handful.

"Are they any good?"

"The proper selection of herbs helps to maintain a proper balance in the body."

"Such as cool as a cucumber or hot as a pepper?" she asked, mocking him.

"Yes, my lady."

"Can a fool be cured by binding herbs around his neck with a red cloth when the moon is waxing in the sign of the bull?"

"My lady—"

"Does the dry root of asparagus break the spell of a witch and cure toothache and bladder trouble—and should you pluck it just before sunrise and hold a mirror over it?"

"My lady likes to tease doctors because we know so little."

"It looks like my husband will die of itch and running sores. Do you have any cure for those?"

"I have prescribed—"

"Oh, never mind. I don't want to talk about the old boar. Do you have a young man named Richard living with you?"

"Yes, my lady."

"Why?"

"Because I need a scribe. Richard—"

"He went away. How long has he been back?"

"About a month, I think."

"He's very handsome," said Elienor, as though musing. "I told him to come and see me when he returned. Why hasn't he?"

"I cannot say, my lady. Perhaps he thought you were jesting."

"Tell him I wasn't jesting."

"I will tell him."

"Are you teaching him?"

"In a way but he is too intelligent to need much teaching."

"Aren't you aware that our holy Church doesn't believe in learning?"

He met her gaze a moment and saw that she was not serious. She was still mocking him. He said quietly: "I'm not an authority on the doctrines of your holy Church."

Abruptly she said: "Do you know that my husband is a brutal man?"

"His highness—"

"Oh, to hell with his highness. He has—well, he's a false wolf's tooth. If he ever turns on you—" She narrowed her eyes, looking at him.

What does all this mean? he wondered. He said: "I have always done my best."

"Of course, but he cares nothing about that. He cares only about his itching and his bellyaches." Her hawk returned and she attached it to her wrist and hooded it. "Do you know what they have done to Jews in England?" She arose and turned down the path but after a moment she looked back and said: "Tell Richard to come see me. It's a command."

"My lady, I will tell him."

Deeply disturbed, Hillel followed the path toward the castle gardens. He knew that there had been something sinister in her words, some menace or threat or warning. Why had she mentioned the Jews in England? Not long after Hillel was born there had been a dreadful slaughter of Jews in England and the horrible persecution had spread through cities and over the land, all because it was said that when Richard First was crowned and Jews came bearing gifts and pledges of allegiance they were trying to destroy him with their magic. Throughout southern France no devout Jew any longer dared to cleanse the public oven for the Passover baking; and if fire broke out in a Jewish house the owner was usually mobbed and killed as a sorcerer who was plotting against Christians. Jewish doctors everywhere were accused of feeding poison to Christians: had she intended to suggest that he was poisoning the baron? He doubted that this was so, for she had always been friendly toward him, though gently mocking him now and then, as she had done this day. But he was convinced that she had intended her words to convey some meaning.

What a lonely man this Jewish doctor was as he took his way down the path to minister to a Christian who tolerated him only because he needed him! Possibly, Hillel thought, he should go away; for like doctors of all times past, even under the Romans, he had no social rank above that of butcher or tanner; and if he cured a patient he got no credit, and if a patient died he was looked on as an assassin. Had Elienor meant that if Guillem died Hillel's life would not be worth a fig? What a wretched predicament he was in—an accursed Jew trying to heal a Christian who at best looked on him with suspicion; a member of an outcast people who had been suffered only because of his medical skill, whose life would be worth nothing at all if that skill failed. To compound his misfortunes he had taken to his bosom, as friend and brother, because his loneliness was so great, one whose Church would leave in him ignorance and would hate Hillel the Jew for his kindness!

When ushered into the baron's private ill-smelling chamber Hillel found him naked to his waist, sitting on a bench and morosely surveying his huge overhanging paunch. He did not look up or speak for some moments and Hillel knew that he was in an ugly mood. So Hillel stood back, respectful, silent, waiting; and it was a measure of the man's character that he felt neither hate nor contempt but only a doctor's concern for his patient.

"Well," Guillem growled at last, "so you finally got here! Why do you neglect me?"

"Your highness—"

"It has been weeks since you came."

"I was here only day before yesterday."

"You abominable liar. Don't you think I have clocks to measure the passing of time and clerks to record it? Have you been with some slut?"

"Your highness knows that I have no woman."

"By the eyes of God," said Guillem, a very blasphemous man, "you should be glad for that. You've been doctoring me for years and you haven't done a damn thing for me. It's women. It's women, you stupid dog, that have brought me to this misfortune. It was a woman who plunged this whole world into sin. It's women who suck out our substance until we are all itches and sores. Women are the curse of this earth. Are you so ignorant you haven't found that out?"

"Your highness—"

"Don't stand there like an ox in a bog. Do something!"

Hillel hastened over and Guillem looked up at him and said: "I'm worse. I have a pox. I think I'm dying."

"Your highness, I don't think you are worse, but better. You have good color today and your voice is strong."

"Have you found some new medicines?"

"Your highness—"

"Aren't there doctors anywhere who know more than you? Who is the smartest?"

"Many doctors know more than I."

"Who?"

"Jacob ben Abbamari ben Simeon ben Anatoli."

"Where is he?"

"At the court of the Emperor Frederic. The emperor has commissioned him to introduce all of Arab learning to Europe. Anatoli is a great philosopher but not a doctor in the proper sense of the word. He is translating—"

"If he's not a doctor then why by the nostrils of God do you bother me with him? And if he is introducing Arab learning what does the Pope think of him?"

"Your highness, I don't know."

"A hell of a lot Frederic would care what the Pope thinks! That brigand! Can this Anatoli cure the itch?"

"I don't know. He's a learned man—"

"How learned? Does he know that women are the cause of disease?" Guillem raised his cold gray eyes to look at Hillel. "Do you know it? I covered one of these damned peasant sluts last year and now I have boils and itching all over me and stuff runs out of my tube. You have no cure. Then why in hell do you grab my gold every time you come here? Am I paying you to torture me?"

"I can only prescribe," said Hillel a little impatiently. "You won't do most of the things I would have you do."

"What?" asked Guillem glaring at him. "You mean I should soak myself in hot baths? The Pope would excommunicate me if I did. And by the teeth of the Holy Ghost I'd rather be excommunicated than die like a dog in his shit. Go prepare the bath."

Hillel prepared a warm salt water bath in a big earthen tub and Guillem stripped off his clothes and entered it. He lay half-sitting, for the tub would not allow him to stretch out, and was immersed save his head. After a few moments he began to feel soothed and he looked up at Hillel and growled, "You blockhead, why haven't you had me do this before?"

"Your highness—"

"What did you put in this water?"

If Hillel had said nothing but salt Guillem would have been outraged. Hillel lied. He said he had put in the juices from certain healing herbs.

"I'm itching more," said Guillem.

"You will itch more and then less."

"Bring me a flagon of wine."

Hillel had a servant bring wine. Lying in the tub Guillem drank wine and said he was beginning to feel better. Suddenly like a white river-monster he clambered out, hurling water all around him, and stood, dripping and looking down over his sores and with curious interest at his penis, which he could not see under his paunch without leaning forward. Gently with a silken cloth Hillel dried him and gently he rubbed into Guillem's sores a salve made of mutton grease, salt and the juices of plants. He wondered if Guillem had the disease known as the King's Evil.

"Your highness, if I may further prescribe—"

"What in hell do you think I'm paying you for?"

"I suggest that you do not sleep in your bedchamber behind those heavy curtains but that you sleep outside."

"You idiot. Would you have me catch all the night-fevers?"

"The night air will do you good. I also suggest that you be anointed all over with oil and then go out into the sunshine, a little while each day."

"Are you trying to kill me?"

"And I suggest that you do not drink the water from the moats or the river. If you'll let me prepare drinking water for you a servant—"

"With poison in it?"

"And I suggest that you take a warm bath each day, such as you have just had, and that you have your garments washed daily and hung out in the sun before you put them on. And I'd not put on any armor for a while."

"By God's coif," said Guillem, "you're stark mad. If I do what you suggest I'll be dead in a week."

"I think you'll feel much better. One other suggestion I would offer, that you do not eat rich food for a few days, such as roasts and sauces and puddings, but only bread and cabbage and a little milk, if you like milk."

"You're determined to poison me or starve me."

"Your highness, I can only suggest. It is for you to reject."

Guillem bawled for a servant and when the man came he roared, "You fool, bring me my purse." When the purse was brought Guillem tossed it to Hillel, saying, "Take what you want, take all of it. If you don't cure me it will do you no good. If you do, I have underpaid you. I'll do what you say but not till tomorrow, for today the saints are merciful and a man may sin."

XVI

That evening Hillel said to Richard, "I didn't speak to Baron Guillem about your problem. Another idea occurred to me. You know the Baroness Elienor?"

"I've seen her."

"You've done more than that apparently. Didn't she ask you to come see her after you returned?"

"Yes."

"How was she? Friendly?"

"Yes. She gave me money."

"Oh, so that's where you got your money. She must have taken a fancy to you."

Richard colored. "I don't think so," he said. "Why should she be interested in me? She has handsome knights all around her."

"You don't seem to understand. For one thing you're a handsome young man. For another thing any highborn lady with intelligence and spirit gets pretty tired of the patterned love-making of knights."

"I'd never thought about it," Richard said.

"She sent you a message. She wants to know why you haven't come to see her. Do you realize that her invitation was really a command?"

"But why does she want to see me?"

"Are you as stupid as you seem to be? You don't know why she wants to see you?"

"I honestly don't know. She asked if I'd like to be a knight."

"I suppose she asked you a number of questions, as women will of men who interest them. She wants to see you."

"But why?"

191

"Peace be upon us!" cried Hillel. "Don't you know anything about women? She wants to see you because she thinks her husband is an old boar and she's sick and tired of him. She wants to see you because— Look, Richard, haven't we had enough of this?"

"You mean—?"

"She wants you for a lover, of course. Are you interested?"

"No."

"I thought you'd say that. Wait till I bring some wine." Hillel brought wine and filled their cups. Then he looked at Richard, his eyes studying him.

"You think I'm a fool?" Richard asked.

"I think you don't understand. I think I'll have to make it very plain to you." Hillel took a basin with water in it and went outside and hurled the water out while furtively looking all around him. After he had returned and sat he said, "You have a problem with Father Luce. I have one with the baron. He's sick and he's getting sicker and like all sick tyrants he expects a doctor to work miracles and if the doctor doesn't his life isn't worth a skinned owl. Don't do anything you don't wish to do but do understand that we're both in a danger that is growing. Ideals are fine. I have them too. But our enemies have no interest in ideals.

"Baroness Elienor is interested in you. There can be no doubt about it. If you don't handle her with tact she'll become your enemy. If you do, she might become a very powerful friend. In that case she would be able to protect your sister."

"You mean I gaff this fat old woman to save my sister?"

For a moment Hillel showed a touch of anger. "What friends do you have? Father Raoul, a fine and worthy man but he wouldn't lift a finger to save a heretic. You have me. I'm a Jew and what influence I have may soon be gone. You have no powerful friends. Do you understand me?"

"I'm not sure I do," said Richard, feeling more and more unhappy.

"Do you have any choice?"

"You mean with Baroness Elienor?"

"Is there anything you can do but yield?"

"I could go away."

"Tyrants have long arms. Is the thought of intimacy with her so distasteful? I think her very attractive."

192

"It seems to me pretty damned funny," Richard said, "if a Christian has to gaff a woman to save his neck."

Hillel smiled.

"How long before she would kick me out? Then what do I do?"

"That would depend on what kind of lover and man you were. You could be more than lover to her. She's quite intelligent, quite perceptive. What she probably needs is companionship, someone who can talk about more than to flean a hart, case a hare, strip a boar, rouse a buck, bay a marten, dig a badger or bolt a coney— more than hawking and hunting and jousting, more than the dismal and tiresome jargon of men devoted solely to their own pleasures. Maybe she's interested in poetry. Maybe in learning. After all, you know, far more Christian women can read than men. I doubt there's a man in the baron's household who can read."

"Can she?"

"Yes but not well."

"But if I become her friend what will the baron think?"

"Leave that to her."

"And what if she should insist on my becoming a squire or a knight or some damned fool thing like that?"

"I think she's completely fed up with squires and knights."

Richard drank his wine off and stared into the cup. In a low voice he asked, "This is what you think I should do?"

"I don't think there's anything else you can do except to go far away. She has asked you to go see her."

"Then I guess I'll have to."

"I don't know how much you know about her. She's very strong-willed. She has been pampered. Knights and jongleurs have composed verses for her and sung them for her, not only a few times but hundreds of times. Knights have gone forth to battle wearing her chemise and garter. Men have been gallant and courtly, they have entranced her with enchanting flummery, they have turned her head with every superlative in the language. I suppose that she liked it many years ago. Possibly it's a measure of her character that she can stand it no longer. But she is a woman, of course, and she has that very personal vanity so perculiar to women. You won't find her easy."

"I'm stupid," said Richard despairingly. "I know nothing about women or love. She'd find me more tiresome and dull than a knight."

"Not if you'll be yourself. Don't try to compete with the high-born in their empty graces. Just be Richard, who loves learning more than he loves life."

"What if she asks me all kinds of questions? What if this is a trap?"

"No no."

"What if the baron finds us together?"

"I don't think he'd mind. Highborn Christians believe that love and marriage can't exist together."

"Can they?" asked Richard cynically.

"I'm no authority on that."

"Isn't there some country we could go to where people are more civilized?"

"I know of none."

"Not England?"

"God no, not England. There they butchered my people like pigs."

"Spain?"

"You must be feverish."

"Naples?"

"Richard, we just have to make the best of the situation we're in. We have to match wits against wits, cunning against cunning."

"Will it always be this way?"

"I'm no prophet. As far as I can see into the future truth will be fighting for its life."

"Have people always been tortured and thrown into dungeons and all that?"

"Socrates was forced to drink poison. Seneca was forced to kill himself. Jesus was hung on a tree. It's a long list. God knows how many thousands have died to make it possible for us to have the little freedom we have. Other thousands will die for it. Look at my people," Hillel said. "Most of them were killed, the others were dispersed, homeless, hated and they'd all have died if they hadn't developed a kind of armor of their own."

He filled the cups and said: "Life is sometimes sweet—in the ringing of church bells, in the magnificent color and design of great art, in great music; in the humble prayer of a Father Raoul kneeling at an altar; in the devotion of a Jew to the customs of his fathers; in the love of mother and child or husband and wife; in the pledge of brotherhood we made, here under the darkness

194

of the sky and the deeper darkness of human ignorance and superstition; in that occasional devotion to truth which God made inherent in his world leaving the discovery of it to his children. Yes,
there's some sweetness, there's a little light. But under these is the
immense struggle between human wills and passions, the engulfing powers of rapacity and greed and sloth and vanity—a
struggle that goes on all over the earth. There'll never be many
men perhaps who will dare hell and tyranny to try to light a torch."

"I'll go," Richard said. "I'll do what I can."

"I thought you would. Be prudent."

"I'll try."

Hillel returned to his studies and Richard sat in thought.

The next morning he bathed in the river, combed his hair out
with his fingers, with Hillel's razor shaved his beard and with a
piece of rag wiped the dust off his boots. He tried to smile when
he said, "Do I look like a man a baroness would be interested in?"

"It's an idle question. We know that she is."

"Pray for me."

"May your memory be a blessing for good and may your light
shine on."

Richard turned away and set his course toward the pennon fluttering from the tower.

Sensing that Richard would come this day Elienor was being
prepared by two maids, while she looked into a mirror. With most
highborn ladies the favorite color of hair was blond, neither dark
nor golden but a very light brown. Elienor's hair was too dark
and she had found no good way to lighten it. The favorite color
of eyes was vair, that is, blue or azure. The teeth of a lovely lady
should be white, her chin dimpled, her neck and hands and arms
white and long. Her eyes, the poets said, should be filled with an
alluring look, keen and seductive; her lips should be redder than
cochineal. Her nose should be long and straight. Elienor fulfilled
none of these completely but she had been a beautiful girl.
Though now stout from idleness and overeating she was still an
attractive woman.

Her undergarment was a chemise worn next to the skin; its
plaited turned-down collar rose above the rest of her attire and
dandies of both sexes took pride in the way the collar was arranged. Over the chemise was the cote, a long tunic with close-
fitting sleeves; and over this was the surcote, the most important

195

article of dress. It was of rich materials and brilliant colors, embroidered with silver and gold. Sometimes over all these she wore the siglaton, named for the precious Eastern stuff of which is was woven. This garment was a kind of mantle.

It was in the head attire that extravagance was most fully displayed. Now and then Elienor wore the chapel de paon, a kind of crown or hat embroidered with gold and pearls and surmounted with a peacock feather. A simpler headdress was a circlet of gold and silver or a filmy veil that fell over shoulders or a fillet or wreath to confine the hair. Today she wore only a wreath. Her gloves were of soft kid, her shoes of soft leather. Very important in the dress of highborn ladies was the girdle, for it was a mark of rank and dignity which common women like Elise sometimes affected, if with no more than a rag. It was made of rich ornamented materials and was buckled tight around the waist. "Pull me in," she said to the maids. "My God, I'm not that big." When she was robed and ready she daubed saffron in her armpits and ears and over her throat and neckpiece. She decided to take her hawk, the most distinctive mark of a lady or gentleman. Elienor's hawk, a merlin, wore small bells of pure silver on its legs, which gave off a fine tone; two straps of the finest leather by which it was held; and a richly ornamented hood with which it was hood-winked when not flying. Having no children she was very devoted to her hawk but wondered if its presence would make Richard ill at ease.

Hillel was right in thinking her a terribly bored and unhappy woman: she perceived that the whole system of romantic chivalry had been contrived to enhance and adorn the man's ego while it made woman merely the foil. It was always to the married, never to the single, woman that the most elaborate love sentiments were addressed. There were highborn men who would not think of marrying a woman who had not proved her popularity with a host of amours, or at least with a host of superficial and purely perfunctory devotions. On April 29, 1174, a case had been brought to a Court of Love, presided over by the Countess of Champagne. The question had been: Can real love exist between married people? The Countess had rendered a judgment that had become famous and that Elienor and many other ladies knew by heart: "We declare and affirm agreeably to the general opinion of those present that love cannot exercise its powers on married people. The following is proof of the fact: lovers grant everything mutually and gratuitously, without being constrained by any motive of necessity. Married people, on the contrary, are compelled as a duty to submit to one another's wishes, and not to refuse anything to one another. For this reason it is evidence that love cannot exercise its power on married people. Let this decision, which we have arrived at with great deliberaton, and after taking counsel of a large number of ladies, be held henceforth as a confirmed and irrefragable truth."

How many times Elienor had said those words over!

Guillem had wooed her with insane ardor but the moment they were married he had transferred his devotion without ever losing stride or a breath to another lady. After the marriage vows she had been taken for granted by her husband, as one to be wooed and won by every other gentleman who came to the castle. She had had sung to her hundreds of sentimental ditties; she had had knights strive to turn pale at sight of her but only look red and strangled, as, kneeling at her feet, they uttered the most preposterous vows of eternal devotion. One of the laws of love for the high-born said that jealousy intensified ardor: the ridiculous fellows had imagined themselves wildly jealous over her and had sworn to rush away and die in battle if she so much as frowned on their stuttering supplications. Because another law of love said that marriage was no excuse to refuse an ardent offer she had felt constrained to play the foolish game; and though at first when she was young and giddy and disappointed in her marriage she had enjoyed it, more and more it had wearied her, particularly when fat lords with offensive breath and puffed eyes had dissembled the fevers and woes of the love-stricken and cried despairingly, "If you deny me, beautiful lady, I will put on my armor and ride forth, never to pause until I am slain and my body is thrown to the wolves!" The absurd fat things couldn't have stood up with a full load of armor, much less ridden away. Well, she had taken a number of lovers before learning that every one of the clowns wooed and loved, not from inner compulsion and desire, but according to the laws, as these had been determined by the Courts of Love.

A law said that the real lover turned pale at sight of his lady: she had seen them struggle desperately to turn pale at sight of her and achieve only a woebegone strangled look. A law said that at the prospect of surrender the lover's heart beat wildly and shook his frame: she had discovered that the hearts of most of them did not increase by a single beat, not even in the embrace: love for them was a game played according to rules, as jousting was, and they played the game. A law said that a man when the prey of love ate little and slept hardly at all: her gluttonous lovers had grown so fat they could hardly get into their armor, and the moment the embrace was consummated had turned over and snored like an exhausted hunting-dog. A law said that a man could find no happiness in life save in pleasing the beloved: not one of her lovers after she yielded had shown the slightest concern for her but only for their own strutting and arrogant manliness. A law said that the image of the ladylove never left the lover's mind: she had learned that out of sight was out of mind for every one of them. A law said that an easy surrender made love cheap and passionless but another law said that favors yielded unwillingly were insipid. A law said that if one of two lovers died the other must not love again for two years: she had seen knights divested by death of their ladylove rush at once with redfaced and flute-tootling ardor to the first married woman in sight.

For Elienor it was all empty and unspeakably childish and she was sick of it. Younger knights, imitating their fat and short-of-breath elders, now wooed her; and she would look at one of them, kneeling, pleading, stuttering with self-induced passion, and think, "You poor dumb bastard! So this is man, out of whose rib woman was made. This is man, the fallen angel. This is man, created in the image of God, panting there on his knees and trying to remember what according to the rules he should say. This is man, whom woman must pity, since she cannot possibly love. . . ."

And so it was that she had turned away from the highborn, to seek some man in whom emotions were genuine, in whom there was some hardness of mind, some ambition besides hawking and hunting, gluttony and drunkenness, and arrogant boyish insipidity. So it was that on that day in the road she had turned to Richard, for she had liked his earnest face and his pride and his wish to make something of himself.

They met again on a walk leading to the garden, where there were benches and fountains and pools and flowers. Without speaking she took his arm and smiled up at him and led him to a secluded spot. When they were seated and Elienor was feeling the emotion of a young girl with her first love and Richard was horribly ill at ease and tongue-tied she said:

"Why did you wait so long?"

He was about to say that he had been busy but realized that this excuse for a lady accustomed to command would be an affront. He coughed and swallowed and said nothing.

"Tell me."

"I—" He shrugged. "Well, I just didn't believe that you wished me to come."

"Why not? Why, then, should I have given you money?" She turned her hawk free, saying, "Beat it, go find a quail—only, poor thing, there are no quails now. Go find a heron." She turned to Richard. "What have you been doing?"

"Learning to write and—and to read Latin."

"I know some Latin," she said. "Amor vincit omnia. Do you know what it means?"

"Yes."

"What?"

"Love conquers everything."

"Do you think it does?"

"I don't know."

"Richard, have you ever been in love?"

"I thought I was once."

"Did you turn pale at sight of her? Did your heart beat wildly? Were you able to eat and sleep? Who is she?"

"She—she's dead."

"Oh? Poor dear," she said and covered one of his hands with a palm. She felt him tremble. Lord, in twenty years she had never known a knight to tremble at her touch! Delighted she was silent a few moments, enjoying this new and miraculous sensation. An emotion stirred her that she had not felt in a long time. "Richard?"

"Yes?" he said, staring at the earth.

"Look at me. Look into my eyes.." He turned with a kind of convulsive movement and met her gaze. "Tell me what you see."

"What I see?" he said, frowning.

"Oh, don't be so shy. Tell me."

"I see that I amuse you."

"Oh?" she said, set back. "But is that all you see?"

"You have nice eyes."

"Others have told me that. Anything else?"

"I—I don't know." He did know and he looked away.

Tactfully changing the subject she said: "What would you like to be?"

"A scholar."

"Then become a monk. Monks are scholars, aren't they?"

"I guess some of them are."

"Aren't all scholars heretics?"

Great God, he thought, here it is so soon! Was this why she had summoned him?

The irrespressible Elienor continued: "Do you think Mary was a virgin?"

"I believe—I believe the doctrines of our Church."

"Richard, you liar. Why do you lie to me? Is it because you don't trust me?"

"I trust you," he said.

"Let me tell you something. You'll be forgiven by our Church if you have love-affairs by the dozen—discreetly; but you'll never be forgiven if you have one hair of doubt about Mary. You can be a thief, murderer, plunderer; you can rape, you can kill, you can curse your mother and for all those you will be indulged; but if you ever say Mary was not a virgin they'll burn you alive. You can rob your best friend and still receive the holy communion; but if you say Jesus was a poor man who owned only the garment on his back they'll pull you apart on the wheel. Do you know all that? . . . You're afraid to speak but I'm not afraid." She squeezed his hand and said: "What do you think of men?"

"How?"

"You think they're the image of God? Do you know what the first thought of every knight is when he meets a woman? I'll tell you. If he finds her unprotected and alone his first thought is to throw her down and rape her. Not even the beasts are so vulgar. Have you ever watched cattle? Have you seen the ram and the bull and the stud? They approach the female; if she wants them, all right, if not they go off about their business. They never rape. Only man who looks like God ever rapes."

"I suppose," he said, thinking of his mother.

"Do you admire men?"

"Some men."

"Ah, some men! You mean like Hillel?"

"I admire Hillel."

200

"So do I but I can't understand Jews. Do you think men are brave?"

"Some men."

"Let me tell you. I've been watching them a long time. A few of them are brave. Most of them are cowards. I've seen them come in and gulp wine and boast of their heroism in battle when they never got within ten miles of a battle. I've seen them show their battle-scars, which they got when the fat awkward things fell off their horse into a bramble thicket. At a safe distance they shoot off their arrows and hit nothing and then sing to me their songs of valor. In the crusades are they brave? They strap on their trinkets and sail away to free the Holy Land and they cut off noses and ears and balls by the tubful for the glory of Jesus. They burn, pilliage, murder, rape. They sing their songs of battle but I have another song. Shall I sing it for you?"

"Yes," he said.

In a low sweet voice Elienor sang:

> Who will come running, arms held out, for my kisses?
> Big as you were I carried you, so dear, so light.
> So many times I kissed you in your sleep.
> You gone, it is from other children's faces
> that I must kiss the tears!

Embarrassed, he turned to look at her and saw a mist in her eyes.

"That's how it is with me," she said. "I had two children. They both died. Do you love children?"

"Yes." Seizing his opportunity he said: "I have a sister, she is only a child. Could she come here to live?"

"Here?"

"She could work. She could be one of your maids or something."

"But why do you want her here? Is she in some danger?" When he did not reply she said a little sharply, "Is some man after her?"

He nodded yes and wished he had never been born.

"Some important man? Someone in the Church?"

"Please don't ask me," he said.

"You foolish man. If you don't wish to reply you have said yes, haven't you? I imagine I know who it is. Is your sister lovely?"

"No. She's pale and scrawny and—no, she's not attractive."

Elienor rubbed caressing fingers down the sleek feathers of her

201

hawk. "All right, you may bring her here but you'd better not be stupid about this. If it's the man I suspect he'll never forgive you."

"I know it."

"Are you willing to take such a risk for your sister?"

"Yes," he said.

"Then you must be a very brave man."

"I'm not very brave," he said.

"Or stupid but I'm sure you're not stupid. Very well, you bring her over. And when will you come again? Do you need money?" She reached into her purse and at once he moved away from her and she clasped one of his hands, crying, "Oh, don't be so silly!" With her two hands she opened his hand and placed the coins on his palm. Then she closed his fingers over them and with both her hands squeezed his hand shut.

XVII

Richard went again. He became a little infatuated with Elienor. She was intelligent, intuitive, vivacious, charming and kind; he had not known that there were highborn ladies like her. And she was disconcertingly frank. On his third visit to the garden she faced him and put arms to his neck and looked into his eyes and said:

"Do you want to be my lover?"

He choked and sputtered. Her laughter was spontaneously merry.

"Good heavens!" she said. "Don't tell me you've never had a woman! . . . You haven't?"

"No," he said, looking away.

"I didn't know there were such men." Still holding him she moved as if to dance and said: "Have you ever danced?"

"No."

"I love to dance," she said, looking up at him, "but our Church says the Devil invented dancing. Did he?"

"I don't know," said Richard miserably.

"Our Church says his favorite instrument is the violin, with which he can set whole communities dancing. Is that wicked?"

"I suppose," he said, aware that she was teasing him.

"It's Satan who fills us with love of learning and liberty and all that. Our Church says so."

"I know it," he said, conscious of her fingers tickling the back of his neck.

"And the Jews—but you know what they say. They say it is the fallen angels, the Devil's imps, who teach men the arts and sciences and all that. Azazel, they say, taught women how to make themselves beautiful with jewels and paints and powders and scents; and Kawkabel taught man how to read the future from the stars. But why does Satan teach all these nice things instead of God?"

He forced himself to look down at her face. "I don't know," he said.

"Maybe you'll know after you're a scholar. Does Hillel know?"

"I've never asked him."

Teasing him gently with a knee she said: "When you become a scholar you'll be Satan's agent. Did you know that?"

"I guess that's what our Church thinks."

"Well, our Church has never erred and will never err. It says the sun up there moves around this earth but scientists say the earth moves around the sun. That means the scientists are wrong. Isn't that so?"

"Yes," he said, not knowing what else to say.

She laughed merrily and said: "I won't tease you any more." She led him to a bench and they sat and he drew a breath of relief that amused her. "My fat husband is going to ride away and show what a brave man he is. Then you can come."

Under Hillel's treatments Baron Guillem soon felt so good that he buckled on his armor and rode away with his knights to seek a foe. During his absence Richard became Elienor's lover. He was wretchedly selfconscious and timid and ineffectual and he knew it and he sweated with shame; but Elienor, disgusted with goatish knights and play-love, seemed to like him. She taught him how to give her deep and voluptuous kisses; how to caress her body and which parts to kiss, when to play at intimate dalliance, when to embrace and how to hold himself back in the embrace.

After the embrace she would stretch like a huge lazy cat, relaxed, self-indulgent, smiling, and she would reach over to pinch his nose or rising to her elbows she would kiss him full on his mouth, pressing her own soft ripe lips in until he struggled to be free. She would lie back then and clasp his hand and after a few minutes she would sink into slumber but he was too disturbed for sleep. He had brought his sister over and Elienor had been very sweet to her; she had given her pretty clothes and nourishing food, trinkets and ornaments and a bed of her own. Fleur was blossoming out as she put on weight and lost a little of her sadness. Elienor was also very sweet to Richard; she gave him more money than

204

he knew what to do with, even after he had given a part to his mother, to Old Noelle and to Father Raoul. She gave him handsome garments and offered jewels which he refused to accept; and she begged him to buy any rare old books that he coveted, no matter what the price, and parchment and writing materials. She was good to him and she was more than lover—mother, he thought, an angel of kindness.

But he was deeply worried. About two weeks after Fleur went over Richard one day came face to face with Father Luce. The priest came up abruptly and without speaking looked into Richard's eyes and Richard was never to forget what he saw. The priest's eyes were small and black and hypnotic and crafty and cold. Richard felt an impulse to flight. Father Luce did not say a word; he only looked hard and deep and turned away. Richard knew that the look was a warning, or possibly more than that, yes more than that: he felt that in the man's eyes he might have read his future if he had had the power.

He tried to forget his fear and anxieties by devoting himself more earnestly to his work and by going now and then into the chapel to pray with Father Raoul. Spring came with its breezes and fragrance and passed and summer came and he was becoming rather proficient in Latin and he was a good scribe. He wrote a fine and wavering but legible hand and was now copying parts of the book which Hillel was writing on the history of medicine and its development under the Arabs. Richard found wonderful things in the book; they sometimes so absorbed him that he forgot his troubles. Hillel had the notion that some diseases came from the water people drank. He had written a whole chapter about that. He seemed to think that water from the wells and rivers was polluted with a kind of tiny organism that caused disease. He suggested that boiling the water might destroy them but admitted that he was not at all sure about it. He said there was a lot of experimenting to be done. Hillel, it seemed to Richard, was a fine scholar, tentative, searching, questioning but never dogmatic: he advanced theories, he flung out queries, he offered suggestions, he proposed lines of advancement. "I also wonder," Hillel wrote in his book, "if there is not some possible connection between certain diseases and stale air that has been too long confined. There may be disease agents not only in water but in air also, too small for the human eye to detect. In any case we medical

205

men can put no faith in Saint Appolonia as a cure for toothache, or believe there are serpents in the body of women that can be extracted by Hugo the Holy; or that monks have been saved from strangling on fishbones by Saint Agnes; or that mutes learn to talk at the shrine of Saint Anthony; or that a journey to the altar of Saint Gaul is a cure for gout. We dare not believe that hunchbacks are straightened when they kneel at the tomb of Saint Andreas, or that suffocated infants are returned to life through the intercession of Saint Coleta. . . ."

Richard read such words with dismay and horror, knowing that they were the rankest kind of heresy; he trembled when he took his pen to copy them and he was troubled by them in his dreams. He had not realized when he wished to become a scholar that he would have to deny so much of what his Church held to be inerrable and sacred. He had never imagined that the scholars were scoffing at the miraculous doings of dead saints. He did not dare to discuss these matters with Hillel: he felt like a crippled man in a morass or a blind man groping over the earth: he had got himself deep into heresy without having been aware of what he was doing, and now there was no turning back nor any certainty that he had the strength and the courage to go on. His admiration of Hillel was boundless, for the man rejected what he took to be superstitions in his own people as fully as in any other: his mind was leading him, it was his only light, and he seemed to have the courage to follow the light. But Richard was afraid. Suddenly, when he was copying a passage whose heresy was as unmistakable as a gallows, he would see that look in Father Luce's eyes as clearly as though the priest stood before him; and choking back a cry he would break off in his labors and shut his eyes. Am I a coward? he would ask himself. Hillel had told him what he would have to face; he had warned him again and again; he had said that the price of learning, of daring to think, might be a man's life. Richard had said with the folly of youth that he would pay the price, yet now he faltered like a craven and wished to undo what he had done.

If he was working in the morning or in the evening when the bells rang he would begin to tremble uncontrollably. He would rise and go outside and stand looking at the church steeple; and if the shrewd and observant Hillel understood what torments and doubts and agonies were in his pupil he gave no sign. He never

206

interrupted his own labors when Richard bolted from the house, though one day he did observe quietly: "Twelve centuries of persecution by Christians, and centuries before that by the Romans and other people, should have given the Jew courage to face anything; whereas men from a dominant and powerful group, protected in its own self-interest, and in possession of all the torture chambers and executioners, might now and then falter a little, though some even there have not faltered." Richard understood the rebuke and though he deeply resented it he allowed its justice.

Matters came up in his dreams until he would roll and toss in his sleep all night. Sometimes he would hear Father Raoul praying for him, the voice gentle and sad. More commonly he would see the black hypnotic eyes of Father Luce. Often in his dreams he would hear the bells, so mournful and sweet and pure in their holy music. When daylight came he would be up, his nerves shattered, his face haggard, and would plunge into his work. Always during the forenoon they would eat a little breakfast but they rarely spoke and Richard never met Hillel's eyes. He hated and despised himself for this. His loathing of self became so deep that he thought of fleeing and one day he did make an effort to flee, going three or four miles toward Toulouse before absolute horror of himself and his weakness forced him to turn back. He then knelt by the road and prayed but reflected meanwhile that he seemed no longer to receive any consolation from prayer. He murmured holy verses from the Scriptures but they did him no good. He was somewhere midway between the irrefragable anchor he had turned from and the deeper truth he was seeking but had not found. He would be stronger soon, he told himself. Abelard had had to go through this Gethsemane. All who sought truth and its light, all who dared to seek those revelations which God reserved to the bold, had these agonies of soul somewhere in their journey, before the light broke and the meaning of God became plain. . . .

Most of what Hillel had written did not disturb him. He was merely curious and enlightened on learning that, great man though he was, Aristotle had believed some very preposterous things; that Chrysippus had rejected something called venesection because he had thought blood was the food of the soul; or that Hirophilus after inventing an instrument called the catheter had concluded that blood moved in tides because of the beating of the heart. This Hirophilus, Richard decided, had been a great man and Hillel's reverence for him was obvious. Hirophilus had named the small part of the intestine the duodenum, had discovered a gland which he called the prostate, had studied the ovaries in the female, and had separated the nerves of sensation from those of motion. But he had also accepted the doctrine of Hippocrates that there were four fluids in the body, blood, phlegm, black bile and yellow bile and that all diseases were caused by disturbances in these fluids. This notion Hillel rejected. Erasistratus had turned from drugs and prescribed rest, exercise, a proper diet and vapor baths, all of which Hillel approved and to which he added suggestions of his own. When reading about Hirophilus Richard yearned to be an anatomist; but when he read that one named Hero had been able to open doors without touching them, make wine flow from a jar or stop at will, or a lamp trim itself or a mirror distort an image he wanted to be an inventor.

It was when Hillel scoffed at prevailing notions of the cause of disease, notions that Richard had heard from earliest childhood, that he felt his spiritual anchors melting away. Hillel had written: "It is generally believed today that the powder from a human mummy is a cure for all ills but it is probably no more effective than unicorn horn dipped into wine as an antidote to poison or the gallstones of goats as a cure for melancholy or moss scraped from the skull of a dead criminal as a cure of the wasting disease. These belong with such superstitions as crushed body lice, incinerated toads, the sole of an old shoe and menstrual blood." Hillel did not believe in blood-letting, which was so popular and usually accomplished by barbers. On such matters he employed the full powers of a caustic mind: "To draw a pint of blood from the right arm; to incise the shoulder and cup it and suck out an additional pint; to give the patient, next, strong emetics and purgatives and dreadful enemas containing antimony, bitters, salt, mallow, camomile, fennel, violet, beet root juices, cinnamon, cardomom, saphron, cochineal and aloes; and to follow this by shaving his head and blistering his scalp and making him sneeze violently with hellebore seems all designed to murder him in the quickest possible time. Considering the doctors they had, that any king lived to be thirty is one of the riddles of history. . . ."

Hillel seemed to have only scorn for one named Galen, who had thought the body was composed of fire, air, water and earth;

whose practice was to keep these in proper balance with drugs that would cool, dry, moisten or heat; and who prescribed potions that contained as many as two hundred drugs. "The wonder of it all," Hillel commented, "is that the human race has survived." He scoffed at the idea that the root of the orchid, because it happened to resemble the human testicle—Richard perceived that in Latin orchid and testicle were the same word—was a cure for diseases of the male genitals; or that the black spot in the flower euphrasia was a cure for diseases of the eye because it resembled the pupil. "I think," Hillel wrote, "it is time to take analogy out of medicine and confine it to art."

Hillel pointed out that for violent bellyache a common prescription even by doctors in the universities was this: take a sheet of parchment and write on it the first sign Thebal, Suthe, Gnthenay. In the name of the Father, the Son and the Holy Ghost, Amen. Jesus of Nazareth, Mary, John, Michael, Gabriel, Raphael. The word was made flesh: after every word make a cross within a square, thus: $\boxed{+}$ "Whoever carries this charm, these doctors tell us, will never again be troubled by cramp, but possibly an emetic of mustard or a physic of warm salt water would produce better results." Richard shuddered when he read such words, for he knew they were blasphemous. "The practice of invoking God and the angels," Hillel wrote, "may be on a par with curing a man of smallpox by bundling him in a red blanket, or making a man wealthy by fixing under his garment the withered heart of a vulture, or easing an abdominal swelling by blowing pepper up the nose. In ancient times surgeons were regarded as man-killers, thieves and frauds; today the status of the doctor is scarcely higher. They generate pus in wounds, use urine instead of a scalpel, and dung as an ingredient in half their prescriptions. Surgery has fallen into contempt because a certain Church, taking its sanction from a foolish verse in the Bible, proscribes against the shedding of blood, and thus in execution turns to the dungeon and stake, garroting and strangling. . . ."

Such a passage made Richard feel that an inquisitor had touched his shoulder. He would rise and go outside and walk around, hoping to see Father Raoul, though not for the world would he have mentioned these things to him. He had no one to discuss them with, not even Elienor. When, overcome by feelings of suffocation and evil, he would try to discuss them with Hillel he always got that quizzical look in the eyes and that austere expression on the face.

One day Richard came on this: "Possibly medicine some day will solve the riddle of the widespread belief in virgin birth, which captured even some of the wisest of the ancients. Basil was convinced that some animals were spontaneously generated; that many birds had no need of sexual union; that grasshoppers and many other insects and sometimes frogs and mice were produced without mating; and that mud alone was necessary to produce an eel. In popular lore. . . ."

At this point in copying Richard's pen began to tremble and he laid it aside. Hillel saw at once his perturbation and looked over at him.

"What is it?" he asked.

"This about virgin birth."

"Does it upset you?"

"You think, then— I mean," Richard went on desperately, "it says here in your book—it says—". He lowered his voice to a whisper. "Then Mary was not a virgin? After she bore Jesus?"

"A scholar, Richard, bases his conclusions on evidence."

"But what is evidence?"

"Yes, what is evidence? Is it taking you so long to learn? Evidence is that which displays itself to the sense of men, on which men trained in research in general agree. Evidence has nothing whatever to do with beliefs. Haven't you discovered yet that the scientist must have no preconceived notions?"

"But if a thing isn't true why do so many people believe it?"

"Because of ignorance."

"Are a lot of things that people believe untrue?"

"What man knows?"

"Then how can we tell?"

"Many people say that wrapping a person in a red blanket is a cure for smallpox, yet if all people so wrapped die, as they do, is it a cure? We can dismiss the more obvious fallacies one by one."

"But would men agree on the more obvious ones?"

"If a certain stone is put in a wife's bed to keep her chaste while her husband is away, yet it is discovered that such wives do not remain chaste, is that one men should agree on?"

"Yes."

"If the common people say that if a crystal held over flames remains cold it is a cure for certain diseases, yet it is discovered that it never remains cold, is that another?"

"Yes."

"If to learn the language of birds you eat the flesh of snakes, yet eat a lot of snakes and do not learn the language, is that another?"

"Yes but I didn't mean such things."

"I know you didn't. Like all persons you are most concerned about those matters that touch your emotions most deeply. If we can't find anywhere in the world a female that can conceive without the male are we to assume without evidence that woman can? I don't know what that idea came from. I suspect it has something to do with male vanity. It seems to me quite an irony that Christian men have developed a cult of the Virgin, of a pure woman untainted by sexual intimacy, yet believe that a woman is responsible for the low condition of men and make seduction of women a major interest. Or don't you see anything ironic in that?"

"I'd never thought about it," Richard said. "Is there nothing, then, that a Christian can believe?"

"Oh, a great deal. He can believe that mercy and charity and forgiveness and love are virtues. But to believe in these does he also have to believe in the ancient myth of the virgin? To believe in honesty and honor does he have to believe that Jesus raised Lazarus from the dead? If I believe in certain things in Isaiah do I also have to believe in witches?"

Looking down at his hands Richard considered a few moments and said: "Is there anything in medicine that you are sure of?"

"Not much. Doctors some day will know so much more than we know now. But that's not the point. The point is that we must accept truth as we discover it, abandon error as it becomes plain. That's this new scientific spirit."

"Is there anything in life that we really know?"

"We seem to know that we are born and we die. Food appeases hunger and water, thirst. But for the most part we grope in darkness, in a vast accumulation of error from the past. Fiat lux, you have said, is your motto. Very well, let there be light. Or have you changed your opinion about that?"

"No."

Hillel turned back to his work but he was secretly watching

211

Richard and after a few minutes he said: "Is my book disturbing you so much?"

Richard looked up quickly. "Some," he said.

"Maybe it's because you don't yet understand the scientific spirit."

"Maybe."

"Hippocrates, the father of medicine, lived almost two thousand years ago. He laid down three principles. First, there is no authority except facts. Second, facts are obtained by accurate observation. Third, conclusions are to be drawn only from facts. If those three principles had been followed think what a different world we would have today."

"I can see that," Richard said, wondering what Hillel meant by a fact.

"Hippocrates also formulated an oath for doctors. I swear, he said, so far as power and discernment shall be mine, that I will strive for the benefit of the sick and keep them from harm and wrong. Guiltless and hallowed will I keep my life and my art. Into whatsoever house I shall enter I will go for the benefit of the sick, holding aloof from all voluntary wrong and corruption.

"He set quite a light on the earth, Richard, but doctors after him let it go out. Men have lifted torches that other men have refused to carry. It's our task to find them and rekindle them and hold them aloft again."

"Thanks for talking to me," Richard said. "It's when you talk to me that I feel better. When I'm alone I feel weak."

"But when you read this book I'm writing you're not alone. Aristotle is with you, Hippocrates and Hirophilus, Hero and Hypatia and Euclid, Isaiah and Job, yes, and Jesus, they are all there, speaking to you. Many men and women are speaking to you who suffered horrible death because they dared to say, Let there be light. So much has been preserved to us in books and one who can read should never be lonely."

"And Francis says we should not read!"

Richard felt strong enough to face anything when Hillel talked to him but the anguish of doubt and fear returned when he was alone. His fear was that he would be found out and tortured. One day he saw Father Raoul going to the church and he followed him and Father Raoul saw him coming and turned and waited.

212

"Did you wish to see me?"

"Yes, Father Raoul. Are you going to pray?"

"Yes, Richard."

"I want to pray with you."

They went to the altar and knelt there and prayed in silence. Richard prayed to God for guidance, for humility and strength, and on rising he thought he felt strengthened, though a part of him seemed to be standing off, looking. He waited but Father Raoul continued to pray and Richard wondered if he was praying for him. After a while he turned away and went softly out.

What did Hillel think of prayer? He put the question to him.

"If a man rises from prayer a better man," said Hillel, "I suppose his prayer is answered. Most people have a need to unburden their souls to a larger power."

"But you've said you don't pray."

"Oh, indeed I do, in my own way. It is a prayer in me when I put my finger in rose water and then touch a great poem."

"I thought prayer was asking for something."

"All right," said Hillel, smiling. "I think of it this way, that in humility a man accepts God, in arrogance he denies him. I think arrogance is the greatest of the sins—greater than avarice or sloth or lying or murder. Those are sins of the passions. Arrogance is the sin of the mind. The spirit of inquiry teaches humility and so is godlike. Dogmas breed arrogance. When both Christians and Jews say that man's supreme beatitude is his intellectual vision of God they speak more profoundly than they know."

In this moment it was borne in upon Richard that when Hillel talked to him he spoke as Gerart had spoken, like one who had before him a group of disciples. Then one day he realized that often Hillel was uttering certain passages in his book. Having discovered this, Richard copied with even greater devotion, for as he wrote the words down Hillel was speaking to him; and now and then he was startled because he thought he actually heard Hillel's voice. In his dreams he did hear it, clear, gentle, firm, skilfully choosing words and formulating phrases. Sometimes he would hear the voice when with Elienor.

"What troubles you?" she asked him one day. "You look worried."

"I do?"

"Have you some trouble?"

213

"I hear voices," he said.

"Voices?" She was astonished. She turned to look into his eyes. "Whose voices?"

"Men. Great men who are dead."

"Saints?"

"I guess they were saints in their way."

"Angels?"

"Great men who are dead."

She continued to look at him. She had been amused at first but now she was anxious. She looked at his eyes, serious, gentle, deeply troubled eyes; and then her gaze wandered over his countenance, searching it: his tender and boyish mouth which she so loved to kiss; his cheeks, on one of which she again observed was a mole; his nostrils, which he kept tidy, unlike some of the knights who always looked as if they had just blown their nose; his strong chin that was slightly dimpled. She framed his face and looked into his eyes and then kissed his mouth.

"Dead men don't talk. Or if they do what do they say?"

He did not want to tell her. He thought it very silly of him to say that he heard dead men talking but he did hear them, not only in his sleep but sometimes when wide awake. Their voices were always low and murmurous, quiet, unimpassioned, grave, like the voices of men who had gathered to discuss mankind, his problems and his future. He seldom understood what they were saying; it was like hearing voices in another room or somewhere out in the night. The tone of the voices communicated to him a host of anxieties.

"Richard, what do they say?"

"Oh, I can't really tell. They seem to be wondering."

"About what?"

"Us."

"Us?"

"All people."

"You mean it's their ghosts?"

"Their minds," he said. "Their intellectual vision of God."

She was silent a moment, looking at him. "But what is it that worries them?"

"A lot of things, I guess. Such as why men are so brutal with one another. Such as why they still prefer error to truth. Things like that."

214

"Who are these men?"

"Oh, Aristotle, Hippocrates, Hirophilus, Euclid, Isaiah and Job and—and Jesus."

"You mean Jesus is worried about us?"

"Don't you think he might be?"

She kissed him again. "Did I tell you my fat boar of a husband is coming home?—and what I'm going to do? No, I didn't tell you. When he returns he always has a great feast. Would you like to come?"

"No."

"Why not?"

"I wouldn't belong there."

"Of course you would. I'll dress you up as a steward and he'll never know it. And now in heaven's name forget about the voices. Let's not worry about the dead. Lord, O Lord, we have enough to worry about with the living!"

"That's what they think," Richard said.

XVIII

Richard was out by the well in the baron's garden. He had seen
Fleur there. He had seen her stealing to the well in a guilty way
and had seen her throw something into it. When he came up
she was bent over, peering at the water; for she had cracked an
egg on the head of someone and thrown it into the water. It was
said that if a girl did this she could look into the water and see
there the image of her future husband.

"Do you see him?" asked Richard.

Confused, she drew away. She looked very pretty, Richard
thought, with blood suffusing her cheeks; she had on a silken dress
fastened at the shoulders with a gold clasp, and a small cap
trimmed with fur. On her feet she had soft leather shoes. As she
had blossomed under Elienor's kindness Richard had worried
about her, afraid that one of the squires or knights would seduce
her.

"Did you see him?"

"No."

"Are you hoping he will be a knight?"

"Why do you tease me?"

He put an arm across her shoulders and walked with her in the
garden, and suddenly, in one of those strange illuminations that
came to him, he saw himself as a kind of Jesus in Gethsemane. He
knew the thought was blasphemous but Hillel had said to him one
day, "I think Jesus is a symbol, a symbol of all good men who come
to teach and die. How many times has he come and under what
names? How many times will he have to come before mankind
accepts his message?"

"Fleur, are you happy here?"

216

"Yes."

"Are they all kind to you?"

"Yes."

"Would you like to spend all your life here?"

"Yes."

"Fleur, I must tell you something. I've a feeling that I will go away soon. I may never see you again. I want you to know—or do you know it?—that men will desire you, men who will wish only to be with you a few times and then forget you. You'll have to be very smart or they'll trick you with flattery and gifts. If any man begins to make your life difficult go to Baroness Elienor. She'll protect you."

"Richard, where are you going?"

"I don't know."

He did know, for again in an unexpected meeting he had looked into Father Luce's eyes and had read his future there. He knew that Father Luce had been talking again to Elise and that he had talked to Pascal and Chretien and Simone and Old Noelle. When he left Fleur he went to a secluded corner and knelt in prayer and again there was borne in upon him the feeling that he was in Gethsemane—for was not Gethsemane, Hillel had asked, only another symbol?—a symbol of man's utter loneliness when enemies overtook him and he refused to deny his God. Socrates, said Hillel, had had his Gethsemane. How many great men had not! Hidden and kneeling, Richard addressed himself to Socrates and to Jesus and to the voices of dead men in the night.

Guillem and his men came thundering back over the earth, their horses lathered and their own bodies lathered under their armor. Whether they had been jousting or warring Richard did not know. The castle and its grounds had been quiet during their absence; now these awoke in tremendous life. Guillem called to his barber and for two days the barber was busy trimming dusty and matted hair and beards. With this task done he set himself to blood-letting. It was thought by such people as Guillem and his knights that by drawing off blood a man was emptied of his accumulated fevers and ills. A vein was opened in the baron's arm and a pint of blood was extracted. "I don't feel very good," he said, groaning. "Take some more." Another pint was drawn. The squires and knights were also blood-let and preparations were made for a huge feast.

Elienor had given Richard garments to dress himself as a steward and it was as a steward that he appeared. He had heard that
the feasts of the idle rich sometimes lasted from noon until dark.
He had tried to imagine, when toiling in the baron's fields, starved
and enfeebled, what they were like.

Guillem and his men had brought with them beasts laden with
flesh. Granaries were plundered for their stores of spices and
wines. A dozen cooks were busy. There would be stag, roasted
whole, crisped and larded and drenched with steaming pepper
sauce. There would be boars' heads larded with herb sauce and
rabbits floating in gravies spiced with onion, cinnamon and saf-
ron; a pottage of drope and rose mallard; pheasant and capon;
pasties of small birds; teal, woodcock, snipe, partridge and heron;
pork pies; patties of egg yolk, cheese and cinnamon; cheeses spiced
with marjoram, sage, sweet basil and pepper; thrush pies with
bacon, sour grapes and salt. There would be geese, duck, trout,
frog-legs and Senlis cabbage, renowned for its odor, and garlic,
walnut, poppy and olive oil sauces and basins of rose water and
rose petals. There would be great flagons of the finest wines: St.
Pourcain, Cyprian, Lesbian; Aquilian from Spain, Rhenish from
the north; and vats of beer for the servants, spiced with resin,
juniper, cinnamon and gentian. Some of the meat, saturated with
spices to preserve it, would be half-decayed, and some of the gluttons, Elienor told Richard, would be as sick as dogs.

The feast was laid out in the huge central room on the second
floor, with its deep accumulation of straw, withered flowers, food
scraps, vomit and dung. Before noon the revelry began, with singing, music and the telling of tales. Baron Guillem was a prodigious braggart as well as glutton and with his applauding syco-
phants around him he liked to tell of his great feats in battle, in
the tournament and the hunt. Everyone knew who heard him
that his stories were shamelessly embellished and that with each
retelling his valor and prowess took on more heroic proportions.
He was fond of a kind of claret composed of wine and honey and
he drank deeply of this and was half-sick before he began to eat.
The table at which he sat, with Elienor, was covered with fine
linen, and on a wall a number of shelves set with pieces of silver
plate and golden bowls proclaimed his rank and wealth. A hors
d'oeuvre in a majolica bowl of milk pudding was passed around;
and when the silver dishes came with capon breasts they were

decorated with his coats of arms and with mottoes. A fountain of scented water was sprayed over the food. At a feast a gentleman and his lady ate from the same dish and used the same flagon and the eating was very noisy with smacking of lips and loud guffaws and belching and farting, because it was believed that those who most enjoyed their food made the loudest noises eating it. There was a story told by jongleurs that a feast in Paris could be heard in London.

Richard had been prepared for an unusual scene but his powers of imagination, he was soon to realize, had been too feeble. He was by turns astonished or abashed or dismayed by what he saw. Standing by in the garb of a steward, whose duty was to oversee the servants, he was speechless and he felt witless.

The feasting began a little after noon and all afternoon the great steaming and garnished dishes were brought in—now stuffed birds looking almost alive and bearing in their beaks the host's coat of arms, attached by silk ribbons to their breasts; and now enormous silver bowls holding a concoction covered with waxed sugar on which was emblazoned the coat of arms and the motto under which the baron rode away to war. The guests were choosing among fifteen different wines and watching them pour the lovely colors down Richard doubted that any of them would be able to walk when the eating was done. Once in a while he caught Elienor's gaze and she winked at him. Most of the time he looked with discreet but fascinated interest at Guillem, for he had never known that a man could eat and drink so much. Sometimes Guillem fed his mouth with both hands, his hands dripping, his mouth and face smeared with greases and sauces and gravies; and when he had his mouth filled he would raise a flagon of wine to wash the food down. "Feast!" he would roar. "Tempus fuggit!" he said and bellowed with laughter. "Tempus e-dax ree-rum!"

Richard thought of the serfs, his kind of people, who lived on barley bread, roots, herbs, a few vegetables and water; of their long hours of toil, their scrawny bodies and their bleak eyes. Here was a man who took and squandered the fruits of their labor, who spent it on a host of worthless parasites who had nothing to do but pursue their own idle pleasures, seduce the wives of their friends, boast of their feats and eat and drink until they were unable to stagger. For them the common people were not even human beings but an order of creation a little above that of beasts.

219

For them religion was only a multitude of rules and rituals and dogmas which they faithfully observed, believing that they would be elevated in another life to a glory of feasting and drinking and hunting that would endure forever, while for minor amusement they would gaze across the parapets and down to see the agonies and hear the screams of the eternally damned. They fully approved a Church Father who had said that for Christians one of the blessings in the hereafter would be a view of the tormented in hell's fires. Among Hillel's papers Richard had seen the words of another Father: "In order that nothing may be wanting to the felicity of the blessed spirits in heaven, a perfect view is granted to them of the tortures of the damned." Well, did it not say in the New Testament that the damned would be tormented in fire and brimstone in the presence of the holy angels and that the smoke of the torment would ascend forever and ever. These, then, he thought bitterly, were Christians, these belching and farting gluttons who would never be punished for heresy, for they attended Mass and prayed and followed the rules, while wringing from the toil of the poor the substance for their castles and silks and jewels and feasts.

He watched them until he felt sickened and then slipped away and changed into his own garments and fled. If he had remained he would have seen one of the drunken knights summon Fleur and then hold her in his lap and kiss her; he would have seen Baron Guillem tumble backward off his bench like a foundered ox and rest on his hands and knees while snorting and blowing and trying to puke; and he would have learned that before darkness came Guillem was deathly ill. Hillel told him about it. Hillel was called over and spent the night with Guillem.

"He acted like one poisoned," said Hillel, pale and shaken. "I did everything I could think of. I poured emetics down him and made him vomit until he was too weak to spit. But he sank rapidly and it will be said that I killed him. God knows, Richard, what will happen to us now."

"You think—someone poisoned him?"

"Oh, not necessarily. It might be so. He had all the symptoms. But perhaps it was the food. Decayed meats may have poison in them but I don't know and I don't know what kind of poison it would be. In other times he has been sick the same way." Hillel looked at Richard and listened, as if for footsteps. "Now—"

"What?" Richard whispered. "What now?"

"Who stands between us and doom?"

Richard began to tremble. "Should we flee?"

"Flight for everyone out there would be a confession of guilt. Is the Baroness Elienor really fond of you?"

"She seems to be."

"Then perhaps you had better talk to her, very discreetly, you know, to find out how she's feeling about it." He was still looking at Richard. "Will you?"

"I'll do anything you suggest."

"Surely you realize the mess we're in, you a heretic, I a Jewish doctor who lost a patient who happens to be one of the most powerful lords in the Kingdom of Arles."

"If we fled what would we be suspected of?"

"Poison, of course. Weren't you there?"

"Yes."

"Did you leave before he became sick?"

"Yes."

"Then don't you see how bad it looks? You'd better talk to her but be very prudent. She was dreadfully upset when I left. She asked me what the trouble was and I made the mistake of saying that it looked to me— Well, you see, you were the only one there who slipped away."

"God!" said Richard. "You don't think I poisoned him, do you?"

"Of course not. It's what somebody else may think."

"I'll go," Richard said. "I'll learn what I can."

Elienor looked like one who had been weeping. On hearing that Richard wished to see her she had had him ushered into a small room and came in almost at once and marched up to him. She looked into his eyes.

"Well?" she said and Richard felt that his position was hopeless. He read the suspicion in her eyes. "What do you mean by well?"

"Why did you run away yesterday?"

"I was sick. I guess it was the wine I drank."

"Do you always run away when you feel sick?"

"I just wanted to be alone," he said.

"Why? Sit down." He sank to a bench and Elienor sat and faced him. "Do you know that my husband was poisoned?"

"No, I didn't know that."

"Didn't Hillel tell you?"

"You mean Hillel thinks that?" he said, trying his best to be prudent.

"He said he had the symptoms of poisoning." She was looking into his eyes. "Richard?"

"Yes."

"I have loved you. I've tried to be very kind to you."

"You have been."

"Have you thought that if the baron died I'd marry you?"

"No! My God, no! I swear it by everything under heaven!"

"You're not lying to me?"

"I swear I'm not," he said, trying to quiet the trembling in his limbs. "I swear by our Father in heaven that I'm not lying to you."

"Then why did you run away?"

"I told you I was sick."

She looked away from him and seemed to be thinking. "If he was poisoned who did it?"

"I wouldn't have any idea."

"Did you see anyone put anything in his food or drink?"

"No." There came to him suddenly a thought that looked like a road to freedom. "You ate from the same dishes and you drank from the same flagons."

"I didn't eat some of the things he ate."

"You—" Richard drew a sharp breath and forced the question out. "You're not suggesting that I poisoned him?"

"I'm asking why you ran away."

"And I've told you and I've sworn it by our Father. Hillel says it could have been from the meat."

"The meat!" She was incredulous. "He has eaten meat all his life. How could poison be in his meat unless someone put it there?"

Was he being prudent? "Hillel thinks that half-spoilt meat may sometimes be poisonous."

"He thinks! Does he know?"

"I think he's a very wise doctor."

"You mean he's trying to protect you?"

"My God!" said Richard, appalled. "I tell you I swear by our Father and by the Virgin and all the angels and saints that I had nothing to do with it!"

"Even if I believe you there are some who may not. Hillel has poisons. He knows all about poisons. You live with him. Don't you see what some people may think?"

"I have sworn," said Richard, feeling again that his position was hopeless. "What more can I do?"

Looking again into his eyes, her own eyes steady and searching, she said: "I believe you. But if there are some who won't believe you there's nothing I can do to protect you. If only you hadn't run away. Well, you go now and I'll let you know what happens."

Terrified, Richard returned to Hillel. His face was so ashen that when he looked at it Hillel abandoned hope.

"I can tell," he said, "that you bring bad news." But he smiled. "I'll bring us some wine for we may not be drinking wine again." He filled their cups and said: "Now tell me."

Richard told him.

"Did she believe you?"

"She said she did but she may have some doubt." And again, almost supplicatingly, he asked: "Why don't we flee?"

"Where to? West to the Kingdom of France? East to Lombardy? North to the Duchy of Swabia or Franconia or Saxony? Where in this world could a man hide? And how long would we hide if we could? My people learned long ago, Richard, that flight is no good. They learned that there is no place in all the earth that they could flee to."

Richard said: "I'm the only one who would be punished. There's no charge against you."

"There always is," said Hillel, indicating the yellow badge. "A Jew is always guilty. Now and then he has a powerful patron but patrons die."

"What could they arrest you for?"

"Anything."

"If it will protect you I'll say I'm guilty."

"Oh no, friend and brother. Won't you ever learn what it means to be dedicated to truth? We'll say nothing but what we believe to be true. That must be so with us, no matter what happens. Have you the strength for it?"

"I think so."

Again Hillel smiled. "Do you hear the voices?"

Richard hesitated a moment and said, "Yes."

"As long as you hear the voices that long you will have the

strength, no matter what they do. What did Jesus say on the cross?"

"He said, Father, forgive them."

"In another way that is what Socrates said. That is what we must say. We may never lift a torch. We'll never know if men some day will hurl down the last tyrant and have a free world. Are you afraid?"

"No," said Richard but he was trembling.

"I don't know what will happen to us. We may as well prepare for the worst. If they throw us into dungeons I don't know if we'll ever get out. So before they come there is something I should tell you. In the corner there," said Hillel, rising to show Richard the exact spot, "buried in the earth is a lot of money, all gold. If you get out and I do not, it is yours. Remember that in this world money can buy anything."

"You mean—?"

"Remember it. Here, let us fill our cups again." Hillel filled the cups and raised his and said—and Richard observed that his hand was steady: "Let us drink to all the men and women of the past who died for truth. Let us keep the memory of them close to our hearts and souls. Let their devotion to what is true, their abhorrence of what is false, warm and strengthen us, no matter what comes. I'll remember that a Jew and a Christian were friends. That is a torch that not all the tyranny under heaven can extinguish."

Richard was silently weeping.

Hillel stood up and drew Richard to his feet and embraced him. He kissed his forehead. "Most of my book," he said, "is buried with the money. It may never be found. But if not, it will always be there in the earth, making, I like to think, a small spot of earth holy ground."

"Our Father—" Richard murmured, trying to pray.

"Don't weep," Hillel said. "Tears leach your strength." He poured wine into the cups. "Let's have one more drink before they come."

XIX

They did not come as soon as Hillel expected them and he went quietly ahead with his studies while Richard tried to prepare himself for the ordeal. When the blow fell it was as sudden and shocking for Richard as though he had not expected it at all. The time was early morning. They had risen and Hillel had washed his hands and face and was sitting at his table with a page of his manuscript and Richard was still sitting on his bed when the door was flung open without warning and two armed men thrust themselves inside. Without a word one of them strode over and seized Richard and yanked him to his feet and the other seized Hillel. The burly giant who had taken Richard hustled him toward the door and in that moment Richard looked back at his friend and a cry escaped him, "Oh, Hillel!" As he was forced outside and away sobs burst from him and once more there came his cry of bitterness and heartbreak, "Oh, Hillel!" He was to remember Hillel standing by the table, one hand on the page of writing, a look on his face of quiet contempt and disdain.

On the way from Hillel's house with his guard Richard passed Father Luce and for a moment looked into the priest's eyes and saw there a light of triumph. A little later he passed Chretien and saw in his face what he was never to forget and never to understand. There was great excitement in Patres, as there always was in any place when word went out that a heretic was to be seized. The common people hated the inquisitors as they hated nothing else on earth. They would gather and they would look and they would hate but they did not dare to move or speak, though now and then an inquisitor carrying the records of a doomed man was set upon and slain with frenzy so violent that he was actually torn limb from limb.

Richard was led to a horse and told to mount; and after he was seated he was manacled, his wrists chained and made fast to a chain around the horse's body. Two guards, each mounted, were going with him, one before and one behind. He was only dimly aware of them. He was looking back for sight of Hillel but he could not see him. He was also looking round him for a chance to escape but he knew there was no chance to escape. He was to remember later that for a moment he saw the round frightened eyes of Simone and the wrinkled weeping face of Old Noelle. For a moment he again saw that strange look in Chretien's eyes. He was never able to recall the presence of his mother.

The guard in advance led off down the road past the castle. He sat in a saddle but Richard rode bareback, his manacled hands before him resting on the beast's mane. To the halter of the horse on which Richard was mounted a rope was attached and the other end was around the horn of the guard's saddle. They had gone only a little distance when the church bells began to ring and their sad music was almost too poignant for Richard to bear. He was weeping, the tears falling to his hands, and he heard the sound of the bells long after they were silent. He told himself over and over that he had to be brave now. Hillel had warned him that this might come and it had come and he had to be brave now. He had to be as brave as Hillel. But all the thoughts that he summoned to give him courage and comfort seemed only to open the wells of bitterness and terror in him and he shook with grief and wept until he was blinded, until the world around him was only a mist of trees and sky.

An hour later he had wept his heart out and was calmer. Because he was unable to reach up to wipe the wet from his eyes he shook his head to throw the tears off his cheeks and lashes. He looked back to see if other guards were coming with Hillel but saw only the brutal bearded face of the man behind him and the soft eyes of the horse. He saw the other guard tip his head up and back but he did not know what he was doing until much later, when he was half-dead with thirst in the awful heat. He tried to look with interest at the chain on his wrists. He tried to study his inner sensations and was conscious first of sweat and heat under his thighs and then of his hanging feet which seemed to

226

be numbed or dead. He was in pain, he told himself, and then became aware that it was a childish thought: he had been thinking of the torture ahead of him and it had seemed strange to him that he was not now in pain. He wanted to look back many times to see if Hillel was coming but he was afraid that if he kept looking back he would anger the guard behind him; and he understood how childish that was too, how stupid, as though by deferring to the guard he might win him to compassion and mercy! Yet this wish not to anger his guards but to be agreeable was strong in him, because it fed on hope, though he knew there was no ground for hope; because it fed on a prayer for mercy, though he knew there would be no mercy. Were they taking him to Toulouse?—or to Arles or Narbonne or Carcassonne? As though it made any difference at all! Was one dungeon less dreadful than another?—or one inquisitor less implacable?—or the instruments of torture less terrible? Who would accuse him and of what? Who would be the two witnesses against him? Would Baroness Elienor intercede?

Before dark the guards turned aside to a grove of trees. One of them unlocked the chain around the horse and told Richard to dismount and then led him to an oak and made the chain secure around the tree. There chained to the tree, he realized, he would spend the night. A little later one of the men brought to him a piece of stale bread and a little water. He gulped the water and wanted to ask for more but the wish in him to be agreeable was too strong. The men tethered the beasts and at a little distance from Richard sat under a tree and ate and then stretched out to sleep. A full moon had risen.

Though numbed with dread Richard tried to examine his position. Could he escape? How stupid it was to have such thoughts! The chains were heavy and they were securely locked. His mind turned to the money Hillel had buried and he wondered if he could bribe these men. How foolish his thoughts were! If he betrayed the fact that he had money they would torture him to make him reveal its hiding-place or they would tell the inquisitors that he had money and the greed and rapacity of inquisitors was known all over the land. Besides, he had no right to the money. For an hour, two hours, most of the night he kept looking back up the road, hoping and praying that Hillel would come in sight; for even if he came in irons and with guards it would be happiness greater than heaven's own just to see him. I can never escape, he thought. I am doomed. Tomorrow I will ride again and the next day until I am brought to a dungeon and thrown in. It was thought of the dungeon that made him tremble. Gerart had said that no form of death was as horrible as murus strictus in the small black hole where prisoners lived month after month and year after year, with their own excrement and the rats, until they went mad or died of loneliness and terror. Women had died of terror after being walled up in that small black place, with only a hole in the door or wall through which they were fed. Sometimes, Gerart had said, the rats practically ate people alive, chewing off parts of their feet and hands, their nose and ears and cheeks, when at last from utter exhaustion they slept.

Because his faculties of the imagination were intuitive and vivid he was living in advance the agonies whch he knew would soon come. He tred to quiet his emotions and his body and make an orderly arrangement of his thoughts. He would look up at the moon or around at the trees and the earth and think, Soon I'll never see these again. Would Fleur be a witness against him? Would they torture her? Well, there would be no lack of witnesses against him. It needed only two, Gerart had said, to convict and both of them could be absolute liars, because inquisitors accepted the lie as quickly as the truth, refusing to distinguish between them or to care. And there were low vicious informers who would testify against anyone for a coin or a jug of wine. Would Hillel be tortured? The punishment of Jews was sometimes as dreadful as that of Christians; they were hung by their feet over a cable between two savage dogs that tore them into pieces or they were boiled to death. . . .

He looked up at the bright night sky and wondered if there was God. If there was, how could he allow his children to torture one another in such fiendish ways for the glory of his name? How could the gentle Jesus look down and tolerate the sight of the gallows and dungeons and torture-chambers? How dared any man call this land Christian! All over Europe the inquisitors were busy. In how many hundreds or thousands of places at this moment were people screaming under torture or lying in their filth like half-rotted beasts? In how many places were bishops in their coslty raiment and silver and gold making war on one another or corrupting the wills of timid women? This was not a Christian land, he thought bitterly. Not even the heathen, Gerart had said, had ever been as vile and vicious as these people who called themselves followers of Jesus. Not even Rome under its worst emperors was as degraded as this. What were human beings anyway, that they could be more savage than the wolf and the boar, more merciless and vindictive than any other creature on earth?

He was chained so close to the tree that he could not sit with his back against it. He could kneel before it or he could half-sit sidewise. A hundred feet away the two guards were sleeping and he could hear their snores but he could not see them clearly. He studied the chain on his wrists and twisted a hand up to feel of the lock; and as far as he could reach either way he felt over the chain around the tree, hoping to find a weak link. But there were no weak links, these chains were bright and strong. Father Luce had seen to that. Father Luce would now have his way with Fleur. He would tell her he was a holy man of God and that she must trust him and put herself in his care; and he would have his way with her as he had had with Madelon. How many Father Luces were there in the Christian world? How many Father Raouls? Not so many Father Raouls, he supposed; even the inquisitors who were disciples of the lowly Francis now rode around in state like lords of baronies, though they were supposed to go barefooted and in simple dress. Still, these were not, Gerart had said, so cruel and vindictive as the disciples of Dominic. God, he said, praying, grant that I may be delivered to a follower of Francis! Grant me the strength to endure everything and to die in the truth! Above all, our Father, be merciful to Hillel, for he has done no wrong and he is a good man. Let me suffer if I must suffer but protect him, our Father in heaven. . . .

He was weeping again but from thirst and exhaustion rather than from fear, and from the great love which he bore Hillel. He prayed again, kneeling against the tree; and again in his last bitter hours as so many men had been. Our Father, he said, protect Hillel, watch over him, let him complete his book and leave it to men who will come after him, to be a light for them, another torch in this awful night where men do not understand but persecute one another, shaming your name and the name of Jesus. Please watch over Hillel, for his love of Jesus is greater than that of the men who have taken him away. And protect my sister. . . .

His poor little sister! She could be punished, as any Christian could, merely for having spoken to a heretic, merely for having seen one.

He prayed and then exhausted he tried to sleep but he could not sleep. He was as wide awake as though he had taken a powerful drug. He watched the course of the moon across the sky and looked round for signs of daylight, yet why should he want the morning to come! He would ride again, chained to the horse; he would ride until he came to some city and then he would be taken into a building and led through gloomy chambers and down a dark and gloomy stairway. A door would be opened, he would be thrust inside, the door would be closed and locked. After a while, after weeks or years, he would be taken to a chamber where the preliminary proceedings were held: this might be the convent of the Order to which the inquisitor belonged or an episcopal palace if he were in a cathedral city; or it could be a church or a municipal building. There would be one inquisitor or two and their assistants, who would have prepared the case against him. The chief assistant might be a bishop or a prior of the local convent. There would be absolute secrecy. He would have no right to ask for a person as counsel, he would have no right to speak in his own defense. The evidence was supposed to be taken in the presence of two impartial men, sworn to secrecy but Gerart said there were no impartial men. He would be questioned and a clerk would write down the questions and answers and everything that he said would stand against him, even if he later denied it, or even if, in the confusion and fright of the moment, he were to say something that he did not mean. No one else would be allowed in the room. The accused was completely in the power of his enemies and if he did not reply to questions he would be taken to the torture-chamber and shown the instruments and they might show him some person being tortured. So it was, Gerart had told his students. They would find him guilty, for nobody had ever been known to escape, once he was in an inquisitor's grasp. They would find him guilty no matter what he said or did not say and the degree of his guilt would determine the form of his punishment. He might be burned alive. If this was his punishment the people roundabout would make the occasion a holiday; feeble old women, eager for a few more days or weeks of indulgence, would bring fagots for the flames and do what they could to see that the agonies were prolonged. Sometimes a person had a part of his feet burned away and then was taken to his dungeon for a day or two and burned again; with the ordeal continuing day after day until his feet were burned off and his lower legs. It was a wonder, Gerart said, what a human being could stand. Or his punishment might be imprisonment in a dungeon until he died, and this, the people believed, was a form of death worse than fire. Or if he were found guilty in a less degree and if he abjured he would be freed with a cross on his back and a cross on his breast, to become a lonely wanderer to whom nobody would dare to speak. He would have to give some kind of property security against relapse; for though it was said that the Jews were a rapacious people there was no greed on earth, Gerart had said, like that of inquisitors eager to fatten their purses. If he were a person of wealth he might be let off with a fine that would bankrupt him. The Pope had rebuked inquisitors for their confiscatory fines but inquisitors, who knew a way to enrich themselves when they saw one, paid no attention to the Pope. . . . And all his people, all his relatives and friends, would be hounded and persecuted to the day of their death, from the moment he was found guilty.

What else had Gerart said? Well, he could get off with a lighter punishment if he would bear witness against others, if he would accuse others, especially those with property; but he would die rather than do that. He could get off with a lighter punishment if with the craftiness of his judges he would lie, if he would deny the truth as he saw it, if he would at once admit himself guilty. But this also he was resolved not to do. He would be faithful to Hillel and Hillel's book and to the voices and to his own motto. He was doomed, there was no way out. If he was not to be a coward there was no hope for him. Could he endure the torture without betraying Hillel? Gerart had told them that some well-known inquisitor, proud of his instruments and his methods, had said that he could make the Pope himself confess to heresy, once he got him into the chamber. It had been said, and the people in general believed, that no person on earth had the strength to endure the strappado, the wheel, the rack, the boot, the fires—that even those with the greatest fortitude broke down at last and babbled insanely and confessed to anything that was demanded of them. If that was so, how could he expect to endure? But he would, he told himself, he would! He was now trembling so vio-

231

lently that his chains rattled and he looked at the chains and thought, I'm not brave, for see how I shake, even before the ordeal! If he trembled now what would he do when he saw the instruments? He was a coward, that was all. Trying to quiet his shaking body he prayed again.

At the break of day he watched the wonder of light as it softened and filled the lower sky; and his thoughts turned to what Hillel had said about a great man named Hipparchus. Hipparchus had decided that the earth rotated on its axis, that the sun did not rise at all but that the earth rolled over once in twenty-four hours; and that it had some kind of irregular movement at the poles which caused the variations in the seasons. Hipparchus must have been a dreadful heretic, for that was not what the holy Bible said. The sun is not rising, Richard was thinking, for he had to get his mind off himself; the earth is turning, though we cannot sense it or see it. He was trying to sense the movement when one of the guards came over, with a cup of water and a piece of bread. Richard looked up at the man's face, hoping to find there a friendly expression but it was sleepy and scowling and brutal. He took the bread and water and while chewing the bread with a dry mouth and swallowing it with difficulty he thought of Anaximander, another great man, who had thought that all life, plant, animal and human, had evolved out of the slime of the sea. That also was heresy. All new truth was heresy, Hillel had said. All great men were heretics. . . .

He rode again all day long and suffered intolerable thirst. He tried to think of things that would give him courage but in spite of his will his mind kept returning to the ordeal ahead. This night he dozed a little and he dreamed. In his dream he saw a heretic led to the flames. The man was forced to ascend a ladder to a post, around which was piled dry grass and wood; and he was bound to the post with stout ropes, around his ankles, below the knees, above the knees, at the groin, the waist and under the arms. Around his neck and the post a chain was made secure. Two priests, who were there to snatch his soul from Satan if possible, observed that he faced the east, which no heretic was allowed to do. The man was unbound and turned to the west. The overseer of the execution then approached and asked him for a last time to deny what he believed to be true; and when the man dully shook his head no, the executioner clapped his hands and

232

men dashed in to kindle the pile. In the dream Richard seemed to be standing close to the man and he was watching his face for the first signs of agony. The fire enveloped his feet and lower legs. Richard smelled burning flesh and the odor of burning hair. Pale yellow flames licked upward, burning off the loin cloth and exposing the pubic hair and the genitals; and Richard saw the genitals curl and shrivel and blacken. He looked again at the face. The man had set his upper teeth over his lower lip and clenched them and had closed his eyes. No cry had yet escaped him. The flesh as it burned burst open as though rotten; a wave of yellow went up the belly and chest mixed with smoke, consuming the hair; and then there was fire in the beard and in the hair on the head. Richard then knew that the man was dead but they were not done with him; with stout green poles and iron hooks they prodded and tore at him, dragging his organs down into the fire, bursting his bones and pulling them downward. Everything must be destroyed, lest some fool preserve a fragment and foist it off as the relic of a martyr.

When Richard awoke, gasping and convulsed and tortured, he had his upper teeth so clenched on his lower lip that blood had run down his chin and his jaws seemed paralyzed. He bent downward to clutch his face with his hands; he struggled to loosen his jaws, and only after frantic effort was he able to release his teeth from his mutilated lip. He was recalling every vivid detail of the dream and in the atmosphere around him he could smell the odor of burning flesh and hair. He knew that he had been the man bound to the post. When he realized that he had died nobly without a murmur, without recanting, without betrayal, he felt a little pride in himself, he felt stronger, he felt that he would be able to suffer it through. It was as though he had already suffered death. It was as though he had sought this test of his courage and his strength. "Hillel," he murmured, "I'll do it!"

But when at last he came to the great stone building, whose ugly wall was blind but for a door, and his guards unchained him and each seized an arm to hustle him inside; and when he was taken down a dark stone stairway and caught the first odors of the gloomy dank depths and sensed the horror of the blackness and silence; and when an iron door was opened, grating on its hinges, and he was thrust inside and as though in a nightmare heard the door closed and bolted; and when he knew that at last he was in

233

a dungeon deep underground and that this had happened to him which, when copying the luminous words of Hillel's book, he had believed could never happen, his spirit broke, his courage failed him, his mind went dark and he sank to the damp cold stones of the floor and lost consciousness. He half-sprawled, his back and shoulders against a wall, his head fallen forward, his hands spread palms downward as though to brace himself. And there he remained for hours, knowing nothing. . . .

XX

When he regained consciousness he came out of woe and horror so deep that it took him several minutes to know where he was, to recall what had happened. His first sensations were of hunger and thirst, his next of cold and damp. His hands moved before he opened his eyes. The fingers of his right hand moved slowly back and forth over the stone and his sensations from his fingers were of chill and of a substance that was soft and sticky. Only dimly aware of what he was doing he brought his fingers to his nostrils and smelled the odor of dung. He let his hand fall. Then the fingers of his other hand began to move. They moved back and forth and he was vaguely conscious of dampness.

Minutes passed before he slowly opened his eyes. He could see nothing. He opened and closed his eyes, opened and closed them, wondering in a sunken numbed way why he could not see. He was half-awake, half-sunk in horror and chill. I cannot see, he thought at last, and he brought his right fingers up to examine his eyes; but smelling again the foul odor of human dung he let his hand sink. He had the notion that he was in his father's shack and was half-reclining on a bedmat in a corner. It was a pitch-black night. Something had aroused him from sleep. He listened, for there would be snoring, yet he could hear no snoring. "Father?" he whispered, and felt pain in his lip. He brought his left fingers up and felt over his chin and mouth. In a slightly louder whisper he said, "Fleur?" There was only silence.

He then struggled and sat up, still trying to see. He reached out to feel of the wall against which he had been leaning and it was not the wall of his home. This wall was of stone but the wall of his home was was of timber and matting. He began to feel alarm. "Father?" he said more loudly, and was aware of strange echoes. Still struggling to realize he staggered to his feet. He thought he would grope toward the doorway and more light but he could feel only a blank stone wall. He moved around, feeling over the wall, until he came to the door; and he felt over it until his fingers came to a hole. He reached into it but seemed unable to put his arm through it. With a forearm he swept his brow and back over his hair. Then he listened. And while he stood there, listening and wondering, realization flooded his mind with the suddenness of shock and the awfulness of certainty; in one horrible paralyzing moment it all came to him, it all opened up around him, it all went through him with shock and sickness and horror. He knew where he was. He remembered.

He felt so weak, he felt such dreadful vomit in his whole being, that he closed his eyes and leaned against the door for support. "Hillel!" he whispered. "Hillel!" He was struggling silently in an effort not to vomit, not to faint and fall. He put both hands up and found the small hole and clutched it to support him. His head was bowed, with his hair pressed against the door, his legs spread and back; and in this position without moving and almost without feeling he stood for several minutes. Then he became dizzy and began to sway a little and he sank slowly to his knees, with his forehead on the stone floor. He was trying desperately to keep from dying, for it seemed to him that he was dying. It seemed to him that he would again be engulfed by blackness out of which he would never emerge if he did not try with all his strength to remain conscious. He was aware of his palms spread on the cold stone and of the sickening odors under his face and of the chill against his forehead and of the hardness under his knees. "God," he whispered, "help me!"

He arose and stood, weak and trembling, staring round him and seeing nothing. At the hole in the door there was a faintness which he thought must be light. He put his face to the hole and tried to look out but there was nothing to see. He turned, his hands outstretched. He groped until he found a wall and he felt over it from the floor as high as he could reach. It was of rough stone and of what he took to be mortar between the stones. He followed the wall to a corner and then moved back to the other corner; he stood facing the wall and stretched his arms out either way and touched the two opposite walls. This way, he thought, it

236

is only six feet wide. He went to the corner and felt over it to the other corner and stretched his arms to span it; and he thought, It is only six feet wide the other way. He measured the other walls and knew that he was in a dungeon cell about six feet square. He looked up but could see no ceiling. This, he thought, is the kind of dungeon they die in who love truth. How many persons at this moment were in dungeons like this? He stretched an arm upward but could touch no ceiling. He knelt. He felt over the floor. He found only the excrement of those who had been there before him. Trying not to foul his hands he moved around on his feet, his rump against his heels, and examined the floor, thinking that there might be some kind of mat to lie on. But there was no mat. There was only the cold stone and the wetness of urine and the messiness of the dung. What kind of man had recently been here? —or woman. Was he dead now or was he somewhere in a torture-chamber? No, there was no mat. He moved around until he had examined the entire floor. There was no dry spot. There was no spot that had not been fouled. The whole thing was a filthy mess and he thought, I'll not be able to sleep, I'll have to stand day and night. Day and night! As though it were not all night in a place like this!

He was shaking from the chill. With an effort he would quiet the trembling a moment but it would recur, more violently for having been checked and he began to pace to warm himself. With a hand outstretched to keep from striking his toes or his face he would take two steps and turn and take two steps. Great God, how could a person live in a place like this, year after year? No wonder the people said they would rather die, they would rather be burned alive, than to be sentenced to one of these holes. No wonder there were stories of people who had gone mad in these cells. He would have to keep calm, he told himself. Would it help if he uttered words aloud? He would try it but what would he say? He said, "Hillel, my friend and brother, where are you? Are you in a place like this?" Echoes devoured the words and he could understand nothing. He said, "I will not betray you, Hillel. I will be faithful to what we believe. . . ." His voice was too loud even when he whispered and it frightened him. If he talked aloud would there be spies to listen? He thought there would be. He needed to hear a sound in the awful silence and he decided to utter only such words as could not be used against him. "Call now,

237

if there be any that will answer you; and to which of the saints will you turn? I would seek unto God, and unto God would I commit my cause. Job answered and said, Oh, that my grief were thoroughly weighed, and my calamity laid in the balances together! For now it would be heavier than the sand of the sea: therefore my words are swallowed up! Call now, if there be any that will answer you! Oh, that I might have my request, and God would grant me the thing that I long for! Even that it would please God to destroy me; that he would let loose his hand and cut me off!" How well Job had understood! "My God, my God, why have you forsaken me?" How well Jesus understood the bitterness of the ordeal! "Then I said, I have labored in vain, I have spent my strength for nought! I the Lord have called thee in righteousness, and will hold thine hand and will keep thee, and give thee for a covenant of the people, for a light of the gentiles; to open the blind eyes, to bring out the prisoners from the prison, and them that sit in darkness out of the prison house!" And them that sit in darkness! How well Isaiah had understood! "For there is no more remembrance of the wise man than of the fool; seeing that which now is in the days to come shall be forgotten! And how dies the wise man?—as the fool." How well the Preacher had understood!

He must not give way to bitterness, Richard told himself; for if he died embittered he would die a coward. Father, forgive them, they know not what they do! Men had suffered greater ordeals than this; men had suffered every thrust and depth of horror and pain and never cried out. It was the few who suffered to redeem the many. Was that the meaning of the Jesus story? He was standing by the door with his ear to the hole, listening, for he liked to stand by the door. He was no nearer freedom there than at the opposite wall but he liked to think he was. There was a kind of intimation of light through the hole or did he imagine it? There was a stairway somewhere out there. Beyond this wall were other walls, other depths, other darknesses. Was there a person in the cell on his left, on his right? He supposed there was. The effort to exterminate the Albigenses was going on and though tens of thousands had been destroyed other thousands remained. The work of torture and slaughter would go on unabated until the last man, woman and child was dead. No doubt this dungeon was filled with the accused: through that thick wall, through this, here, there, someone trembled in the cold and darkness, listened, waited. Call now, if there be any that will answer you! Oh, if he could only speak to the person so close on this side, so close on that!

He stood tiptoe and stretched his arm up, trying to find the ceiling. He jumped up, reaching, but touched nothing. He strained his eyes in the blackness and could see nothing. He could not see his own hand when he moved it before his face, he could see nothing, he could hear nothing. When he put his ear to the hole he thought that now and then he could hear the grating of a door opened but he could not be sure. How long would they leave him here before they took him up for trial? Gerart had said that sometimes, when they had a large number of heretics, they forgot people in the cells and found them dead. Those, he had said, were the lucky ones. Richard wondered if he could extinguish his life by holding his breath or by refusing to eat. He began to move around, feeling a sensation of soft dung or of wetness under his feet, wondering if it was day or night outside. He would never know, for it would be night here all the time. Would he sleep after he was completely exhausted or would he just stand or sit night after night staring blindly and seeing nothing, listening, listening and hearing nothing?

He went to the wall opposite the door and with his fingers tried to examine the mortar. If he had a sharp instrument could he pick the mortar out and remove a stone?—and would there be earth beyond it through which a man could tunnel or was there another cell? It was the proud boast of the Church that no person ever escaped from its dungeons and Gerart had said that no man had ever heard of one who escaped. How stupid he was, for he had only his fingernails and the mortar was as hard as stone. The *in pace*! If his punishment should be confinement in a dungeon, on bread and water, his guard would be allowed so much to buy the bread and the less he gave his prisoner the more he could pocket himself. It had been told all over the land that some of the guards were so rapacious that they starved their prisoners to death. He must not come back here, after they took him out, for it would be better to confess and be burned than to become a skeleton feeding its miserable self with hope. What would he confess? Would he deny the things which Hillel had said were true? No, he would never do that. He would dare to quote Augustine

239

right in their faces: "No man should be compelled to accept our faith by force." He would say it to them and keep saying it. If they quoted St. Paul, "But, though we, or an angel from heaven, preach any other gospel unto you than that which we have preached, let him be accursed," he would fling at them Paul's other words, "Brethren, if a man be overtaken in a fault, you who are spiritual, restore such a one in the spirit of meekness." He would tell them what Hillel had said: "This terror upon the earth is not religion." He would tell them that today's heresy is tomorrow's dogma. Or would he dare?

It now seemed to him that he had been in the cell many hours and that a deeper darkness had come. He was weak from travel, despair, undernourishment and he was weary with standing; but when he moved to a corner and sank slowly to the floor he felt the chill on his flesh from his thighs to the base of his skull. His feet were drawn back with his knees up and he rested his arms across his lap and closed his eyes. He was sitting thus, breathing words of faith and hope, praying for Hillel, when he heard a faint sound, a kind of scratching sound like bird claws over stone. He opened his eyes and stared and listened. Was the person in the next cell trying to make him hear? He listened in silence until with shock so terrible that a cry escaped him he felt something at one of his feet. At once he reached out but nothing was there. Again he sat and listened and waited and again some living thing touched his foot. He arose, shaken, his being filled with the mad wild notion that another person was in the cell with him. He walked all around, his hands groping and seeking but there was nothing. He paused, he listened. Then he heard a scurrying sound above him and shuddered with horror, for he knew that the thing that had touched him was a rat. He looked up, listening, and slowly, as though spelling it out like one learning to read, he understood that in some part of the masonry there was an opening at least large enough for a rat to come through. He clasped a wall and tried to climb but there was nothing to get hold of and he only tore his flesh and sank. He went all the way around the cell, reaching up to find a crevice, some kind of hand hold, but there was none. If only for a moment he had a light to see what was above him! Were the cells built so that rats could enter? All his life he had heard stories of rats in dungeons, that they sometimes ate prisoners alive, little by little, piece by piece, until only bones remained to be taken away, bones and hair. He was so filled with terror that he wondered if he could back up to a wall and hurl his skull against the opposite wall and kill himself. . . .

He tried standing in a corner, his legs spread out a little to brace him, his back and head against the stone. If a rat came he thought he might bend over quickly and seize it, though the thought of grasping the thing filled him with shudders. He had seen many rats; Patres was full of them and they sometimes had entered his father's hovel to slink along the ceiling timbers, rapping with their long hard tail, peering down with their tiny black eyes. All the people he had known hated rats more than they hated lice. It seemed to him now that he had grown up with the sickening odor of the creatures in his nostrils and all through him. It seemed to him that he could smell them now, and the stink of mice and bats. He was standing thus, tense and waiting, when he heard a sound at the door and he hastened over with the insane notion that Baroness Elienor was there, or Hillel. Looking into the hole he listened and heard a scraping sound: something was being pushed forward into the hole. He put a trembling hand in and touched something that had not been there. It was a small stone cup. Very carefully he put a finger over its brim and down and touched water. Then slowly, carefully, he clasped the cup and drew it out and while holding it in his left hand he reached into the hole and felt another object and drew forth a piece of hard bread. He stood with the cup in one hand, the bread in the other, and listened but he could hear no sound. The guard had come and gone.

He stood there a few minutes clasping the cup and the bread. Should he eat and drink? Why should he not set them back in the hole and starve to death as the quickest and most merciful way? Hardly aware of what he was doing he raised the bread to his mouth and bit into it and began to chew, his lips tightly closed so that no crumb would be wasted. He raised the cup in the darkness until the brim touched his lips and tipped it and drank. He bit into the bread with great care so that he would waste none of it and he drained the cup. All the while he was telling himself that he was a fool to eat. What was it in a man that made him cling so desperately to life, even when that life had nothing more to offer but pain and horror? He set the cup back into the hole. After a moment he reached in and seized it and tipped it up to

241

drink again but it was empty. He had known that it was empty and he was disturbed by his irrational behavior. Was Hillel somewhere drinking a cup of water and eating a crust? Were prisoners all around him in this deep black dungeon standing alone with their pitiful meal, listening, waiting?

He thought there was something terrible in human beings that he had never been aware of until now. Gerart had said that most people loved to watch the sufferings of their fellowmen: you had only to look at their faces, he said, when a heretic was burning, to see the gloating, the cruelty, the evil joy. Sometimes they would burst into wild cries or dance like demented things around and around the screaming victim. Why was that? What in the world was it? He had asked Hillel and Hillel had shaken his head sadly and murmured, "I don't know why."

It is either evening or morning, Richard thought; each morning and each evening until they are ready for me they will bring me a cup of water and a piece of bread. If I take them from the hole they will know that I still live, if I leave them there they will open the door to see if I am dead. They did not want him to die. Merciful Father, no: they wanted him to live so that they could take him to the dark chamber with the shrouded walls and triumph over him in the name of Jesus. He put a hand up and sniffed it. His hands were stained with human filth, yet he had held the bread and had eaten it, he had even licked a finger because he thought a crumb was on it. It was easy, Hillel had said in his book, to reduce a person to a level below that of beasts. He would have to take care of his needs and he would choose some corner and squat, and add to the stench and the filth. But which corner? Which corner, he wondered, and felt all through him the tang of bitter mirth. Cattle and hogs would lie down in their dung but a cat would not. No meat-eating animal, Hillel had said, would lie in its own dung. . . .

He was standing again in a corner and was dozing a little when he heard the clear sad music of church bells. He came instantly awake and listened. The bells seemed far away but he could hear them distinctly; and then deep under the mellow tones he could hear human voices. The voices were talking in low murmuring as though they dared not be overheard and he could not understand what they were saying. He knew they were the voices of great men who had died long ago. Then he heard Hillel's words

242

as clearly as though they had been spoken at his ear: As long as you can hear the voices of Socrates . . . Hirophilus . . . Hypatia . . . Jesus . . . you will have the strength . . . no matter what they do. What had Jesus said on the cross? But it was not Jesus, it was Hillel: How many times will he have to come. . . . Hillel, he said, whispering, keep speaking to me! Talk to me, Hillel! And he seemed to hear Hillel's quiet voice saying, The wonder of it all is that the human race has survived. . . . He could hear him: To believe in honesty and honor does he have to believe that Jesus raised Lazarus from the dead? If I believe in certain things in Isaiah do I also have to believe in witches? . . .

The voice faded and Richard listened. He whispered, "Speak to me, Hillel!"

Thousands have died to make it possible for us to have the little freedom we have here. . . .

"Yes!"

If we could raise another torch in the darkness. . . .

"Yes!"

There's some sweetness, there's a little light. But under these is the immense struggle between human wills and passions . . . a struggle that goes on all over the earth. There'll never be many men perhaps who will dare hell and tyranny. . . .

"Speak!"

. . . . devotion to that truth which God made inherent in his world, leaving the discovering of it to his children. . . .

"Yes, go on!"

. . . . life is sometimes sweet—in the ringing of church bells, in the color and design of great art . . . in the prayers of Father Raoul kneeling at the altar . . . the devotion of a Jew to the customs of his fathers. . . .

"Yes, Hillel!"

. . . . in the pledge of brotherhood that we have made. . . .

"Yes!"

. . . . here under the darkness of the sky and the deeper darkness of human ignorance and superstition. . . .

He sank without knowing it to the floor, still hearing the sad quiet voice of his friend and under it the voice of music and bells. Some will always dare hell and tyranny. Yes! Hillel, I feel stronger now! He was weeping but he did not know it. I will keep the faith, he said. He was sitting now, his back to a corner, and his teeth were chattering and he was shivering but he was filled with a warm drowsiness, a drowsiness of comradeship and brave words and brave men, who had loved the dignity of man and the freedom of his mind more than they had loved life, more than they had loved life. They were with him now and he was not afraid. He was not afraid of loneliness and rats and torture. Speak to me, Hillel, his lips said, half-asleep from weariness and exhaustion. And Hillel kept speaking to him all night, all night, as half-asleep, half-awake he sat there and did not know that the rats were nibbling at his feet; did not know that he was alone in a dungeon. All night, all night, as he dozed and awakened and dozed, hearing when he dozed the music of bells and his own voice praying as he knelt with Father Raoul; hearing when he half-awakened Hillel's quiet sad voice reading from his book—for in this fight for freedom and the liberation of the mind it is doctors, among the few, who must lead the way; and the Jews who have suffered most of all people must teach how compassion is born out of persecution; and science must build a rational world above this darkness. . . . Hearing the bells far away and lonely . . . hearing Hillel's reading . . . hearing the voices of dead men out in the night, speaking to one another of things that must be. . . .

But he was at last fully aroused to pain and he rubbed at his eyes, trying to understand where he was; and as before the shock of it went through him but not so deep as before, for he was still warmed by music and voices and he did not feel alone. He drew a bare foot up and felt over it and felt a wetness; and then he drew both feet back under his thighs, knowing that the rats had been chewing on them yet not caring so much about the rats now. For what was the body but the house of the mind, and the mind no rats could chew on, not even human rats—not as long as great men did not die but left their souls in their books, in their art, in the truths that they dared hell and tyranny to set as lights on the earth. It did not matter now, he thought; he would be brave, for in his most terrible agonies Hillel would be speaking to him. Somewhere out of his own pain he would speak and across the distance they would hear one another and understand. God bless Hillel! God bless all the great men who would speak out of the night and comfort him, for they were a part of God and he would be a part of God. . . .

He wondered if it was morning. He arose and staggered a little

244

from weakness and groped his way to the door and reached up to the hole. The cup was there but was it empty? Carefully he put a finger over the brim and down and felt water and he knew then that he must have sat in the corner a long time. He bent over and on the lower part of his garment he tried to cleanse his hands. He would wipe and scrub a little and then sniff, and wipe again. Of all the stinks in the world hard to get off hands he thought that human filth was worst, worse than that of sheep and rats and mice. There was no need to keep wiping and rubbing; the smell was in his pores and under his nails. He took the cup of water and then reached in for the bread, and as before he stood bent over a little and in the pitch blackness he ate the bread and drank the water. Then he put the cup back. He must have slept, he thought, for so much time had passed. Or had they brought him more bread and water during the night? No, they would never do that, he had been asleep a long time. And he had dreamed a number of dreams.

He had been with Fleur. She had squinted her eyes at him and he had rebuked her; and she had said, It is considered modest to squint. All highborn ladies squint. She had looked at him with her lips tightly closed; and when he asked her why she did that she had said that if Christians had their lips tightly closed it was a sign that they were honest. She had clasped him lightly by one finger and he had known that she was imitating highborn ladies, who thought it the height of great refinement to hold one another lightly by one finger. He had been distressed, for it had seemed to him that his sister was making herself ridiculous with the airs of the highborn.

He had been with Hillel. They were not in Patres but in some city with clean wells and streets and Hillel was a famous doctor there and he had discovered the reasons for nearly all diseases; and people came to him looking healthy and happy and acclaiming his name. Hillel was writing another book, a larger and even wiser book, and Richard was his devoted scribe; and he was making many copies of the book and these were being buried in different places, so that sometime in the future they would be found, after all the book-burning by Christians was done. Some day—he could hear Hillel's word again—some day there would be a rational world above all this darkness, and men would be brothers. Yes, Hillel!

245

There were fragments of other dreams. In one he had been with Madelon and she was well and sweet and happy, and around her there was no aura of evil; and in another Chretien had come up to him and given him that strange searching stare and had said, We are on the same side but you will never know it. . . .

He was standing, eyes closed, trying to recall other dreams when he saw something astonishingly beautiful. A great spray of pink-rose blossoms was limned against a sunset sky of deep burning gold. While he stared, the gold very slowly lightened and faded and at the same time all the pink deepened to pale rose and then to gold that darkened little by little until it seemed suffused with blue. He opened his eyes and saw it like a lovely blooming light in the cell. He closed his eyes and it was there in the same intensity of loveliness, so delicate and pure, so untouched by any evil of earth. But while he looked at it, noting how on all its margins it faded into paler blue and from blue into gray and darkness, the whole light went away. After it was gone he could smell the odor of the blossoms and the smoke of burning oak leaves in autumn.

XXI

How much time had passed he did not know. Sometimes it seemed to him that he had been in this dark prison for days or even weeks; and again it seemed to him that he had been there only a long day and a long night. He had forgotten how many times he had taken bread and water from the hole. He had forgotten what it was like to see daylight on the earth. He was unable even with an effort of will to measure the passing of time. It seemed to him that there no longer was time, neither past nor future but only the moment in which he stood or sat. He was losing his mind, he thought; he would become mad and he would know nothing, he would only exist, and there would be nothing, neither life nor death. At times he heard the voices; at times he saw things, no matter if his eyes were closed or open, as though on his eyelids there was a continuous panorama of changing faces and scenes. He saw all the faces he had ever known, sometimes very dimly, sometimes with startling clearness; and all the scenes of the earth and sky; and he smelled all the odors he had ever known. He was enveloped by these sensations of his former life which he seemed to have brought with him into the dungeon; even the taste of things when his hunger pains were most severe; and the touch of things besides rats. Most of the time he sat in a corner, his feet drawn under him, his head back to the wall or his head bowed to his arms across his thighs. His sleeping was only half-sleep, only the twilit margin of sleep; and his waking was only half-waking. Sometimes he would go to the hole and reach in without knowing what he did, or to a certain corner where he voided himself, like a blind animal that had become accustomed to its maze.

All the while he strove to remain rational.

And when at last there was a rattling of chains at his door he did not understand what it meant. He was sitting and he did not rise. The door was swung open and a man with a light was looking in, and dimly he saw the man in the lighter darkness of the doorway. They had come at last, he thought, but he did not seem to care. When the voice in the doorway told him to come forth he staggered to his numbed feet and slowly went forward, and a strong hand grasped his arm and roughly drew him outside. The strong hand guided and led him and they went up a stairway and came to light and Richard was blinded by the light and could not see. He kept opening and closing his eyes. When he opened them there seemed to be flashes of lightning and wide reaches of sky, and when he closed them he could see a multitude of images. He thought he could hear screams somewhere around him. The guard had taken his clutch off Richard's arm and gone away and he now stood alone in what seemed to him to be a huge gloomy chamber. The light hurt his eyes but after a while he could make out figures in the chamber; and a little later he could tell that the walls were draped with enormous loose shrouds of black cloth and he could see no windows but there was light and it seemed blinding and he could not tell why. He became conscious of murmuring voices—and of a cleaner air which he was breathing—and of a long silence that at last had been broken. I am now to be tried, he thought; I must be brave, I will be brave. He felt weak and he wanted to sit but he sensed that several pairs of eyes were steadily watching him, though he could not see the eyes, only the figures of men in black shrouds. There seemed to be nothing in the room that was not black except the lights and he was not sure there were any lights. The figures of men he could tell now were shrouded from their heads to their feet, in loose hanging folds of black cloth like that on the walls. How long, he wondered, must he stand here? He moved his toes, feeling of the floor and understood that it was carpeted. The chamber was much warmer than his cell and he began to tremble as the warmth penetrated him. He felt a need to vomit. He still opened and shut his eyes, trying to accustom them to the light; and he was sure now that he could hear screams and he supposed that the torture-chamber was somewhere not far away. What questions would they ask him? What witnesses would be brought against him? Had they tortured Fleur to make her confess? Had they questioned Elienor? He looked round him hoping that Hillel would be here and instantly was shamed by his weakness.

He could not have said how long he stood there, shivering and waiting; but at last a man came over and led him to a table and told him to sit. It was a long table draped in black and around it sat a number of persons and other persons stood back, looking at him. There were two inquisitors and their assistants and two men sworn to eternal silence who would be witnesses and two guards. The guards stood back and after a few moments they went away. Richard was at the end of a long table and now a man stood at the other end facing him. On the table were papers and several books and Richard did not know that these were the Gospels. A man prepared himself to write and Richard supposed that he was the clerk who would take down everything said.

The man facing Richard cleared his throat. "You are Richard, the son of one named Victoir and his wife Elise. You have a brother named Pascal, a sister named Fleur. Your father's father's name was Peire and he was a heretic in Beziers. You were infatuated with a girl named Madelon, a heretic now dead. You were born a serf but you consorted with a Jew who bought your freedom; and you lived in Patres, the village where you lived, and went to Toulouse and there became the student of a heretic named Gerart. You returned to Patres and became the scribe of this Jew whose name is Hillel." It was a strong deep voice speaking to him. It now asked coldly: "Do you deny any of these statements?"

Richard tried to speak but choked up. He was shaking. He said something and it seemed to him that his voice was very loud.

"Lower your voice," the inquisitor said, "and answer me."

"I—" O God, if he could only speak! "I know nothing about my father's father."

"You understand that you must give evidence against all persons you suspect?"

"I—"

"Do you understand that?"

In a voice that still seemed loud to him he said, "I suspect none."

"Wasn't your father a heretic? Didn't you hear him express doubts of the holy Church?"

"No sir."

"Do you know why you're here?"

"I—no sir."

"You're here accused of heresy. You're accused of believing otherwise than as our holy Church believes. Are you guilty or innocent?"

Trembling, Richard bowed his head and murmured, "I don't know."

"You mean you don't know what our holy Church believes?"

"I—I don't know if I believe all of it."

"Do you know that doubt itself is heresy? . . . Do you know that?"

"I've heard it is."

"Then you've already confessed to heresy. Do you realize that?"

"I only said—"

"Answer me, yes or no."

Hillel, he whispered, deep in him, be with me! He glanced up and gasped, "I can't answer yes or no! Truth for me isn't that simple."

"Truth is not that simple? Then you don't believe that all truth has been revealed by God to our holy Church?"

Struggling desperately to quiet his trembling frame, his trembling voice, he said: "I think God made truth inherent in the world he created." He met the black eyes a moment. "I think he expects us to discover the truth. I think that's one form of revelation."

There was a moment of silence, save for the pen scratching on paper. Then the cold voice spoke again. "You think every person should determine truth according to his prejudices? Is that what you think?"

"Augustine said no person should be compelled to accept our faith by force." Inside he comforted himself with the thought, Hillel, I had the courage to say it!

"The great Augustine said nothing of the kind. He said, Quid est enim pejor, mors animae quam libertas erroris? I'll translate it for you. Which is worse, the death of the soul or the freedom to err? You think men should have the freedom to err and lose their souls?"

Richard drew a sharp breath. He was telling himself, I must be brave, I must speak up! He said: "Some of the popes have said things other popes denied. Were some of them heretics? Pope

250

John said it was heresy to say Jesus and his apostles were poor. The canons of the Decretum say simony is heresy. Then are Christians guilty of simony heretics? Hildebrand said that fornicating priests are heretics. Was he a heretic, or are the priests?"

"Simony," said the cold voice, "is heresy."

"Then are all the people heretics who buy religious offices?"

"You're not here to ask questions. And I warn you that your spirit of intransigence will be taken into account when your punishment is determined. Have you believed in any faith but the Christian faith?"

"I believe with Jesus that truth will make men free."

"Do you accept the faith of our holy Church?"

"I—I don't know."

"Do you believe in God the Father and in the Son and in the Holy Ghost?"

"Yes, in what they mean to me."

"We want no evasions here but straightforward answers. Do you believe that Jesus was born of a virgin?"

Richard turned a little, as if to escape. He was sweating. He felt weak and trapped and helpless. But he forced himself to look up at the black eyes and say, as calmly as he could: "The word in Isaiah, translated virgin, doesn't mean virgin but girl or young woman."

"Who told you that?"

"Jews say it. They know what their own language means."

"Then you don't believe that Jesus was born of a virgin?"

"I don't know."

"You don't know if you believe?"

"I just don't know if such things are true."

"Then you're no Christian. Do you believe the bread and wine in the Mass is changed into the body and blood of Christ by divine virtue?"

"In a symbolic way." Again under his breath he said, Hillel, be with me!

"Do you believe priests are holy men?"

He thought of Father Luce and said: "Not all."

"Have you known one who is not?"

"I've known one who is."

"Answer the question."

"Yes."

"What is his name?"

Richard turned again and glanced round at the silent faces. "He's one of my accusers."

"I warn you again that your arrogance and contempt—"

"O God!" Richard cried, speaking with passion, goaded beyond endurance. "I know you'll burn or destroy me but I won't deny the truth!" He broke for a moment and sobbed. He looked up again at the face and cried: "Why don't my accusers face me? Is this Christian justice? Why isn't someone allowed to speak for me? Did Jesus say the accused should be faced only by his enemies and not even know the names of those who accuse him? Did he say that if they lie their lies are to be accepted? Is this Christian justice?"

"You are very stubborn," said the voice, "but we have ways to deal with that. Shall we show you the instruments?"

Fighting to control his emotions Richard said as quietly as he could: "I've supposed that you'd torture me. But you can kill me and I'll not deny what I believe is truth. I don't think this is Christian justice."

"You won't deny?" asked the voice, deadly in its quiet. "We have ways to make you deny, for if you do not recant and abjure your soul is damned forever. What did Saint Paul say?—that if a man preach another gospel and you believe you are accursed."

"He said we should bear one another's burdens."

"Do you think we're not bearing yours? Aren't we spending our time to persuade you to turn from your evil ways and accept the truth which God revealed to our Church and to our Church alone? If you persist in heresy you'll lose your soul. We would bring you back to truth. We do it for your sake. What does it say in the Book of Revelation?—we have somewhat against you because you have left your first love. Remember therefore from whence you are fallen and repent, else I will come to you quickly and remove your candlestick out of its place, except you repent. What did the blessed Apostle John say?—If a man abide not in me he is cast forth as a branch and is withered; and men gather them and cast them into the fire and they are burned. You do not abide. You have strayed so far that you have consorted with a Jew, yet it is written in the Gospel, You know how it is an unlawful thing for a man that is a Jew to keep company, or come unto one of another nation. You—"

252

"This Jew," said Richard, "is a noble man. I don't know what you've done with him but I know that God loves him and is with him."

"If you persist in such wicked words you will be cast forth as a branch that is withered and you'll be cast into a fire and burned. But first you will recant, so that your soul may be saved."

"A soul isn't saved if the mind isn't convinced."

"Your soul will be saved. We can promise you that. We have ways to save it. Now I must continue with the questions. Did this Jew Hillel try to turn you away from the only true Church?"

"No!"

"Did he express contempt for believers in the Christ?"

"No. He said there are good things in the Christian faith."

"Did he admit to you that he belongs to an accursed race?"

"No. He doesn't."

"Do you understand what you're saying and that all your answers are being written down?"

"Yes."

"Did the Jews deny the Lord?"

"Jews have no son of God."

"Was Jesus the messiah and Lord and son of God?"

"I—I don't know."

"You understand that doubt is heresy?"

Richard hesitated. Then simply he said, "Yes."

"Is it true that you love the books written by the heathen?"

Richard looked up at the eyes and said: "Was Peter Damiani, Cardinal of Ostia, a holy man?"

"I'm asking the questions. You'll answer them."

"I'm answering. This Cardinal said, Cicero was music in my ears; the songs of the poets beguiled me; the philosophers shone upon me with their golden phrases. He was a cardinal, yet that is what he said. If books by the heathen meant so much to him—"

"You will answer. Is it true that you love books by the heathen?"

"Some of them."

"Do you know that love of such books is heresy?"

"Then Cardinal Damiani was a heretic."

"I must warn you again that we have a way to deal with arrogance. You—"

"I'm not arrogant. I've been trying to learn."

"You'll learn before we're done with you. Answer my questions simply and briefly and don't try to instruct me. Do you believe that God delights in the destruction of his enemies?"

"No."

"Then you don't believe the Bible. Was Saul punished for sparing Agag? Did the prophet Samuel have him hewn to pieces? Did God command the slaughter of the unbelieving Canaanites? Did he praise Elijah for killing four hundred and fifty priests of Baal? Do you understand that mercy to enemies of the only true faith is disobedience to God? . . . Answer me."

"No."

"Very well. That is better." The inquisitor was silent a few moments, looking at Richard. Then he said, quietly, patiently: "How did David cry out?—I hate them that hate thee, O God! Christians must hate those who reject the only true faith. Now I have some other questions to ask you, for we must determine the full extent of your heresy to know what your punishment should be. Answer simply, for I cannot be with you all day." He turned to the other inquisitor. "Do you wish to question him?"

Richard now looked at the other man and was shocked. He had paid no attention to him since coming to the table. Now he looked into the black eyes of Father Luce.

"I think not," Father Luce said. "Continue."

"Have you ever said that a wicked priest pollutes the holy sacraments?"

His mind going swiftly to Fleur Richard looked again at Father Luce.

"Answer the question."

"I think the sacrament is holy but that—"

"Don't try to instruct us. Answer the question."

"Yes."

"Do you realize that you are confessing to arrant and abominable heresy?"

"No. I think—"

"Please don't evade. Just give simple answers. Now you knew a girl named Madelon, a heretic now dead. Did you seduce her before you ran away to Toulouse?"

"No!"

"But you did run away?"

"No. I wanted to see the university."

"Who bought your freedom for you?"

"I don't wish to tell."

"Was it the Jew?"

"I don't wish to tell."

"We have ways to make you tell but in this instance we know. Does this Jew have a lot of money?"

"I—I don't know."

"We think you do know and we have ways to make you tell that. Now you seduced this girl and ran away and when you returned you told around Patres that Father Luce had seduced her. Did you?"

Richard glanced again at Father Luce and said: "She was pregnant when she died."

"Did you say that Satan doesn't copulate with women?"

"I don't know."

"Do you think he does?"

"No."

"Then if you didn't and Satan didn't you think Father Luce did?"

Richard turned and looked full into Father Luce's eyes.

"Answer the question."

Still looking into the eyes Richard said, "Yes," and inside him he said, It is all over with me!

There was a terrible silence. The inquisitor looked at the scribe, as though to give him time to write the answer down. "You just told us you think Father Luce seduced this girl. You understand what you're saying?"

"I'm saying," said Richard, again speaking with passion, "that it's known all over the Christian world that some priests do seduce helpless girls and it's said that some of the convents are nothing but brothels and have piles of infant bones—"

"Who told you that?"

"These stories are told everywhere."

"Who told you?" asked the deadly voice.

"I've heard them all my life."

"I ask again, who told you?"

Richard thought, My father is dead, they can't hurt him. He said: "My father."

The inquisitor turned to the scribe. "Note that," he said. "We'll dig up this heretic's bones. Who else told you?"

"No one." Richard thought, It's all over with me, does it matter now what I say!

"Have you said some priests have concubines?"

"The people believe that."

"Who told you?"

"My father."

"Did the Jew tell you?"

"No. He always spoke of Christians with kindness."

"Have you said that women are of the same order of creation as men?"

"Yes."

"You don't believe women are inferior to men?"

"No."

"Then why did God make woman out of man's rib?"

"I don't think he did."

"Again you doubt the holy Bible."

"As Abelard said—"

"We're not interested in what the heretic Abelard said. Have you praised the Jewish attitude toward women above the Christian?"

"I admire it more."

"In what way?"

"Jews don't think sexual love is vile. They don't prey on helpless girls. They—"

"That is enough. Have you accepted the religion of the Jews?"

"No."

"Do you think there is truth in it?"

"If not," said Richard, looking up at the eyes, "why did Christians steal their holy books?"

"Steal them!" The voice had risen. He turned to the scribe. "Do you have that answer written down?" The scribe nodded. The inquisitor turned to the two witnesses. "Did you mark that well?" They bowed assent. The inquisitor turned to Richard and said: "Have you said that if a scientific opinion contradicts our holy faith it should be determined which is true?"

"I think—"

"Answer the question."

"I will. Our Church says the sun moves around the earth. Science says the earth moves around the sun. Which is true?"

"You think God erred?"

256

"No. I think men err."

"Our Church says that if science contradicts an article of our faith science must be abandoned. Do you believe that?"

"No."

"You think science should be allowed to overthrow our faith?"

"When it is true."

"The blessed Apostle Paul said, If any man is ignorant let him be ignorant. Do you believe that?"

"I don't think God wants us to be ignorant."

"You think Paul wasn't speaking for God?"

"I think that time he was speaking for Paul."

Again there was silence. Then: "Are you a Cathartist?"

"No."

"Do you think there's any truth in what these people teach?"

"They teach that Jesus didn't wear velvet and silk and gold and jewels. I think that's true. They teach that the Old Testament and the New Testament contradict one another a lot of times. The Old says, I'll put enmity between man and woman but the New says God will reconcile all things unto himself. In the Old the children of God sin but the New says, Whosoever is begotten of God does no sin. In the Old—"

"That will do." He looked over at Father Luce. "I see no reason to question this heretic further. Do you wish to?"

"No."

The inquisitor turned back to Richard. "Richard, you've confessed to the blackest heresy I've ever heard in this chamber and I have questioned hundreds of them. Do you now recant and abjure these evil things, these abominable beliefs?"

"I think—"

"We know what you think. You have told us. You've said enough to condemn your soul to eternal perdition. It is our duty to save it. Do you understand that?"

"I understand that you believe that."

"Do you recant and abjure?"

"I'll not deny what I think is true."

"We'll see about that." He looked at Father Luce and his question chilled Richard to his marrow: "Are all the instruments busy?" Then, with almost fatherly compassion, almost with gentleness, he said to Richard: "We're going to show you mercy. We're going to give you a little while to think this over. I be-

257

seech you, as though I were your father, to humble yourself, to pray, to ask God for guidance. You are young, Richard. If only you will pray, if only you will ask our Father to show you the light." He went to the door and summoned a guard and said, "Take him down."

XXII

He was taken down and thrust into the cell, the guard propelling him with such force that he staggered and sprawled. He crept over to the corner where he customarily sat, his strength drained, his mind darkening, and for the moment his courage gone. During the long ordeal he had kept Hillel's name in his thoughts and Hillel's face before him. He knew now that he was doomed and he whispered again, Hillel, be with me!

What a strange thing a Christian was! He cared nothing about the body, nothing at all; it was only the temporal house of the soul, it could be tortured, mutilated, burned, destroyed and thrown into a grave to be forgotten. But the soul had to be saved. With calculated thoroughness they would force him to recant and abjure. They would starve him, they would leave him here with the rats; they would take him up and torture him and return him to the cell and torture him again. This would be his ordeal until out of agony he denied what he believed to be true or until, unable to endure more, he died. According to Church doctrine a man could be tortured only once but inquisitors got around this by saying that torture was not completed but *continued*.

He understood now in his woe that the inquisitor was not really an evil man. That was what made it so terrible. He saw himself as a very good and holy man, a man who wanted to save other souls as well as his own; a kind of angry and impatient and frustrated father, wearied by the stupid stubbornness of heretics who would blindly damn themselves to eternal torments rather than confess their errors and come to God. It was his duty and his unpleasant task to save them. That was the way, Richard now understood, that the inquisitor looked at the matter. That was the only way he could look at it, once he accepted all the Church's dogmas as infallible and changeless truth. The matter for him was very simple: man had fallen, God had revealed all truth to the Christians, it was there, it was to be accepted without doubts or questions. If you did not accept all of it you were headed for hell and your more determined brothers were determined to save you, as a great kindness. How could they force you except with torture? If persuasion and pleading failed what could they do but burn your flesh off and break your bones? Thinking of the inquisitor he had a kind of feeling of friendliness for him, almost of respect, even while loathing his fanatical blindness. . . .

He tried to recall now other things that Gerart had said. If a man refused to confess they sometimes gave him wine mixed with drugs to weaken his will. Or sometimes they slipped a person into his cell, who to gain his confidence pretended to be a heretic but who actually was a spy. Or they tortured your relatives and friends to force them to testify against you. But with him they did not have to do these things. He had confessed to heresy so black and infamous that the inquisitor had actually been shocked. Looking back, Richard realized that, and he tried to recall all the things that had been said. He recalled a number of things, any one of which was enough to send him to the stake or to the dungeon for life. He had said—and he remembered how the inquisitor had shuddered—that if a Church belief and a scientific opinion did not agree it should be determined which was true. He had said that a wicked priest polluted the sacrament. He had said that Christians had stolen the holy books of the Jews. He had said that women were of the same order of creation as men. Lord!

He was doomed, he thought, and bowed to his arms. It was only a question now of how long he would be made to suffer. They would never let him go until he recanted and he would never recant. Or would he? If they could make the Pope confess to heresy, what chance had he? How dared he imagine that he could endure the agonies and keep his lips sealed? He would, he would! But could he? Gerart had said that no man had ever been known to endure all the tortures without recanting—for they had so many ways, all fiendishly contrived to make the body suffer unendurably. If he could not endure it why should he not recant now and get it over with? But what if under torture he was asked about Hillel's money or Hillel's beliefs? What if they were determined to destroy him also?

Could he kill himself? He held his breath as long as he could, until blackness was swallowing him and things were ringing in his ears, until he almost fainted; but at the moment of losing consciousness he gasped and came up, stricken, sucking air. He wondered if he could smash his skull against the wall, or if he struggled with the guard next time the man came if he would mercifully drive a knife through him. He wanted to die now, while he could still think, for he knew that he was not a strong man and could not endure all the torture. But he could think of no way out. He would live. He would have to endure it. If only they would give him more to eat, so that he would have strength—but no bread and water were brought to him this night or what he took to be the next day. He went again and again to the hole but nothing was there.

He could not tell how much time was passing but his thirst had become intolerable and hunger pangs moved from his stomach down through his bowels and convulsed him with cramps. He tried to sleep to gain strength but he could not sleep. He tried to pray. He would kneel with his face to the wall and pray to God and turn away from prayer no stronger than before. He would recall Hillel's words and hear his voice speaking—Aristotle . . . Hippocrates . . . Hirophilus . . . Hero and Hypatia and Euclid . . . Isaiah and Job, yes, and Jesus are all there, speaking to you. Scores of men and women are speaking to you who dared to say, Let there be light. . . . You have the fellowship of the greatest who have lived and taught and died. . . . He thought, There is no worse death than crucifixion, yet Jesus endured it. Jesus had thought that God had deserted him but he never denied God. Yes, but Jesus had not been thrown into a dungeon and starved for days or weeks; he had not had to sit in black loneliness night after night, with his feet drawn under him to keep the rats from chewing, with his hands moving blindly out in sleep to strike them away. He had been taken in his full strength to the cross. But here he sat, growing weaker and weaker and they would starve him until he was too weak to rise and then they would take him to the torture-chamber. They knew what they were doing! They had tortured so many that they had made torture an art or a science. He had no chance against them. . . .

261

Now and then a little bread and water were brought and he ate and drank but they were slowly starving him. He could not even guess how much time had passed. He could hardly be sure of his own name. Too weak to stand any longer without feeling dizzy, too empty any longer to have any need to void, he would sit in the corner, struggling to keep his mind clear, fighting to preserve his courage which he felt dissolving into the suffering and emptiness of his being; murmuring over and over words of courage and light. . . . I think arrogance is the greatest of the sins . . . greater than avarice or lying or murder . . . these are sins of the passions but arrogance is the sin of the mind. . . . God reveals his purpose to each of us to the extent of our understanding . . . our capacity to understand his will is the measure of our godliness. . . . But as he whispered the words over and over they became meaningless, they were not words at all, they were not even memory, as his energies waned and his mind darkened. He tried to keep them in full stature in his thoughts but they were shrinking. Endlessly, endlessly he told himself to keep talking or he would lose consciousness and sometimes when he dozed off his lips kept moving. Now and then with a sense of sickening horror he would recall the widespread belief that often the delays were long between questioning and torture—months, even years. He no longer cared about himself. But what if they tortured him to force him to betray others?—for if they had learned that Hillel had money they would stop at nothing to get it. If he could only die now. If only they had forgotten him. He prayed to God to let him die. . . .

When awake he heard almost continuously now the sound of bells. Most of the time they were low and sad and far away, as though all the bells all over the land were softly tolling; but once in a while they would come in so loud and clear that he was startled. Mingled with the sound of bells was the murmur of voices as of people everywhere talking but he could not understand what they said. He thought that among them he could hear his father's voice and that of Father Raoul praying and that of Fleur crying. He wondered dully if Hillel was dead.

And he saw faces more and more plainly as he grew weaker; and this was so whether his eyes were opened or closed. Even when his head was bowed and his eyes shut tight he would see the face of Father Luce; it would come in from darkness and he would see it coming, see it slowly shaping and becoming clearer, until it was there before him, the black intent hypnotic eyes looking into his eyes and the whole face lightly touched with a smile. Or it was the sad pale frightened face of Fleur; or it was the face of Hillel, looking at him earnestly, the eyes searching him for doubt and weakness, the eyes saying, We made a pledge of brotherhood, neither as Christian nor Jew but as two men . . . never to betray one another . . . to be faithful to the truth . . . never to deny it. . . . May God's light shine upon you to be a blessing. . . . Or he would see the wrinkled face and sad eyes of Gerart and hear Gerart saying, God reveals himself to those who inquire and those afraid to inquire he leaves to their folly. . . . Or he would see a multitude of faces, of all the people he had known and of people he had never known, as if all the people of earth were gathering to a great assembly. They would come and fade and return, sometimes bathed in strange lights, sometimes very dim in enveloping darkness. . . .

When he dozed he dreamed. In one dream he was climbing a ladder. It was a very strong ladder made of oak poles with oak rungs. The rungs were so fat and strong that his hands could not close around them. He could feel their strength under his bare feet. He climbed for a long while and knew that he was far above the earth, for he could see the earth spread out below him in a vast expanse of valleys and mountains; and still he climbed, for the ladder seemed to extend endlessly beyond him, to pierce the sky and stand up and up in pure light. He climbed until he came to the topmost rung and above him he saw Jesus smiling down upon him and Jesus looked like a Jew and he heard Jesus saying, Suffer all truth-seekers to come unto me. He stood on the topmost rung and heaven seemed to be all around him; and he stretched his arms out as though they were wings and stepped off; and then he was floating, suspended, in peace and all around him were the choirs of heaven, singing. This dream was so sweet and strong and good that on awaking he tried to move back into its atmosphere as into the shelter of a mother's arms.

There was another dream that was so utter in its horror and dread that it made him sob in his sleep. He seemed to be standing before Hillel's house in Patres, though in one moment it was his house and in the next it was his father's hovel. While standing there, alone, he sensed some imminent disaster. He listened. He heard vast explosive but muffled sounds far overhead and saw a prodigious convulsion of the whole upper atmosphere. There were stupendous gray eruptions of what seemed to be billowing clouds and smoke but they were pale and wan like some strange atmosphere that had risen from innumerable graveyards. The earth under them was filled with light as from hidden fires and the light was darkening, slowly. All this was terrifying but the worst terror was from what he could feel but not see: a kind of enormous engulfing loneliness but more than that; an approaching menace, a vast and sinister thing, but with no threatening sounds, no apparitions. It was a sense of the end of something, even of the end of all things. It was a sense that all of death had gathered here. The most horrible part of it at this stage of the dream was the way all the familiar aspects of sky and earth were changing, until, though he recognized them, they were not what he had known all his life but were being suffused and filled and darkened with an alien and menacing power, the power to consume and destroy or the power to blight and wither, as though gaseous poisons had filled the earth. There was an odor that was strange and evil. But the awful thing that broke him to sobs was the absolute quiet.

He stood looking into the west; staring up at all the moving masses of wan unearthly light; listening; and there was no sound. Then, above Hillel's house, something that had been hidden until this moment slowly came in sight. It was a strange blackness that resembled cloud or smoke but was neither, for it was not of this world. It was two or three hundred feet above the earth. In shape it was a few hundred feet long and a hundred feet or so in depth; and it moved out from its hiding and then seemed not to move at all, but lay there in the sky, its power complete and supreme; and some kind of atmosphere or spirit seemed to emanate from it and this began to fill all the sky roundabout. The whole of earth and sky was being conquered by it, as a mind by loneliness or a graveyard by night. Richard stared at it and all of hope died within him. Everything seemed to die within him and he knew that this was his end; and all the despair and heartbreak of his soul, for him and for the whole human race, broke forth into awful bitter sobbing. . . .

Then he was awake and trembling with the horror of it. He sensed that the blackness he had seen was a symbol of death and that death had filled the whole earth and sky; and that when he stared at the sinister force of it that was like nothing in the world and felt the force seizing and paralyzing him he was face to face with his end. There was nothing that could be opposed to that vast and enveloping substance that had filled all existence and needed only to become visible to make men cry out and sob like children, as Richard was sobbing now. This dream was such a terrible thing in its finality, in its soft implacable insistence, in its quiet assurance of its mighty and conquering powers, that he could not shake off the nightmare of it, the smell of it and the horror of it, but shook with sobs that strangled him, gasping out, "O Hillel!", gasping out his tortured soul.

This dream was never to leave him to the day of his death. Life had its powers, its lights and joys, the warm full substance of all that it was; but this other and greater power, rising from its hidden places, had engulfed and overwhelmed it, until there was nothing left but the sinister gray pall and the softness and soundlessness and the blackness in the heart of it, as though a fire covering the earth had burned without flame and without ashes.

The next time he dozed off he reached out in sleep, as had become his way, to ward off the rats; and while he slept his hand closed on one of the furry creatures and held it. The rat bit his hand and this aroused him but he was stuporous, and though his hand did not relax its grasp it took him some moments to realize that he had a rat in his clutch, to become aware that the rat's sharp teeth were set in his flesh. He put his other hand out and from the underside gently took the rat by its throat. With one hand clasping the throat so that the creature could not bite and with his other hand closed around its back and haunches he drew it to him, drew it to his lap and held it there. He was trying to think about it. He was trying to understand that this creature would devour him but that he now had it in his power, to choke to death or to crush. The rat's claws were digging at his garment and going through to his flesh and the soft furry body was writhing and struggling to be free. And Richard was feeling only tenderness for it. Merely to hold it and feel its wild heart beat and to sense kinship in its terror was almost as sweet as freedom itself. Still clasping its throat he moved his fingers down to capture the hindpaws. When he was secure from claws and teeth he held the rat against his face to feel its warmth and its heart. He gently rubbed the fur back and forth across his cheeks, his mouth, his closed eyes and then he moved the rat down and held the wild beating heart against his own heart.

An hour later he still held it, for he did not want to let it go. It was a living thing and he loved it because he had such need of life. He wondered if he could tear off a part of his garment and make a kind of house for it, and so keep it with him. He began to talk to it, saying all kinds of foolish and tender things. He put it again to his face and kissed its fur. It had stopped struggling now but he had not hurt it. He kept its face away from him, knowing that it would bite, but all the rest of it was friendly in its living warmth and he loved it. . . .

He was sitting with the rat in his two hands when the door was flung open. He looked over and knew that a man was there but he could not see the man.

"You in there!" said a voice. "Come out."

With difficulty Richard got to his feet and went over and through the doorway, still holding the rat. He held the rat so that the guard would not see it or know about it. With a hand on his arm he was led up the long stone stairway and into a lighted room but as before he was blinded by the light and could see nothing. He stood there, holding the rat under a half-fold of his garment, hardly knowing where he was but knowing that he had a living thing with him which he would not betray. He did not know that a number of men were staring at him. He did not know that his companion had been discovered until a hand roughly jerked his two hands away from his body and a voice cried, "He has a rat!"

Richard heard voices. He was swaying because he was very weak.

"Take it away," a voice said.

"No!" Richard said and turned blindly to flee.

He would have fled back to his cell but two men seized him. One wrenched his clutch off the rat, and with a sense of having been outraged Richard knew that his hands were empty and he felt the loneliness in his hands.

XXIII

He was taken to a bench and told to sit and he sat until his eyes became accustomed to the light. He could tell that the walls of this chamber were thick, but even so, he could hear gurglings and moanings beyond them or now and then a scream.

He was summoned to the table where he had sat formerly and the one who had examined him said: "Richard, your confession will now be read to you." The clerk who had written down the questions and answers now stood at the end of the table and read word for word everything that had been said.

The inquisitor spoke again. "You've heard the confession. Are the answers as you gave them?"

Richard heard himself say in a low voice, "Yes."

"You confessed to the most abominable heresy. If you will now recant and abjure your wickedness and throw yourself on the mercy of our Father and of the Holy Office your punishment will be determined. If you have fully perceived your errors mercy will be shown to you. If you have not you will be delivered to the secular authorities." He paused, as though waiting for the scribe to catch up. "Do you acknowledge the errors of your ways?"

Richard said: "I won't deny what I think is true."

"You mean that you know more about what is true than the Holy Office knows, which received its authority from our blessed Lord the Christ?" Richard gave no reply. He was staring at the table and trying to strengthen himself for what was coming. "Richard, do you realize that if you stubbornly persist in your evil ways you will damn your soul to eternal perdition? . . . Do you?"

He thought the voice was rather gentle. This man, he thought, thinks he is a good man. He would say that his only desire is to save my soul.

"Richard, do you?"

"I understand that that is what you believe."

"You're multiplying your sins, for you have now challenged the wisdom of the Holy Office. You're forcing us to take the most extreme measures for the good of your soul. Are you aware of that?"

"I'm aware that that is what you think."

"I don't know," said the voice, sounding perplexed, "how well you understand these matters. I'll explain them. You confessed to many kinds of heresy, not only willingly but, it sometimes seemed, gladly. Heresy is a dreadful sin. Even if committed through ignorance a return to the light is not enough; your evil ways must be admitted and then abjured before you can be considered as a penitent, entitled to any thought of mercy in your punishment. But you cannot be allowed to abjure before you confess the wickedness in the things you believe. Denial of that wickedness is obduracy, which must be punished by death with fire. You must confess your sins and then you must abjure them. Do you understand?"

Richard looked up and met the eyes. His mouth was dry and it was with difficulty that he spoke. "I know that you're doing what you think is best for me. If I confess and abjure I'll then be burned alive or left to rot in a dungeon. In that case I'd be a coward. If I do not confess and abjure I'll be tortured." He paused a moment to gather his strength and then said: "I can see no choice between what you will do to me. So how foolish I would be to deny what I believe to be a part of God."

Gently the voice asked, "And what is that?"

"I believe God made truth inherent in this world. I think scientists are discovering some of that truth. I don't believe all truth was revealed to our Church."

"What you mean, Richard, is that in spite of our pleadings and prayers you will persist in your heresy. Is that what you mean?"

"I mean—" He licked his dry lips and tried to swallow. "I just mean I won't deny what I think is true, no matter what you do."

The fatherly voice said: "Don't you understand that we have ways to save you?"

"I know you have ways to torture me."

"Well, Richard, we'll show you some of those ways. We ask you again to humble yourself in prayer and in meditation to God."

Richard gasped: "I wish you'd kill me now!"

"We have no wish to kill you. We have a great wish to save your soul." He looked at Richard and seemed to be considering. "You're very stubborn." He turned and summoned a guard. "Show Richard the instruments and what they will do."

The man who now took Richard in charge was thick and rugged, with a low forehead and heavy features and a short black beard. He took Richard through a door and into a hall and through another door; and with one quick glance Richard knew that he was in the torture-chamber. By the garb of the three men who first fell on his vision he assumed that bishops and inquisitors or both were present, as under the rules they were supposed to be.

The torture room's appearance was in keeping with its purpose: the walls were of huge stone blocks, blackened by the smoke from fires. There were no windows. The floor was of stone. In the center of the room was a long table covered with a cloth as red as blood. In the far end was a fireplace with a glowing fire, which was the only light except a few torches held by human hands, and a candle on a small table where a man sat, writing.

The man took Richard aside and stood by a wall. He was staring at Richard; he was studying his face and he was grinning his evil grin. "See," he said. "Look all around."

Richard's second glance had shown him that a number of persons were being tortured. He caught a glimpse of the awful ugly agony in a human face and closed his eyes, and at once the man prodded him in his ribs and said, "Look. If you can't stand to look what'll you do when they put you on the rack. You come here to look, so look and then I'll show you the things."

"Take me away!" Richard whispered.

"Take you away? Oh no. You come here to see and you're going to see. So just look and listen." When Richard did not open his eyes the man said sharply: "I said look! If you don't look we'll put the boot on you. If you look and see what it's like then maybe you'll do what they ask you to do." The man gave him a savage poke in his ribs. "I said look!"

Richard opened his eyes, thinking, I may as well look, I'll be dead soon. . . . The scene came to him through all his senses. He saw, rather dimly, as in a terrible dream, the one they had hoisted

269

with his arms behind his back . . . the one on the rack . . . the one being tortured by fire. He heard the awful groans and the sudden nerve-shattering screams. He smelled the burning of human hair and flesh. He felt his own flesh quivering all over his body and smarting and stinging as though struck with nettles. And he could taste the thick atmosphere of the room, its smoke and burning meat. . . .

"First," said the man, "I'll show you the instruments not being used." He grasped Richard's trembling arm. "Come," he said. When Richard did not move he angrily jerked him forward and seized both his arms and shook him. "I said come!"

He took Richard to a corner where a number of instruments stood. "Look," he said and he picked up a pair of heavy boots that would reach to a man's knees. "You put your feet in these," he said. "Then they pour them full of melted lead or boiling water. Then you talk." All the while he was studying Richard's ashen face. "If you don't talk, see here." He picked up a boot made of iron. He explained that a person put his feet and lower legs into these boots and then wedges of wood or iron were inserted between the boot and the flesh and driven down with a mallet, driven clear to the bottom of the boots. All the flesh, he said, was stripped off the bones as the wedges went down and the bones themselves were splintered and crushed, until a person's feet and lower legs were only mangled flesh and bones and blood. "They talk," he said, "when we use the boot. We don't use it until we've used all the others." He was studying Richard's face. "Can you feel it? Can you imagine what it's like?"

He said: "How'd you like to be buried alive? Did you ever hear of the sister of Aymeric, governor of Le Voeur? She was buried alive. But that ain't so bad," he said. "A person don't last so long when we do that. He chokes to death pretty quick. We won't bury you alive. We got other ways for you. Look at this," he said and he took down from a spike on the wall a *san benito*, a penitential garment of yellow cloth that fell to the knees. If they burned him alive, the man said, on the san benito would be painted his picture, burning in the flames, with dragons and devils all around him, fanning the fire. He would have a rope around his neck and he would carry in his hand a yellow candle. If he abjured just before being led out the flames would be painted licking downward; this would indicate that he was not to be burned

270

alive but would be strangled first. On his head he would wear a *coroza,* a pointed pasteboard cap three feet tall; and on it would be painted flames, devils and crosses. He might have a gag in his mouth to keep him from insulting good and holy Christians while he was led to the stake. "Like her," said the man and jerked his thick thumb toward a woman being tortured. The woman was screaming, "Thieves and fornicators!" and Richard became aware that he had been hearing her cry, repeated over and over.

"Here," said the man, delightedly watching Richard's trembling body and white sweating face, "is what we'll probably use on you first." In this form of torture, he explained, the person was forced to lie at full length on the floor and was bound. Two pieecs of iron concave on one side were affixed to the heel of the right foot and a screw was then turned inward to the flesh and bone. This, he said, was the easiest form. It was all some heretics needed. While Richard heard him dully as from far away he went on to say that next they would use water. They would make him lie down and open his mouth and they would let water trickle into his open mouth and he would almost choke to death and he would burst blood vessels in the violence of his efforts to breathe and blood would run from his nose and ears; or they would make him drink a huge quantity of water and would then beat him over his belly with a board; or they would bind a piece of linen cloth over his face and pour water on it and he would strangle. This was also an easy form, the man said, proud of his knowledge of these things. Richard was leaning against a wall while the man explained these minor forms. "You ain't very strong," the man said, studying his face. "Water or the dice will take care of you. But if you're stubborn—Well, I'll show you."

When Richard did not move the man again seized him and jerked him forward. He propelled him over to a man being tortured with the strappado or pully. The wrists had been bound together behind the man's back and a rope had been tied to the cord that bound the wrists. In the ceiling was a pulley, through which the rope ran, and grasping the other end of the rope were two powerful men. They would pull the man seven or eight feet off the floor and then suddenly slack the rope and drop him but without allowing his feet to touch. His arms were drawn back and up and the drop was calculated to dislocate his shoulders. If it did not, weights were tied to the feet.

271

Shuddering, Richard looked up at the poor thing's face and knew that the man was unconscious. He knew also that the shoulders were out of joint, for the arms went straight up past the base of his skull. Standing close by the man and looking up at his face with interest untouched by emotion was one who, Richard thought by his dress, was a bishop. Sweat was pouring off the hoisted man and his whole body, naked but for a short pair of drawers, looked drained of blood and life.

Then Richard felt horribly sick and weak, felt that he would vomit if there was anything in his stomach. He was trying to keep a rational mind and trying to keep from fainting but the pictures here moved like nightmare in his vision and the sounds numbed his senses. The guard was whispering to him with cold glee that they might yank the man's arms off his body and surely would if they put weights on his feet; and Richard was wondering why they tortured a man who was unconscious.

He was now propelled over to the woman on the rack. This was a structure made of planks spiked to the wall: she was upright on it, her arms outflung, with the wrists bound, with her legs spread and bound at the ankles. Her weight was supported only by the cords around her wrists. A man was on either side of her with a torch that was fed from a candle of mutton-fat. She had on only a loin cloth. They had burned her breasts until they were blackened and smoking and now they were burning the flesh under her armpits. Then they held the flames to her ribs and Richard smelled the frying. This was the woman who from time to time had been screaming, "Thieves and fornicators!"

Richard looked for a moment at her face. It was distorted and hideous. Sweat was pouring off her face and body and mucus and slobber were falling from her lips. When the pain became unendurable she would strike her skull back against the rack, and her lips, white and moist and curled with hate and contempt, would shriek: "Thieves and fornicators!"

The two men torturing her were calm and methodical. When applying their torches they would bend forward and peer with critical interest at the burning flesh and they would move the flame up and down or from side to side. They would look up at her face and study it a moment, as though waiting for her to speak; and when again she flung her furious bitter words at them they would quietly, firmly apply the torches again. She was writhing in dreadful agony but she seemed to be fully conscious. A man came over with writing materials and the men with the torches stepped back. The man studied her face a moment and asked:

"Do you confess?"

Without opening her eyes she spit down at him and cried, "God's curse upon you!"

Another man came over and said to the men with torches: "Put her belly down on the table and bind her."

They set the stems of their torches in small holders and freed the wrists and ankles. She slid down and crumpled to the floor. The two men seized her, one by her wrists and one by her ankles, and carried her like a dead thing to the table; but at this moment the quiet voice of the second man who had come over said, "No, take her to the wall and bind her wrists to the spikes." They carried her to the wall and tried to stand her on her feet but again she crumpled. Then one of the men took her from behind and held her up and the other man bound each wrist to an iron spike. When the man released her her body sagged, its weight supported by the wrists. Now a man came with a whip. It had a haft of bone to which was secured a strip of tough hard leather about three feet long. One of the torch-men took a position, holding the whip ready, and turned to his superior for instructions.

"Give her twenty lashes and cut them deep."

"Thieves and fornicators!" she muttered, her face to the wall, her body sagging from her wrists.

Taking the whip with both hands the man struck her high across her shoulders, and Richard, still trying to keep from fainting, stared at her and saw the long red line which the whip left. It cut into the flesh over both shoulders and opened the flesh and blood ran but it did not cut into the depression across her backbone. Again the whip fell. There were three bloody lines, four, six, eight, ten across her shoulders and her lower back. She writhed and struggled feebly to release her wrists and with contempt and bitterness and loathing she breathed against the wall, "Thieves and fornicators!"

The cloth around her loins covered her buttocks. The man flogging her now pulled the cloth down to expose her buttocks and across them the lash fell, cutting deep. Blood was running down her back, down over her rump, down her legs. She was hanging entirely from her wrists. After the twenty lashes had been given

273

the man with the pen and paper came up to her and as before asked quietly, "Do you confess?"

Gasping, choking, she muttered, "God's curse upon you!"

"She's a tough one," the guard said to Richard. "But we have other ways."

Richard had just become aware of a new horror. Leaning against a wall, his mouth open, his eyes almost glazed, he became conscious that something soft and warm was on one of his lips. He touched it with his tongue and knew that it was a piece of the woman's flesh, flung off by the lash.

The man with the paper and pen came over to Richard and studied his face. "Do you abjure?" he asked.

Richard was unable to speak.

"Do you abjure your heresy?"

The woman had heard the question. She could not see Richard but she understood that someone had been asked to abjure and with all her strength she cried, "Tell them to go to hell!"

But for this woman's incredible fortitude Richard would have fainted. Her magnificent will gave him a little strength and he stared at her mutilated back and wondered what they would do with her now. Would they break her at last or would she die unbroken? How brave she is! he thought, feeling great compassion for her, a warm fellowship. The guard now took his arm. The guard led him to another part of the big chamber. The guard was saying, "We have other ways. They all confess before we're done with them."

He took Richard, dizzy and stumbling, to a man who was lying on a low table on his back, his arms pulled down under the table and bound and his feet bound. Two men were with him. A long thin strip of leather was drawn across the man's mouth between his teeth, to force his mouth open, and one of the men came with a small funnel and a pouch of water. The funnel was placed just above the man's mouth and water was poured into it and at once the man began to struggle and choke. When he seemed likely to throw himself off the table the other man flung one leg over and sat upon him, astride his belly. The other man continued to pour the water and soon the one on the table was so strangled that blood was bursting from his nostrils. . . .

The guard was saying to Richard: "If you abjure now you'll save yourself all this."

274

Richard wanted to ask him to take him to the cell but then he thought it would be better if they put him on the rack now and killed him and got it over with. The next moment he fainted. Blackness engulfed him suddenly and he fell, his skull striking the stone floor.

When he came to he was in the chamber where he had been questioned. He was lying by a wall. He knew by the wetness around him that water had been flung over him. Maybe he was dying, he thought; maybe he could just lie there a little while and die. . . .

But the guard had been watching him. The guard saw him open his eyes and he spoke to someone, his voice sounding far away: "He has come to."

As from far away another voice said, "Make him stand up."

The guard kicked Richard lightly and said, "Get up." When Richard did not move the man seized his arms and dragged him to a sitting posture. Then he took Richard from behind and lifted him to his feet. Again blackness engulfed him and he swayed and sagged and the guard held him up. Someone came over and said, "Make him drink this." While supporting him with one powerful arm the guard pressed to Richard's lips a small stone cup, forcing his face up and back, forcing the liquid into his mouth. Richard was faintly conscious of the taste of wine. His senses cleared a little. The man now carried him over to a table and set him on a bench and Richard sank forward, his head and shoulders on the table. He was never to know how long he sat there.

After a while he became conscious of a question and of someone shaking him. Someone was trying to make him hold his head up. Someone was asking him if he abjured. Hands were beating on his skull and fingers were forcing his eyes open. A hand slapped his face and shook him. As in a nightmare Richard was thinking, They won't let me die, they won't let me die. . . .

"Do you abjure?" The voice was angry. Someone was behind him now and was roughly massaging his face but he did not care. Someone was forcing his eyes open and pinching and twisting his lips. Then a voice said, "Take him to his cell. Give him bread and water and be sure that he eats." They won't let me die, he thought, they won't let me die.

Someone picked him up and carried him out. He had no sense

of where he was and not much sense of what was being done to
him. He knew that stuff was forced into his mouth. He knew
that a rough hand was massaging his throat to force him to swallow. He had a sense of being carried but the world was swimming
in darkness where there was no light or sound and no meaning
but his prayer for death. He was trying to recall the name of his
friend but he had forgotten it. He had forgotten everything. His
effort to think and to realize was so feeble that he could bring
nothing into light but knew only that he was being carried and
then that he had been dropped and that everything was still.

XXIV

He had almost lost all sense of time, all sense of being, but after a while he knew that he was back in the dungeon. He knew that food and water had again been forced down his throat for he had a taste of bread in his mouth and sharp pains in his stomach. As though he had never seen her but had found her in a dream he recalled the woman flinging her taunts even after they had burned off a part of her breasts and riddled her back and he thought that compared to her he was a coward. He was a coward compared to the man whose arms were being torn off.

After another while there came to him a thought that gave him a little strength. He had been thinking about the wrong kind of people during these days or weeks in the dungeon—about those who tortured instead of those who endured. Let there be light and this was the light. For, though some could be so brutal, some could be so brave; so mean, but so noble; so evil in their connivings and designs but so inflexible in purpose and will; so much lower than the beasts, but so much higher! That was the meaning which he had almost lost. That was the strength that he must find again. It was not the brutes holding the fire but the woman who in her scorn flung the taunt; not those hoisting the man but the man who endured until his senses failed. That was it. That was what he would die for. And he could go in peace, in faith, having known how noble a human being could be at the highest reach of his strength and his aspiration, having learned that in such an ordeal a man could stand with God.

"Life," he said, shaping the words with his lips and whispering them, "life can be good . . . some day . . . some day when people learn that God is that part of them above the beasts and hell that

277

part below. . . ." That was the meaning in it all. If he could only keep that meaning with him and not lose it, if he could keep it in his heart and his thoughts and his emotions, he could endure anything and die without bitterness. Was that it?—and he heard Hillel speaking. . . .

. . . . some day hurl down the last tyrant and build a world for free men. . . . A crimson sky at dawn; and rain; at evening, light. . . . How many times has he come and under what names? How many times will he have to come. . . .

Yes, Hillel!

He had been afraid but now he felt that he would be afraid no more. He recalled now that Jesus had said in John's story, Follow me. What had he meant, save that men must accept their suffering if they would find the truth? I am with you always, Jesus had said, even unto the end of the world; and what had he meant but that he was in dungeons, on crosses, at stakes, and in all the places where men suffered because of the ignorance of men? Yes, he understood now the parable of Peter when he cursed, saying, I know not the man. How simple and profound the story of Jesus was for those in whom agony and loneliness had opened the heart and the mind—and how literal and foolish it was for one in a bishop's robes who looked up at a ghastly face and had in his heart only that arrogance which Hillel said was the one unpardonable sin! He thought he understood now what Jesus had meant when he said let the dead bury their dead. He understood the great words in Isaiah, that he would open the blind eyes, to bring out the prisoners from the prison, and them that sit in darkness out of the prison house. Who was more deeply immured in that prison than the bishop fingering his cross and looking with calculating eyes at the anguish in a face? Father, forgive them.

Those were the words he had been searching his soul to find. Father, forgive them. Will you have the strength? Hillel had asked and he had said, I will. Hillel had smiled and said, Do you hear the voices? Yes, he could hear them again, the murmuring voices out in the night, of dead men talking about what must be. He could hear the church bells again, he could hear Father Raoul softly praying. He now prayed and he was not alone, for Hillel was with him, and Father Raoul, and many whose names he would never know, yet who were part of him, having given their best and highest to that for which he would die. Father, forgive them, and open the blind eyes and bring out the prisoners. Father, give me the strength and the courage not to deny you. . . .

He became aware an hour or hours or days later that they were bringing him more food. The guard had come in how many times to force him to eat but now the bread and water were placed in the hole. He stood, starved, exhausted, trembling by the door and ate and drank, hoping to gain strength to accept his ordeal. He would need to be as strong as he could be. He would need to quiet his emotions and seek tranquillity. He took the bread and held it carefully in his cupped hands, to waste no crumb, and he put his mouth down to his hands and ate. He drank the water. When again he heard a sound at the door he went over and was surprised to find more food there and this time a small piece of cheese. But why be surprised? In their own way they were doing the best they knew how for him. He ate again and drank the water and felt a little refreshed.

He thought of the Easter hymn, Zyma vetus expurgetur, a symbolic prefiguration of Jesus in the Old Testament; and he understood now that Jesus *had* lived in those times and in all the times of men; that he lived in Socrates when that great man comforted his friends while he was dying; and in Epicharis when she suffered the agony of scourge and rack and fire and the dislocation of every limb; and in so many more, so many more. Christ's blood blunts the sword, said the hymn. That your grace may save us from the second death, said the hymn. He understood now but never till now what that second death was: it was the death the bishop would die, that Father Luce would die, but it was not the death that the woman on the rack would die.

He slept a little while and when he awoke he strove to nest his emotions and mind in tranquillity. Father Luce would say that Palestine was the central province of the earth and Jerusalem the center of the earth and the universe, for so they were shown on maps; but science knew better than that, science knew that they were only the center of Christian ignorance. He thought of the heresy of Joachim of Flora: Joachim had said that Christianity up to his time had been a failure: vices were as unchecked, the clergy was as carnal, the social evils as rampant as they had ever been. Christianity, he had said, was only an intermediate stage in mankind's march to the light; and though some popes had prized Joachim's writings he was now looked upon as a heretic. Yet, as

Hillel had pointed out, he had spoken the truth. No man, Hillel had told him, could say what God was, save that he was the best of what people aspired to, the collective conscience of all that was good. Gerart had said that Jews had a deeper sense of God than Christians had. Indeed, he had said that Christians were pagans at heart. Most of their rituals, sacraments, vestments and holy days they had taken from the pagans; and the one deep religious principle, which they might have taken from the Jews but lost when they lost Jesus, they now rejected, that arrogance was the greatest of all the sins. In lonely contemplation this truth came into Richard and for the first time in his life he could say and fully know what he was saying: Father, forgive them.

Augustine had known that truth. He had also known that Jesus had always been; that when man lifted himself above the beasts and discovered his power over them and over his weaker fellows he had had to have Jesus to save him from himself. Augustine had known that revelation was progressive, that in any age as much of truth was revealed as men could grasp. He wished that he had told the inquisitor that! While wondering about Augustine he thought of the world beyond this pile of stones and he heard birds singing, he smelled the fragrance of wild thyme and hawthorn. A man never knew how sweet life was until he had lost it: all persons knew who were in dungeons: then they could hear song as they had never heard it before, and laughter, and the joy of children before they knew evil. Then they could smell the sweet earth as they had never smelled it before and feel its warmth under their feet, who had stood for weeks on stone; and they could see it when they closed their eyes, in all its splendor of form and color. He could see and hear and smell and touch it now and marvel at the wonder of it. I am stronger, he thought; memory of these things is making me strong. I will have the courage. . . .

How long he waited this time he could never know, for time now had no more meaning than for a bird on a nest or for a child. They had given him more to eat and he was stronger. He was ready. And when at last the door was flung open and a voice called to him he arose without trembling and walked out. He was not able to see but he walked with a firm tread.

He was shockingly emaciated, haggard and white; his hair was matted with filth; and the stench of him would have been overpowering to men not used to it. But his mind was clear, his emotions were quiet under his will. He was allowed as before to sit for a while to become accustomed to light and he sat, waiting, and looking into his emotions. In another minute, he thought, in another minute . . . over and over.

The guard then led him to a table and he sat there. He saw the inquisitor who had examined him and the same clerk; and again the confession was read to him. The inquisitor said in a voice that was not unkind:

"Richard, we have been very patient with you. We've given you time to pray and meditate and humble yourself. Have you prayed?"

"Yes."

"Have you asked our Father to guide you?"

"Yes."

"Have you humbled yourself?"

"Yes."

"What do you say now?"

"I say what Jesus said, Father, forgive them."

There was silence. Then: "Do you persist in your errors? Do you still believe these things you confessed to?"

"Yes."

"You understand, Richard, that the only purpose we have is to save your soul. If you are going to be stubborn we have no choice but to turn you over to the secular authorities. You understand that?"

"Yes."

"You understand that if you abjure you'll not be tortured?"

"Yes."

"That we must force you to recognize your wickedness?"

"I'll not deny what I believe to be true."

"Is that your final statement?"

"Yes."

"If we gave you more time would that still be your final statement?"

"Yes."

With a sign of weariness the inquisitor turned to a guard. "Deliver him over," he said.

The guard took Richard's arm and led him to the torture-chamber. While they were walking the guard studied Richard's face and said: "You're a stubborn one but we have ways to deal with stubborn ones. What do you say to that?"

"I say, Father, forgive them."

"You'll say more than that before we're done with you."

In the chamber a man came forward who seemed to be the secular overlord. He too studied Richard's face, as though to calculate the strength of his resistance. He looked Richard up and down. He then turned as though to see which instruments were in use and called a man over and said: "Make him ready."

This man now took Richard in charge. He led him to a corner and said: "Take off your clothes." When Richard made no move to take them off the man roughly unrobed him. Richard had on a short pair of drawers and after taking the outer garment off the man said: "Leave your drawers on."

For Richard the scene was taking on the aspect of nightmare. He was beginning to feel faint and dizzy and he fought to remain calm and keep his mind clear. He kept telling himself that this was his supreme moment, in which he would be true or in which he would break. It seemed to him that the chamber was suffocating with heat and flames and smoke. He could hear someone screaming but he did not look at those who were being tortured. He did not want to see them, lest what he saw might weaken his will; but he did want to see them, for they were his only fellowship in this room or on this earth. He kept saying under his breath, Father, forgive them. He would keep these words in mind, even when the agony became unendurable.

The man who had studied his countenance came up again. For a moment Richard met his eeys. They did not seem to him to be human eyes. They were the eyes of a man who had spent years in this place and for whom all the instruments were commonplaces and all the torture a routine part of his life. Richard looked into the eyes and he could well have been proud of himself, for his gaze was unwavering. The man turned and summoned two men and said, "Begin with the thumbscrew."

The two men led him to a strong wooden chair and one on either side seized a hand and Richard could feel them putting on his thumbs something that felt like iron. He had heard it said that the thumbscrew was one of the most dreadful forms of torture. He was vaguely aware that the men were very businesslike. They were kneeling, one on either side of him. They were putting the two thumbscrews in place and binding them to his hands. He could hear screams and the sound of voices and the sound of something falling. It was all nightmare now. He tried to keep possession of his senses. He felt very faint but he thought his mind was clear. He was aware of the two men when for a moment they paused, as though they had the instruments in place and were ready to begin. With an effort he turned and met the eyes of one of them. He turned and met the eyes of the other man. They were both the eyes of men who were saving souls and who knew no other way of life. In his breath he said, Father, forgive them.

The two men now began to apply the pressure. In this form of torture an iron screw was turned in upon the thumb. The men were turning the screws. At the first thrust of pain Richard murmured, Hillel, be with me! The pain was stabbing through him now in hot blind flashes. It flashed up his arms and through his shoulders and caused a nightmarish suffocation in his chest. At the next partial turn of the screws agony convulsed the whole upper part of his body and was like an imprisoned violence in his skull trying to burst the bone asunder. He was still dimly in possession of his faculties. He had set his teeth hard and through his teeth with a desperate effort he whispered, Father, forgive them. He was vaguely aware of hot tears falling down his face and of sweat bursting from his whole body. The pain seemed most awful now in his belly and it shot like flames from his belly down his legs. A goan escaped him. He shuddered and writhed and sobbing with agony he whispered, Father, forgive them! There was more blackness than pain now. There was horrible black agony all through him, rending and convulsing him from head to feet. He was only a shuddering thing with his mind and senses reeling and turning dark as the fires consumed him. . . . And then he lost consciousness. His head and shoulders slumped forward, his mouth open and drooling, blood running from his nose.

The overlord came up and looked at him. To one of the men he said, "Did he speak?"

"Yes."

"What did he say?"

"He kept saying, Father, forgive them."

A bishop came up and stood by the overlord and looked at Richard. The overlord bent down to see how deeply the screws had penetrated and he perceived that they had mangled the flesh and crushed a part of the bone. He straightened and looked at the bishop.

"Did he abjure?" asked the bishop.

"No, my lord."

"Did he speak at all?"

"Yes, my lord. He said, Father, forgive them."

"Is that all?"

"Is that all?" the overlord asked one of the men.

"That is all."

But the other man said, "He called out to someone."

"To whom?"

"My lord, I do not know."

The overlord said, "Take them off." The two men turned the screws out and unfastened the irons. The overlord bent forward to look at the thumbs. He said to the bishop, "He is a very stubborn heretic. Not one in a thousand can stand the thumbscrew."

"You have other ways," said the bishop.

"Yes, my lord. Unbind him," said the overlord to the men.

Unbound from the chair, Richard toppled forward on his face. He was still unconscious. "Throw water on him," said the overlord to one of the men. A pail of water was fetched and Richard was turned over on his back and water was dashed into his face. In the ghastly pallor of it there was no sign of life. The overlord knelt and put a hand on Richard's chest. "He's still alive," he said, looking up at the bishop.

"I'd take him back to his cell for a while," the bishop said.

The two men gathered Richard up and carried him unconscious out of the chamber. They took him into the other chamber and there the inquisitor came over to look at him.

"Did he abjure?"

"No."

"Where are you taking him?"

"His holiness the bishop said to take him back to his cell."

"What form did you use?"

"The thumbscrew."

The inquisitor looked down at Richard's thumbs. "Did he say anything?"

"He said, Father, forgive them."

"Is that all?"

"He's a very stubborn heretic, my lord."

284

"All right, take him down."

The two men carried him down to the cell and laid him on the stone floor.

He became conscious first of a great throbbing through his whole body but he was not really conscious. For an hour or more he was not conscious of where he was or of himself as a man but only of vague memory of pain and of the deep throbbing anguish within him. His entire body was twitching and jerking with spasms and tremors. Before he became fully conscious his lips began to move and they whispered the words that he had fixed so deep in his mind, so deep that they possessed his subconscious; and over and over without knowing it he whispered, Father, forgive them. He came slowly and painfully into consciousness whispering those words. Even after he had opened his eyes he was not really conscious but lay sunk in pain and memory of pain, while little by little the darkness thinned and moved away; while little by little he became aware of local areas—first of a strange numbed sensation in his thumbs and then of an awful aching in his arms and shoulders and then of the suffocation in his chest; for as he came into wakefulness he was reliving the moments before he fainted. Next he felt the hot blind stabbings down through his torso and up into his brain; and the pressures trying to burst his skull open; and the wild ringings in his ears. He licked his tongue over his lips and tasted the salt of blood. He swallowed. He moved one hand and felt a stab of pain. He raised a hand and brought it up to his face to wipe his lips and knew that there was something wrong with his thumb. Gently he put his hand back down. He swallowed again and made an effort to realize where he was. He closed his eyes and shuddered and the shudder went through him and again through him and gathered into a spasm so violent that it shook him like a blow. Where am I? he thought and tried to understand where he was. He moved his fingers over the stone and knew that it was stone. He gently turned his head and heard his hair grating on stone. When his lips, through no will of his own but drawing on that deep reservoir of courage that he had taken to the chamber, murmured aloud the three words, it all came back to him with an overpowering rush of terror and pain and nausea, and he knew what had happened.

Slowly he sat up with sickness engulfing him. He swayed and then turned a little, until he could lean his back to the wall. His head sank forward. His eyes were closed. He could feel the throbbing in his thumbs and up his arms and through his shoulders. He knew now that they had crushed his thumbs but he cared little about that. What had he said? Had he denied the truth, not knowing that he was denying it? Had pain broken his will and heart and mind and made him confess the words they wanted to hear? If only he had been strong, if only he could still utter without shame the names of Socrates and Abelard, he would endure the next torture, and the next.

Tell me, Hillel, he whispered, was I true, was I true? . . .

XXV

Hours might have passed, or days, for he had lost all sense of time and all sense of life and reality, when he heard Hillel's voice saying, "Richard, are you in there?" He knew of course that it was not Hillel. He thought he had lost his mind; but again the voice came, clear and insistent, "Richard, can you hear me?" But of course it was not Hillel. He had not heard the door open and he was sure that it was not open. . . .

He seemed now to hear feet entering his cell but he knew that he did not hear them at all. He seemed to feel a hand on his shoulder but he knew that he did not feel it. The whole thing was strange and he wished he could go to sleep now; for why should he hear and feel so vividly when there was nothing to hear or feel? Yet the hand seemed to be there, the voice seemed to be saying, "Richard, can you speak? It is Hillel." How crazy it all was! But Richard said, "Yes, I hear you." "Then rise and come with me. Can you walk?" And Richard, knowing that it was nothing at all, said, "Yes, I can walk." "Then rise," the voice said, "and come." Richard staggered to his feet, thinking, "I'm lost, O God I'm lost!" Thinking, "Why must I hear these things when there's nothing to hear?"

He felt an arm around his shoulder but he knew that the arm was not there. He felt himself walking with an arm around him but he knew that this could not be. It seemed to him that he walked out of the cell. And then the voice was saying, "I've come for you, Richard, my brother." Richard said, "I'm going with you" but knew that he was not going. He knew that he was sitting in his cell in the dark and loneliness and that he was hearing a voice that was not there and feeling an arm that was not there.

It seemed to him that he was walking across a stone floor and that an arm was guiding him and that a voice was speaking to him; and he again told himself that he had lost his mind. He thought that he must get control of himself or the next time they tortured him they would make him say what they wanted him to say. How strange it was to be walking with this person—with Abelard, was it?—with Socrates, was it?—or was it Hillel?—and to hear him saying in that firm but gentle voice, "Richard?"

"Yes?" Richard said.

"I've come for you, Richard. I'd have come sooner but I couldn't. I've also been in a dungeon."

"Yes!" Richard said. "I knew you would be."

"I came as soon as I could. Did you know I would come?"

"Yes!"

"Have I been with you?"

"Yes!"

"We'll go away," the voice was saying, the strong arm pressing him with friendship. "We'll find a place for men who want to be free."

O Lord, how sweet it was! But Richard said, "You have told me there is no such place."

"Men must make such a place, Richard. Did they torture you?"

"Yes!"

"But you were true, for I knew you would be."

"Yes!"

Richard was weeping. How strange! he thought; for I seem to be walking and Hillel is with me, and he is speaking to me and I can feel his arm! But then he thought, I've been hearing voices a long time. I only imagine this—and wondered then if he was imagining the hot tears flowing down his cheeks. He raised a hand to his face to learn if the tears were real and felt the shock of a mutilated thumb. He thought, Is my thumb hurt or do I imagine that? He paused then and the arm pressed against him to come. But he insisted on halting here, for he would examine his thumb; he would determine whether he was dreaming or awake; in a nightmare of horror and hope and memory, or walking with Hillel. With either hand he tried to examine the other hand; then he felt two hands examining his own and he heard what he thought was a cry of horror. He heard Hillel's voice saying, "My poor brother, they did this to you!" It seemed to him that a warm

288

gentle mouth was kissing his two thumbs. Richard thought, Hillel would have done that! Hillel would have said those words and kissed the wounds. . . .

Lord, he must get control of himself now! Did he wake or sleep?

"With the thumbscrew," the voice was saying. "Yet you were true and truth was with you. You are another of the great men, Richard. . . ."

Yes, he thought; Hillel would utter such words if he were here. It seemed to him now that they had left a building, for there was light; and he seemed to be stumbling; yet the firm arm was still across his back. Was there light now, or did he dream?

"Hillel?" he said.

And the voice replied, "Yes, Richard."

"You seem to be with me, Hillel. I asked you to be. I prayed day and night that you would be. And now you seem to be with me, even more than you have been, yet you were always with me in the way Abelard was with me. . . ."

Father, forgive me! he thought; day and night I spoke such words in my cell and I am only speaking them again, and he is not with me!

But the voice said, "I am with you, Richard."

"You seem to be," Richard said, troubled by what he took to be a great light, a light that was opening and growing, to show a world that had been lost. He said, "They'll torture me again but I'll try to be true."

"They'll not torture you any more, Richard."

He was sobbing bitterly now and hating himself for this weakness. His eyes were blinded but he knew that some sort of light was dawning. "They'll torture me again," he said. "And millions of men after me, as long as men are afraid."

"Others they will torture, but you no more."

"If you are here," Richard said, "how is it that they let you come?"

"Money, my brother. Money can buy anything. It was the man called Chretien who at last got to me."

"Chretien?" Richard said. He said, "I did not tell them about your money."

"I know. I knew."

"They'll torture me again," Richard said. "But if you are with me I'll not care. It's only my body they can kill—"

"That is all."

"Can they ever destroy the truth?"

"No, Richard, only themselves for being afraid of it."

How strange it is! Richard thought; for I am in the cell waiting, yet he seems to be walking at my side and talking to me; I can feel his arm and hear his voice, and a light seems to be waking. He asked, "Do I see a light?"

"Yes."

"But there's no light in my cell."

"There was always a light in your cell, Richard. You were the light."

"But this before me seems to be the light of day."

"It is the light of day, of a new day. . . ."

Yes, he seemed to be walking in light with Hillel's arm around him and Hillel's gentle voice in his ears. He thought he saw hills and trees and buildings and the sky. He thought he saw stars. In all his days or weeks in the cell he had never seen stars.

"Do I see a bright star?" he said.

And Hillel's voice said, "The star of morning. That bright star up there, Richard, is the star of morning."

Richard thought, How strange that is!—for that was the meaning of Hillel's name, and that was the name the Christians called Satan by! The Star of Morning! If he had not known that it could not be true he would have thought he was walking over the earth and toward a hill; and he would have thought that he was climbing a hill. But all this could not be. Oh no, he was in his cell, waiting to be tortured again, and he was dreaming that Hillel was with him. And Hillel was saying:

"I will dress up your wounds, my brother. Your poor thumbs, but I have salve and will bind them. What did Paul say? You have fought the good fight, you have kept the faith. What did Isaiah say? To open the blind eyes, to bring out the prisoners from the prison, and them that sit in darkness out of the prison house. . . ."

What noble words! Richard thought, and stumbled. It seemed to him that he was walking and was climbing a hill; and it seemed to him that day was breaking. He was sure that he could smell the clean fresh air of morning and feel the wind of morning on his

290

face. Yet it could not be! There was the arm of friendship and love firmly around him, a strong arm supporting his weary wasted frame. Yet how could this be! Had he ever known Hillel? Had there ever been a Hillel, or had he dreamed all this during his months in the dark?

He was weeping quietly now. He said, "It seems that day is breaking."

"Day *is* breaking," said Hillel's voice. "All those in the dungeons are its light."

Richard thought of the words and said inside him, There must be a Hillel. There would have to be! For how out of centuries of persecution could there come anything but compassion? He looked down, and was sure he could feel the earth. He was sure he felt the throbbing in his two crushed thumbs, yet persistently wondered if he was dead. He could feel the arm around him, and its pressure seemed to be all the goodness that he had ever hoped for, for himself and for all men. He looked up at the star which Hillel had said was the star of morning. He was sure now that a light was breaking. . . .

NOTES AND COMMENTARY

My extensive reading in the records of the past has discovered no subject that has called forth more distortion and misrepresentation of the facts than the Christian Church of the Middle Ages. Its apologists are many, and include some scholars who are able and detached when their theological prepossessions are not engaged. Most readers and many writers, says Coulton, have taken their notions of this period from such wholly untrustworthy sources as Montalembert and Chesterton. Coulton has proved conclusively in his many volumes that certain Catholic historians have deliberately distorted or suppressed some of the facts. Coulton has been accused of favoring those facts which support his 'preconceptions'; and has replied: "I must repeat here that I shall be very glad to print the supposed rebutting evidence, if only my critics will show me where it is to be found." Of Cobbett's widely read history of the Reformation he says: "For popularity and inaccuracy combined, it would be difficult to find any book so conspicuous." Of Cardinal Gasquet: "he does not hesitate to lend his authority to statements which are not only absurd, but which we know that he himself knew to be absurd." Michael's picture of rural prosperity "depends for most of its effects on the omission of notorious facts." O'Brien's *Economic Effects of the Reformation* "is possibly more wildly inaccurate than his earlier volumes." A typical O'Brien statement is that the Middle Ages witnessed "the building up of a beautiful and harmonious civilization." Other scholars whom Coulton exposes include Janssen, Pastor and Hurter. He quotes Cardinal Newman: "Unless one doctored all one's facts one should be thought a bad Catholic . . . a man who is not extravagant is thought treacherous." Lord Acton, famous British Catholic of the 19th century, was almost excommunicated for publishing such statements as this about papal infallibility: "It not only promotes, it inculcates distinct mendacity and deceitfulness. In certain cases it is made a duty to lie." The curious reader who would see for himself with what thoroughness Coulton exposes certain untrustworthy scholars is referred to various appendixes in his *Medieval Village* and to his *Five Centuries of Religion.*

The apologists lay great stock by a 16th century anonymous writer who said that the monks "never raised any rent, or took any incomes or garsomes of their tenants," a statement repeated by such as Gasquet and Chesterton. Chesterton goes so far as to say that harsh treatment of tenants was "practically unknown wherever the Church was landlord." Leadam's exhaustive researches in Star Chamber records found only one case of sympathy by an eminent ecclesiastic, the abbot of Croxton in 1530.

The greater scholars include Coulton, Delisle, Guérard, Lamprecht, Lea, Maitland, Michelet, Taylor, Sée, Verriest. Not all the scholars quoted in the following Notes are of the first order, and a few are often quite untrustworthy. I quote the latter now and then to show that even they concede some of the more terrible facts. A word must be said in the defense of Lea, possibly the greatest of them all, for he suffered the most violent abuse. Let Prof. Coulton say it—and he published these words (*Medieval Panorama*) as late as 1938: "Lea's monumental work has been so unscrupulously handled by popular controversialists on the Roman Catholic side. . . .A certain school of journalist-historians is adopting nowadays the policy of attempting to laugh Lea out of court. . . .Lord Acton, the most learned of modern British historians, who claimed that his Roman Catholic faith was dearer to him than his life, testified to Lea's accuracy and general impartiality. . . .The fact is that Lea's bulky work has never been corrected except on an almost negligible minority of details; and if he had lived twice as long and been able to read twice as much, he could have doubled the mass of his already overwhelming evidence."

The topics, as in former volumes in this Series, are in alphabetical order, so that the reader can quickly find those items that interest him. CE, where these letters appear, indicate the monumental *Catholic Encyclopedia.* In the space here I have tried to give a fair picture of this period, as the abler scholars have made it out, but I obviously do not accept the magazine *Life's* characterization of it as "that time of singular sweetness."

ABELARD Waddell: "Abelard is the first of the new order: the scholar for scholarship's sake. . . .whom the love of God and the hate of men had broken, yet left greater in his ruin."

AGE, THE CE: "The wonderful efficacy displayed by the religion of Christ in purifying the morals of Europe has no parallel." Elsewhere CE many times contradicts that statement; as: "The desperate moral barbarism of the age"; or: "The Lateran was spoken of as a brothel, and the moral corruption of Rome became the subject of general odium"; or: "the condition of the clergy, and consequently of the people, was a very sad one"; or: "an age of terrible corruption and social decadence." Prestage: "Let us try to forget for the moment that we are living in an age, in which men and women all over Europe have different religious creeds, or none at all, and imagine an epoch when there was a Christendom united in belief under the successors of St. Peter; when life beyond the grave was known to be of supreme importance and the present a passing show . . ." Meyendorff: "In dealing with a period so obscure . . . it is essential for us to avoid as far as possible the use of preconceived assump-

tions and the reading back of modern conditions into medieval times."
CE says "only the clergy were generally able to read." James Harvey
Robinson: "For six or seven centuries [after 476] very few outside of
the clergy ever dreamed of studying, or even of learning to read and
write. Even in the 13th century an offender who wished to prove that
he belonged to the clergy in order that he might be tried by a church
court, had only to show that he could read a single line." Lea: "It was
rare for knights to be able to sign their names."

This period's ignorance of geography is fantastic. Strzygowski:
"Western Europe is treated already as the center of the world . . ."
Newton: "true views of the shape of the earth had almost disappeared
and had given place to fanciful ideas of symmetry based upon the
speculations of Hebrew poets"—that is, of the Bible. (See Newton,
Travel and Travelers of the Middle Ages or Beazley, *Dawn of Modern
Geography*). It was an age, says Meller, "in which Force was para-
mount, and the sword, and not the law-courts, the chief arbiters of
justice." It was, says Rudwin, "a perpetual spiritualistic *seance* with
lights lowered" when Satan "was the Prince of this world." Louandrae:
"The history . . . may be summed up in three words: War, Plague
and Famine." You follow, said Voltaire, its "scenes of absurdity and
horror with pity; you find nothing like them among the Romans, the
Greeks or the old barbarians. They were the fruit of the most infamous superstition which has ever degraded man." Jackson and Lake:
"a period in which good men showed a fanatic zeal, a lack of self-re-
straint, which seems incongruous today." Peter Damiani (11th cen.)
said: "the world is so filthy with vices, that any holy mind is befouled
even by thinking about it." It was, says Prentice, "not until well into
the Middle Ages that infanticide was considered a crime." Delisle:
"adultery was frequent, and often it was the parson who seduced his
parishioners. . . .The Middle Ages honored only the noble, who lived
by exploiting the lower classes." It was a period, says Reinach, "which
ignorant and fanatical people are still apt to admire." "An evil weary
age," says A. V. G. Allen, "in which ecclesiastical scandals abounded,
which was rife in intrigues and dark suspicions, when the reputation
of good men was destroyed, and even the darker crimes of murder and
implacable hatreds which were worse than murder stained the records
of the Catholic church." Robertson: "the Christian world seems to
present a relative paralysis of thinking, due largely to the very ac-
ceptance of the gospels as a super-human product . . ." Morgolis: "In
the sharp struggle to maintain life all scruples are overcome, neighbor

295

is against neighbor, and the strong are ruthless toward the weak. With wonderful force of simplicity does a 13th century Russian chronicle relate the horrors of the famine in the Novgorod province: 'We were all in a fury of irritation; a brother rose against his brother, a father had no pity for his son, mothers had no mercy for their daughters. . . .There was no charity left among us, only sadness, gloom and mourning . . .' "

Michelet: "we find always and everywhere the same ferocity of folly. . . .this horrid shelving declivity, down which a man slips from free man to vassal—from vassal to servant—from servant to serf, is the great terror of the Middle Ages, the basis of its despair." Again: "When mankind has completely awakened from its prodigious dream of two thousand years, and can coolly and quietly take stock of Christian society in the Middle Ages, two astounding facts will become apparent. . . .*Adultery was one of its recognized institutions,* normal, established, esteemed, sung and celebrated. . . .Incest is the ordinary condition of serfs . . ." Day: "A grown ox seemed to have been little larger than a calf of the present day, and the fleece of a sheep often weighed less than two ounces. Many of the stock had to be killed before winter, and those that survived were often so weak in the spring that they had to be dragged to pasture on a sledge."

The picture is not wholly dark. J. H. Robinson: "The so-called Renaissance offers nothing comparable to the achievements of the 12th and 13th centuries." That statement would seem to be exaggerated—as well as Dubnow's: "In this abysmal night . . . the lamp of thought was fed and guarded solely and alone by the Jews." Taylor: "Men were then opening their eyes a little to observe the natural world, and were thinking a little for themselves." Abba Silver: "The 13th century was one of great spiritual ferment and mystic exaltation." Lea: "The human intellect had awakened, but as yet the human conscience slumbered, save in a few rare souls who mostly paid in disgrace or death the penalty of their precocious sensitiveness. . . .The results of that hundred years of effort [13th cen.] are well symbolized in the two popes with whom it began and ended—Innocent III and that pinchbeck Innocent, Boniface VIII, who, in the popular phrase of the time, came in like a fox, ruled like a lion, and died like a dog." To comprehend it, says Lea, we must realize that "passions were fiercer, convictions stronger, virtues and vices more exaggerated. . . .The age was a cruel one. . . .We have only to look upon the atrocities of the criminal law . . . to see how pitiless men were. . . .The wheel, the caldron

of boiling oil, burning alive, burying alive, flaying alive, tearing apart
with wild horses, were the ordinary expedients by which the criminal
jurist sought to deter crime." But it was a century, Jackson reminds
us, that saw most of the cathedrals built, gave new impetus to learning, and laid the foundation of our modern universities.

ALBIGENSES were, says Legge, the "bitterest and the most dangerous enemies that the Catholic Church in Europe
ever had to face." Their dislike for the clergy was so intense, says
West, that the old byword, I had rather be a Jew, became, I had rather
be a priest. Fisher: "Innocent proclaimed a crusade, offering the
sunny lands of the South, and heaven hereafter, to all who would engage in the holy war. The crusaders . . . fulfilled their commission with
inhuman cruelty. Their thirst for blood and their unbounded rapacity . . ." Proctor: "the indulgences which he lavished upon all who
assumed the Cross in that atrocious warfare, were more extensive than
any which had been promised for the deliverance of the Holy Sepul-
chre." The best of these people, says Packard, "were so far superior to
the clergy of southern France as to make the latter ridiculous." Their
real offense, says Adeney, "was opposition to the sacramental mate-
rialism of the Church." Newman: "Their cultural life far outshone
that of any other locality. . . .Nowhere in Europe were the clergy more
negligent of their duties or more despised. . . ." In manners, morals
and learning, says Bennett, they deserved respect "to an infinitely
greater extent than the orthodox bishops and clergy. . . .the court of
Toulouse was the center of a higher type of civilization than existed
elsewhere in Europe." Jackson: "The strong town of Beziers was taken
in 1209, and every living creature in it was put to the sword. . . .The
Albigensian War, which lasted twenty years, and ruined the most
civilized nation in Europe. . . ." Allen: "this massacre of a large part
of the population of France with the sanction of the papacy . . ."
Lea: "the pitiless cruelty and brutal licentiousness habitual among the
Crusaders, who spared no man in their wrath, and no woman in their
lust. . . ." One Arnaud, a participator, wrote the pope: "Our men
have spared neither rank, nor sex, nor age. About twenty thousand
persons have been put to the edge of the sword. After the slaughter
was finished, the city was first sacked, then burned. The divine vengeance has been admirably displayed." Peter of Val-de-Cernay recorded that the leader Simon de Montfort condemned to dungeons
to die of starvation those who could not raise 100 sous as ransom.

"Sometimes he had them brought forward half-dead and thrown into cesspools before his own eyes. . . .he forced the father to hang his own son." Barnes: "No Roman, Hunnish, Muslim, or Mongol conqueror ever wiped out a Christian community with greater savagery." The Albigensians, some say to the number of 100,000, were completely exterminated.

ART   Though Racine, Moliere, Goethe, Voltaire and many others denounced Gothic art as barbarous, we know now, as Prentice says, that the cathedral has been revealed to us as a "palimpsest whose facade has been many times written over; on whose walls, portals, capitals and windows the thoughts and beliefs of many generations and diverse races, from the days of Sumer and Accad, are curiously intermingled." In other words, the art was derived from many pagan sources. Coulton: "Medieval art . . . was strictly collectivist. The men who worked at the great cathedrals were under a discipline comparable to that of an army; indeed they were often actual conscripts."

AUGUSTINE   It has been pointed out that apparently it was Augustine who applied the words, Compel them to enter in to religious persecution. Humphrey: "Augustine's works became the great source of justification for intolerance."

AVERROES   Coulton: "Arab philosophy furnishes an almost unique example of a very lofty culture suppressed almost instantaneously without leaving any trace behind . . ." His Commentaries, says Taylor, "tended to supplant the work commented on, whether that work was Holy Scripture or a treatise on Aristotle."

BASTARDY   Taylor: "there was then no line of disgrace as now between bastard and lawful issue."

CASTLE, THE   This subject of 'romance' was, says Davis, "a most uncomfortable place, with its cavernous halls barely lighted by tiny loopholes, frigid in winter, stifling in summer, unsanitary—in short, almost intolerable for habitation . . ."

CATHEDRALS   Lea: "While these structures were in some degree the expression of ardent faith, yet more were they the manifestation of the pride of the prelates who erected them, and in our admiration of these sublime relics of the past . . . we must not lose sight of the supreme effort which they cost—an effort which inevitably fell upon the suffering serf and peasant. Peter Cantor assures us that they were built out of exactions on the poor, out of the unhallowed gains of usury, and out of the lies and deceits of the *quaestuarii* or pardoners . . ."

CHIVALRY   Sir Walter Scott said it produced a permanent difference between ancients and moderns; and C. P. R. James that it was "the most glorious institution that man ever devised"! But Thomas Arnold: "If I were called upon to name what spirit of evil predominantly deserved the name of Antichrist, I should name the spirit of Chivalry." It was, says Buckle, "a mischievous institution that enlivened the superstitions of monks with the debaucheries of soldiers." For Freeman it "substitutes purely personal obligations devised in the interests of an exclusive class for the more homely duties of an honest man and a good citizen." J. R. Green dismisses it as "picturesque mimicry of high sentiment, heroism, love and courtesy." H. W. C. Davis: "that peculiar and often fantastic code of etiquette and morals which was grafted upon feudalism." Schofield: "less an institution than an ideal." Lacroix: "the Christian form of the profession of arms." Barnes: "Novelists and, within recent years, the cinema have managed to create a romantic and unreal picture of the social life of the feudal noble." Stubbs: "the gloss put by fine manners on vice and selfishness and contempt for the rights of man." Michelet: "*Ivanhoe* is an equally feeble and entirely artificial portrait. The author has not dared to face the foul actualities. . . .The Romances of Chivalry give exactly the opposite of the truth." Lippert: "The celebrated 'woman cult' of the Middle Ages . . .was . . . a dying echo, though often a shrill one, of a decadent form of life." Dean Church: "Our poetical notions of a gay and gentle chivalry fade away cruelly, we had almost said ludicrously, before the frightful realities of European life as drawn by the Middle Age historians." May: "Christian asceticism denounced women as evil and dangerous. Chivalric romanticism praised them as worthy of love and reverence. Both of these sets of ideals were beyond hope of attainment in the comparatively crude society. Both degenerated into folly and vice." Traill and Mann: "To judge from contemporary poems and romances, the first thought of every knight, on finding a lady unprotected and alone, was to do her violence." John of Salisbury: "Each is boldest in the banquet-hall,

299

but in the battle everyone desires to do the least; they would rather shoot arrows at the enemy than come to close fighting—if they return home without a scar, they sing triumphantly of their battles and boast of a thousand deaths." Abrahams: "the same events which gave chivalrous romance a commanding influence in the marriage customs of Christian Europe produced an exactly opposite effect in Jewish circles."

CHRISTIANITY   What had it become? Just before the Reformation, says Réville, "nothing short of a terrible perversion of true Christianity." Jackson: "had tended to become a cult of relics and holy places, martyrs, and sacred symbols." Klausner: "the religion has stood for what is highest ethically and ideally, while the political and social life has remained at the other extreme of barbarity and paganism." Gilbert Murray: "The polemic literature of Christianity is loud and triumphant; the books of the Pagans have been destroyed." Robertson puts it best: "It is not Christianity that has civilized Europe, but Europe—the complex of political and cultural forces—that has civilized Christianity."

CHURCH, THE   Abelard: "I am called religious at a time when most religion is hypocrisy . . ." Pope Gregory VII (11th cen.): "The Roman Church has never erred, nor will it err to all eternity." Leo XIII: "the sacred writers could never have made a mistake." Joachim of Flora's writings, says Lea, prove that "the most pious minds confessed that Christianity was practically a failure." Every human advance, said Macaulay, "has been made in spite of her, and has everywhere been in inverse proportion to her power." Still, all popes, says Lea, "were not like Innocent IV and John XXII; all bishops were not cruel and licentious; all priests were not intent solely on impoverishing men and dishonoring women." St. Bernard asked, "Whom can you show me among the prelates who does not seek rather to empty the pockets of his flock than to subdue their vices?" Robert Grosseteste, Bishop of Lincoln, in 1250 drew up for Innocent IV and his cardinals a list of the Church's vices; and 10 years later the inquisitor of Passau drew a list which, says Lea, "is awful in the completeness of its details. A church such as he describes was an unmitigated curse, politically, socially and morally." It was in the 13th century that Bernard said: "Today, foul rottenness crawls through the whole body of the Church." One scholar has called him the greatest monk of the Middle Ages. He says again: "The cardinals are full of

300

avarice and evil living; without faith or religion they sell God and his Mother, and betray us and their fathers. Rome sucks and devours us, Rome kills and desroys all." Innocent III: "The corruption of the people has its chief source in the clergy. From this arise the evils of Christendom."

Coulton: "parishioners pushed and brawled for precedence in church, to vindicate what they considered their social consequence. . . .Not one-tenth of those to whom the Catholic Church now prays can be claimed, with any show of probability, as coming from the less wealthy three-quarters of society." Rudwin: "whatever was displeasing to Rome in any field of human thought or activity was regarded as the Devil's work." Davis: "An excommunicated person is next door to an outlaw. . . .most people will shun him as they would a leper . . ." Jenks: "from the 9th century to the close of the Middle Ages, not the most autocratic monarch of Western Europe . . . would have dreamed of denying the binding force, within its proper sphere, of the Canon Law." CE: "prelates were the most powerful and the wealthiest subjects of the State. . . .The luxury of bishops and the wordly possessions of monks." Thompson: "The Roman Church in the Middle Ages was a governor, a landed proprietor, a rent collector, an imposer of taxes, a material producer, an employer of labor on an enormous scale, a merchantman, a tradesman, a banker and mortgage-broker, a custodian of morals, a maker of sumptuary laws, a schoolmaster, a compeller of conscience—all in one." J. W. Thompson: "The Church was the greatest landowner of all." Taylor: "the *Unam sanctam* of Pope Boniface VIII., fulminated in 1302, arrogating for the papacy every power on earth. . . .a senile outcry." Lea: "The history of mankind may be vainly searched for another institution which has established a spiritual autocracy such as that of the Latin Church." Munro: "difficult to realize the extent of the influence of the Church in the Middle Ages." H. W. Smith: "a vast corporation ruled by the pope and the Holy Congregation through coercion, force, fear and theological formulas. . . .concubinage and its implied hypocrisy were the accepted rule, and indolence, mendicancy and extortion were characteristic of the clergy generally." Wright: "a very considerable portion of the clergy, down to a very late period, so far set the regulations of the Church at defiance, that they lived with concubines, who were acknowledged by the parishioners as their wives, and were commonly spoken of as the 'priestesses' . . ." Bennett: "From the Roman court to the simple parish priest, the majority were idle and corrupt where

301

not actually vicious. . . . In the parishes the priests were seldom respected." Hearnshaw: "the Church itself was deeply tainted and infected with the virus of gross immorality." Maurice: "monstrous corruptions. . . . more bloodthirsty than any nation had ever been." Toynbee: "the relative deadness of societies that are consolidated into universal churches or universal states: a condition in which . . . the stimulus of multiplicity and variety and emulation is absent." Machiavelli: "the evil ensample of the papal court robbed Italy of all piety and religion." Conditions did not improve in the following centuries. Lea: "The world has probably never seen a more defiant disregard of all law, human and divine, than that displayed by both the Church and the laity during the pontificates of Sixtus IV. and Innocent VIII. and Alexander VI. . . . Pope and cardinal were used to reviling, and endured it with the utmost good-nature, so long as profitable abuses were not interfered with." Taylor: "scholasticism has no sense of humor."

CLERGY, THE   And see under Church. Pope Leo X: "What profit has not that fable of Christ brought us!" Coulton: "The priest, with the hierarchy at his back, was in theory almost everything to his people." Lea: "the deplorable character, intellectual and moral, of the medieval clergy." Hannay: "the most licentious body of men known to history." Buckle: "The prosperity of nations depends upon principles to which the clergy, as a body, are invariably opposed." Dr. Vctor Robinson: "If Hildebrand had emasculated his clergy instead of merely forbidding them to marry, he would have deprived the Middle Ages of their choicest scandals. The celibacy of priests became a grim jest. . . . People who did not know Latin knew enough to protest against the expulsion of women from the monasteries, since these concubines in some measure protected the wives and the daughters of the peasantry from monkish lust." Lagarde: "The clergy, which did not enjoy prestige in any quarter, were particularly despised and detested by the people of southern France." Even in earlier centuries "the clergy afforded a spectacle of thorough-going immorality. They shook off the yoke, not merely of celibacy, but of the commonest decency." Davis: "If knights exploit the peasants, the clergy do so hardly less." Even much later, says Hayes, a third of the land of Europe, half the revenue and two-thirds of the capital "were in the hands of Christian churches." Bishop Guillaume la Maire said in the 14th cen.: "in very many districts the lay folk hold the priests as viler and more despicable than Jews." Nine centuries earlier, says McNeill, Salvian of Marseilles had drawn an "unrelieved picture of a depraved society . . . scarcely paralleled in literature." Cardinal de Vitry said (early 13th cen.) : "I have seen that men crossed themselves at once on meeting a priest, saying that it is an ill omen to meet one." Erasmus said it was an unpardonable insult to call a layman a priest. Two friars, whom Coulton calls earnest and orthodox, wrote about 1400: "By such hypocrisy, under the color of poverty, they maintain their pride and their avarice and occupy greater lordships than do many dukes, earls and barons, to great hindering of the land and great disease of the poor people." *Annales Colmarienses*: "almost all the priests had concubines." King Wihtred: "If a priest . . . is too drunk to discharge his duty, he shall abstain from his ministrations, pending decision from a bishop." Palgrave: "Scarcely could the priest at the altar, reeking from the debauch, stammer out the words of the Liturgy." Lea: "the vices of the clergy were so universal that those who adhered to the rule of chastity were the objects of the most degrading and disgusting suspicions. . . .Nunneries were brothels, and to take the veil was simply another mode of becoming a public prostitute." May: "By the time of the Reformation there were said to be 100,000 prostitutes in England. Upon the ecclesiastics they were largely dependent for their patronage." Michelet: "It is impossible to realize or understand the enormous power exercised by the Confessor over nuns. . . .the priest sanctifies by his priesthood those he loves, and sin with him is a form of consecration. . . .The ecclesiastical seigneur, no less than the lay, possesses this foul prerogative. . . .in practice he was quite willing to sell his wife's virginity to the husband for money down."

Rudwin: "Satan's power of impersonation was so great that women often gave birth to children that . . . perfectly resembled the parish priest." Robertson: "the clergy as teachers had two specific tendencies. . . .One was the disparagment of women; the other the encouragement of cruelty." Power: "the history of ecclesiastical celibacy is one of the tragedies of religious life." Lundberg and Farnham: "The bulk of the sexual immorality of the Middle Ages is attributed by all authorities to the bachelor priests." Ecclesiastical court records, says May, show that sexual offenses were fifty times as common among the clergy as among the non-clergy. Lecky: "Pope John XXIII was condemned for incest; the abbot-elect of St. Augustine, at Canterbury, in 1171, had 17 illegitimate children in a single village; the abbot of St. Pelayo in

Spain in 1130 was proved to have no less than 70 concubines; Henry III Bishop of Liege who was deposed in 1274 for having 65 illegitimate children. . . ." And so on, ad nauseam. On the priesthood see such books as Luchaire, *Social France* and Seignobos, *The Feudal Regime*.

CONFESSIONAL   Lea: "penitents are instructed to use language as decent as possible so as not to excite the sensuality of their pastors. . . .the seduction of women in the confessional has always been a source of anxiety to the church. . . .The doctors of both the Dominican and Franciscan schools were unanimous in saying that a woman seduced ought not to confess to her paramour and that he ought not to absolve her from their mutual sin, but that if he did so the absolution is good, the only objection urged against this being that it relieved the woman from the shame, which is a wholesome concomitant of confession."

CRUELTY   CE: "The custom of burning heretics is really not a question of justice, but a question of civilization." Aquinas: "In order that nothing may be wanting to the felicity of the blessed spirits in heaven, a perfect view is granted to them of the tortures of the damned." Gregory the Great, says Lea, "had argued that the bliss of the elect in heaven would not be perfect unless they were able to look across the abyss and enjoy the agonies of their brethren in eternal fire." The Old Testament is replete with passages which gave to Christians their sanction for every form of cruelty: "And if a man take a wife and her mother it is wickedness; they shall be burnt with fire. . . .And the daughter of any priest, if she profane herself by playing the whore . . . shall be burnt with fire. . . ." Constantine, first Christian emperor, decreed that a slave who had intercourse with a free woman should be burnt alive.

Farrer: "nor has the history of the Church from the time of its conquest under Constantine onwards for more than a millennium been anything else but the history of cruelties, riots, wars, persecutions, the horror of which in its entirety the human mind is incompetent to grasp, but the like of which may be searched for in vain in the pre-Christian annals of the world." Sumner: "The Middle Ages reveled in cruelty to men and beasts. . . .The Church was venal, sensual, gross and inhuman." Meller: "To torture prisoners, to slay women and children wholesale . . . was held by the Christian knight as lawful. . . . Robert Fitzgerald, near Antioch, brought back into camp a hundred heads of Turks. . . .Saracens' noses and ears were spitted on a lance as a trophy. A boat's load of Greek noses and thumbs were sent to Byzantium. . . .Bohemund killed and roasted some prisoners as a jest. . . .Some of the Christians (it is stated in their own chronicles) ate the flesh of Turks. . . .Knights who on first catching sight of the Holy City . . . slaughtered so vast a number of unbelievers in the Mosque of Omar that the reins of their horses were bathed in blood." Scott: "The populace, instead of rearing up in hot indignation at the cruelty, the barbarity, and the inhumanity of burning alive the victims of the Inquisition, cheered with gusto. . . .In the early days the feet and hands were often amputated *in toto,* but Justinian tempered the severity of this law, restricting it to the amputation of one hand only." William the Conqueror: "We decree that no one shall be killed or hung for any misdeeds, but rather that his eyes be plucked out and his feet, hands and testicles be cut off."

Reinach: "I execrate these judicial murders, the accursed fruits of a spirit of oppression and fanaticism. . . .There are zealots still among us who glorify these crimes, and would wish to see them continued. If they attack my book, they will do both me and it a great honor." The extermination of the Albigenses is, says Whittaker, "by general consent the most atrocious in the annals even of Christendom." Lecky: "what strikes us most in considering the medieval tortures is not so much their diabolical barbarity, which it is indeed impossible to exaggerate, as the extraordinary variety, and what may be termed the artistic skill, they displayed." H. W. Smith: "extraordinary variety and elaborated with artistic skill by men who pondered long on the best methods of evoking the most intense and prolonged human suffering." Barnes: "it was not uncommon for the victim to be snatched from the flames after being thoroughly seared, left to suffer with his burns and then be returned to the flames." Michelet: "The judge is always sure of doing justice; anyone brought before him is inevitably guilty, and if he defends himself, doubly guilty." Lea: "At best the jails of the Middle Ages were frightful abodes of misery. . . .a living death far worse than the short agony of the stake." Women, says Michelet, died "of the terror of being walled up in the little black hole. . . .One word recurs continually, like a bell of horror tolled, and tolled again, to drive the dead in life into despair—always the same word, *Immured.*" Jurgen: "The largest lake in Hell is formed by the blood which the followers of the 'Prince of Peace' have shed in advancing his cause."

CRUSADES   See also under Cruelty. Lea: "It was a commonplace of
the *jongleurs* that the crusader, if he escaped the perils
of sea and land, was tolerably sure to return home a lawless bandit."
Hearnshaw: "their progress through Constantinople to the Holy Land
was marked by orgies and excesses, murders and debaucheries, which
were a disgrace not only to their religion but to humanity itself. . . .
we hear of nothing more absolutely wanton than the crucifixion of the
captives in Edessa, or the sending to the Greek emperor . . . of a whole
cargo of sliced-off noses and thumbs." CE: "These Holy Wars were
essentially a papal enterprise. . . .the Christians entered Jerusalem
from all sides and slew its inhabitants regardless of age or sex."

DISEASE   Davis: "The sufferers from nervous complaints make up
small armies. . . .lucky is the mother who does not have
from one-third to one-half of all her offspring die in the act of birth."
Augustine: "All diseases of Christians are to be ascribed to these demons; chiefly do they torment fresh-baptized Christians, yea, even the
guiltless new-born infant." Haggard: "physicians . . . apparently tried
to make the deaths of their patients as unpleasant as possible; when
Cardinal Richelieu was on his death-bed a female charlatan prescribed
for him a mixture of horse dung in white wine, and the cardinal drank
it. . . .Fauchard . . . advised his patients to use their own urine as a
mouthwash in case of toothache. Urine was an old remedy . . . Madame
de Sévigné recommended it highly . . ." Michelet: "The diseases of the
Middle Ages . . . were predominantly hunger, languor, and poverty of
the blood. . . .The war persistently waged against the flesh and against
cleanliness was bound to bear fruit. More than one female saint is
commended for having never washed even her hands. . . .We may be
quite certain not one of those knights, those fair and ethereal ladies,
the Percivals, Tristrams, Iseults, ever washed. Hence . . . the furious
itches that tortured our 13th-century ancestors. . . .terrible and cruel
ills. . . .womankind were stricken with detestable eruptions that were
looked upon as the visible sign of sin or a direct punishment from
God."

EDUCATION   Coulton: "there is nothing that can be called an edu-
cational system in the Middle Ages. . . .It was only
heretics who possessed anything beyond the merest smatterings of
Bible knowledge. . . .The ignorance of many medieval clergy, as described, or statistically recorded, by their own superiors, is almost in-

credible. In 1122, out of 17 priests serving dean and chapter livings under the cathedral of Salisbury, five were found unable to construe even the first sentence of the first prayer in the Canon of the Mass."

FAITH   Clifford: "Aristotle whose writings had been found to be so disastrous to the temper of faith." CE: "The integrity of the rule of faith is more essential to the cohesion of a religious society than the strict practice of its moral precepts." Tennant: "The medievalist calls the times of darkest ignorance and superstition the 'ages of faith', the same subjective psychological process is involved as led half-civilized man to dream of a simpler and happier world long before his time." Coulton: "society oscillated between this childish credulity and childish indifference or petulance. . . .It is only loosely that we can call the Middle Ages an age of faith; it would be more strictly true to call this period an age of acquiescence."

FORGERY   See chiefly notes to my two more recent novels. Prof. Bergen Evans: "All tyranny rests on fraud." CE: "the forging of papal letters was even more frequent in the Middle Ages than in the early Church. . . .Substitution of false documents and tampering with genuine ones was quite a trade in the Middle Ages. Innocent III (1198) points out nine species of forgery which had come under his notice. . . .In all these departments forgery and interpolations as well as ignorance had wrought mischief on a great scale." Robertson: "corruption of the texts of the Fathers is a scandal since the time of Erasmus." Reinach says the second decretals of Isidore "is a series of impudent forgeries, supporting the pretensions of the Pope and the bishops. . . .Never yet has the papacy acknowledged that for a thousand years it made use of forged documents to its own profit." For the amazing record see Wheless, *Forgery, passim,* but especially 260 ff.

FRANCIS   Jackson: "perhaps the most remarkable Christian who has ever lived." Lea accepts this opinion and adds that it is an irony that he founded his Order on poverty which "gave to the Inquisition an ample store of victims whose heresy consisted in fidelity to the precepts of their founder." Jessopp: "the John Wesley of the 13th century, whom the church did *not* cast out." Coulton: "It is impossible fully to understand St. Francis without measuring the extent to which his gospel was a revolt against the capitalism of the

307

older Orders." Harnack: "he desired to renew the life of the Apostles by imitating the poverty of their life . . ." Taylor: "He had not taken the theology of Augustine; he had not taken the Christ handed over by the transition centuries to the early Middle Ages; he had not adopted the Christ of the ecclesiastical hierarchy. He took Jesus from the Gospel . . ." Workman: "He preached that society should go back to the Sermon on the Mount, at the very time when Innocent III was making the Chair of the Fisherman into the most powerful throne since the days of the Caesars." But Jackson and Lake point out that the literary image of today was created by Franciscan piety; and Robertson "the startling fact that while his active career is almost exactly synchronous with the horrible Albigensian crusades, there is no trace in the records that he was ever saddened by them."

HELL Dujardin: "Hell as a torture-chamber was unknown to primitive religions and to ancient Judaism." C. H. Moore: "the horrors which the medieval Christian loved to depict . . . were first devised by the Orphics." Reinach: "The Greeks even invented . . . a Purgatory, where a certain mild chastisement purified souls."

HERESY Draper: "Persecution is the mother of proselytes." Mackinnon: "Religious liberty . . . cannot be said to have existed at all in the Middle Ages." Michelet: "In the 13th century everything is heresy; in the 14th, magic." The Church, Lea points out, "had always held the toleration of others to be persecution of itself. . . .it could brook no rivalry in its domination over the human soul . . ." Draper: "No one in the dominating party was heard to raise his voice in behalf of intellectual liberty." Loisy: "it came to pass that Christianity, with persecution at an end, soon became master of the house. Would that it had never forgotten the lesson, taught by its own first experience, of the fundamental iniquity and ultimate futility of persecuting men for the offense of religious belief." Taylor: "There were plenty of obdurate heretics in the Middle Ages." Freytag: "the unlimited pretensions of the popes drove many a stout heart to heresy." For ages, says Lea, the Church had taught that poverty was the mark of "exceeding holiness" but "the test of heresy was the assertion that Christ and the apostles held no property." All the heresies, says West, drew "strength chiefly from the popular feeling against the wealth and corruption of the higher clergy." It was a time, says Victor Robinson, "when the intellect of Europe was so clouded by monkish fables that

308

the monasteries were buying milk purporting to come from the breasts of the Blessed Virgin." Everything urged against the medical heretics, says Coulton, was true of the early Christians. Bennett: "Waldo found . . . that the Church said many things for which she had no Scriptural warrant." Capital punishment of heretics was employed as early as 385. Lea: "the highest authorities in the Church admitted that its scandals were the cause, if not the justification, of heresy." A tract under the name of one Peter Pilichdorf argued that "the worst of men who is a priest is worthier than the most holy layman." One principle nearly all heretics held to was that the sacraments were polluted by a priest living in sin. Reinach: "I defy anyone to name a single opinion persecuted by the Church in the Middle Ages, the adoption of which would not have brought about a diminution in her revenues."

INCEST   Michelet: "Incest is the ordinary condition of serfs. . . .
          The eldest only of the brothers married, so hiding under a
Christian mask the polyandry that was the actual fact."

INNOCENT III.   Davis: "the great and wise Innocent III." Taylor:
                "perhaps the most powerful of all the popes."
Wright: "a man exceedingly proud and overbearing." Packard: "he prepared the machinery of the medieval Inquisition." Abrahams: "the persistent efforts of Innocent III had spent themselves in branding the Jews as a race outside the pale of humanity." Gibbon: "Innocent may boast of the two most signal triumphs over sense and humanity, the establishment of transubstantiation, and the origin of the inquisition."

INQUISITION   Robertson: "Religious fanaticism, the last and low-
              est form of moral energy . . ." CE: "the much-
abused Inquisition. . . .the Inquisition marks a substantial advance in the contemporary administration of justice, and therefore, in the general civilization of mankind." Rev. Father Vincent, quoted by Reinach: "The Church has received from God the power to reprove those who wander from the truth, not only by spiritual but by corporeal penalties, such as imprisonment, flagellation, mutilation and death." M. S. Bates: "From the two Testaments taken together the dogmatist, the bigot, the man of faction, the literalist, the bureaucrat, the disciplinarian, the sadist have been able to justify their will, from that day until now." Lord Acton, Catholic, wrote to the daughter of Glad-

stone: "the principle of the Inquisition is murderous" and added that a later time "swept away that appalling edifice of intolerance, tyranny, and cruelty which believers in Christ built up . . ." Catholic Isabel Burton: "I do not know why we find many Catholics, even at the present day, who dislike writing or talking about the Inquisition. I always conclude that it results from a want of reading or from ignorance. . . . I think there is but one opinion for an educated, well-read, honest-minded Catholic to hold upon the subject: Horrors were committed by unscrupulous people in the name of Christ which can never be glossed over and excused." Two popes, Clement VIII and Paul V, declared that anyone should be delivered to the Inquisition who said that kissing, touching or embracing for sexual pleasure was not a grievous sin. Instituted by Innocent III it was not formally founded until 1233, and its complete and dreadful powers were not fully granted until 1252. Newman: "The Dominican Order was in large measure responsible for the establishment of the Holy Office of the Inquisition."

Workman: "the horrible vindictiveness of the Inquisition." Coulton: "The Church anticipated in discipline the Soviet-Nazi theory of Totalitarianism. . . .after 1150, no bishop, I believe, can be found protesting against the ever-increasing severities. . . .burning alive had never before been carried out in anything like this wholesale and official fashion, torture was now being applied with equally unprecedented frequency and cold-blooded cruelty. . . .no clear case of a verdict of *not guilty* seems ever to have been recorded. Accusers were commonly sheltered by anonymity; and unfavorable, as apart from favorable, evidence was accepted even from infamous persons, or was extracted from the man's own children. . . .We are told that, out of the 930 accused before Bernard Gui, 139 were acquitted altogether, and that this is a proof of inquisitorial justice. Yet in fact it is now confessed . . . that this assertion has rested upon a misunderstanding so gross as to be almost inexplicable. . . .It is natural enough that the advocates of a Church which thought and acted for so many centuries on the principles described above, and which has never yet repudiated them . . . should push their apologetics to the point of demonstrable, though doubtless unintentional, *suppressio veri* and *suggestio falsi*." G. R. Scott: "when the Spanish Inquisition was functioning at its mightiest, the horrors of the tortures were sufficient to cause men to go to any lengths to prevent themselves from falling alive into the clutches. . . .an inquisitor had boasted that if he could place the Pope on the rack he would guarantee to induce him to plead guilty. . . .

The vast power of the inquisitors . . .enabled them to secure a conviction with ease against anyone against whom they had a grudge." Lord Acton: "the Papacy contrived murder on the largest and also on the most cruel and inhuman scale. They were not only wholesale assassins, but they made the principle of assassination a law of the Christian Church . . ." Lecky: "the Church of Rome has inflicted a greater amount of unmerited suffering than any other religion that has ever existed." Robertson: "It has been reckoned that a full million of all ages and both sexes were slain. . . .No such reign of terror and horror has occurred in any other period of European history." V. Robinson: "countless victims accused of heresy to enable the Church to confiscate their property; rapacious cardinals attending the tortures and executions with troops and merry-making prostitutes . . ." Jastrow: "a code of inconceivably barbarous cruelty to extort confession, of a procedure of trial that gave the accused no chance—all under the sanction of a glorious crusade for the redemption of mankind." McSorley: "The aid of legal advisers was refused to the accused, and—contrary to the usual custom—the testimony of heretical and excommunicated witnesses was accepted." Lagarde: "Whoever was denounced as a heretic by two witnesses was found guilty. Criminals, who by the common law, were not to act as witnesses, were admitted to denounce heretics; and their denunciations were believed. The accused . . . was not brought face to face with his accusers. . . .He . . . could not commit his cause to any advocate." And after being tortured it was declared "that he admitted his guilt 'of his own full accord, without having been constrained'. . . .Sometimes to please the civil power, it even consented to condemn persons who were not heretics at all." A scholar as able as Waddell repeats the widely published falsehood that the inquisitors recommended mercy; but even such Catholics as Lepicier and Vacandard admit that if they sometimes affected to hope that death might not ensue, they were bound, says Coulton, "to excommunicate any secular judge who should neglect to inflict death." Though CE says the barbarous penal codes originated in the State and not in the Church, it admits that civil authorities were "enjoined by the popes under pain of excommunication to execute the legal sentence that condemned impenitent heretics to the stake" and adds that excommunication was "no trifle" because if the one excommunicated did not within a year free himself from the ban "he was held to be a heretic, and incurred all the penalties." All civil rulers were forced to swear on oath that they would destroy heretics to the full

311

extent of their powers; and as for the punishment CE further admits that "lenient measures were resorted to only where power to apply more severe measures was wanting." It would appear that such scholars as Waddell haven't read the *Catholic Encyclopedia*.

Newman: "the triumphant Church did not hesitate to make use of the death penalty whenever it could prevail upon the temporal power to enforce it." Reinach: "Not only was the papacy responsible for the Inquisition; it actively encouraged and excited its ferocity. . . . Frightful as were the punishments inflicted by the Inquisition—and imprisonment for life in pestilential gaols was perhaps worse than death at the stake—its methods of procedure were still more abominable. . . .indulgencies were promised to those who provided faggots. . . .As a well-meaning old woman at Constance deposited a faggot at the feet of John Huss, 'Oh! sacred simplicity' said the martyr." Abbe Vacandard: "It is proved beyond question that the Church, in the person of the Popes, used every means at her disposal, especially excommunication, to compel the State to enforce the infliction of the death penalty upon heretics."

The standard authority is still, of course, Lea's three monumental volumes. I now offer a few sentences from him: "inquisitors would pass calmly on, leaving a neighborhood well-nigh depopulated—fathers and mothers dispatched to distant shrines for months or years, leaving dependent families to starve, or harvests ungathered to be the prey of the first-comer, all the relations of a life, hard enough at best, disturbed and broken up. . . .It required courage to foolhardiness for any one to raise hand or voice against an inquisitor, no matter how cruel or nefarious were his actions. . . .fanatic zeal, arbitrary cruelty, and insatiable cupidity rivalled each other in building up a system unspeakably atrocious. . . .the trained inquisitor left no method untried which promised victory in the struggle between him and the helpless wretch abandoned to his experiments. . . .one of the most efficient was the slow torture of delay. . . .everything that could affect the accused injuriously was eagerly sought. . . .the most devout Catholic could never feel safe for a moment. . . .Wives and children and servants were not admitted to give evidence in favor of the accused, but their testimony if adverse to him was welcomed, and was considered peculiarly strong. . . .withholding from the accused all knowledge of the names of the witnesses against him. . . .a witness who withdraws testimony adverse to a prisoner is to be punished for falsehood, while his testi-

312

mony is to stand. . . .the only source of disability in a witness" was mortal enmity and there "must have been bloodshed between the parties. . . .men of wealth whose whole property was at stake might well consent to divide it with the papal court, whose all-powerful intervention would thereby be secured. . . .if he would not abjure and give satisfaction he was to be handed over to the secular arm; if he confessed and sought reconciliation he was to be imprisoned for life. . . .He was tied living to a post set high enough over a pile of combustibles to enable the faithful to watch every act of the tragedy to its awful end. . . .the accused was treated as one having no rights, whose guilt was assumed in advance, and from whom confession was to be extorted by guile or force. . . ."

The "much-abused Inquisition" in "that time of singular sweetness."

JEW   The ghetto, Abrahams points out, was at first a "privilege rather than a disability." He says the Jew "was not harshly judged by his contemporaries" and on another page in the same book says "there dawned on the Jews of Europe a new era, dark with degradation and misery." Leroy-Beaulieu (quoted by Abrahams) : "Beaten, reviled, scorned, abused by every one . . . he was made to swallow abuse like water, he was not allowed to take offense at anything." Coulton says Aquinas followed the "orthodox view that all Jews are by nature 'slaves to the Church, who may dispose of her property as she chooses'." Lecky: "The wretched Jews, stung to madness by the persecutions of the Catholics, furnish the most numerous examples of suicide in the Middle Ages." Adcock: "the Church waged war on them as a group of infidels." Rudwin: "The Jewish synagogues were regarded by Christians as temples of Satan." Rabinowitz: "the policy of the Church aimed at degrading them ruthlessly from holding a recognized position in European society and reducing them to an unwanted and despised element." Davis: "the Jews continue despised, maltreated, and mobbed every Good Friday." Meller: "the outcast and downtrodden Jew. . . .The law forbade him to sit among Christians without invitation from an ecclesiastic." J. W. Thompson: "Cruel and variable treatment of the Jews . . . all over Europe." Rare in the Middle Ages were such as Rulman Merswin a rich banker and Nicholas Lyranus, who argued that there must be a place in heaven for Jews. In England Langland and Juliana of Norwich were concerned over the matter, and More was inclined to mercy.

JEW AND
CHRISTIAN   See above. H. F. Stewart: "the medieval churchmen, who declared that to learn Hebrew was to turn Jew, can scarcely have sought help from the Talmud which they burnt wholesale without reading." Some Jews, says Newman, who became Christians, "proved valuable allies to the Dominicans in their assault upon Jewish books . . ." Coulton: "In some ways the Jews approximated more to modern ethical conceptions than did a good many Christians. . . .had many virtues which honest Christians could not help recognizing." Whittaker: "Without the Hebrew spirit of insurgence it may be doubted whether the rediscovery of classical culture would have broken the yoke of the new theocracy in Europe." Sachar: "papal bulls thundered anathemas upon those who permitted Jews to sit in places of trust." As Marini and others point out many Christians preferred Jewish doctors and called them at the risk of excommunication—as in this novel.

LOVE   Taylor: "medieval dogmatic faith regarded the emotional impulses between one human being and another as distracting, if not wicked."

MONASTICISM   Guérard: "The great monasteries of France were real states." The coming of the friars, says Workman, is "one of the great spiritual epochs of mankind" but Bennett says "Monasticism was essentially selfish." There is truth in both views. Reinach: "the literature of the Middle Ages sufficiently proves that both monks and nuns were unpopular . . ." Lea: "Maceration and mortification were the surest roads to Paradise. . . .In too many cases the abbeys thus became centers of corruption and disturbance, the nunneries scarce better than houses of prostitution, and the monasteries feudal castles where the monks lived riotously and waged war upon their neighbors. . . .for the most part the abbeys were sources of evil rather than of good. . . .we hardly need the emphatic testimony of the venerable Gilbert, Abbot of Gemblours, about 1190, when he confesses with shame that monachism had become an oppression and a scandal, a hissing and reproach to all men." Lecky: "writers of the Middle Ages are full of accounts of nunneries that were like brothels, of the vast multitude of infanticide within their walls, and of that inveterate prevalence of incest among the clergy, which rendered it necessary again and again to issue the most stringent enactments that

314

priests should not be permitted to live with their mothers or sisters." But Lecky points out that monasteries rendered a great service in preserving many writings of the ancients. Michelet: "Everywhere he finds the monks leading the bold, bad life of feudal nobles, going armed, drinking, duelling, hunting . . . the nuns living with them in indiscriminate concubinage, and everlastingly with child by them. . . . The poor girls they immured within monastic walls as a way to get rid of them, died off promptly . . . of sheer ennui and despair. . . .ten years is the average duration of life in monastic establishments." Power: "there were not wanting men to abuse it and to use the nunnery as a 'dumping ground' for unwanted and often unwilling girls, whom it was desirable to put out of the world, by a means as sure as death itself and without the risk attaching to murder. . . .Nor were the clergy loath to embrace this opportunity of removing the fruit of a lapse from grace. . . ." Jessopp: "It is often said that the monasteries were the great supporters of the poor, and fed them in times of scarcity. It may be so, but I should like to see evidence for the statement." When Benedict XII came to the throne, the King of France sent an embassy to call his attention to 18 complaints against the clergy, one of which asked for abolition of the custom "whereby the parish parsons in Anjou and Maine take upon themselves to seize all movable goods of their parishioners when these die; whereby their heirs become beggars."

MARRIAGE Taylor: "Marriage was holy in the mind of Christ. But it did not preserve its holiness through the centuries which saw the rise of monasticism and priestly celibacy." Lea: "Deprived as was the priesthood of the gratification afforded by marriage to the natural instincts of man, the wife at best was succeeded by the concubine; at worst by a succession of paramours, for which the functions of priest and confessor gave peculiar opportunity. So thoroughly was this recognized that a man confessing an illicit armour was forbidden to name the partner of his guilt for fear it might lead the confessor into the temptation of abusing his knowledge of her frailty."

MUSIC Dickinson: "musical culture was soon assumed everywhere by the Christian Church, which for a thousand years succeeded in restraining music within the antique conception of bondage to liturgy and ceremony."

PAGAN   It is by this time well known that the Christians
ELEMENTS   adopted pagan holy days, sacraments and liturgy, inventing practically none of their own. Carus: "The
rosary is unquestionably of pagan origin." E Carpenter: "the festival
of John the Baptist in June took the place of the pagan midsummer
festival of water and bathing; the Assumption of the Virgin in August
the place of Diana in the same month; and the festival of All Souls
early in November, that of the worldwide pagan feasts of the dead and
their ghosts at the same season." And so on: see Notes to my preceding
Christian volumes.

PAPACY Hobbes: "If any man will consider the original of that
great ecclesiastical dominion, he will easily perceive that
the Papacy is none other than the ghost of the deceased Roman Em-
pire, sitting crowned upon the grave thereof." Coulton: "The Papacy
was a great bureaucracy, a network of officials from top to bottom."
Many of the popes were incredibly corrupt; Lea says of one in the 12th
cen.: "Apparently his children by his sister Tropea, and his being ac-
companied by a concubine when traveling in the capacity of papal
legate, had not proved a bar to his elevation in the Church."

PENANCE Plummer: "The penitential literature is in truth a deplorable feature of the medieval church." Watkins says
it is difficult to obtain any "satisfying evidence that the public confession of sins by word of mouth ever . . . formed part of the formal
discipline of penance." McNeill: "The ideal was founded in monastic
asceticism; the reality in primitive brutality. . . .It is difficult to appre-
ciate the fact that a literature now so obscure had formerly an extensive circulation. . . .This public procedure, in which the penitent in
his humiliation implores the intercession of 'all the brethren', was
later to be replaced by a private and secret rite involving confession to
and absolution by a priestly confessor."

POOR, THE Such Catholic apologists as Allard have argued that the
selfs owed all their progress to the church, but it
was non-clerical landowners who took the lead in improving their
lot. CE: "an epoch when many fanatical or designing persons reaped
a rich harvest out of the credulity of the populace." It has been said
of Aquinas "that no man has ever fallen into error by following him,
nor has any man attacked him without incurring suspicion of error."

He explicitly justified slavery. The great jurist Heineccius long ago summed it up: "We see that only layfolk freed serfs gratis . . . the clergy who felt sufficiently secure in their own eternal reward, granted liberty only for hard cash." Brons: "We shall not go wrong if we find the main object of these manumissions in the frequent deficits of the monastic treasury." Coulton: "Aquinas never erred worse, perhaps, than when . . . he judged the ideal state to need a peasantry strong in arm, dull in intellect, and divided among themselves by mutual distrust." Even eloquent apologists like Imbart de la Tour admit that improvement of the peasant's lot "en un mot, transforme le serf en personne humaine." Peasant catechism (15th cen.) : "What part of speech is peasant?—A noun. What sort of noun? Jewish. Wherefore? Because he is as silly and ugly as a Jew." Typical of upper class sentiment is that of Malvitius, canon of Bologna: "for base and coarse foods are to be given to base persons, and delicate foods to noble folk."

The Church, says Caggese, "was the most tenacious and inflexible maintainer of seignorial rights over the bondmen of the soil." Inama-Sternegg: "This concentration of lordship over the productive forces of the soil resulted in a steady increase of the propertyless classes. . . ." Pollock and Maitland: "There is plenty of evidence that of all landlords the religious houses were the most severe . . ." Coulton: "the great centuries of serfdom were the centuries of clerical, and especially of monastic, power." "The advantages accruing from the acquisition of bondfolk," says Herter, "rendered the monks somewhat negligent of the means whereby they acquired them." Sée: "the Church landlords were essentially attached to the manorial system; and they exploited their peasants no less harshly than the laity." Lord Acton: "Medieval liberty differs from modern in this, that it depended on property." Guérard: "la condition d'un individu se détermine bien moins par l'éducation, par le mérite, par la naissance même, que par la propriété."

Coulton: "The irreligion of the peasant is a medieval commonplace." Lea: "Under the guidance of a Church such as this, the moral condition of the laity was unutterably depraved." Lamprecht: "Kinship within a manorial population rose to an extreme degree." Davis: "the pitiless ravaging of the lands, farms and villages of the helpless peasantry. . . .Of the moral condition of many of them it is best to say little." Furnas and Furnas: "a fearsome huddling into permanent and utterly filthy villages and cities. . . .food hopelessly inadequate. . . .Cast over it all was the enervating influence of the Church, which

317

convinced everyone that the more he suffered today the greater his happiness would be in the world to come." Gautier de Coincy said (13th cen.) the "serf is poor, sad, downcast. . . .Many serfs hate the clergy even as Esau hated Jacob. . . .little they love them, and still less do they believe them." West: "The poorer inhabitants were miserable in body too, beyond all words—fever and plague stricken, dying slowly of want and filth and wretchedness such as no modern city knows." Ernle: "droughts, scarcities, famines, crime, violene, murrains, scurvy, leprosy, typhoid diseases, wars, pestilences, plagues. . . ." Lea: "The helpless and hopeless state of the lower classes of society in those dreary ages has probably never been exceeded in any period of the world's history." Hayes: "the sufferings of the poor European peasants and serfs can hardly be exaggerated." Coulton: "the peasant labored ordinarily from dawn to dark." Evans: "Even the serf's children were not his own."

Vinogradoff: "of all manorial exactions, the most odious was incontestably the *marchetum*." Of the Church's claim that it saved the serf from the bloodsucking moneylender Coulton says: "This has been asserted, and is now being repeated with increasing boldness and frequency from year to year, by writers who seem to draw the historical bow at a mere venture, and who would certainly disdain to treat their fellows in money-matters with that reckless irresponsibility which they display wherever the Christian religion is concerned." If serfs were ever treated decently, say Pollock and Maitland, it was to see "that no one shall make an ill use of his property." Guizot: "go backwards in French history and stop where you will; everywhere you will find the feudal regime looked upon by the mass of the population as an enemy which must be fought and exterminated at any cost."

E. P. Prentice: "The history of the world has been the story of a struggle for daily bread."

RELICS   There was a huge traffic in relics; the sale of them, says Fisher, "grew to be a lucrative branch of trade. Vast sums of money . . . were expended in the purchase of pieces of apparel or other objects believed to have once belonged to Christ or the Virgin. . . .For the disputed possession of relics there were fierce contests between rival monasteries." A statute of the Seventh General Council (787) said: "If any bishop from this time forward is found consecrating a temple without holy relics, he shall be deposed as a transgressor." Robertson: "To find what might pass for the bones and relics of saints and martyrs, to frame false tales concerning them . . . these were, by the grieving admission of many Church historians, among the common activities of the Church from the second or third century onwards. . . .abbots and monks who sold the privilege of seeing and kissing holy relics. . . .an intense anxiety to possess or benefit by holy relics, the easy manufacture of which must have enriched myriads . . ." Lea: "How sedulously this fetichism was inculcated by those who profited from the control of the fetiches is shown by a thousand stories and incidents of the time." B. Z. Goldberg says that until recently there were 12 holy prepuces of Jesus in European churches and one of them "the pride and possession of the Abbey Church of Coulomb, in the diocese of Chartres, France, was believed to possess the miraculous power of rendering all sterile women fruitful." Goodenough: "The revering of the bodies of martyrs and other saints led to their use as charms in the old pagan magical fashion."

SAINTS Reinach: "the worship of the martyrs, the origin of the worship of saints, took the place of the worship of the Greek heroes, and sometimes adopted even their names and their legends."

SANITATION H. W. Smith: "The most admired saints were those who had become a clotted mass of filth. . . .Self-mortification, squalor and physical uncleanliness became esteemed Christian virtues." Davis: "The peasants 'almost live on the manure heap'. The clergy . . . seldom preach the virtues of bathing; indeed . . . discourage the practice." Prentice: "no knowledge of the simplest forms of sanitation." Reynolds: "In the Middle Ages habits of cleanliness were held in such low esteem among most of the peoples of Europe that to wash in hot water, and more particularly to immerse the body in it, was considered a matter of sinfully indulging the flesh." Meller: "We find in the 'Testamenta Vetusta' Earl Humphrey of Hereford bequeathed 'a silver basin in which we are accustomed to wash our heads,' by which term no doubt he meant his face—washing the head being then not practiced." Even so, he thinks, the medieval knight was cleaner than the ladies and fops of Louis XIV's court, who "never washed but greased their faces." Cunnington and Cunnington: "it has been less than 200 years that bodily cleanliness has been considered important. Men and women, even of high rank, were generally dirty and often verminous. Heavily perfumed undergarments imperfectly distracted attention from less agreeable odors." But many Jews, says Abrahams, had the habit of bathing every Friday.

SATAN Aquinas: "All the changes capable of occurring naturally and by way of genus, these the Devil can imitate." Lecky: "It was firmly believed that the arch-fiend was for ever hovering about the Christian; but it was also believed that the sign of the cross, or a few drops of holy water, or the name of Mary, could put him to an immediate and ignominious flight." Anatole France: "The Middle Ages frightened us with a lugubrious phantasmagoria of devils snapping at a sinner's soul as it passed." Lea: "We cannot understand the motives and acts of our forefathers unless we take into consideration the mental condition engendered by the consciousness of this daily and hourly personal conflict with Satan." Barnes: "Medieval peoples feared above all else the activities of the Devil and his evil associates." Jastrow: "The same scholastic ingenuity . . . could calculate, as did Weirus, by methods beyond our comprehension, that there were just 7,405,926 devils divided into 72 companies, each under a captain." Rudwin: "Of all the myths that have come down to us from the East, and of all the creations of Western fancy and belief, the Devil has exercised the strongest attraction upon the human mind."

SCIENCE St. Francis: "Books are a temptation; the brethren who cannot read shall not seek to learn." CE: "When a clearly defined dogma contradicts a scientific assertion, the latter has to be revised. . . .Moorish Spain had 19 colleges, and their renown attracted hundreds of Christian scholars from every part of Europe. Herein lay a grave menace to Christian orthodoxy." Reinach: "Victorious Christianity waged war upon science." Robertson: "It was left to the Church as such to frame for the suppression of free thought in religion a machinery never paralleled in human history." Lea: "the very number of the defenders and the vigor of the defense show the danger which was recognized as dwelling in the spirit of inquiry which had at last been partially aroused from its long slumber." Rudwin: "Every discovery of science, every invention of material benefit to man, was believed, during the Middle Ages, and in Catholic countries for long centuries afterwards, to have been secured with the Devil's help." Michelet: "Name me one science that has not been a rebel! Every new one has been Satan. . . .the Church has declared accursed, the vast edifice of the sciences and of modern institutions which she has excommunicated stone by stone. . . .Is there one science you can name that was not originally a revolt against authority? . . .Medicine above all was truly and indeed Satanic, a revolt against disease, the merited scourge of an offended God. . . .It is expressly forbidden to invent, to create." Lecky: "An elaborate process of mental discipline, with a view to strengthening the critical powers of the mind, is utterly remote from the spirit of theology; . . .it is difficult to look upon Catholicism in any other light than as the most deadly enemy of the scientific spirit. . . .It is indeed marvelous that science should ever have revived amid the fearful obstacles theologians cast in her way." Draper says of Pope Gregory the Great that he insisted on the maxim that ignorance is the mother of devotion and "expelled from Rome all mathematical studies, and burned the Palatine library founded by Augustus Caesar." Even Roger Bacon, says Taylor, accepted "to his detriment the universally prevailing view that the end of all the sciences is to serve their queen, theology." Bennett: "The new learning was in the air of the 13th century. . . .The two things most feared were philosophical *subtilitates* and the dreadful dangers of all kinds that beset those attending the schools." Barnes: "The remarkable Muslim culture gradually permeated Christian civilization and encouraged the rise of scientific knowledge . . ." Döllinger: "the whole of modern civilization and culture is derived from Greek sources. Intellectually we are the offspring of the union of the ancient Greek classics with Hellenized Judaism." Newman: "Anatolio and Scot together, under the influence of Frederic, opened to the western world the treasure-house of Arabic learning." Coulton: "medical science stood still—or even, to some extent, went backwards, from AD 200 to nearly 1500." Rashdall: "by the beginning of the 14th century Arabic medicine was everywhere in full possession of the Medical Faculties."

Reynolds: "what we call the Middle Ages long had the Renaissance in its belly." Wright points out that it was women far more commonly than men who were able to read and write.

SEX   Lea: "As for chastity, the whole history of the Church shows the impracticability of its enforcement." Martin Luther: "There is nothing unusual in princes keeping concubines; and although the lower orders may not perceive the excuses of the thing, the more intelligent know how to make allowance." E Carpenter: "this contempt of the body and degradation of sex-things went on far into the Middle Ages, and ultimately created an organized system of hypocrisy and concealment and suppression." But of course phallic symbols were every-where, especially in architecture and ecclesiastical garb. Hannay: "The Christian Church has also an Ark of God in the Monstrance and Pyx, a lingam-yoni combination." Bayley: "Roman Catholics are taught that St. Gertrude was divinely instructed, and that, as often as the Angelic Salutation is devoutly recited by the faithful on earth, three efficacious streamlets proceed from the Father, the Son, and the Holy Ghost, most sweetly penetrating the Virgin's heart." Inman: "a confessor of the Roman church, who wears the *crux ansata,* the Egyptian symbol of life. . . .It is remarkable that a Christian church should have adopted so many pagan symbols as Rome has done." Such a statement has been made by many, all of whom overlook the fact that there was no Christian church, as distinct from paganism—that the church was a slow accretion of so-called pagan elements.

Barnes says that in the MA people slept with their clothes on; but Davis: "Nightdresses are no more used in the 13th century than are table forks" and Wright: "it was the custom in those times for both sexes to go to bed perfectly naked."

SIMONY   CE: "Simony . . . was the evil so prevalent during the Middle Ages." A. L. Smith: "You could buy off every-thing . . ." Simony, says Lea, "was the corroding cancer of the Church throughout the whole of the Middle Ages—the source whence sprang almost all the evils with which she afflicted Christendom. From the highest to the lowest, from the pope to the humblest parish priest, the curse was universal." Waddell: "the *Beginning of the Gospel according to the silver Mark* has blasted the entire Roman curia with one triumphant breath." Sée: "what specially interests the wielder of justice is the sanctions, i.e., the fines, which form one of his steadiest revenues." Lombroso: "In other cities, the right to commit fornication with impunity for a lifetime could be obtained by payment of a quarter cask of wine to the bishop's officer, who drew this privilege from the canon *De Dilectissimis* in the decretals of the Pope." Allen: "the buying and selling of ecclesiastical offices, especially of the great sees and abbecies, was a sin and temptation of the age, and indeed it remained the characteristic vice of the Middle Ages under the later regime of the popes . . ." Jackson: "the corruption of the Church, the worst aspect of which was its shameless venality. All great positions—abbacies, bishoprics, even the papal office—were purchasable." Imbart de la Tour: "the sale of the sacraments was one of the regular sources of the parochial income."

SIN   Cassian (just after Augustine) determined the principal vices as gluttony, fornication, avarice, anger, dejection, languor, vainglory and pride. Michelet: "they were one and all arrested, let us rather say, blinded, hopelessly intoxicated and made cruel savages of, by the poison of their first principle, the doctrine of Original Sin."

SUPERSTITION   Until 1250 says CE Christians were "almost wholly absorbed in the supernatural." Lea: "St. Augustine, who did so much to transmit pagan superstitions to succeeding ages . . ." Coulton: "the Church deliberately inculcated further ignorance of great portions of human life. . . .A modern antiquary has unearthed documentary evidence for 86 cases of animal excommunication. . . .the medieval custom of condemning and executing criminal beasts—the sow which has devoured a child, or the ox which has gored a man." (The Greeks also did, of course). Barnes: "The most eminent philosopher, say an Aquinas, was as much absorbed in the supernatural as was the most superstitious peasant." Halliday: "Respect for authority . . . completely shackled criticism." Farrer: "Philosophy . . . ceased to operate as a moral influence over the lives of men; and human reason was given over entirely to the uncontrolled tyranny of priests and monks and to the wasting debility of insoluble theological discussions." Pico della Mirandola: "No science yields greater proof of the divinity of Christ than magic . . ."

VIRGIN, THE   Lippert: "The celebrated 'woman cult' of the Middle Ages was . . . a dying echo . . . of a decadent form of life. . . .The image of this cult, only rarely beautiful, fluctuated between extravagant fantasy and crude reality." Michelet: "The Virgin, exalted as virgin, and not as Our Lady, far from raising actual womanhood to a higher level, had degraded it." Bayley: "The worship of the Queen of Heaven was flourishing long before the time of Jeremiah, and when the Christian Church appointed its festivals, it fixed upon the 25th of March as 'Lady Day' for the reason that this date was celebrated throughout the Grecian and Roman world as the festival of the miraculous conception of the 'Blessed Virgin Juno'." Jacques de Vitry (13th cen.) : "some of these women dissolved with

323

such a particular and marvellous love toward God . . . that they languished with desire, and for years had rarely been able to rise from their cots." As for the virgin birth, Augustine had written that there were "many proven instances that Sylvans and Fauns, who are commonly called Incubi, had often made wicked assaults upon women, and satisfied their lusts upon them: and that certain devils, called Duses by the Gauls, are constantly attempting and effecting this impurity." Hartland: "The Fathers had dwelt upon the physiological details of the Incarnation with prurient rudeness. They were as familiar with at least the negative results of the miracle, as minute and positive in their description, as if they had made an obstetrical examination. In their zeal for the virginity of the Savior's mother they insisted that he was conceived and born without any physical changes in the body that bore him." On the virgin birth see Notes to my novel *A Goat for Azazel*.

WALDENSES Of this body of 'heretics' Lea says that they "sought only to restore Christianity to its simplicity." Coulton: "tenets were founded upon Bible-reading and upon the attempt, more or less successful, to recapture the spirit of the early Church."

WARFARE Luchaire: "war was the normal state." Meller: "constant warfare, whether between conflicting countries, or the petty feuds hardly ever ceasing between neighboring barons and knights . . ." Boisonnade: "When the peasants were unable to take refuge in the heart of the woods they were seized, fleeced, tortured, mutilated, hanged. Sometimes their hands and feet were cut off, or they were flung upon the fire; captives had their eyes put out, women were violated and their breasts were hacked off."

WITCH Michelet attributes the spread of witchcraft among the lower classes to their despair at finding (as Rudwin puts it) "that the Church had become even more tyrannical than their lay oppressors." Robertson: "If the merits of Christianity as a civilizing force are to be in any way determined by its influence in working bloodshed, its record in the matter of witch-slaying alone would serve to place it, in that regard, lower than any other creed. Classic paganism knew no such infamy." Of course the sanction was taken from a barbarous passage in the Old Testament.

WOMEN Dr. H. W. Haggard: "The Middle Ages were the most unfortunate period in the history of womankind." Crump and Jacob: "women found themselves perpetually oscillating between a pit and a pedestal." Power says the attitude of the wife to the husband "may be summed up as submission, obedience, and constant attention." Hearnshaw: "in feudalism love and marriage were as completely divorced as was piety from ecclesiastical office. . . .Chivalric gallantry . . . was a gigantic system of bigamy." St. Bonaventura said that it was not infrequent for priests to persuade women that intercourse with them was no sin. As Prentice says, the monk might bend his knee to the Virgin "but in his inmost thoughts woman had her place, and wherever that place might be it was no fit place for man." When Christine de Pisan protested the contemptuous portrayal of women in the immensely popular 'Romance of the Rose' she was attacked by various men, including prominent monks. Bennett: "the conventional medieval contempt for women, which regarded them practically as a lower order of creation." *Corpus Juris Canonici*: "It is a natural human order that the women should serve their husbands and their children their parents; for there is no justice where the greater serves the less." Gower said women were inferior and intended to be, else the Creator would have fashioned them from man's head instead of his rib." Evans: "In the early days of chivalry their life was almost incredibly hard." Meller: "Her surroundings, too, in the gray weather-beaten castle, hardly tended to the cultivation of maternal duties—the hall and entrances and tiny sleeping apartments filled with armed men, or giddy pages, often, except a bower-woman or two, she the only woman in a household of rough men, who looked upon her with favor only when she carried on those strange passages of feigned love the knights expected." Wright: "ladies even of the highest rank were exposed to dangers of all kinds." Barnes: "wife-beating was common . . . and was fully recognized by law. The feudal nobility possessed a notoriously low esteem for the chastity of women of the lower classes or of non-Christian birth." The Council of Toledo (400) had decreed that "if the wives of any clergy have sinned" the husbands were privileged to "keep them bound in their house, compelling them to salutary fasting" and "macerating them with stripes and hunger." The *Book of the Knight of La Tour-Landry* a popular manual of the duties of the upper class tells approvingly of a husband who, scolded by his wife in public, "smote her with his fist down to the earth; and then with his foot he struck her in the

325

visage and brake her nose, and all her life after she had her nose crooked." Michelet argues that so many women surrendered themselves to Satanism because Satan elevated them above the position assigned to them by the Church. "The Church keeps her down at the lowest level of degradation—she is Eve, and sin incarnate. In the house she is beaten. . . .At bottom she is nothing, and has nothing. . . . This is the horror of the Middle Ages." Sprenger, most notorious of the witch-murderers, said that Fe-mina came from fe and minus, because a woman had less faith than a man. It is little wonder, as Taylor says, that many a woman "felt a passionate love for the spiritual bridegroom." The first plea for the emancipation of women came, says Coulton, not from Christians but from the Arab philosopher Averroes.

Readers familiar with the records will be aware that my Madelon-Luce scenes are based in part on the infamous case of Father Girard and Charlotte Cadière.

That time of singular sweetness! "We may well ask ourselves," said the great James George Frazer, "whether there is not some more general conclusion, some lesson, if possible, of hope and encouragement, to be drawn from the melancholy record of human error and folly." Well, yes; for another great scholar, Henry Osborn Taylor, says, "Men had new thoughts; the power of the popes was shattered. . . .Wicliffe had risen; Huss and Luther were close to the horizon; a new science of observation was stirring, and a new humanism was abroad. . . ."

DATE DUE

DEC 15 1999	